TURNAROUND

John P Warren

ISBN: 069234067X
ISBN 13: 9780692340677
Library of Congress Control Number: 2014921277
PineLands, New Wilmington, PA

The right to vote—and have it count—is the sum of all our rights in the US Constitution and all its amendments. If we lose that right, we lose everything.

~John Whitaker,
Speaker of the House
TurnAround

AUTHOR'S NOTE AND DISCLAIMER

*T*urnAround is a story unto itself, although many readers may see it as the conclusion of *Turnover*. Both are works of fiction in all respects. Any resemblance to any persons, living or dead—public, private, or journalist—appearing in either novel, is purely coincidental and unintended. Although real events are used as texture to the story, any errors in historical fact and any opinions reflected are the author's alone.

The core of both *Turnover* and *TurnAround* involves the potential for massive electronic vote fraud—the theft of a national election. What is not fictional is the real threat to our right to vote as free Americans in any election across our country. That it is possible for electronic signals to be intercepted and manipulated is well understood and all too tempting for those with more ambition than appeal.

Can any responsible authority guarantee our citizens that widescale electronic vote fraud cannot happen in America? That it hasn't happened?

~Jack Warren
New Wilmington,
Pennsylvania

DECEMBER 2012

1.

Commander Jeremy Bolling, White House physician, could wait no longer. His chief patient, President Averell Harriman Williams, newly reelected, had kept it secret, but time was running out. *Will the president survive the cancer that's killing him?*

As Bolling strode across the wheat colored carpet of the Oval Office, he saw more signs of change. The blue-and-mustard striped chairs that had defined the space in front of the fireplace during the Bush era and most of President Williams' first term had been replaced with a brown leather pair. Yet, the eight-foot grandfather clock retained its place where the ceaseless rhythm of time seemed to race faster than at any other spot on the planet. Bolling chided himself for noting the banal while the president faced a peril to which he appeared oblivious.

"Jeremy." The president looked up from his paperwork on the Resolute desk that achieved its stardom during the Kennedy Administration and had been used by several occupants of the office since. "Come sit by me while I finish up. I suspect you have a thing or two to say." He winked, and a half smile highlighted his mottled ebony face, deeply creased by the pressures that consume each occupant of the office.

Bolling took the chair to the right of the desk, from where he could better admire the sideboard's Remington sculpture of a horse bucking its rider—a metaphor for the Williams Administration striving to tame the special interests tainting its every initiative. He was drawn back to the president, who'd aged ten years in the space of four while the nation struggled to lift itself from economic gloom.

As the president's sinewy hands wrestled the paper pile down with each signature, Bolling's gaze wandered to the brace of nine-by-nine windows backdropping the Resolute. Outside, leafless branches stirred into a *danse macabre* by the whining, winter wind. He wondered if the chill outside the window might describe the conversation he was about to have. Bolling sat up straight, his dress uniform as crisp as could be, his game face in place. He was ready. *Is the president ready for what has to come?*

After a minute more of furious writing, President Williams—AHW to the print media—lifted his attention to his physician, a man he'd been dodging for weeks, and the medical issue could no longer be avoided. Uttering one of his favorite phrases, he said, "OK, let's review the bidding."

"Sir, you'll remember that when we first talked about a diagnosis of prostate cancer in February, I mentioned that, in your case, the disease had already taken an aggressive turn."

"Let me stop you there. For posterity's sake, you don't need to remind me—or the recording devices—that you warned me early on." He smiled. "Relax. It's just us, and no one can fault you on this. The decisions along this road were all mine, not yours."

"Thank you, Mr. President. Not to be dramatic"—Bolling arced his head and eyes toward the ceiling—"but history, indeed, is listening."

"I take your point."

It was clear Williams did not wish to rehash their previous exchanges. It had been his decision to withhold the cancer diagnosis from the First Lady, White House and campaign staff, and indeed, the nation. Bolling recalled his shock at the president's insistence the secret be kept. Reluctantly, Williams had agreed to monthly blood tests, and to biopsies taken by a Johns Hopkins urologist. Bolling could only hope his patient's delay would not prove fatal. "It was a long election season, sir, and then, in the fall—."

"Yes, how could I forget our meeting before the first presidential debate? I know, I know—I put you off, and you had an update to give me. The public still doesn't know the real reason why I performed so badly in that first session with Governor Hardy." He laughed. "I'll let my biographers find that little tidbit."

"I'm glad you can laugh about all this, sir, especially given what I laid out for you at that time. Your PSA numbers and the Gleason score resulting from the biopsy were not good—and sir, you promised we could act immediately after the election. It's now December third—almost a month later, Mr. President."

"I know a verbal finger wag when I hear one, Jeremy. You gave me two surgical choices: either alternative on the eve of a tight election would have given the Republicans the best ammunition they'd ever had: that the incumbent might have a life-threatening health problem." The presiden't voice lowered to a whisper. "So, you see, I did not forget."

Bolling sat motionless but lowered his eyes. "Let's not mince words, sir. You now have very little elbowroom. We have to act—and soon."

Williams nodded, and then looked directly at his doctor. "Well, I guess you're not going to like the rest of our conversation then."

"Why is that, sir?" Bolling's words sounded tremulous in his ear. He shifted in his seat.

"The US Constitution. Yes, the election is over, but not in a legal sense. You see, each state's electors meet on December seventeenth, two weeks from now. At that time, they will cast their votes, but, whether most people know it or not, not all of them are bound by state law to assign their ballots for the majority winner in their state. They may bolt if they think I am, for some reason, unable to serve my term."

Bolling's body tensed as if in reaction to a fast-approaching lightning storm.

"It gets worse. Let's say that because we've kept this under wraps—by the way, the First Lady and Vice-President Morrison now know about this, but nobody else—the electors will do what they're supposed to do on the seventeenth. That's just the first hurdle. On January fourth, both Houses of Congress meet in joint session to count those ballots and certify the election. It may be a formality and a nice bit of ceremony, but the law states that if only one member of either House objects to the ballot, the whole process stops, and what happens then, God only knows."

"My God. Are you telling me we have to wait until after the fourth of January?"

"Actually, my dear friend, I'm telling you I'd rather wait until after the Inauguration on the twentieth. That would be optimal."

Blood rushed to Bolling's cheeks. "Mr. President, I know I may be out of turn here, but, as your doctor, I strenuously object to further delay—that's another six weeks." He paused. "Sir, do you not understand that if we fail to operate soon, you are risking everything? Everything! As it is now, your chances go down by the week, and by late January..." he said, his voice rising.

"Yes, Doctor?" His voice was steady, as if to suggest nothing would surprise him.

"I'd have to give you a no better than fifty-fifty shot. Sir, is that clear enough?"

Williams took a deep breath. "There are few people I can say this to, so listen closely." His voice grew more determined with each syllable. "You may not be politically attuned—and I'm damn glad you're not—but here's one simple fact, remembering that like cut diamonds, every fact has many facets—if, I do not persist in my plan, there's a chance that on December seventeenth, the Electoral College might go for Governor Hardy. The country would survive that choice, I suppose, but what if they chose to bypass him and vote for Joseph P. Morrison?"

As if jolted by an electrical charge, Bolling's words came with difficulty. "You mean we'd be better off with Hardy—a Republican?—than your own handpicked VP?"

"Only you and I and the recording device heard that, and please don't remind me that I picked Joe Morrison. He may have some good qualities, but he's a mile wide and an inch deep. If it's the last political thing I do on this earth, I can't take the chance that he will become President of the United States."

"But, sir," Bolling said, "if...if the...unexpected were to happen—Sir, I can hardly say the words—wouldn't your vice-president succeed you in any event?"

"This is why somebody coined the phrase, 'between a rock and a hard place,' and that's exactly where I put myself. You have no idea the tortured dreams I've had since Election Day. If I throw myself on the mercy of the public and the electors now, I feel virtually certain that

I will lose my party's grip on this political moment." He exhaled. "If I wait, as you say, my odds improve by at least fifty percent." The president's voice carried compassion, and his eyes, a bit of a twinkle. "Isn't that what you said, Jeremy? Fifty-fifty?"

Paul Gladston and Mare Burdette found time for private talk only in bed after all the work on the Pennsylvania Amish farm was done, and the sun went down. They rose at sunup with all the Schenks to work the 240 acres without the benefit of electricity or powered farm implements. That they had adjusted well, but to different degrees, was a minor miracle. They had both been raised and educated in a modern world that was vastly different from this Amish community steeped in customs and traditions still firm after nearly three centuries of practice.

That this was winter may have meant a shorter day, but there had been plenty to do around the barn, and Paul's muscles knew they'd been used. As he readied for bed, he had to admit that his high school and college summers spent with the Schenks had prepared him well for Amish life. For the five foot four Mare Burdette, though a farm girl herself, the reversion to truly rural life must have been an unwelcome surprise.

Despite the early December cold and the unheated room, he was clad only in his long, flannel nightshirt. Laying his six-foot length down on the old mattress, arms behind his head, he studied the lamplight's flickering shadows on the ceiling. Since their escape from a killer the Sunday night before election day, when the largest electronic vote fraud in US history had been perpetrated upon the American people, they'd been warmly welcomed by the kind and unworldly Andy and Sadie Schenk. Because they presented themselves as a betrothed couple—a bit of a stretch, Paul had to admit—the Schenks permitted them to reside together in the separate little house originally built for Sadie's parents.

Although he and Mare were content to be off the grid for the present, safe and far away from the blond killer in the black Tahoe, both knew that Amish life was not theirs. *So what was next?*

Paul shivered with the possible answers to that question when Mare entered the room, her long auburn hair in a braid, apparently ready for "a long winter's nap," as Clement Clarke Moore had described it.

"What's on your mind, Paulie boy?" she said, more in invitation than question.

"You already know what's always on my mind, little one," he answered in the same way, "but we need to talk for once, and"—he paused to smile into her limpid green eyes—"play later."

"I'm listening, but you'd better talk fast, Mister." She mussed his brown hair, a month uncut.

"Seriously, Mare, we need to talk about what our life will be about— a week, a month, a year from now."

"That question would be a whole lot easier to answer if you'd quit stalling and ask me to marry you." Mare's tone was playful, not bullying, but there was a seriousness underneath.

A smirk upended his jaw. "You little stinker—you beat me to it. Are you planning to manage our entire life together?"

"You bet, Paulie boy, so you'd better decide early on if you're going to fight it, or enjoy it." She climbed under the covers and, with both arms, lifted her nightgown over her head, and snuggled up next to him. "Well?"

Paul doused the lamp and did the same. After a minute under the down quilt with Mare, no further protection against a full December frost was necessary. Having teased each of her pleasure zones and letting her indulge her own desires, they captured their love with a slow rhythmic pulse that for him, ended with a minds-eye sparkling eclipse.

As they lay panting under the quilt, now damp from the gleam of their bodies, Paul said, "I love you, Mare, and I don't think I could have gotten through this without you."

She squeezed his ribs with one hand and nestled further into his shoulder, her braid lying softly on his extended right arm, trim but muscled. She gently stroked his chest and murmured, "That makes two of us, Paulie boy." Silence punctuated the room, brightened only by a wash of moonlight.

"I think we need to talk to the Schenks."

"How does this work, anyway? Do we do this here, or come out of hiding and let our families do the whole shebang?"

"Here," Paul said. "It'll be safer that way, for us and for them. We'll have a simple ceremony and blessing by their minister, and that's good—the event won't draw any attention in the English community."

"You've thought this all out." She chuckled. "I love the way the Amish refer to everyone who is not them as 'English.' But you know all this stuff because...?"

Paul laughed in their quilted cocoon. "Don't give me any credit, short stuff! Hey, I may have been a dumb kid when I worked for the Schenks all those summers, but I wasn't deaf and blind. There was even a pretty girl or two, I remember."

She poked him hard. "Don't you start, big boy. Remember, I may be a little thing, but I grew up on a farm and haven't forgotten my way around a cow barn." She went on with mock emphasis, "And you're one skinny dude, so don't think I couldn't knock you back on your heels if I had to. Just keep those big olives on me."

"Not even married and you're already getting darn possessive. Hah." He hoped she could feel his broad smile in the dark. "And, by the way, I can't seem to take my eyes off of you, even in the moonlight."

"Uh-oh. Get us back to the wedding plans, Mister, before you tire us out for tomorrow's work."

"Yes, ma'am." He cleared his throat. "As I remember it, when a young couple begins to court, it's a big secret, even from the parents and sibs, until around July or August. Then the couple announces their intention only to their own families. There's no ring or engagement party or anything. It stays a secret until a month before the actual wedding."

"I'm liking this plan already."

"Most Amish weddings take place in November or December, after all the harvesting is done and the community has time to prepare and celebrate. We might see one in the next few weeks."

"Hm. We could be right on schedule," she said, a soft giggle in her voice.

"You're right, come to think of it. We missed the July/August part, but we've sure kept things a secret."

"So how do they do the weddings then?"

"They take place in the girl's home, usually on a Tuesday or Thursday."

"What? Why would that be? They do weekends, like us."

"Haven't you noticed, though? Sunday is a total day of rest, so a wedding cannot be on a Sunday, and neither can it be on a Saturday because of the late-night celebrating before the Lord's day. That also means a Sunday cannot be used to prepare for a wedding, so that lets out Monday out completely. Over time, they've settled on Tuesdays or Thursdays."

"And?"

"Usually the Amish bride makes her own wedding dress out of blue or purple fabric and, along with the prayer shawl, it's saved for her to be buried in."

"That's pretty neat." She snuggled even tighter beside him, her breasts against the side of his rib cage. "You know, if you put some meat on you, my poor boobs would have a softer pillow."

"Want me to make them feel better?"

"No! I want to hear more about the wedding. What will you wear?"

"Men wear a black suit, white shirt, high black boots, and a black bow tie. And by the way, there are no flowers, rings, or veils."

"Oh, now I get it. You want to do it here to save on expenses—and no ring." She tweaked his private parts with her fingers.

"Hey." He shifted his position as a physiological change began to occur. "Don't start what you can't finish."

"Just finish up with the wedding stuff, Mister Ever Ready."

"At the ceremony itself, hymns are sung, scripture is read, and the minister counsels the couple—there's no divorce allowed in this neck of the woods, so if we go through with this, I'm holding you to it, shortie."

"Don't 'shortie' me, Paulie. Two can play that lifetime game, so don't get any other ideas."

"Then there's usually a sermon." He laughed. "And it's not by you to me..."

"Yeah, those services will come later."

"Then it's party time, Amish style. There's tons of food, followed by games, songs, and chitchat. They're always a lot of fun, and you can actually hear yourself talk because there's no DJ pounding a beat through your eardrums."

Mare laughed softly. "I'm loving it even more. Do you think our parents will go for it?"

"We'll have to find out. We can promise them a nice church thing sometime down the road if we can get past Crew Cut."

"Oh, God, don't mention my worst nightmare."

As Mare lapsed into silence, Paul wondered how the two of them made it to this point. It seemed unlikely, to say the least. Who would have thought that operatives for the National Investigations Service could have uncovered a plot by the Vice-President of the United States to steal the election? Who would have thought one of their own NIS brethren would have been murdered for his views? Who would have thought that Paul and Mare could have outwitted the practiced killer controlled by that same Joseph P. Morrison?

When you get right down to it, he wondered with a smile, *How could a Presbyterian boy from Grove City College have found himself matched with a little Catholic girl from Indiana?*

When he catalogued the list of improbabilities, he thanked Almighty God for having spared them an early death. *But why?* Now, after their whirlwind escape up the northeasterly byways of Ohio, some twenty miles into Pennsylvania, what were he and Mare to do? Leave their Amish sanctuary? *Where would we go? What would we do?*

Without God, karma, and the invisibility of the Schenk farm, they would have been killed the month before, and their brush with mortality wasn't over. The murderer they knew as "Crew Cut" would come for them again. *But when? Where?*

Finally, Mare spoke again. "I guess that solves another problem, though."

"Crew Cut?"

"No, smart guy—the wedding. I may be crazy in love with you, but I'm one Catholic girl who's not giving up her faith, and I'm bettin' you're sticking to your Presby guns as well."

Paul chuckled. "You put it right out there, don't you? You're right though. We can solve that little dilemma later, and perhaps our folks will accept this outside-the-box alternative for that reason alone."

"Don't be silly. They'll accept it because we want to get married, and this is the only way we can do it without endangering our lives—and theirs." After a moment, she added, "There's one thing we haven't talked about, Paulie, my man."

"And that is?"

"What do we do for the rest of lives?"

"Maybe that can wait for tomorrow night." Paul brought his left hand up to her cheek and kissed her deeply before finding her breast, taut with desire.

Sleet pelted the Palladian window above and behind Vice-President Joseph P. Morrison as he sat, brooding, in the deep Moroccan leather chair. Alone in the study of the official residence at the Naval Observatory in Bethesda, he let his legs stretch out before him, one crossing the other at the ankle, and rested his head against the soft leather. For a supposed rough-and-tumble Texan, he had long, thin, spatulate fingers fit for a surgeon that he steepled so that his thumbs touched the tip of his narrow, prominent nose. It helped him concentrate.

The staccato plinks against the glass punctuated the thoughts nagging at him. Here he was, arguably the second-most important man in the world, yet, in fact, he was the most powerless. In the room, stilled except for furnace heat fluffing the air, he felt totally alone. Splendored though it had become by Nelson Rockefeller's personal funds, it was not the White House, and this walnut-paneled library was not the Oval Office.

He was surrounded by shelves of books he'd never read, but placed there to let visitors think otherwise. A few feet from the left arm of his chair was a complete stock of the best liquors—favorites of the guests he'd tried to impress over the last four years—though he himself never touched a drop. All the trappings were his, but no substance made them real.

On a night early in the Washington Christmas season, he should have been looking forward to the political theater at the galas he and his wife, Sharon, would attend, all of them celebratory of the holidays and, by extension, the victory for Democrats at the national level on November 6. He couldn't shift his mental ramblings in that direction, but gave in to the streams of thought that kept badgering him. With no one to trust with his musings, least of all Sharon, he knew he'd have to sort things out himself.

He recalled the night several weeks before the election when he'd entertained Attorney General Norton Sweeney and Senator Harrison Riordan, majority leader from Missouri. On that occasion, the book-shelves still held election memorabilia and other Texas doodads, which he realized left a wrong impression. That, however, wasn't the only impression he came to regret. Full of himself, he had strongly suggested to his guests that he could influence the election by accessing the skills of his other visitor at the time, Ricky McCord. *Would they remember what he said? To what, exactly, could they testify?* he demanded of his memory.

Morrison hoped that neither Sweeney nor Riordan would ever connect that conversation with the McCord's sudden death in Cincinnati on election night. The magic of vote manipulation had occurred in McCord's SoftSec's offices to make the difference in Ohio, Virginia, Florida, and Colorado, and a few more states, to be sure. He also hoped the two men never stumbled across the fact that several other people in Cincinnati disappeared that same night.

Like Benghazi, the sacrifices were for the greater good—the reelection of Averell Williams and Joe Morrison. Fortunately for everyone—except the dead, of course—what a Republican guru called "State Media" remained remarkably incurious about Benghazi, the election results, and the IRS matter.

Morrison laughed to himself when he thought how foolish they were, but grew serious when it came to News Global, an outfit he would go after when he became president. He hoped the State Media lemmings would dutifully echo his talking points when the time came.

Retracing his acts, conversations, and travel before the election had developed into an obsession, he knew. The greatest threat to his future was one of the men dedicated to protecting him. Agent Marty Cox of the Secret Service had served Morrison's every need, including the one to rid the election season of those who might burst the bubble of total choice and utopian socialism. Cox would have to be dealt with, but, for now, he was a necessary evil. Morrison had always liked that turn of phrase.

His more immediate calculation was whether to release to the media the tidbit that the president may be dying of cancer. Would the state electors honor the choice of the voters, albeit one obtained by fraud, and remain with the Williams–Morrison ticket, or would they bolt to the GOP's Hardy–Smith? They had been worthy opponents, but Governor Win Hardy and Senator Olivia Johnson Smith were the losers, and they never knew why. They thought it was the Latino vote and the so-called Millenial vote. Self-satisfied, he grinned. *If they only knew it was the Morrison magic!*

More specifically, if the electors wavered, would they take the constitutional risk of casting their ballots for Joe Morrison? *Probably not.* The more he thought about it—in his craving to succeed the man who bore him and the great state of Texas so little respect—the more he thought they'd stay the course made clear for them by Morrison and McCord in their electronic machinations. That Williams was a shoo-in, coupled with his worries over the crimes he'd committed, threw any seasonal merriment he might have enjoyed into a funereal funk. He felt like a man on a runaway luge, with no idea how quickly it might crash him into political oblivion.

At that moment, Sharon Morrison entered the library. "Honey, do you want to say goodnight to the kids? A good Christmas story might be in order. Oh"—she hastened to tease—"or am I supposed to say holiday story, because we're Democrats?"

Morrison looked at his wife, still beautiful after two children and too many Washington dinners. Trying to lever himself out of his funk and the leather chair, he managed a vacant, "Whatever you want, honey."

She leaned down and planted a soft kiss on his coal black hair. "Joe, what's eating at you? You've been morose for three weeks now, and you should be one of the two happiest guys in America."

"I know, Shar, honey, but the world is never perfect, is it? There's always a fly takin' a shit on the picture."

"Now Joe, keep that cowhand talk out of this house, y'hear me? Let's keep that for Texas backrooms when we go home."

"This is home now, hon, whatever that means."

Bishop Mast's mid-December mood was frostier than the snowstorm gathering fury outside the farmhouse of Andy and Sadie Schenk. He wasted no time after the usual greetings. "I do not like this one bit." Though both his hosts were in the room, he addressed his comments to Andy alone, as he was the head of the household.

"I understand," Andy replied meekly, stroking his rapidly graying beard and eyeing Sadie, who sat impassively across the room, closer to the second stove alight that evening.

"You say they are like your own family," the bishop said, "but truly, they are not of our way. They have been with us—a month, Andy? There was no intent to marry expressed to you in August, as is customary, because they did not live here." His voice ticked in exasperation. It was rare for an Amish bishop to surrender a calm demeanor to ill-tempered commentary, but this was different. "I do not like the precedent this sets. Soon every English couple in Lawrence County will want to get married in one of our farmhouses because it is 'cool.'"

Andy remained silent as the bishop's sarcasm iced the air.

"The rest of our people are surprised at you, Andrew Schenk. That you would allow your household to be a part of such a break with tradition and custom is extraordinary." The last word was traced with the German accent the elders of the community retained. "These are English people, and they should get married in their church, apart from our community."

"There are reasons, Bishop, why that is not possible at present. For this moment, they are family to us and, after praying upon it, Sadie and I—we think it best for Mr. Gladston and Miss Burdette to be married here in our house, as if the young woman were our daughter."

"But she is not your daughter," the bishop persisted, his hair plastered to his head from the heat of the wood-burning stove immediately next to his chair. "And the two of them haven't been betrothed in accordance with our custom."

"Yet, they have, Bishop. They were pledged to one another before they arrived here. That was plain enough for Sadie and me to see. When their betrothal occurred is not important to us. What is more, they asked our permission nearly two weeks ago, and they are content to wait the full month for the news to be announced in our community."

"There is another matter," Bishop Mast continued, not unlike a prosecutor. "It has been said that these two have been hiding on your farm because the English authorities are searching for them. They have brought danger here, whether you wish to say so or not."

"You may have forgotten, Bishop, that young Paul lived with us for many summers in his youth. Now he is a responsible man and the woman, too, was raised on a farm. They are good people. If someone in this particular government chooses to chase them, there must be a good reason for us to protect them."

Bishop Mast was silent, his teeth clenched against the possibility that he might say something highly regrettable to a most-respected man in the community.

"I might add, Bishop," Andy said quietly, his head bowed in humility, "that when our people came here nearly three hundred years ago, it was to escape the authorities. Was it not?"

The older man sat by the stove, pondering. The crackle of wood turning to glowing coals splintered the silence.

"In any event, Bishop," Andy said, his head still bowed, "Mistress Sadie and I have taken Paul Gladston and his betrothed, Miss Marlyn Burdette, into our hearts, and, for their safety, the wedding must not be performed in an English church for all the world to know about. It should be celebrated here—with your blessing."

Somehow struck by a memory of his own youthful passion when he and his wife of sixty-two years fought custom to marry early, resistance melted away with the last crystals of icy snow on the bishop's black, frock coat. "They will dress and marry according to our ways?" he asked quietly. "And there will be no electricity and no loud English music from a radio?"

The Schenks nodded, a slight smile lifting each of their faces.

"The words and the hymns will be ours?"

"Yes, Bishop. Both are Christian and will choose scriptural readings appropriate to the service."

"Well," he said, weakening, "perhaps..."

Andy Schenk seized the opening. "Only their parents will come—no brothers or sisters—so we will not be overrun with English that day."

"And the couple will seek my blessing?"

"Yes, Bishop," Andy said with a tone intimating acquiescence to an idea not at all his own.

"And they will wait until the first week in January?"

"Yes, Bishop. I know that is a bit later than our custom, but it is not overly late. Do you agree?"

"That will be fine," the elder said, feeling he got his way in all things. "Let us remember, Andy and Sadie, that this is a sacred moment, and they must realize the permanence of marriage. It is not a hobby, as some of the English think. If there is any notion that these two do not take this seriously, why, I expect you to call an end to it. That is understood?"

Sadie nodded.

Andy said, "Understood, Bishop Mast. With these two, I have no doubt. If they had been born to our community, I would not know the difference."

"So be it, then." The Bishop rose as he spoke. Looking toward the door reminded him he was getting too old for buggy trips in a blizzard.

"Bishop," the host said quickly, "you could stay the night, or my Jakub could drive you home in our buggy."

"My Martha will worry if I do not return," he said, "but she will know I am with you tonight, if I may bed down here."

Sadie's gentle face lit with a smile. "We will make you comfortable, Bishop, and then you can see for yourself how this couple goes about the morning with us." Her deep blue dress rustled as she moved to prepare a bed. "I am sure you will be pleased."

"We must be," the bishop said, eyeing his host over the round, frameless glasses perched on his nose.

It was not often that Norton Sweeney and his oldest daughter, Maddie, home from boarding school, had a day together without all the limousine hoopla attached to high public office. Clad for winter weather, they braced for the cold air as they exited the DC Metro at the Gallery Place/Chinatown stop and began their short walk to the National Portrait Gallery on F Street NW.

Sweeney pushed his middle aged self along as he and Maddie chattered about school and boyfriends. He was annoyed when the cell phone purred in his pocket, and he didn't want to answer because doing so would subtract moments from the rare opportunity to spend real time with one of his three children. Deirdre, his wife of thirty-seven years, was home with the other two, so an opportunity to visit one of Maddie's favorite places was not to be missed.

When his cell interrupted a second time, he assumed it must be Deirdre telling him to pick something up on the way home. He reached an ungloved hand into his black North Face jacket, retrieved his phone without looking at the caller ID, and answered, expecting a familiar voice. Instead, the first syllables both frightened and unnerved him, and he listened closely.

"Norton Sweeney?" inquired the hard, electric sound.

"Yes," he answered. "And who's calling?"

"Never mind, you fruitcake. Just listen up."

"Who the hell are you?" Sweeney demanded, his voice out of its natural timbre. Then he noticed Maddie's fearful looks as she stood on the sidewalk next to him, her blonde curls brushing across her cheek.

Suddenly, he felt alone, and wished the black Lincoln Town Car was right at the curb.

"Like I said, you don't need to know. What you should know is that others know about your sexual preferences, and those could be made public any day, any way."

Sweeney's face felt flushed, but not from exposure to the weather. "You don't know what you're talking about." His tried to control his voice.

"Oh, yes, we do," the caller said. "I know you're with your daughter right now—it's Maddie, isn't it?—so you can't say anything, but just listen. We know all about you and your friend from your Air Force days, the same friend you still see periodically. Remember now, Norty?" The caller spoke his nickname with derision.

"N-no one cares about that any more. W-what do you want?"

"You care. We know you care. Even liberals like to keep their secrets, but we want what you want—that all of this stays in the closet, so to speak." The caller made a cynical noise that nearly passed for a laugh. "All you have to do is be careful about the past, and be careful about the future."

"What does that mean?" Sweeney demanded, panic beginning to overcome him.

"You'll figure it out," The caller paused before adding, in the same mocking whine, "Norty."

"Wait. I don't understand..." But the line went dead. Sweeney looked all around, but no one stood out as watching them. No one was out of place. He pulled Maddie close and put his arm around her. He was scared to death for her; his past; and now, the future.

The antediluvian desk phone with multiple lines, each with its own light, occupied a prominent spot on House Speaker John Whitaker's desk, making it easy for him to reach the instrument when he chose to do so. A bright spot caught the corner of his eye as he perused a piece of legislation doomed to the trash basket. Line one meant his assistant would announce a call from God only knew; line two signaled a call from a select number of politicos, friends, or large donors—they would be announced as well; line three meant his wife, Janet, couldn't wait for him to come home to tell him who said what to whom; and line four trumpeted a call directly from the president, vice-president, or their chiefs of staff.

With Williams and Morrison in office, however, line four had remained largely unlit for four years, and, once or twice in that period, Whitaker had a maintenance man check to see if the light for the line actually functioned.

It was line two. "Yes, Lynne, what is it?" He listened for a moment as she told him what he needed to know. "Really? Give me ten seconds, and I'll talk to him."

Whitaker was always surprised by this caller, and knew from experience that composing his thoughts would serve him well. When he picked up the phone once again, he couldn't get beyond, "Hello," before the voice on the other end took command.

"Why, is this the vaunted Speaker of the United States House of Representatives, congressman from Ohio's Eighth District?" came the gravelly voice of the ancient Harrison Riordan, top Democrat on the Hill.

"I hear the unmistakable voice of my colleague in the other body, the esteemed Senate majority leader from the great state of Missouri." Whitaker finished with a laugh.

"John, it's always a pleasure to make this call, because I know you're one Republican who always has time for civil conversation," Riordan rasped with a voice corrugated by decades of cheap cigars and even cheaper bourbon. "By the way, I noticed you used the term, 'other body,' instead of the 'upper chamber,' as some might think customary."

"Why, you old rascal, I don't want you to keep thinking 'upper' somehow suggests superior, wiser, or more collegial. Lordly, perhaps." Whitaker chortled.

"Lordly, my ancient ass, John Whitaker," Riordan said. "I don't mind telling you that I enjoy our talks more than I did when the Maryland congresswoman from my party sat in your chair."

"Now, Harry, let's not be disrespectful of the lovely Angela Tesoro," Whitaker said in mock chastisement. "But I know you didn't call to daub me up with warm butter on a cold afternoon, so what's on your mind, you old schemer?"

"That's what I like about you, John. Get right to it and cut the bullshit. Heh-heh." Riordan paused, inhaling loudly and deeply.

Whitaker imagined him sucking in the delicious poisons of the old man's favorite cigar. "If you're smokin' over there, Harry, I'm gonna call the General Services Administration and create a big scandal over such an egregious violation of the rules your administration imposed."

Riordan chuckled and exhaled at the same time. "You do that. I'm glad you mentioned a scandal because that's what I'm calling about. Just how far are you going to let the Tea Party push you on all this IRS stuff?"

"Don't start that anti-TP stuff with me, Harry. You're one of many Democrats who believes in fiscal prudence, adherence to the constitution, and, perhaps, respect for life. If you're not careful, I'll out you as a closet TP guy."

"And I'll return the favor by letting people know how damn reasonable you can be—for a Republican."

"Ah, more butter," Whitaker said.

"Seriously, how far are you going to take this IRS business?"

"As far as it goes, and you'll be damn glad we do, because you'll want to get together with us to make sure it doesn't happen to you."

"Maybe...maybe, but don't tell me the rumors are true that you're also going to make a big stink about this Benghazi thing," Riordan said, his Missouri drawl grinding the gravel in his throat.

"That's another matter. I know you'll have to support the president on this, but there's an awful smell there, and we're going to have to find out where the rot is."

"Now, John, don't talk like that. Averell Williams is an honorable man."

"And a decent one, too, but he probably ranks number one in the category of 'Ineffective Foreign Policy Leader,'" Whitaker said. "The American people will one day figure out we were safer and more respected under George Bush than with your guy."

"Our guy, you mean. He's *our* guy."

"Point for your side, but we're going to dig, so get ready." Whitaker stopped, and switched the phone to his other ear.

"You were about to say something else."

"You know, Harry, there is something else, now that you called. It's the strangest thing. Sometime before the election, some of us heard the faintest rumor that your protégé had developed some sort of relationship with a Mr. Enrique McCord."

"What of it? I've met the man—both Texas boys, as I recall," Riordan said.

Whitaker sensed the change the old man's tone, as if he'd shifted his creaking bones to the edge of his chair. He knew Riordan's words would be chosen with care. "You may be aware, then, that McCord is dead, reportedly killed in some sort of road-rage thing late on election night."

"I'm sorry to hear that, John, but I'm not connecting the dots on this."

"I'm not connecting anything yet, either, but the odd thing is that, unlike what was on the news, the police haven't closed the file on this one yet. We'll be keeping an eye on it."

"A coincidence, I'm sure," Riordan said.

"I don't believe in them, and neither do you. All this happened in my district, or close-by, so some people in Cincinnati are curious."

"What might this have to do with House committees?"

"Nothing yet." Whitaker sensed an even higher level of tension creep into Riordan's voice, like the audible tightening of a bowstring.

"Anyway," Riordan said, "I wish every conversation with the dark side was as cordial as this."

Mock scorn marked the Speaker's laugh. "You're right, and we slobs in the House bask in the wise words of our Senate friends." Laughing still, Whitaker said, "See ya, and give Angela a big hug for me."

As he replaced the receiver, Whitaker felt a chill in the room that had nothing to with the weather. Shuddering his six foot two frame and swiveling his chair to peer at the winter sun's glare on the limestone framing his window, he wondered what rime-ridden ghosts haunted his chambers.

In some ways, the five hundred miles from Cincinnati measured the distance he had come from his origins as an every-man-for-himself individualist. The days of the lone wolf were over, and his challenge as a Republican was to acknowledge the needs of neighbors without sacrificing rights and responsibilities.

Where is that not-so-straight middle road? One that would allow us to purge the evils from a politicized IRS and lay bare the hypocrisies of a foreign policy, of which Benghazi was but one icon, yet welcome the unstoppable, new generations of would-be citizens seeping through the porous southern borders? Where was that path that would allow reason to feed and educate the poorest of us, yet allow those with talent and drive to thrive without guilt or undue burden?

The nation had become more than polarized. It had become so fragmented that each two-person lobby seemed to think it had a lock on all the right answers and was unwilling to give up anything in their zealotry for a misty goal. Gridlock wasn't only in the legislative body Whitaker managed. It lived in every town and hamlet, in every borough and city. Indeed, the US House of Representatives reflected the political tastes of the nation, as varied and eclectic as they had become.

What the country needed was a politician who insisted that those individuals and clusters still possessed of reason and rational compromise find a way to build on the essentials on which they agreed, and then take step by reasoned, patient step toward a logical and fair outcome. Whitaker was sure he had done his best to let the waters of the partisan divide resume their natural level without marginalizing those out of the main.

But would the ghosts of Webster and Clay, of Lincoln and Teddy Roosevelt guide him on the treacherous lanes he had to travel?

2.

S now softened the air as Andy, his eldest son, Jakub, and Paul trudged to the large, white barn, their boots leaving a trail of whitened foot prints.

"Soon it will be Beltznickel," Andy said, puffing little clouds as he talked, "just like what you English call St. Nicholas Day. We will have some fun in town that day!" He watched for Paul's reaction.

"We'll be happy to tend to the place for you," Paul said.

"Nonsense. You and Mare must come, too."

"It might be better for us not to leave the farm, Andy."

He put his hand on Paul's shoulder. "You have been here nigh on a month and we do not want you and your Mare to go crazy with the cows," he said, smiling wide through his beard.

"I'm not so sure. Mare and I want to be completely invisible to the English world."

"And Beltznickel is the perfect day for that." His enthusiasm for the idea grew with each word. "We will go into town for a shop at Gilliland's Market, and then to the auction barn north of the borough to see what all the sellers might entice Sadie and me to buy."

"How would we fit in then?"

"It is good, do you not see?" Andy asked with the German-Dutch lilt at the end of the question. "We will take one buggy and a covered flatbed wagon. You and Mare will be dressed like us, and you will be taking care to see the children do not eat too many donuts and crullers at the auction." Mirth filled his face.

"As I remember it, they sell good food there," Paul said with a widening smile of his own.

"Oh, yes, and there will be so many Amish in black and purple and blue, no one will notice you. It is"—Andy stretched his arms wide—"a big day for selling, eating sweets, and celebrating Beltznickel with the children."

"I trust you, so we'll go."

When Thursday came, all the Schenks bundled up against the cold and readied the horses for the buggy and wagon they would need to carry everyone the four miles into New Wilmington. Paul and Mare enjoyed the canter into town as the horses clopped and snorted in the thin, cold air. In town, they shepherded the children up and down Market Street, while the elder Schenks tended to bank business and bought a few things at Gilliland's. The winter air protected all the food from spoilage.

Then they all headed north, where the long, broad auction house sat close by the Mercer Road. Constructed of hewn beams, cedar planks, and galvanized, corrugated steel roofing panels decades before, the whitewashed, open buildings had seen their best days. Already, a sea of buggies and wagons, along with a scattering of cars and trucks, filled the unpaved parking area.

Lunchtime and early afternoon marched along as the elder Schenk had described it. Nothing was amiss until shortly after one o'clock, about when the Paul and Mare purchased freshly deep-fried and glazed donuts for each of the children. That's when Paul looked across the crowd and saw the sharp jaw of the nameless man he hoped he'd never see again.

"Mare," he whispered, bending low. With one hand on her shoulder to steady them both, he wiped the sugar from little Joshua's chin with the other and said, as casually as he could, "Over to the left, it's him—it's Crew Cut."

Mare stiffened, her face reddened from the clammy cold. "I can't believe he's here," she said, sufficiently self-possessed to take the napkin from Paul's hand and continue to swab Joshua's face. "What should we do?"

"There's no danger to us here. Stay put with the youngest three. I'll take the rest with me and get behind him. He'll be looking for a pair of us and won't be expecting the human appendages."

"What if he sees us?" Her whisper rasped like coarse grit sandpaper.

"He won't do anything here. We'll know. If he hangs around and waits in his SUV, he'll have spotted us and will try to follow us home. If he drives off in a bit, he's given up."

"I hope you're right, Paulie boy," she said, but her usual playful tone was gone.

Keeping his broad-brimmed black felt hat pulled low, Paul stayed several feet behind the yellow-haired giant and hoped for the cover of his new whiskers, assuming as he did that his tracker had somehow secured their government file photos.

Paul had seen Crew Cut only once before and for a fraction of a second, but he was sure that the man stalking them in the barn was the same nameless driver of the black SUV that had chased them on the Columbus outerbelt a month earlier. He would never forget the determined glare, the unyielding energy so evident in that glimpse—and the blond, close-cropped hair. *God, it's him!*

The man hunter didn't belong with the farm people in the barn. Not only his height, but the systematic way in which he circuited the crowd made him stand out. It was if the people somehow sensed the tall stranger meant trouble for someone, and they gave him plenty of room.

At one point, as Paul knew might happen, Crew Cut turned and headed back in the opposite direction, at the far side of the folks clustered toward the center. He was headed toward Mare and the children.

Step after step, Crew Cut moved closer to his prey. Paul hoped the killer had not spotted her. He motioned to his own charges to find the hot pretzel counter and wait for him. Paul closed the distance between him and Crew Cut. Thankfully, Mare remained stooped, scrubbing little faces free of sugar glazing. Crew Cut stopped within a foot of them.

Paul's heart nearly stopped when the killer put one hand on Joshua's shoulder. Absent-mindedly, he patted it, much like an uncle does a favorite nephew. Crew Cut scoured the crowd one more time. Finally, he moved away.

Mare kept busy with her chattering charges, their eyes big with the black and blue crush of Amish all around them. With her long, bright dress and stark, dark blue woolen bonnet, she looked like an eldest daughter tasked with caring for the children while the parents saw what bargains were available to them elsewhere in the barn. Several times, she reached to the back of her neck to make sure each strand of her auburn hair was tucked in under the stiffened wool.

She startled when Paul returned and said, "He's gone."

"How do you know?" Her voice trembled as if trying to slow a pounding heart. "You've been gone nearly twenty minutes."

"I turned the tables and followed him around. A few minutes ago, he was within inches of you. Good thing you're a natural mom. When he went outside, I watched him walk across the road toward the hardware store where the black Tahoe was parked."

"Then it was him, for sure?"

"Definitely. I took the older kids, and we walked as close as I dared."

"And?"

"Virginia plates. What's more, I have his number."

The bright, primary color set for the News Global evening broadcast was lit up and ready to go when Forbes Flannery settled himself into his usual chair and rocketed into the opening monologue right after his famous intro.

"My friends, the election may have come and gone, but, like the smell of bad meat from a shuttered butcher shop, some issues won't go away. One that I'm talking about involves the continuing reports of bias and discrimination by the IRS in how they treated conservative nonprofit groups in the run-up to last month's election. What's more disturbing is the Benghazi mess. I say 'mess' because this administration can't even decide when it knew there was a terror attack that killed four Americans, including our distinguished ambassador.

"After the din following most election celebrations dies away, the partisan issues in play before the voters decide also go away. Not so the IRS and Benghazi matters. With me here tonight, after the unexpected loss by Governor Hardy to President Williams, is the former campaign wizard to President George W. Bush, Gardner Stewart."

Flannery pivoted his chair to the right, and the camera followed his gaze to the guest chair where the ineffable guru from the state of Texas sat. "What have you to add to that, Gardner?"

"As always, Forbes, you covered it well, but I'm here to predict—more accurately than I did the election outcome, I might note—that neither of these issues is going away, much as the State Media is laboring hard to make them disappear."

"Why is that?"

"Unlike a lot of preelection stuff that gets put up for the public to chew on, these two scandals and accompanying cover-ups not only have credible bases in fact, but each week that goes by reveals another piece that makes our suspicions stronger."

"Do you have any specifics in mind?"

"Let's take the IRS. After many weeks of silence, the Democrats have trotted out one or two liberal organizations for which the IRS slowed the process, as opposed to the dozens and dozens that claimed to be conservative. Illegally, the IRS even quizzed some of these groups about the prayers they said before meetings. And Benghazi is in a whole different realm, in my humble opinion, Forbes."

"You'll have to say more on that."

"Because to date, the administration has not acknowledged the cover-up where Benghazi is concerned. There was no video, there was no demonstration—nothing happened the way the administration said it did on countless television shows, in presidential speeches—everywhere you look, there is a prevaricated statement."

"Why are they stonewalling to this degree?"

"Simple. If they admit one single thing they said was false, their whole narrative before November 6—that General Motors is alive, bin Laden is dead, and al Qaeda is on the run—was a lie."

"There you have it, ladies and gentlemen—the world according to Gardner Stewart."

The towering grandfather clock chimed softly as Joe Morrison strode into the Oval Office at exactly two o'clock on December 12. Across the expanse of thick carpet, the president knocked out some deskwork and didn't look up right away. Morrison was surprised that the president's alter ego for administrative matters, Mary Beth—Freddie—Frederick wasn't standing by his side, sliding one set of documents after another under his hand, pen at the ready, for his famous signature.

The top of the president's head seemed grayer, perhaps, with white hair invading what had been jet-black territory not so many years before. When Williams lifted his gaze, Morrison could almost see the weight of Western civilization lying astride his shoulders as he bent again to the paper carpeting his desk. Then, Williams stood up and walked briskly toward him, hand extended in greeting. "Joe! Good to see you."

Sensitive to any slight, Morrison was offended that he was being greeted as a foreign dignitary from a small South American country, rather than as the man a heartbeat away. Nonetheless, he shook the president's hand, and the two of them headed toward the seating enclave where the president held court. Williams went to his favorite leather chair, nicely positioned so that he could find the oversize clock standing against the wall with a slight leftward glance. Morrison sat on the couch immediately to the president's right, where he faced the same clock straight on. He knew from Freddie that the president wanted his guests to be mindful that their time together would be short.

"Well," the president began, "five more days, and we will have jumped another hurdle. How do you feel?"

"Fine. The real question is, how do you feel? I mean," Morrison stammered, "I mean, you know, in reference to our private talk on election eve." Relieved that he finally got the words out, he sat back and waited for the president to lead the conversation.

"How I feel is apparently at odds with what the blood work and biopsies tell us," Williams said, pausing for effect, "and that's that I should be feeling a bit poorly. It seems, according to our good Doctor Bolling, that I've pushed the treatment envelope to its outer limits, and that we must act soon."

"Is that what you want to do, sir?"

"No, it's not. Neither of us wants to consider the alternative choice the electors might make, and for that matter, we can't risk what the joint session might do when they come up to bat on the fourth. Whatever treatment I receive will have to wait until after the twentieth, and that's that."

"So, then, you're sure you want to push it?"

"I am not at all interested in having our second inaugural footnoted in history as the only one the president-elect did not attend. Besides, in the public mind, I do not officially enter my second term until I place my hand on the Lincoln Bible and take the oath. That's our answer. The calendar dictates it to us, and that's why I wanted us to talk today."

"Yes, sir. How should we proceed?"

"First, we should go on as if this little problem didn't exist, keeping it a total secret lest some fool decide to upend the electoral process for the moment's fame it gets him—or her. That's why it's imperative that we're together on this."

"You can count on me, Av."

"I know I can, and that brings us to the second reason for our talk today: how we handle things while I'm under anesthetic."

"I recall you mentioning that we'll invoke Section Three of the Twenty-Fifth Amendment."

"Actually, I will invoke it," Williams said, and paused, as if regretting his choice of words, "when I transmit to the president pro tempore of the Senate and the Speaker of the House that I will be unable to discharge the powers and duties of the office. Bolling tells me that the duration should be eighteen hours or so, at which time—barring any medical circumstance—I will transmit notice that I intend to resume the office."

"Seems pretty straightforward to me."

"In conversation, yes. In practice, no. Ronald Reagan refused to invoke the amendment when he underwent minor surgery, while George W. Bush did so on two occasions. Think about that for a moment. Dick Cheney was actually president—with all the powers attached thereto—for a total of some twelve hours. Hah! Nobody will think twice when you hold the reins this time around." He beamed at his Number Two.

Morrison saw that the president's smile was intended to be real, but masked some discomfort. Pain? Quickly, he said, "Thanks for that, Av."

"It's all in the wording of the documents and the care with which we walk through the process with the media and the public, and that's why I wanted to give you a heads up so that when the two of us meet with Sweeney on the particulars, you'll be totally comfortable with the drill."

"Of course."

"Joe, you may be surprised to know that aside from Commander Bolling and the First Lady, you're the only other person who knows about my medical condition." He paused for a moment. "All the more reason we need to keep to our respective scripts for other ears between now and sometime shortly after Inauguration Day."

"Got it, sir. You can depend on me to keep mum." Even as Morrison spoke the words, he hated Williams. The real purpose of this meeting, he concluded, was not to give him a warm fuzzy about the upcoming surgery, but to make sure he kept his mouth shut. *Does he think I'm a fool?*

"What's wrong with you?" In her coy manner, Mare Burdette put the emphasis on the *wrong* without making it sound as if she thought there was something evil about the man she loved.

"Wrong? Wrong? You little tease." Paul pulled her close in the one location on the Schenk farm where they weren't chilled to the bone. Despite their own farm life experiences, neither of them could get used to what Amish folks were inured to from birth. "C'mon. Let's warm up the way you like best."

"Me? It's you who think that sex is your sole occupation in life." She couldn't help but laugh out loud when she said it.

"And I've found a most willing companion."

"I thought all you Presbies were too stiff-necked to—"

"Say no more. Let me demonstrate." Not an intelligible word was exchanged for the next twenty minutes. Paul used every tactic she had taught his hands and fingers, and her sounds of satisfaction suggested she might give him a passing grade.

"Do you think" Paul whispered in her ear, "the Amish think about sex all day when they're working in the barns and in the fields?"

She poked him in the ribs. "Change the subject, Paulie boy, or that prized tool of yours will wither away and fall off."

He put his lips on hers, a transparent attempt to get her in the mood again.

"Seriously," she said, and she was, indeed, serious, "is there a plan for us when we take a break from farm chores and intercourse?"

"Oh, all right. If you absolutely insist on a halftime in the sport we play so well, I've been thinking about this a lot. Don't mock me. I do think about things other than sex—not too many, I admit, but the important things, yes."

"Well, then?"

"After what happened the other day, we can't stay here. Besides us, it puts too many people in danger. He might come back."

"So?"

"We have a throwaway cell phone and, much as I hate to do it, I think I should make a call or two. We've been so cut off from things, I have no idea what's going on in the English world out there."

"Yeah, it's kinda strange, actually. In some ways, it feels good not to have all the political crap poured all over you every single day. I've enjoyed this in ways I never thought I would."

"What I was going to say is I found out how best to get in touch with Pete Clancy. Last we heard, he was being dumped by NIS and was actually going to retire. I can't believe a guy like that would put his credentials in a drawer, but who knows. Maybe Pete, being in DC, can help us navigate without running into Crew Cut."

"Jesus, Paul, don't mention that guy's name. We came too close, and we know he's still out there—and still looking for us. We really don't know much about him, do we?"

"Except that he's still driving the same black Tahoe he had last fall. We now have the Virginia plate number, and there's no doubt in my mind it was the same vehicle that ran down Nelson Evers. And"—he said the word with a trump—"we know he's somehow connected to Vice-President Morrison."

Mare didn't respond right away. When Paul mentioned Nelson Evers's name, it triggered too many memories of her mentor in Cincinnati. The older black investigator had trained her in the craft and along the way, treated her like a younger sister. He held strong views, especially about the need for his people to get off the "new plantation," as he called it. He had never been careful about what he said or to whom. She was sure that his views about the IRS mess in Covington and the plan to steal the election had gotten him killed— by the man they knew only as, "Crew-Cut." Evers had been honest and brave, and she had to wonder, *How can I get justice for him?* Mare forced her focus back to the moment, but could not filter the emotion from her voice. Softly, she asked, "How do we know that again?"

"You must be sleepy. Enrique McCord and Morrison were buds— that we knew because McCord himself made a point to tell us—and when we worked through the logic on Nelson Evers's murder, the threats later on, the same guy, apparently, stalking Amber Bustamente, it had to be Morrison himself pulling the strings."

"But no smoking gun, right?"

"Not exactly, but if we eliminate the IRS crowd and the Office of Personnel Management types, he's the only one who makes everything fit together. Nobody else."

"God Almighty, Paul, I wish it didn't go that high. Makes it so hard to believe in the big things, you know? And Crew Cut's still on the loose."

"I know. That's why I thought Pete could help us."

"OK," she said, "I can live with that. I'm starting to chill." Her speech husky, she asked, "Got any ideas?"

Playing a game of one-on-one basketball on the half court tucked amid the trees near the West Wing was almost always fun for the participants. The court itself was relatively invisible to the public outside the fence and to visitors who traversed the nearby walkways.

Agent Marty Cox of the Secret Service was not looking forward to the match, however. Play could be downright miserable on the gloomy days approaching the official start of winter. The two reasons guys—mostly—came out to play were simple: either they were die-hard jocks who wanted to get their heart rates up in an activity other than politics or sex, or they wanted to have a totally private—and unrecorded—conversation.

The latter reason prompted the outside meets for Agent Cox and Vice-President Joseph P. Morrison. Neither man trusted the interior spaces of the West Wing, both of them knowing all too well how both Lyndon Johnson and Richard Nixon had come to regret their penchant for recording history.

Though he had just begun a few warm-ups, Cox was sweaty and nervous. His chest was full of air, but it was hard to take a breath. It wasn't the cold. It was Joe Morrison. He and his boss, the man he was assigned to protect against any attack, were murderers in the truest sense of the word, and Cox—who feared nothing—was afraid of what might come next.

He recalled vividly the March day on this very court, the tipping point, when he knew that what the vice-president asked him to do was utterly criminal, and he didn't turn back. It wasn't a gray area at all. What he told himself then was that he had a pension and a family. He told his conscience that he was simply doing the bidding of the second-most powerful man in the land. That would be weak in any venue other than his own mind. The soft crunch of gravel alerted him to the arrival of the only other player that day.

"Do you remember how the president ran this court the first year of his first term? We couldn't keep the media away—they loved it, and so did we." The vice-president's voice was conversational, almost casual.

"Yes, sir, I remember," Cox responded, wondering how the chatter between two conspirators could be anything but deadly and serious.

"That first year, you had been assigned to him, if I recall correctly."

"Correct, sir."

"Do you want to be assigned to the president's security detail again, Marty?"

"I'm happy serving you, sir."

"That's loyal of you, Marty, but I meant as a member of my detail."

Cox hesitated, wondering if Morrison was playing a head game. "Sir, I'm not following. You told me last fall that you expected to have more responsibilities in a second term, but..." He let it hang there.

Morrison caught his eye and held the connection. "There could be a change, Marty, if the president has a health problem..." It was his turn to let the thought drift unfinished. He took the ball above the key.

"Am I supposed to connect some dots here, sir?"

"Out here, Marty, it's always Joe, and yes, there are a few dots I'll let you pencil together. But for now, that's all that needs to be said."

"Got it." Cox wanted to process Morrison's suggestion. *Or was it a revelation?*

"Now, let's shoot a few hoops to keep our blood flowing. It's only thirty-seven out, for Christ's sake, and there's something I want to go over with you."

"Shoot." Cox meant the ball.

"Witnesses." He dribbled.

"Well, sir, you know that your friend, Mr. McCord, met with a fatal accident election night—I guess he was on his way home." Cox couldn't help choosing his words carefully. *You never know who's listening.* "Then there was the IT guy, Nathan Somebody, and the guy your campaign sent out to Cincinnati—those two disappeared, as did Nathan's girlfriend. Too bad for them."

"Yeah," Morrison hissed between his teeth. "Others?" He shot and missed. "Christ!"

Cox shrugged and gave up the pretense. "Well, sir, there are the two young NIS investigators. They've gone off the grid—completely."

"How do people actually do that? You've tried everything? Credit cards? Phones? Family?"

"Yes, sir. I drove up to Pennsylvania recently and watched the Gladston house, snooped around, and asked a few questions downtown. There was a rumor about him having worked for some Amish farmer, so I drove out to New Wilmington where they all live and hung around town and the auction barns. Nothing." He retrieved the ball.

"Is this something"—Morrison chuckled—"we should ask the National Security Agency to check? They can damn near peek into your underwear without you knowing it." He turned serious. "By the way, were any of your Secret Service pals involved with you?"

As casually as two men discussing a Ravens-Steelers game, Cox dropped the circumspection with which their conversation began. "A techie who did the electronic eavesdropping—he was with me when the black investigator became a hit-and-run victim in a parking lot. Come to think of it, he was with me on the other actions as well."

"He will have to be neutralized." Morrison's voice seemed colder than the air temperature.

"There are, perhaps, two more, sir."

"Who?" Morrison stopped and held the ball.

Cox caught the surprise in the VP's voice. "Didn't you call someone to make arrangements for our nighttime visit to McLean last summer? And there was a guy at the safe house. I don't know who those people were, sir."

"Shit! You're right. And they're a couple of people who can't simply disappear. Ah, that reminds me, Marty. A few weeks ago, I mentioned that the attorney general needed to be put on notice. Did you take care of that?"

"Yes, sir," Cox responded but noticed that Morrison's attention seemed unfocused. *Is he thinking about me as a witness to be 'neutralized'?* "I think a phone call did the trick, using the information you gave me about the Air Force connection."

Morrison nodded. "That may be all that's necessary—for him. However, Mr. Andrew Warner could be a problem for us—for us, Marty.

Don't forget the fact—the problem would be for us. Could you arrange something for our CIA friend—something just enough?"

Cox hesitated. *How deep was this hole going to be?* "I guess I can do that, sir."

"No guessing, Marty. This is now about protecting us. Understand?" The ball went in the basket.

Cox rebounded as a nasty question crossed his mind. *Who will he get to kill me?*

Andrew and Nancy Warner never spent much time together, mostly because the CIA director didn't have much time for anyone but his real bride: the agency. A true *Company* man, Warner lived and breathed his work, devoted as he was to the nation's security.

He was thinking about it at Tyson's Corner Mall at around eight in the evening, when he said, "Honey, I thought you said we were stopping only at one toy store for Tony." He knew Nancy thought of nothing else besides the little guy, his antics, and the Facebook pictures she checked every day. They had finished picking up a few more Christmas gifts for their four-year old grandson, and he was relieved when, after visits to three more stores, they could finally leave.

"Don't call him Tony. It's Antonio."

"It's Tony to me and his father."

"But our daughter and I like the sound of his full name."

"Good God, Nan—" And then, as they were about to reach their BMW near the end of a long row, it happened.

As they carried their awkward load of already wrapped boxes, a large, black SUV roared directly down at them. Warner couldn't make out the exact make or the plate. It was not a reckless driver, he knew instinctively. Shoving Nancy between two parked cars, he let the packages fly, but he wasn't fast enough. The large side mirror tapped him at thirty or more miles per hour and knocked him senseless.

When the ambulances arrived several minutes later, the paramedics determined there were no life-threatening injuries, but plenty of heavy bruises and asphalt abrasions. People from the agency were on the spot as well, and the first action item in their report was to never permit the director to go out on his own again, Christmas or not.

There were no other witnesses to the vehicular assault, and neither Warner nor his wife could provide any useful descriptive details. The agency forensic gang lifted some minuscule paint fibers from the back of Director Warner's chesterfield coat, while the local police tagged the incident as a hit-and-run, cause unknown.

US Senator Jordan Marshall of Kentucky groaned aloud when he picked up the phone to call his friend, House Speaker John Whitaker. *I know I'm on a fool's errand,* he told himself, *and why I promised Harry Riordan I'd make this call, I'll never know.* He waited to get through on the Speaker's direct line. In a slow rhythm, he tapped the desk blotter with his pen.

"What do you know, Jordy? I was wondering how long it would take for Riordan to sidle up to you in the cloakroom and offer you something in trade for a call to me about upcoming hearings. Am I reading this right?" Whitaker asked, his voice full of humor.

Marshall returned a chuckle on the inside joke. "He says he'll let me block one of the president's nominees for a judgeship if I would make the call. You'll have to back me up on this, John, so I can collect on the favor."

"Is this someone you really want to block?"

"Hell, no. It's someone Riordan wants to block, but he can't do so because he's supposed to be flogging this guy's nomination for the president." Marshall chuckled again. "So now, I'll be able to remind him that he owes me one, not the other way around."

"Oh, God, the games we play. So, to carry out the deal, what is this conversation supposed to be about?

"Oh, let's see...the IRS targeting conservatives and the inept foreign policy that got us Benghazi, Iran, Syria, and North Korea. How's that for starters?" Marshall was a man of the Senate, and thoroughly enjoyed all the banter, bargaining, and backbiting—all hallmarks of standard senatorial business. He adjusted the round-rimmed glasses perched on his nose, thought about the upcoming midterms in 2014, when with luck, he might assume the role of majority leader and thereby have more legislatively productive conversations with the Republican Speaker.

"I'm not sure what Riordan hoped to accomplish by bribing you to make this call."

"Well, consider the call made, but I'm guessing that if he's willing to trade me a judgeship for a phone call, he's telling us he's open to further bargaining on all these hearings. Do you have a strategy on this?"

"We're gonna let the heat build up under all of them while I attempt to remain above it all. I expect to come under intense pressure to do something official about the hearings, but I also expect there's more evidence out there on the IRS matter and Benghazi. Like a boil to be lanced, I'm giving it plenty of time to get to that point."

"Good luck, John. Do you really think you'll be able to peel the onion on these two?"

"Yeah, I think so. It'll take time for a lot of Americans to see that everyone has a dog in the fight over IRS corruption, and, at the right time, we'll let our South Carolina member do what he does best—prosecute. As to Benghazi, that's a bit trickier. So far, President Williams and Secretary Grantham have managed to keep the lid on the whole thing. They're like a couple of fraternity brothers who've pledged to keep their secrets."

"Grantham has to be careful not to piss off Williams. There are rumors, by the way, that Grantham will announce his resignation, effective early in the second term. If he doesn't fully support Williams, Williams will have no choice but to throw him under the bus, and that'll ruin Grantham's chances for 2016."

"Two comments," Speaker Whitaker answered. "First, shouldn't it puzzle people that Emerson Grantham—who desperately wants to become president so he can show up his hillbilly cousin, Jefferson Harper—is resigning four years before the next election? Does that make sense? You'd think he'd want to stay to burnish his record as secretary and keep himself in the public eye. Unless..."

"Unless what?" the elderly Marshall prompted. He stopped tapping his pen and sat perfectly still in his chair. Whitaker was as smart as they came, and he didn't want to miss a word.

"Unless Grantham figured out that a foreign policy crafted on the basis of not hurting anyone's feelings is going to blow up—and badly—and he doesn't want to be around to take the blame. He wants it all on Williams. Wait, Jordy. It'll be Grantham who throws Williams under the bus—not the other way round. Then, the Benghazi disgrace will wash over Williams, not Grantham."

"You're probably right on that. You said you had a second comment?"

"You've got to admire those two. They've made a devil's pact to protect each other, hoping their friends in State Media—I love that term—will cover for them for four years. It ain't gonna happen! The steam is going to build, and something will blow. Some bureaucrat, some e-mail, some policy paper, something will surface that, like acid, will burn and smoke their tissue of lies. Americans may not be happy with the IRS, but I sense they're damned angry about the big Benghazi lie."

"Jesus, John, don't get too passionate on these two. The Democrats may be willing to give on the budget or even some aspects of abortion to put those issues behind us."

"You deal all you want to," Whitaker said, "but that's the difference between the House and Senate. We're elected every two years, and you, every six, because we're supposed to be closer to the mood of the people. And the mood of the people ain't very forgiving on Benghazi. I think a lot of people think Williams and Grantham didn't protect our consulate so as to not offend the Libyans they put in power, and, on September eleventh, they didn't use the resources they had, because it would have become a larger military incident in a supposedly friendly country."

"I see your point. Embarrassing in the middle of the campaign."

"Yeah. Remember, 'General Motors is alive, bin Laden is dead, and al Qaeda is on the run.'"

"Yeah, I remember," Marshall said derisively.

"And people were beginning to believe that lie, and a few others that put them over the top."

Marshall heard the conviction in the Speaker's voice and matched it. "Too bad Governor Hardy didn't have the political testosterone to go after Williams on Benghazi in the second or third debate. Hardy is way too much a gentleman for his own good, but I believe he'd have made a good president."

"Ditto, that," Whitaker said. "Since you called, Jordy, I have something for you."

"What's that?" About to pick up his cell phone, Marshall put it aside, deciding he could check his email later.

"I know that in Lexington you're too far from Cincinnati to have paid attention to our news, but did you hear about a guy named Enrique McCord being murdered in my town? He was the CEO of SoftSec, the electronic voting company."

"Now that you mention it, yeah, was it a coincidence he was killed the night his company was doing their biggest public service?" Marshall asked, and once again, found himself glad Whitaker was a curious man.

"Some think he wasn't doing such a public service. There's other information about his death that isn't computing with some people."

"Like how?"

"Like murder, maybe," Whitaker said, his voice devoid of drama.

"Murder? My God, John, what the hell is going on?" Marshall pushed his cell phone off the blotter and leaned into the landline receiver.

"Don't have all those answers yet."

"Well, don't forget about Ted McNickle right up the road in Columbus," Marshall suggested. "Maybe he can use the State Police to flesh that one out."

"Nice thought. The Ohio secretary of state is a Democrat, but with Governor McNickle being a Republican, maybe we can go at it from the other end."

"What do you mean?"

"With Ted's help," Whitaker intimated, "maybe we can replay the voting in some way and double-check everything against the data as of November 6."

"Jeez. Oh, man. You're not telling me Williams wasn't legitimately reelected, are you?

"I'm not telling you anything, Jordy, and damn it, don't you go talkin' to your buddy from Missouri." It was a warning dressed in a tease.

"No worry on that score," Marshall said. "I'm not Harry Riordan's fool. And I don't need to tell you that, played well, these hearings could help us in the 2014 by-elections."

"Listen," Whitaker said, his voice rising, "you and I are friends, so I won't tell you what I think of that strategy. What I will tell you is that we're going to zero in on the IRS for every American's sake."

"And Benghazi?"

"Those hearings will be to ensure that those four Americans didn't die for nothing!"

With the election over, some of the pressure was off, and Marty Cox took one of his few leave days in a while. He wanted to spend real time with Natalie and the girls, but she was out running them to soccer and ballet with a stop at the store, and his "alone" time at home was not something he cherished. Without them, it was just a house, and like him, it felt hollow. For them, he would do anything, and did.

As he sat in their the family room of their four bedroom colonial— bought in the early 2000s because Leesburg was how far out of the city they had to go to afford something nice that they would never have to leave—moisture stung the corners of his eyes. At six-four, Cox was a formidable guy and had stood out in every class he'd been in since junior high school. With a chiseled chin holding up the rest of a hard-knock face, his cold, blue eyes welled up nonetheless, and he was glad his Nat could not see him.

Until the summer of 2012, his record with the US Secret Service had been stellar and then some, and, of course, it remained so—at least in his personnel jacket. When he graduated from the Rowley Training Center right after college, he had been regularly assigned high-profile protection details, worked long hours, and was on the road constantly in the United States and abroad.

Nat was good about it, and when the girls were old enough to understand, they were fiercely proud of their dad, a man who'd protected Vice-President Alton Grayson, President Jefferson Harper, President George W. Bush, and, briefly, Averell Williams. Since then, his principal assignment had been Vice-President Joseph Morrison. Being assigned to the vice-president was not a demotion, he knew, but a reflection, to some degree, of presidential preferences, and, he hated to admit, even to himself, his age. As a law-enforcement officer, he was entitled to retire after twenty years of active service, and that date was etched on his mental calendar: September 2016.

In the heat of the 2012 election season, however, claims he might once have made about his spotless record melted into nothing. Because of his loyalty—and what he thought was a special relationship—to Joe Morrison, Morrison and Williams would be in office until his retirement. All he wanted was to get through the last four years of his active career and then move on to some lucrative post in corporate America.

When Morrison first asked him to make a few phone calls threatening the NIS manager in Columbus, he knew it was wrong, but it didn't seem like a big deal. When he had to warn her about her black investigator, Nelson Somebody, that didn't seem like a big deal either. It didn't matter to him the NIS people were former federal investigators, employees of the US Office of Personnel Management forced into privatization. Like many others, the ones he threatened were faceless people who didn't matter much to him—or to Joe Morrison for that matter. When the vice-president suggested that he needed to do it again, Cox's phone call to the manager was nasty, crass, and racist, and he'd hoped it would do the trick.

Could he help it if the black investigator, obviously nearing the end of his career, chose to stand up for something that got in the way of the president's reelection? Could he help it if that man's obstinacy left him no choice when Morrison insisted? And the other murders? Ricky McCord, who apparently had a conscience? And the two election nerds? And the one's fat girlfriend?

Cox couldn't believe he let himself slip down the slope so fast, but after the first, how could he refuse any others? *Now, the bastard has me leaning on people at the cabinet level. Good Christ,* he thought, *does this son of a bitch have any limits?*

"Do I even have a conscience?" he said out loud to the empty room. "Does it matter now?" He tried to force that thought out of his mind with a logic that was easier to handle.

After all, Cox reminded himself, the requests came from the vice-president and, for all he knew, Morrison was merely relaying the wishes of President Williams himself. Even if that weren't the case, if this president could drone people he felt were national threats, was it that big a stretch to consider eliminating people who threatened the survival of the presidency?

His eyes dried, but the feeling of full sandbags resting on his shoulders, of a bear trap clamping him tight, would not leave him. In the stillness, he thought of his gun, that all of it could be over. Then he heard the deadbolt in the door to the garage.

"Honey!" Natalie Cox all but shouted. "You're actually home—and doing nothing! Shall I call the Guinness people and tell them a new record is being set?" she teased from across the kitchen.

Cox mustered a weak chuckle, but didn't move, didn't get up to greet the girl he swept off her feet sixteen years earlier. She was a beautiful woman through and through. Nat and the girls deserved better than they got.

"Hon," she began in a light voice that dropped a few levels as she came closer. "It's only ten in the morning. Are you drinking bourbon?"

"Yeah. Sorry—didn't think you'd be home. You know I don't drink much, but the stress on the job this past year, and, of course, with the holiday season. We'll be out every night with the old man..."

"I know, Marty, and I'm sure we're both thinking about when it'll all be over."

Cox looked at his wife. "Yeah, hon. Over."

She walked over to the brown rattan chair where he sat, stroked his still blond crew cut, and kissed him on the forehead. "We are so lucky, Marty!"

"How's that?" he asked, looking for any kind of hope.

"You're home and today's a great day." She brightened. "We can have a special dinner in with the girls, or we can go out."

"I have a choice?"

3.

Peter Marsden made sure his tortoise-shell glasses were precisely balanced on the bridge of his nose before he signaled the CNS camera crew that he was ready for his midafternoon broadcast. He checked his earpiece and that his foil for the day, Tony Duke, was standing in the right spot in Washington, DC.

"Good afternoon, ladies and gentlemen. Here in the *Control Room*, there's been a lot of discussion about what some are calling the *un*scandals the Republicans and their cable allies are puffing up before the American public. I'm speaking, of course, about the unsubstantiated allegations of wrongdoing by the IRS and the continuing drumbeat of foreign policy ineptitude over the tragedy of Benghazi. Tony Duke, you're in Washington, and I know you have your ear to the ground on these matters. What are you hearing?"

"Well, Peter, I've had extensive conversations with the Democratic majority leader, Senator Harrison Riordan of Missouri, and Congresswoman Angela Tesoro, former Democratic Speaker of the House from Maryland, and neither of them or those close to them can offer any intelligible reason why the Republicans would make so much of these nonissues. The election is over, they say, so let's move on to more important things."

"That seems to sum it up well, Tony, and thank you for your fine reporting."

When Norton Sweeney, a tall, spare man, entered the West Wing for his appointment, he was surprised when he was directed to the

Roosevelt Room, across a foyer from the Oval Office. Sweeney's white shirts with flyaway collars always sported a natty bow tie, and today was no exception. His dark, glen plaid suit served as a backdrop to the iridescent red and green, oversized neckwear he donned, a mere five days before Christmas.

Once inside, he was further surprised to find no one there, and he wondered who might fill the fourteen medium brown leather chairs now arranged, soldierlike, as if to guard the inlaid Stickley table. When on the president's turf, one needed to know the seating protocol. In the Oval Office it was one thing, but, in this room, there were several places—at least four—that fit an alpha description, depending on the occasion. After a moment of lawyerlike analysis, he chose a seat immediately to the right of what would be the head of the table, closest to the entrance door he supposed the president would use. *At least in a royal palace,* he thought, *a majordomo followed you around to give guidance. Here, in the house of the people, you were on your own.*

"Norty!" the president boomed when he joined him a few minutes past the hour. "I hope you didn't mind the short notice Freddie gave you."

Sweeney stood. "Not at all, Mr. President. You're my chief client, and I am always at the ready."

"Many thanks. Today, we'll find out how well you live the Boy Scout motto," Williams said as they both sat.

"Oh, no. Another bar exam." Sweeney laughed. "What's on your mind, sir?"

"Norty, we are old friends, and I had this meeting in the Roosevelt Room for several reasons, one of which was some measure of informality."

"Sure—Av," Sweeney responded. He wondered why, if Averell Williams wanted informality, he didn't use his private study, immediately adjacent to the Oval Office. He kept his eye on the president while he concluded that, perhaps, the official study was bugged while the Roosevelt Room was not.

"Why you're here today, and with no one else present, is that we need to have a conversation about the Twenty-Fifth Amendment, and, specifically, Section Three."

"What?" Sweeney blinked several times, his usual physiological reaction when stress began to crowd him. "What's going on, Av?"

"Take it easy, my old friend. It will come as a surprise to you that this old fox has kept one or two things from you." Williams kept his eye on Sweeney's. "The fact is, Norty, I have cancer, and, aside from the obvious reason for not telling anyone, I needed to keep you out of the tiny circle of knowledge to protect your ability to operate without, shall we say, complications of conscience."

Sweeney grimaced as soon as he heard the president mention *cancer*. "Naturally, Av, I'm terribly sorry to hear your news, but you must know the hundred questions in my mind. What kind of cancer? Is it treatable? Will there be surgery? Who knows about the diagnosis?" His eyes batted along at a furious pace.

The president held up his hand, as if stopping traffic. "I won't bore you with all the details, mostly because it's a bit embarrassing to talk about. It's prostate cancer, and I've known since late February 2012," he said, and paused.

Sweeney felt himself go white, and could bring no words from his throat.

"When I learned of it from Commander Bolling," Williams went on, "I was in no real danger, although we knew the cancer could be of the aggressive variety. I made a decision then—and it was all mine—that no one, not even the First Lady—needed to know about something that was not life threatening."

The attorney general listened with both ears but let his mind begin to absorb the enormity of what he was hearing. He let his client talk.

"So we cruised along, and Bolling performed the usual blood tests— PSA, I believe—and had a urologist take some biopsies. At the height of the campaign, right before the first debate, in fact, Bolling came back to me with the news that the cancer had apparently spread, and he was pressing me to seek treatment immediately."

"Jesus H. Christ, Av." Sweeney put his head in his hands. "Holy shit, what does it mean for...?" but he didn't want to finish the thought. "My God, do we have a stack of problems here!"

"I know we do, but here we are. You can see my dilemma, Norty. I couldn't very well announce it to the public in February, at the beginning of the campaign. That would have ended it for me, I suspect. Then once the campaign hit its peak, I couldn't do it then. And since the election, you are more aware than most of the legal hurdles we needed to jump."

"And we still have one more to go," Sweeney said, referring to the Joint Session of Congress on January 4.

"Yep. And then, there's the Inauguration."

"Jesus, don't you regret not having done something last March?"

"Yes, and no," Williams said. "It would have been over and done with, to be sure, and the consequences to me medically, perhaps, negligible. Politically, well, that's another story, isn't it? Had the Republicans been successful in making an issue out of it, I would have been pushed aside for whom? Joe Morrison? Emerson Grantham? No way, Norty. Should we have given up the White House to the Republicans? Hell, no!"

"I can see your dilemma, but now it'll come out. Poor Jack Sennett—will he get raked in the White House Pressroom!"

"Jack is one of the longest running press secretary's ever, so he's used to it, and, by the way, I hope our many friends in the media stick by us."

"We'll see. What does the First Lady think?"

Williams exhaled and shrugged his shoulders. "What you'd expect Andrea would think. She was mad as hell, especially because I hadn't told her. She learned about it—quite inadvertently—from Commander Bolling. And I told Joe Morrison myself on election eve. He needed to know what would likely happen."

"Av, we can't let Joe Morrison sit in your chair!" Realizing the full import of what he'd said, Sweeney added, "I'm sorry. I shouldn't have said that."

"That's OK. My sentiments, exactly, but we have a Constitution with a Twenty-Fifth Amendment."

"Yes, we do." Sweeney reached up and fiddled with Christmas bow tie, suddenly feeling its noose around his neck.

"So, that's why you're here this morning. What do you know about the legislative history?"

"Quite a lot, actually," Sweeney said, doing his best to keep his voice steady. "It's a favorite topic of mine, especially since we've never used one of its more interesting sections." He paused to look at Williams directly. "Let's hope we never do."

"I have some conversational knowledge myself, but what I'm asking is what will Congress and the public be looking for during the eighteen to twenty-four or so hours I'm under anesthesia, if we want people to feel confident in the process."

"Well, then, you're aware of the few instances George W. Bush and his father deployed Section Three for their procedures. When Reagan was shot, naturally, there'd been no opportunity to prepare anyone, but no one doubted that George H. W. Bush was at the ready. Reagan did not invoke Section Three, and Bush did not need to consider Section Four. Needless to say, there would not have been a hiccup had Reagan not survived his surgery."

"Wasn't there some question about succession early on, because of Article II?"

"Yes, but John Tyler settled that rather decisively when Harrison died in 1841," Sweney said, "and the question has never been raised again. That's why the focus of the Twenty-Fifth is on the VP's chair, not yours.

"Did Congress have any special axe to grind when it voted to send the amendment to the states for ratification?"

"Yes." Sweeney chuckled. "Just one, really. There'd been several attempts in our history to pass an amendment to cover situations when the office of the vice-president became vacant through death, disability, or promotion to the presidency. All in all, such a vacancy has occurred over fifteen times in our history."

"So what was the problem?" the president pressed.

"You'll laugh if you've never heard this one, but it's true. When the Bayh–Celler amendment language was first proposed in early January 1965, Lyndon Johnson was a president without a vice-president. Hubert Humphrey would not be sworn in for several weeks, but, by then, LBJ had already had one heart attack that we know of, and he was not a young man. The next two people in line at the time were John McCormack, who was seventy-one, and Carl Hayden, who was eighty-six." Sweeney laughed, thoroughly enjoying the rock and the hard place between which the politicians had found themselves.

"In any event," he continued, "both Houses approved the amendment, and it went out to the states. Shortly after Nevada ratified in February 1967, it became the law of the land. So, Mr. President, in short, the major concern at the time was the age of the participants and the concern that neither chamber could politically abuse Section Four."

Williams nodded. "Well, okay. So we'll need to prepare all the paperwork relative to Section Three, which puts Joe Morrison in charge for the day or so that I'll be unable to discharge my duties. We'll wait to announce until right before the Inauguration, and I suspect we'll garner more sympathy than anger."

"Constitutionally, I don't see any difficulty, and, given recent precedents, there should be no problem. In fact, for most Americans, it will be just another moonshot and hardly on their radar."

"Now there's a metaphor for you."

They both guffawed.

"Quite accidental, Av. I'm sorry." Sweeney reddened as he centered his bow tie. "Sir, I vote for announcing it shortly before the twentieth—not that you asked for a vote—for the reason you cited and blunt any suggestions of deception." His words triggered a memory of not many months before when he, Harry Riordan, and the vice-president had an after-dinner conversation and Morrison had hinted that somehow he might put his thumb on the scale of the election. Sweeney had almost forgotten that evening, but now he couldn't help but wonder who the people had actually voted for on November 6, 2012.

"Pete, this is Paul Gladston." His greeting was followed by dead silence. He thought he'd lost the call to Alexandria. Finally, the low hiss of the electronic ether reached his ear.

"Paul Gladston? Can't be. Who are you?"

"Why can't it be, Pete? We're not dead."

"We?"

"Mare Burdette and I."

"Where are you? No," Pete Clancy quickly added, "don't answer. Are you both safe and away?"

"We're fine and, if you must know, soon to be married. We'd invite you, but can't."

Pete was emotional. "God, you have no idea how glad I am to know you're alive. I thought"—his voice cracked—"I thought you two were dead, like the others."

"Well, then, Merry Christmas," Paul responded with delight, but then changed his tone altogether. "What others?"

"You knew about Nelson Evers, of course, but maybe not about McCord—he was killed election night in a car accident."

"Jesus!" Paul said in a hoarse whisper. "I know you're not kidding. What about the girlfriend, Amber Bustamente? And Conaway, the techie? Any word on them?"

"Nothing—they've all disappeared."

"Is that certain?"

"Well, no one's actually gone out and checked—I'll get someone to make a few calls."

"Jesus!" Paul said again, assuming the worst. He knew his voice shook. "Mare and I knew all those people—heck, we interviewed them all—more than once. How did you know about McCord?"

"Actually, I don't know much," Clancy said. "Mare's old office assistant in Cincinnati—Gladys, you remember her—sent me the link about McCord's death from *The Cincinnati Enquirer*. As to the others, maybe they went off the grid as well—you two actually told them they were in danger, remember?"

"I wish you were right, Pete, but you'd think somebody would surface, especially after McCord was killed."

"That's exactly why they wouldn't."

"But if they're missing, it's no coincidence," Paul said.

"You're right, I know. For some stupid reason, I'd hoped this election/murder scheme hadn't been so..."

"Massive?"

"Yeah, massive," Clancy said. "Come to think of it, that's a pretty good word—massive election fraud, mass-murder—if you think about Evers, McCord, and maybe, others. And what's more is that Averell Harriman Williams was not reelected president of the United States."

"Unbelievable!" Paul said. "Who'd a thought we'd all be witnesses to something like this?"

"All we can think now is that the vice-president himself has been pulling the strings here. He manipulated, maybe bribed, McCord, who evidently enlisted Conaway."

"But without Amber Bustamente, these guys would have gotten away with it."

"They have!" Clancy said.

"It ain't over yet. And that's why I called. Are you hangin' it up at the end of the month?"

"The end of the month is a few days from now," Clancy said, "and that's a yes and a no. Why do you ask?"

"We want to come to DC," Paul said. "We've got to go somewhere, because we can't stay where we are."

There was dead air on the line.

"Pete, are you there?"

"I'm thinking," Clancy said. Then, "Hell, yes, you should come. And if you two want to stay with me for a bit, I've got an extra bedroom."

"You mean it? You're not kidding, are you?"

"Not kidding. But you two have to understand that in coming here, you'll be putting yourself in danger."

"You're right about that. It's Crew Cut's territory. Can we call you in a week or so?"

"Yeah, sure. Crew Cut?" Clancy asked.

"That's what we call him—the one who killed Nelson Evers. He showed up here, looking for us. All we ever pieced together about the guy in the black Tahoe with Virginia plates was that he had a blond crew cut. I caught a glimpse of him once before, but I never forgot that face. Now we have his plate number."

"Save it. Now you'll be here too—in the eye of the storm. And Merry Christmas to you!"

In the White House Medical Facility a few days before the New Year, Navy Commander Jeremy Bolling hosted his chief patient, who sat like any other, clad in slacks and a T-shirt. Bolling and a registered nurse took blood pressure and pulse, and drew blood for several vials. Next came an EKG and the myriad pre-surgical tests.

When the president donned his light blue, button-down Brooks Brothers shirt, tucked it in, and cinched his belt, Bolling signaled him to have a comfortable seat in his office where the two of them could have a private chat.

Williams began. "Maybe I should start by mentioning that I'd prefer to have the surgery performed on Thursday, January twenty-fourth, as early in the morning as possible."

"Understood, sir." Bolling penned a note. "The surgery will be performed by Dr. Tommy Delano Robby at Johns Hopkins, and I can tell you he's the best in his business. I've already provided all the relevant info to the Secret Service for the background check." He cleared his throat. "When we spoke earlier, sir, I mentioned there were two ways to go about the surgery, officially called a prostatectomy. I'll describe them now, but sometime in early January, I will arrange for Dr. Robby to pay us a visit. Before that time, he will have access—via courier—to your medical records, the results of the biopsies, and all the blood work to date, including the results of all the testing we did today."

"Will he be saying anything different than what you are telling me now?"

"I can't answer that, Mr. President, but I do know Dr. Robby's immediate concern will be the lengths to which he will need to go to remove all of the cancer."

"I see. Give me the broad picture."

"Let's say that you and he opt for doing the work robotically. It's a well-developed process pioneered right here in Baltimore, and the surgery has been successfully performed ten thousand times, to be sure. With that protocol, the surgeon operates on you via robot. Five to six small incisions, half-inch to one inch, are made in your lower abdomen. One or two are for cameras, two for stability and tissue control, and two for the devices acting as the arms and hands of the surgeon. You'll be under a general anesthetic, by the way, and will feel absolutely nothing of the process. The surgeon will remove the prostate, carefully excising all of the tissue, with special attention to nerve endings having to do with bladder control and sexual function."

"Wait a moment. You said, 'bladder control and sexual function'?"

"That's right. For some time after surgery, a year or more, you will have to retrain your bladder muscle for complete control, and the same will be true for full sexual function."

"Are you telling me I will, or won't, be able to have sex?"

Bolling did not answer immediately. "That all depends, sir, on what the surgeon finds, and what he has to do to get it all."

"Oh, Christ!"

"Sir, I should tell you that a standing prescription for Viagra or one of the other similar drugs—the urologist will know which one will be best to prescribe for your particular circumstance—will be of immense assistance to you."

"I don't know why I laugh when we men joke about this stuff all the time. I never thought it would happen to me. Is there more?"

"Yes, sir. Dr. Robby will undoubtedly check all related tissue structures to see—especially in your situation—whether the cancer has spread. He will check the seminal vesicles and the associated lymph nodes and, in all likelihood, remove them to be totally certain."

"So...?"

"You will no longer produce semen."

"Got it. What else?"

"For the robotic procedure, the surgery will take a few hours. You'll be in recovery for a few more and then moved to a room where you'll lie flat on your back with a urinary catheter for the balance of the day and overnight. They will get you up and walking that day, however. The next morning, if all is well, you'll be released into Andrea's care, but, of course, you'll have medical personnel with you constantly."

"Did you tell me I'd be 'out of it' for eighteen to twenty-four hours?"

"By the twenty-four hour mark, the full effects of the anesthetic will have worn off, possibly sooner, and there'll be no drug-induced impediment to your judgment."

"Pain and medication?" Williams asked.

"You'll need to take something—probably Percocet—but, in relatively short order, you could switch to Advil and Extra-Strength Tylenol. The catheter you'll have for about ten days, after which they'll test you for capacity and the ability to flush your bladder without one. No problem there will demonstrate surgical success. From then on, we'll test your blood once a month for six months, then on a reduced schedule after that."

"What will the blood tests show?"

"It'll be the same PSA test we've used up to now, and it will show all zeros if the cancer was successfully removed."

"And the other method you mentioned?"

"The surgeon makes a single, longer incision in your abdomen, large enough to reach in and perform the surgery in the old-fashioned way. The rest of it is exactly the same, except that, of course, it is more invasive than the robotic version, and, some say, recovery is longer because of the larger wound and the disruption of abdominal wall tissue and muscle."

"Why would a surgeon prefer one over the other?"

"I understand that some of the surgeons, including the man who developed this procedure to its present high rate of success, may feel that touching, handling, and manipulating the respective tissues with his own fingers gives him a better sense of what is affected and what is not—even though biopsies are performed as the work is being done using either protocol."

"Anything else I should know?"

"Sir, because you felt compelled to wait, you might be prepared to hear the surgeon say he'd prefer not to use the robot so that he would be better able to make more accurate surgical judgments as the work progressed."

The president nodded, obviously taking in all, or nearly all, of the consequences of his decision to put reelection above his own survival. Slowly he stood, walked forward, and stood directly in front of his doctor. "Whatever happens, Jeremy, my friend, I appreciate the professionalism and loyalty you've shown. My absolute confidence in you has helped me through all of this."

"You're very kind, Mr. President," Bolling said as they shook hands. "And please know that I'll be at your side no matter what."

JANUARY 2013

4.

O n Thursday the third, Paul and Mare woke as the rooster's morning song echoed across the cold ground and hoarfrost webbed the single-pane windows.

Mare elbowed him in the rib. "Well, Paulie boy, this is it. The big day. The last chance for you to jump in your buggy and vamoose."

Paul rubbed his side in mock pain. "Is this how you're going to physically abuse me our entire married life?"

"You bet it is, big shot—just like this." She planted a long kiss on his waiting lips, her soft, flowing hair spread across her shoulders and his chest.

Paul loved running his fingers through what seemed like a river of auburn hues, and hoped he could do the same for another fifty years. "Well, if that's how it's going to be," he finally said, ending the longest kiss of his life, "I guess I'll have to put up with it."

She gave him a mischievous grin, and said, "We'd better get going then before I change my mind."

"You'd better not, short stuff. I like your abuse."

"Then I'll use your line. 'Just wait!'"

"Got me there."

They rose and readied themselves as the rest of the Schenk farmhouse finished their preparations for a wedding, the likes of which had never been seen there, or anywhere else in the community. And, if Bishop Mast had his way, they all knew, one that would not be seen again.

Bud and Joan Burdette had come the farthest, driving as they did from a small farming town about forty miles due west of Cincinnati.

Because they too lived a simple life, they seemed most at home in a white, wooden farmhouse that was plainly adorned, outside and in, with hardly a cushioned seat in the place. Lit kerosene lanterns warmed the stark white walls and seemed to invite in what little sunlight graced the crisp morning.

As for the Gladstons, they only had to drive from their home north of Grove City, on SR 173, but below I-80. The sixteen miles had been short in time and distance, but crossing the threshold into another century made the experience more of a journey, one that Paul senior had made before in his dealings with the Amish, but one that Marissa had never experienced.

Nervously, Paul and Marissa Gladston approached the only other English people there and introduced themselves to their new in-laws, strangers to them in so many ways. "Welcome to our little part of Pennsylvania." With a half chuckle, the senior Gladston added, "I don't suppose any of us ever expected to meet in an Amish farmhouse for a wedding, not to mention that it might be for children we love."

The Burdettes laughed politely. Bud had no hesitation in extending his hand and hastened to introduce Joan to the Gladstons. All four smiled. Angst melted away when they learned what they all had in common. None had seen or talked to Paul or Mare since early November, except to be invited to a wedding with all the hush-hush of a state secret.

"Our Paul is over the moon about your daughter," Marissa Gladston hurried to say, "and he says she's the most beautiful girl, inside and out, he has ever met. When he called us three days ago after two months of silence, we could hardly get a word in edgewise."

Joan Burdette beamed. "We must have had the same conversation. Mare couldn't stop talking about Paul and made us drop everything to be here, all on the qt, of course. We can't wait to meet him."

The two men in the conversation exchanged glances that conveyed a code shared by husbands and fathers everywhere: if the moms were happy, everyone else would be happy.

Andy and Sadie Schenk came in from where they had been supervising the bride- and groom-to-be, and welcomed the English guests into their home. "I am so glad you are here, and warmly dressed," Andy said as he eyed the howling snow squall outside the window. The Schenks spent a minute or two explaining what would soon happen, right after they heard deep expressions of gratitude for harboring the young couple and sponsoring them on their wedding day.

Soon everybody found a place on the wooden benches that lined the walls, and softly, hymns of joy and praise filled the air. The voices of the men, women, and children, grew louder and more in unison as each phrase escaped their lips.

Finally, with no more fanfare than a stirring of those seated closest to the doorway, the wedding couple entered the room from the kitchen where both men and women—the bride- and groom-to-be included—had worked much of the night before to prepare the feast to come. Two of the Schenk girls served Mare Burdette as bridesmaids and, in accordance with custom, had helped fashion her wedding dress of purple, starched cotton, decorated only with a white shawl for her shoulders. Not permitted a veil, Mare wore her striking auburn hair in a simple bun, but nothing could have hidden her joyful tears.

The two Schenk brothers chosen as Paul's groomsmen accompanied him in his black suit and highly polished black leather boots. Another hymn trumpeted through the air, as if to summon God's angels into the flickering glow of the parlor's light, and he and Mare stood together when the Amish men read scripture in anticipation of the bishop's counsel.

His words echoing from a thousand weddings past, Bishop Mast stood before them reflecting upon the special wedding readings of the gospel. He marked their relevance for all times and all persons, not least for the pair before him today. There was no doubt, he noted, that scripture required the bonding of a man and woman for life, there being no such thing as divorce when good times turn to bad.

At last, he asked the bride and groom to speak their intentions out loud for all the company to hear and confirm their understanding of the biblical terms under which they wished to marry. When they had done so, he pronounced a blessing upon them and announced to the gathering their new status as man and wife. In closing, the bishop's face wore the gleam of ancient satisfaction in doing a duty well.

All at once, everyone within hearing stood and sang the joyful wedding hymn *Praised Be God in the Highest Throne* in German. Mare and Paul embraced with a singular passion, eliciting the applause of the elders and giggles of the youngsters.

The Gladstons and Burdettes swarmed the newly married couple and bestowed hugs, kisses, and blessings of their own, as more secular songs and noise took over the room. Andy and Sadie Schenk signaled to family and sundry guests that the English should have some time to themselves, albeit surrounded by the celebratory din of people dishing up the roast chicken with mashed potatoes and all the fixings the season had to offer.

Joan Burdette gave her daughter a long embrace. "I'm so happy for you." She looked around the room. "And you seem right at home here."

"A big change, Mom," Mare responded directly to her mother, with everyone in their circle listening over the din. "See?" She held up her hand. "No ring. They don't do that here."

Paul jumped in. "No worry, Mare. I'll make that up to you."

"You don't need to. I am perfectly content the way things are."

"But they will change, we both know," Paul said and the four parents looked at him closely. "Mare and I will be leaving here shortly for Washington, DC."

Shocked, Paul, Sr. said, "Are you sure it's safe to leave here? The two of you need to be careful, although I've never understood all that's happened."

"Best that you—all of you—do not know the details. The Schenks know we'll be leaving, but they don't know where we're going. We'll write them. For you folks," Paul said, looking at all four parents, "we'll keep it the same as before: occasional, brief calls from throwaway phones to let you know we're safe."

Marissa Gladston teared up. "Will our lives never be the same? Will you two ever have a normal life?"

"As long as things are the way they are, as long as the American people are willing to put up with..." Mare let the sentence trail off. Then, as an afterthought, she said, "It's like what Paul always says to me. 'Just wait!'"

"And that doesn't mean," Paul added, "that you should be patient. It means that something—I'm not sure what exactly—but something will happen."

When Joe Morrison reached his office in the West Wing on Friday morning, his personal assistant, Remy Carlson, came in with a long to-do list, but, as in the previous four years, there was nothing especially noteworthy—or newsworthy.

"Anything that I absolutely must do this morning?" Morrison asked, once he was perched on his top-grade executive leather swivel chair.

"There's a photo op with a delegation of Texas cattle herders at ten, but otherwise, nothing that can't wait." Remy stood at his desk and rifled through the notes attached to his schedule.

"Good. I'll make the photo op, naturally—gotta keep the home folks happy—but there are a few phone calls I need to make. If I'm running late, come get me."

"Yes, Mr. Vice-President."

When the solid walnut door closed behind her, Morrison extended his right hand for the phone, and then pulled it back. These would be extremely important phone calls to Norton Sweeney and Andrew Warner, and he wanted there to be no misstep on his part. He had to find out where their heads were. If either of them had thought through a key contact they had had with him, one or both would have reason to believe Morrison was guilty of a high crime.

His biggest problem in initiating each call was that, in reality, he had little business to talk about with either man. *Hell*, he thought, *I'll have to wing it.*

He picked up the receiver and dialed the direct number for Norton Sweeney, which his personal assistant answered on the second ring. Sensitive about his lack of importance in the scheme of things, Morrison thought it a slight and wondered if a call from President Williams was handled in the same way. He heard a click or two, reminding him of the conversation he'd overheard ten months ago, when the president's physician told him he had cancer, and that it was somewhat aggressive. His heart rate quickened.

For all the world, he wished he'd never overheard those snippets of doctor-patient conversation. Had he remained blissfully ignorant of the president's health, he would never have thought to engage Ricky McCord in a scheme to defraud the American people of their vote. That one step, leading inexorably to each one following, each fueled by greed and ego, took him on a slip-slidy path to bribery and serial murder. Guilty though he was, there was still a good chance he would get away with all the crimes, and, in the end, he'd shrink away in history to the footnote status occupied by most vice-presidents of the United States.

"Hello, Joe," the voice boomed through the ether.

Sweeney's greeting jostled Morrison back to his guilty present. "Nice to hear your voice, Norton. How are things going down the street?"

"Well, thanks. What's on your mind, sir?"

Obviously, Sweeney had no time for small talk, but, so far, so good. "Nothing terribly much, but I have to confess"—Morrison took a fraction of a moment to ask himself why he had used the word *confess*— "I'm a bit concerned about the fuss the Republicans are making about this Benghazi thing." He pictured Sweeney fingering his bow tie.

"Right. They can make all the noise they want to, but it'll go nowhere. We have everything buttoned up tight."

"You think so?"

"You were there, Joe, when the president himself decided how to put out this little fire, and, fortunately for us, most media outlets are with us on this. Heck..." There was a short pause, a break in thought, and then Sweeney cleared his throat. "Did you hear Jon Stewart mocking News Global about its anal persistence in pursuing it?"

"No, I hadn't seen it. Probably after my bedtime." Morrison noticed Sweeney's hesitation, and could almost see the man blinking rapidly, as if he had momentarily forgotten what he wanted to say. "In any event, do you feel certain the administration can keep all the usual leakers dark on this?"

"Oh, I think so. The fact is, no one has asked the right questions of the right people yet—and if that occurs, the people who know the real answers will not likely provide them."

"Music to my ears, Norton." Morrison realized that for the second time, he couldn't bring himself to use the same diminutive for Norton the president used. "What happened in Benghazi was the unfortunate result of events beyond the control of this administration."

"Couldn't have said it better, Joe."

"Thanks." Morrison smiled because he now knew for certain that Sweeney could be counted on as a quiet coconspirator. "I fail to see what difference it all makes, to quote our former secretary of state. Those men are dead, the unfortunate victims of the rabble that seems to dominate Middle Eastern discourse."

"You may be right, sir, but don't put those words in a speech." Sweeney chuckled.

Morrison knew Sweeney to be polite at all times, but he also knew a jibe when he heard one—the reference to what News Global called his 'gaffe-ability.' "As always, I appreciate your advice," Morrison said with more gratitude than he felt. "I'd better let you get back to your work."

When he hung up the phone, Morrison was perspiring. He glanced in the mirror. His coal-black hair, perfectly brushed, clung to his wet scalp. He quickly found tissue to swab his neck and forehead before Remy saw him and thought he was dying of dengue fever. Frustrated at his own ability to control his physiological response to tension, he sensed that, in fact, it was not subsiding. *What about that conversation didn't sound right?*

He sipped a cup of hot tea in the hope that the Chinese were right: you could cool your body on the outside by warming it on the inside. Whether it worked or not, he needed to make another phone call, but he couldn't bring himself to pick up the phone until he deciphered what his subconscious was trying to tell him.

It hit him. When Norton Sweeney mentioned Jon Stewart—no, right before that. There was the slightest hesitation, as if Sweeney forgot what he was going to say. Perhaps when he recalled the events of the evening of September 11, 2012, the date of the Benghazi attack, he remembered another event from around that same time—a dinner at the official residence, when Morrison had intimated more about his relationship with Ricky McCord than should ever have left his lips. *Was it my imagination?*

Morrison couldn't help himself. He had to know. What was Andrew Warner thinking these days? Would there be any difference in his demeanor? He dialed the number of the CIA director's office and waited. In one ring, he heard Warner's voice.

"To what do I owe the honor, Mr. Vice-President?"

"This is your humble Texan calling to see how his friend is doing with all this Benghazi bullshit stinking up the media."

"Wait a minute. Did I hear you say, 'humble Texan'? I would have thought that was an oxymoron outlawed by the state legislature when George Bush was governor!" Warner said with a laugh.

"Ha ha. Nice try, Drew, but you'll have to come up with a better dodge than that. How are things going?"

"That's a broad question, but if you're really calling about Benghazi, I'm just another guy in this town who wants that whole thing to go away. No good will come of raking through that muck."

"Is there muck to rake?"

"There always is, Joe, and you've been around long enough to know it," Warner said. "The agency stands by its original intelligence on Libya during that period. All of us—I mean the western intelligence outfits—pooled our intel, and it all came out the same. Libya was, and is, in some ways like the Pakis and the Afghanis. They all have governments that pay lip service to managing their crazies, but, in reality, they're relatively powerless, and all that means is that those places, including Iraq now, are on the unstable list."

"Why didn't we get the hell out of there, then?" Morrison asked. "Why did Chris Stephens go there, to a consulate that was less protected than a Walmart store in an American strip mall?"

"Now there's a colorful phrase," Warner joked. "But you're right, and maybe we shouldn't pursue this because you'll be asking me to be disloyal to the administration. But then, there are times when people have to count their friends."

Morrison didn't speak immediately. "You've got that right. But for now, you think the matter is contained?"

"As far as this agency is concerned, it is."

"Well, I don't want to take your time when you're busy making the world safe for democracy."

"Yeah, sure," Warner said. "Thanks for the call. Perhaps we'll have time for lunch before long."

"Counting on it." Morrison hung up, having heard the intelligence man's message loud and clear. Warner had spoken candidly on Benghazi only to let Morrison know they now owed each other. *Or did they?*

"Ted, I need some help," Speaker Whitaker said into the landline phone connecting him and Governor McNickle in Columbus, Ohio.

"Of course, it'll cost you," McNickle replied with a chuckle that only long-term political allies would understand.

"This may be a wild goose chase, of course, but I'm thinking there might have been some voting irregularity—to put it nicely—in our Buckeye State this past November, and I'm hoping you might be willing to poke around a bit."

"Tell me why you think so."

"Maybe it's just me and my old partisan bones, but I'm still having trouble believing we lost Ohio to Williams, but put that aside for a minute. I don't know if you had reason to notice it, but the guy whose company has—or I should say, had—a boatload of contracts across the country, including Ohio, was murdered election night. This was right after he left his company headquarters in Cincinnati—on my turf. Name was Enrique McCord. Originally, the police put it down to some sort of road-rage thing."

"And now?"

"Over the past few weeks, a curious staffer of mine has been cruising the Internet looking for related stories, and I'll be damned if she didn't find one, also right in our backyard."

"Talk about baiting the hook."

"OK, OK, I know we're both busy, but this could be pretty big. The other story was another hit-and-run of sorts that took place in a Frisch's parking lot, and it involved a Tahoe running down an older black man. The vehicle had out-of-state plates."

"I'm not seeing the connection."

"Nobody would, unless you drill down a bit. What got my staffer curious was that the older fella was a retired federal investigator who became a contract type for NIS—"

"NIS. The National Investigations Service? The people who do work for the Office of Personnel Management?"

"Yes—OPM. This bit wasn't in the papers" Whitaker went on, "but on McCord's vehicle, the forensics gang found traces of black paint that came off a Tahoe."

"A connection, I'll grant you, Detective Whitaker, but tenuous."

"Again, Ted, how many coincidences do we need to get a little more curious?"

"OK," McNickle said. "What do you want me to do that you can't do?"

"If you have any state resources you can trust—people who report only to you—maybe they could go snooping around a few places around Ohio where the votes that went for Williams seemed out of whack from what history tells us they should have been."

"Even if we find places like that, almost everything's electronic, and where paper may be involved to complete the ballot, it was supposed to have been destroyed."

Whitaker remained silent.

"OK, now I know why you're Speaker of the House. I feel the push, but here's the problem," McNickle said. "I have some discretionary funds to use for purposes such as this, but a lot of the people at the senior level here, including Secretary of State Kathlyn Hopkins, are Democrats, so there really aren't any resources I can trust. Any ideas?"

"You'd put them to work under your direct authority?"

"Yeah, I'll do it, but, like I said, you'll owe me big," McNickle promised.

"I might have an idea. Let me think about it, and I'll get back to you."

"By the way," McNickle asked, "what prompted you to make this call today of all days? It wasn't your staffer's research—which I'll bet you've had since before Christmas—it was something else. What was it?"

"Not that anybody would have noticed, but this morning, the House and Senate officially tabulated all the electoral votes, and certified Averell Williams as president."

"And?"

"When we got to Ohio's eighteen votes, all the little coincidences began a tabulation of their own, and I wondered what really happened on November 6."

At five in the morning, Paul backed his used Volvo out of the Schenk barn, where it had rested since the presidential election. Though he had started it every ten days or so to keep the seven-year old engine fully lubricated, it had gone nowhere, in keeping with the promise he and Mare made to the Schenk family. For the time they were there, they lived as Amish—no exceptions.

This morning, however, was Sunday, January 6, and the agreed upon date had come sooner than anyone wanted. While the car idled to life on the crisp earth, Paul and Mare stood with the Schenks around their kitchen table, all eleven of them having had a delicious breakfast of eggs, cured bacon from the neighbor's farm, warm bread and jam, and, for the adults, strong black coffee percolated on the ancient wood-burning stove. Their goodbyes were laced with tears and words of love and warmth.

True to their word, Paul and Mare had not attempted to inflict English ways on the Schenk family, but the reverse was not true. Paul and Mare looked at each other wearing the clothes they'd worn last in early November, and in some ways, found them strange and affected.

Paul spoke to the elder Schenks first, attempting to manage the mist in his eyes. "You both have been a second mother and father to me again and again in my life, and your examples of the plain and simple will be a part of me always." He threw his arms around them both. "And you have welcomed my Mare into your hearts as you have done for me."

Mare joined them, smiling through a tearful embrace of her own.

"Little Mare," Andy said in his Germanic lilt, "you have added beauty and energy to my household and have demonstrated to all the Schenk children how much one little person can accomplish in one day." His laugh was deep and loud, in contrast to the silent smiles of all seven children.

Not to be outdone, Sadie added a proud smile to her own sentiment. "For such an English girl, you surely know the way of life on a farm, and you will always be welcome in my kitchen or at my supper table." She gave Mare a long hug, and whispered, "God bless you, my child."

The pair of refugees, passengers on an underground railroad for two months, made their farewells, and, bags of sandwiches in hand, they stepped into the frigid air, seemingly thinned by the Arctic gusts slapping away their breaths. Once in the dark green Volvo, they found their way to SR 19 and, via I-79, to the Pennsylvania Turnpike headed east.

"Do you know what day it is, Paulie boy?"

"No, short stuff, is this a quiz?"

"Not at all, but you coming from a true-blue Presby background, I thought you'd see a little symbolism."

"Now you're really workin' me."

"Today is the Feast of the Epiphany. You know, three kings."

"Yeah, well, if you haven't figured it out already, I'm not religious in the same way as you papists." He knew he had to finish that line with a smile.

Mare poked him in the ribs while both his hands were on the wheel, and he was unable to retaliate in kind. "Oh, so you're a cultural Protestant, eh? I thought Grove City College was pretty 'all about it' when it came to religion."

"Some people are like that, but remember, I grew up in town, did not stay on campus, and did not participate in a lot of stuff the other kids did."

"Didn't you have mandatory chapel, though?"

"Sure, but we didn't have to go all the time, and we could choose which ones we attended. Few of them were religious services in the same way you might consider going to Mass."

"That's another thing, Paulie boy. I am not a cultural Catholic, so if you want to roll out of the sack with me on Sunday mornings, I would sure love it, but I won't bug you about it."

"Thanks, I might take you up on that. Rolling around in the sack on Sunday mornings."

"I said, 'roll out of the sack,' you of the one-track mind." She smirked at him nonetheless.

The upper, leafless altitudes of Pennsylvania whisked past the Volvo's windows, and, past Breezewood, the miles-long views of Maryland gave them respite. Before the long slide down I-70 into the metro Washington area, Paul exited the highway and made a right turn. "Hey, tour guide, is this on the itinerary?"

"It is now," he said. "If you don't mind, I want to make a little stop down the road a ways."

"Sure, but don't give me the 'just wait' line when I ask where the heck we're going on a cold day like this."

Paul became silent for a minute. "Something you need to know about the guy you married, Mrs. Gladston. Patriotism and sentiment run deep with me, and there are some things that never cease to inspire."

"You sure like to keep a girl in suspense."

"No suspense," he said quietly and evenly. "We're stopping at Antietam. It might be too cold to walk around much, but given what we've seen and experienced this past summer and fall, I need a booster shot of spirit."

Mare avoided a cute retort, and waited for him to complete his thought.

"You told me you liked history, and that's one of the thousand things I love about you, but it's Antietam and the bloody struggle that occurred on these fields near Sharpsburg that always remind me I must never be swayed by someone else's version of America—like Joe Morrison's—and that I have to live for what these men lived and died for."

"I'm not being a smartass, but you could be the narrator for a documentary on this stuff, and that's one of the thousand things I love about you."

He looked away from the road for a moment and gave her a half smile, one that needed no words. "Thanks, sweet stuff," he said at last, and reached for her hand. "Antietam was the bloodiest single day of the entire Civil War, and, despite that horror, when the Union could have negotiated a peace, they struggled on for two-and-a-half years more, and more bloodshed than anyone can imagine."

"I've never been here before," Mare said, as they drove onto the grounds, and an unnatural hush overcame them.

After parking the Volvo, they wandered to the information center and inhaled what information one of the national park service guides had to offer, which was a great deal. Despite the cold, they took a walking tour with only one stop.

The pair stood in silence and looked down at the space where the Sunken Road became Bloody Lane. "In a little more than three hours on September 17, 1862, over 22,000 men were killed, wounded, or went missing," Paul whispered. Their hands stayed clasped, Mare's left to Paul's right. They steadied themselves against the chill breeze and did their best to soothe the ghosts with silent prayers for their eternal rest.

In Sharpsburg itself, they found a little place for a late lunch of hot soup, grilled cheese, and coffee, and then found their way to I-270.

"Is this the back way into DC you told me about?"

"No." Paul chuckled. "But you told me once you've never been here before, and I want to kill some time before we wander down to Pete Clancy's place."

"Why?"

"Two reasons: I get to play tour guide a bit longer and show you the sights, and," he added, more seriously, "I don't want to get where we're going in daylight."

"Oh, now I get it—that means, Paulie boy, you didn't have to get me up at the crack of dawn and two, you get no credit for showing me around. I can take a freaking tour."

He looked at her, surprised. "Are you pissed at me?"

"No, but I'm trying to get in a little practice." She laughed and gave him a peck on the cheek. "I'm really glad we stopped at Antietam, though."

"Back to the Epiphany thing for a sec," Paul said. "What symbolism?"

"Oh, I don't want to carry that too far," she said, "but three kings is all about the journey to the seat of all religious power and who they thought would be the king of Israel. And here we are, journeying to the seat of temporal power ourselves, corrupt as it might be."

"That's a bit of a stretch, but I see what you mean. To me, we're like lambs to the charnel house. The nation's capital, and maybe Crew Cut himself.

"Do you think Pete Clancy may be able to find something for us to do without exposing us?"

"I guess that's one way of hiding in plain sight," he said, "and I don't know of any other good alternatives. We'll see what kind of friends Pete has."

St. Mary's church in Alexandria drew a wide mix of parishioners, and instinctively, Pete Clancy took note of them as he mounted the few steps to the front doors of a worship space nearly as old as the nation itself. On the raw edge of winter, the eight-thirty Mass was sparsely attended, there being services in the warmer hours for children and late sleepers. Clancy blessed himself and made a right turn to walk up the side aisle and enter a rear pew that was otherwise unpopulated.

He knelt behind a longtime friend. "I suppose the angels of the Almighty didn't bar the door fast enough," he said.

Already seated in the next pew up, the black man shot back, "Obviously, the security detail must be on a long coffee break for you to have broken through."

"Where's our friend?"

"Business with the House. Maybe next week."

"On a Sunday?" Clancy whispered.

"Our buddy never rests. If something's happening, he'll be there."

"Can we chat a minute after?"

"Sure."

Promptly at eight-thirty, not 8:31, Father Michael Pallison entered with three servers and began the rite that had remained substantially unchanged for nearly a thousand years, with some parts of it reaching back to the time of the apostles. Pallison was a few years older than Clancy and his friend, and the two watched him intently as they knew of the torture he had endured in enemy hands. Clancy wondered how Pallison kept up his schedule, but supposed that imprisonment had brought him moral courage along with the daily regimen of physical and emotional degradation.

With it being the feast of the three kings, the priest's homily dealt with the journey each woman and man must make to find the Almighty God that surely exists. He said that each step they took in that quest was unique, and the only gift expected was trust in an eternal plan so much greater than any could imagine or fathom. In a rare reference to his own life, Pallison noted that God's abiding presence with him in the prison camps of North Vietnam was the only company he and his companions had. "He asked nothing of us, but gave us the gift of his spirit, and it made all the difference."

At the end of the service, he blessed the people and said, "The Mass is ended. Go in peace to serve the Lord."

The two men at the back of the church stepped aside to speak quietly in the shadows near the confessionals.

"What's on your mind?"

Clancy knew he couldn't waste his friend's time. Ever since they were warrant officers together in the Army Security Agency—a long since disbanded unit—minutes had always seemed precious to his companion. "I need a favor. You know I'm hangin' it up with NIS—just a few loose ends. But this is a new day, and I want to keep my hand in."

"You're too damn old to be starting with us," said the friend, a man of the same age. He chuckled with each word.

"Not me. I have two capable young people coming to town. When they get here, I want them to receive some off-the-books specialized training of the kind only you guys offer."

It was an unusual request, one Pete Clancy had never made before. There was a moment's hesitation. "Are you sure about this, Pete? We don't usually do this sort of thing."

"I'm sure. They arrive today, and I'll size them up. If I'm wrong, we'll forget it, but I didn't want another week to go by. There may be some urgency."

"You weren't clear about who they are. We're not hiding any bad guys here, are we?"

"Hardly—you know better. These two are the good guys, but right now, I can't tell you more. You aren't ready to hear it, and, if you did, you'd have to do something about it."

"You're tying my brain into a knot with that one, but for you, Pete, OK. We go back to when Christ was a corporal, and, if I can't trust you, who can I? Give me a call tomorrow when you're surer about things—at the usual number—and we'll get something going."

5.

Just at dusk, Paul Gladston steered his green Volvo down Alexandria's South Fairfax Street and found the house a block or two below Wilkes. Following Pete Clancy's instructions, he found the alley behind the townhouse, where a vacant space next to the old man's 2009 silver Lexus ES 350 awaited them.

The rear door of the two centuries-old brick pile opened a few seconds after Paul's soft tap on the heavily varnished wood. Clancy stood there, a bottle of beer in hand and a large smile on his weathered face. The hair on the top of his head couldn't decide whether to remain dark, turn silver, or simply disappear. Without a word, he waved them in. Once the door was closed, however, the silence ended.

"Good to see you two!" Clancy looked them over with an appraising eye.

"Are you checking us out for new clothes or something to bury us in?" Mare asked.

"Mrs. Gladston, I presume? Yes, I'm checking you out, because I may have something for you to do."

"Uh, oh. This is sounding serious."

"It is, Paul. Dead serious." Clancy looked from Mare to Paul. "Hey, I don't mean to put you off, but you've now entered ground zero, if I may be so dramatic—but more on that later. First, let me show you where you can put your stuff, and then we'll order in a pizza or something."

An hour later, when Paul and Mare were unpacked and refreshed, Clancy ordered a pizza and offered them a beer. His guests looked at the bottles and both burst out laughing. "This must be some secret," Clancy said.

"Not at all," Mare said when she caught her breath. "It's that we've been holed up on an Amish farm since early November, so we haven't even seen a beer, much less had one."

Clancy let a smile spread across his face. "So, you're married! That worked out for you, didn't it?"

"You bet," Paul said, "and I won't give her any outs."

Clancy looked from one to the other and became serious. "I remember seeing you two in Columbus last spring at the session we had about the Hatch Act. I was impressed even more with your handling of the SoftSec cases and with what followed after Nelson Evers's death."

"Thanks, but you said something about stuff for us to do?" Mare asked, shifting the topic from Evers.

"Well, yes. You'd have no reason to know this, of course, but when I left NIS—when they canned me—my severance package included a two-year noncompete. However, I didn't agree to not take on certain miscellaneous investigative jobs."

"So the kind of work you're talking about has nothing to do with background investigations," Paul concluded.

"That's correct, but many of the techniques you already know will come in handy." Clancy cleared his throat. "You know, I've made a lot of friends in Washington over the years, and there are always off-the-books, one-off pieces of work to do for smart, persistent people, and it's possible you two might fill the bill."

"Still thinking about it?" Mare asked.

"Well," Clancy said, "I've made up my mind, but we'll have to find out whether you can handle it."

"What does that mean, exactly?"

"I can't tell you, 'exactly,' Paul, but I've arranged for both of you to receive some specialized training. After I make a call or two in the morning, you'll be going down to Camp Peary—what some here call 'the farm.' There you'll learn about handgun use and, perhaps, other interesting skills."

Mare said, "You know, both of us are already fairly proficient with weapons."

Clancy smiled at her. "I'll bet you two could knock a rabbit's eye out at fifty yards, but this is highly specialized stuff and involves two-legged animals." He let that sink in. "For you, Mare, I've procured a Kimber 25 ACP with a three point five inch barrel, and for you, Paul, I have a Walther PPK, stainless steel 380. We'll also secure concealed-carry permits for Virginia, DC, and Maryland." Clancy was glad to see both his charges were speechless.

"That's right, you two," Clancy said, "this is serious business, and better that you understand that now. Some of the work that shows up at my front door may require you both to know how to save your own lives and protect each other—and perhaps, the lives of others."

"Others?" Mare wanted to know.

"There's a VIP protection course that lasts one to two weeks and is put on by certified NRA instructors. We'll get that one under your belts next month if it can't be fitted in at Peary, but, for now, it'll be the weapons course and a defensive driving program. The facility is down around Williamsburg."

"Is this the CIA operation?"

"We'll discuss more about that when I know your security clearances have been validated and upgraded. For now, let's just call it the farm."

"Jesus H. Christ." Mare exhaled. "What what have you got us into, Paulie boy? Some honeymoon." They all laughed until the doorbell rang.

"Pizza man!" someone yelled through the door.

All three froze. Clancy said, "Relax. It's what I ordered, but wait here anyway."

When he returned with a large flat box that was warm to the touch, judging by the gingerly manner in which he managed it, the older man and the young couple inhaled the large cheese and sausage in no time at all.

When Mare took her last bite, she got right to it. "Pete, why are you doing this? I mean, you hardly know us, and you've practically adopted us overnight. What gives?"

Clancy threw down the last gulp of Sam Adams and put the bottle down on the table with a decisive thud. "Like I said, I've liked what I've seen and heard of the two of you over several months."

"But that can't be it. You've seen a lot of sharp people in your day."

"There was something else about the two of you, but I would never have guessed it would all come to this. The biggest stolen election ever. A vice-president as a serial killer. You two on the run. Getting married. Me being forced out of NIS." He paused. "Here I am, a widower with with a roomy place, and when you called, it all clicked. I need a couple of operatives and you need a place to camp. And as to the training you'll receive, well, like I said, you may need it in the weeks to come."

His guests nodded and said good night as Clancy turned to climb the stairs. He stopped and turned around. "By the way, make sure you give me the plate number of that black Tahoe."

Promptly at nine o'clock on the eleventh, presidential Press Secretary Jack Sennett, one of the longest-serving occupants of the position in the last fifty years, appeared, as scheduled, in the White House Press Briefing Room to make what he had signaled were to be routine announcements.

First, he said that President Williams would travel to a G8 Summit in Helsinki in early March, where he expected to make further progress in negotiations regarding Iranian and Syrian sanctions. Second, the president is scheduled to undergo a routine exploratory procedure on January 24 to ascertain the degree of treatment for prostate cancer, if necessary. Third, the logjam of appointments to federal judgeships was cleared to go forward as a result of an arrangement between Majority Leader Riordan and Minority Leader Marshall. "I'll take a few questions," Sennett concluded.

Every hand in the room went up, accompanied by a cacophony of shouted questions. Sennett looked around the room, but couldn't avoid

Lew Michaels, senior White House correspondent for News Global, seated in the second row facing the podium. As was customary, senior correspondents among the entire cadre had first dibs on a question. "Lew," Sennett called out.

Michaels opened with, "Jack, I'm sure I'm not alone in wondering why an announcement about presidential surgery is considered to be routine."

"I didn't say, 'surgery,' Lew. I said, 'routine' because it is routine. Did you have a question?" Sennett's tone was contentious, because he knew that News Global was not among the friendlies in the room—definitely not one of the State Media claque.

"I thought a biopsy procedure was the way prostate cancer was assessed, so why the need for surgery?"

That was the question Sennett didn't want to answer. "I wish I could help further your medical knowledge, but that's the information I have. It may well be a matter of nomenclature, but we felt that in the interest of transparency, we would share what we knew." He attempted to look away from Michaels as quickly as he could, but the hardened newsman squeezed out one more round.

"Is what you're really saying that the president has known he might, or does, have cancer, and he's kept it from the public during an election campaign?"

The decibel level in the room rose ten points. Sennett waited a moment. "That is not at all a fair conclusion, Lew, and I'm disappointed that's the tack News Global would take at this time." He broke eye contact to scan for a friendly hand. *How apt*, Sennett thought. Finally, he saw Continental News Service's Tony Duke and called on him.

"Where will the procedure be performed?"

Already, Sennett owed him one for reinforcing the use of 'procedure' rather than 'surgery.' He smiled at his friend. "Of course, we want to use the best possible resources available in consideration of the president's health, and that's why we chose Johns Hopkins University Hospital."

"Can you identify the surgeon who will be doing it?" Duke asked.

"Not at this time." Sennett smiled deprecatingly at his audience. "We know only too well that you media mavens would dog this poor fellow every day between now and the twenty-fourth." He heard the expected, knowing chuckles, and then offered a postscript. "The president of the United States is in no danger whatsoever, and all of you know that he has maintained himself in excellent physical condition, despite what all of us know was a grueling political campaign in an extremely demanding job. Are there any other questions?"

He looked around the room and took a few more queries on each of his announcements before breathing a sigh of relief as he closed the session. Without a doubt, News Global and a few others would take the news and make it a firestorm of concern about the latest barrage of dissembling from his office. Sennett could only hope there were no leaks about the real state of affairs. Their best defense would be that the State Media crowd would glide along with the oily talking points leaked from other sources primed by the White House machine.

Forbes Flannery knew his nightly audience, and, after the medical news about the president earlier in the day, he threw aside his original opening monologue. "This is *The FactZone*, ladies and gentlemen, where you'll hear no spin or counter spin, just the plain facts. Tonight, I was going to bring you up-to-date on the two scandals that won't quit: the political bias at the IRS and the Benghazi cover-up, but today's announcement about the president's health changes everything." He looked into the camera's eye. "Doesn't it?

"Most certainly, the bombshell by Jack Sennett, tucked into other announcements so it would appear mundane, is most disturbing. When everyone over the age of seven connects the dots here, they will conclude— all except the left-wing loonies, of course—they should no longer drink the Kool-Aid. Who is the White House kidding? It seems clear to this journalist that the president has prostate cancer, that he must have known about it all along—well before the election—and that they've put it out there now to harvest sympathy for the man who continues to be less than truthful with the American people. My staff and I have dissected every piece of information surrounding the Sennett statement, and we have talked to medical experts who have confirmed our suspicions.

"While every genuine American wants the president to survive his battle with cancer and remain in office, Americans would feel more comfortable at his side if they knew he'd been telling them the truth. We all wish you well, Mr. President, but if this is the start of your second term, it does not bode well for our future."

Nine days later, at the fifty-seventh Inaugural, Joseph P. Morrison was sworn in as vice-president of the United States by a recently appointed associate justice of the Supreme Court. Reciting the same oath used by all vice-presidents, senators, representatives, and government officers since 1884, Morrison placed his left hand on a bible and said, "I do solemnly swear that I will support and defend the Constitution of the United States against all enemies, foreign and domestic; that I will bear true faith and allegiance to the same; that I take this obligation freely, without any mental reservation or purpose of evasion; and that I will well and faithfully discharge the duties of the office on which I am about to enter, so help me God."

The white paintwork of the special inaugural structure draped along the west front of the Capitol shone brilliantly through the filtered light of an overcast sky. As the steady breeze stiffened everyone in the forty-degree temperature, President Williams took the three steps to the podium where, placing his hand upon the Lincoln Bible, he swore a slightly different oath and began his second and, constitutionally, his last inaugural address.

Through his own lens, Morrison could easily imagine himself taking the presidential oath, but, in his fantasy, the image he saw was in the quiet of a conference room not long after the announcement of a tragedy. Guilt tried to nag at him for the morbid wishes about the president he continued to despise, but what few qualms he had were easily put aside.

Before the election, Williams promised him the second term would be different, that he would be a vice-president with significant, visible responsibility. All that had happened, Morrison snickered in the silence of his mind, was that Williams said he could be president-for-a-day while he underwent the surgery to purge him of his secret—aggressive, spreading cancer.

Morrison returned to the parallel world in which he wanted to live this January 20th. There, it was not the vibrant, intelligent, well-suited man—Averell Williams—he saw taking the oath as president. No, it was the one-term US senator from Texas whose mark on the pages of election history included his good looks and an unabridged support of total abortion rights on demand. To him, those two qualities were enough to secure his party's base, along with the loyal support of State Media.

Already, the administration's print and broadcast coterie had calmed itself after the announcement on the eleventh about the president's *procedure*. Since the eighteenth, there had been a steady series of stories, sympathetic to the president having to undergo the knife. The adoring public below and in front of them today was clearly in the Williams camp, and their repeated, robust applause showed it.

Morrison scanned the crowd, wondering if their applause would be as hearty were he to become their leader. Then, thinking of the heightened danger to him amid the sea of faces and hidden hands, he carefully turned his head to see where Marty Cox had positioned himself. Seeing his man where he should be reminded him he had yet to make up his mind about how he he should handle him in the end.

Returning to a more pleasant prospect, he knew only that he, Joseph P. Morrison, again vice-president of the United States, couldn't wait for Thursday, January 24, when, in the wee hours of the morning, he would begin his one-day term of office. At present, he could only hope for a much longer tenure.

❖

The phone rang in Pete Clancy's tiny study, and he went in to pick it up, assuming that of the few landline calls he received anymore, this one would either be a telemarketer or a call he had been waiting for. It was neither.

"Pete, this is John. Got a minute or two?"

"For you, sure," Clancy said to the Speaker of the House, "because you never waste anyone's time."

"You mentioned back in December that you might be hanging out a shingle about now, and, it so happens, old friend, there have been a few developments," Whitaker said. "If you have the right people, you can have both pieces that need to be done."

"Exactly the call I like to get. Shoot."

"First, there has been a constant barrage of rumors of trouble at the Veterans Administration and, specifically, I mean Walter Reed."

"I thought that stink blew away in the Bush Administration."

"It's come back, only now it's much worse. In the Bush years, it was a matter of budgetary stupidity and plain incompetence at the agency level. Now, it may be out-and-out fraud of the worst kind."

"Somebody selling them Band-Aids for a thousand dollars apiece?"

"Even worse, Pete. They've apparently developed a backlog of patients, so they've phonied up their records to indicate that veterans are getting prompt, good care for their mental and physical injuries."

"You mean they're not? You and I are vets, and I don't know about you, but I haven't had a problem."

"That's because you and I and our third musketeer are in good shape—we were lucky as hell, so we don't need the care some of these guys need. There have been scattered reports of guys with PTSD committing suicide because they've had to wait for months to see their shrinks."

"Jesus!"

"So that's one. I want a couple of people who are not feds to go into Walter Reed and into the big VA hospital in my home district in Cincinnati and see what they can find."

"It's none of my business, but with all the resources available to you a phone call away, why would you want to go outside like this?"

"Look, Pete, the White House, the Democrats, and the liberal media are on my ass because we're turning up the heat on the IRS business and Benghazi. If I make this 'official' by using fed resources, it'll be out, and, once more, I'll be accused of being on a partisan witch hunt."

"Got it."

"So that's why I thought your guys could snoop around. If there's enough of an aroma there, I can sic the federal dogs on them."

"I have only the two for you, and they're now in some specialized training our friend offers. They'll be ready in a few weeks or less. That OK with you?"

"Yes, and don't tell me any more about specialized training." Whitaker laughed.

Clancy laughed too. "Not to worry."

"That brings me to number two, and this one is right up your alley, but it'll have to wait until you get started at Walter Reed."

"OK—I like a full calendar with top billings."

"Just don't soak me, you old rascal. Since your guys will be in Cincinnati to check out the VA there, another friend of mine needs some work on the qt as well. I won't keep you in suspense. This began with me, but will be under the authority of Governor McNickle. There may be an even bigger stink on my turf that indirectly involves you and your former company. It's about voting irregularities and maybe a homicide or two, all in one of the nicest, most beautiful cities around."

"Holy shit, John! I can't believe what you may be about to tell me."

"Well, here it is. I'll give you a phone number direct to McNickle for credentialing and billing purposes, but, again, this is another one that has to stay under the radar."

"I'm listening. Real hard." Clancy wasn't sure what he should share.

"You know that guy of yours who was run down in Cincinnati last summer?"

"Yeah?"

"That may well be related to the alleged road-rage death of Enrique McCord, the owner of—"

"SoftSec. John, you have no idea how weird this is. You don't have the time for me to brief you now—maybe coffee one of these Sundays—but the two people I'll put on this used to work for me there. They know the whole deal."

"Not everything, I'll bet. As always, there are some forensic details about the McCord killing that are yet to be released. In any event, one of my staffers thinks the two deaths are related, but also important is the possibility that they were killed because they knew something about corrupt voting practices in Ohio and elsewhere."

"We may be ahead of you on this, and there's a lot more to it," Clancy said. "This could go all the way up. So far, nobody with any clout has been interested in this mess except a miserable old warrant officer from forty years ago—you."

"Wish I could laugh about it, but this is pretty fucking serious. If the Democrats and their media buddies are foaming at the mouth now, this will send them completely over the edge. Sounds like we have more to talk about here, but some other time."

"Like I said, we'll be on it."

"As soon as that"—Whitaker cleared his throat—"training is finished, I want them in Bethesda at Walter Reed."

"Got it, and right afterward, I'll point them back to Cincinnati. By the way, this took longer than two minutes."

"Fuck off."

"And we missed you in church on Sunday," Clancy said.

"Being Speaker of the House is the worst curse I could ever wish on anyone, and I can't wait to give this job to somebody else—maybe somebody I hate."

Still laughing, Clancy said, "Well, there is one other job some say is worse."

On January 24, President Williams and the First Lady exited the West Wing and walked across the dormant lawn toward the helipad where Marine One was humming to warm its passenger space. The illumination was bright enough, but neither needed to wave at gawkers. It was four thirty in the morning, and even the homeless did not wander by the White House at that hour. Clad in comfortable wool slacks, a dark blue shirt, and gray wool sweater, the sixty-eight-year-old president did not feel the warmth his lined, leather bomber jacket purported to offer. The First Lady dressed a bit differently, knowing as she did there'd be media contacts and photos later in the day.

As Williams stepped aboard the VH-60N WhiteHawk for the short skip to Johns Hopkins in Baltimore, he saw some humor in the fact that the WhiteHawk was flown by the Nighthawk Squadron for the man who some referred to as the Blackhawk, America's first African American president. He and Andrea belted themselves in, but neither attempted a conversation. Each remained alone in their thoughts.

Always the manager, the president ran through his mental checklist. The all-important paperwork had been executed the evening before. After a light dinner, he met Attorney General Sweeney and Vice-President Morrison in the Oval Office, where they were joined by Freddie Frederick, his assistant; Sondra Thompson, his chief of staff; and Remy Carlson, who was Morrison's assistant. Jack Sennett, the press secretary, and the White House photographer were also on hand, the latter to capture another historic moment in the Williams presidency.

"Let's be clear," Norton Sweeney had said once the usual pleasantries had been exchanged. "The president is invoking Section Three of the Twenty-Fifth Amendment so that the government is in capable hands"—he gestured to the vice-president—"from the approximate time when anesthesia is administered to President Williams until his physician declares that he is physically and mentally able to resume his duties. We expect this period to last no more than eighteen to twenty-four hours."

Everyone in the room nodded, and Sweeney continued. "You are all here to witness the president signing the documents necessary to affect this brief transfer of power to Vice-President Morrison, and I am belaboring this process only so that there is no uncertainty about it, and that there is only one voice speaking for the government while this transition is in effect. Our spokesperson, of course, will be Jack Sennett, and he will brief the media on all medical and personal bulletins. In the unlikely event that Acting President Morrison will have to act as head of state during this period, it will be Sennett who will convey such news. Are we all comfortable with this protocol—the same one used by President Bush, by the way?"

"Enough already, Norty," Williams had said, hoping to lift their moods with his own gallows humor. "There's no funeral yet."

Everyone laughed, but nervously. Williams then affixed his signature to three copies of the document, and Sweeney took possession of all of them.

"All right," Sweeney had said. "This patient needs a good night's sleep, if you don't mind."

Williams remembered the exhaustion he felt as his head hit the pillow.

The rotors began their battle with the air, and, in a moment, the VH-60N, the smaller of the two presidential helicopters, lifted off the pad and rose straight up, the marine pilot making sure to clear all possible obstacles before guiding his craft toward the northeast.

He felt the First Lady squeeze his hand. She was one of only three people in the White House who knew how serious the surgery and associated risk would be, and she made it clear no one should take comfort in the belief this was going to be a yawner. She had told him her love was beyond words, but would never understand how he could put his reelection above everythng else, even his own life. In the cold light of a cold morning, he wondered, *Why did I let Joe Morrison's fate control mine?*

Again and again, the president returned to the one conversation he had with the urologist, Dr. Tommy Delano Robby. The medico had been discreetly ushered into the Oval Office late one evening after a State dinner to which he had been invited as cover. Williams smiled as he recalled his silly idea the doctor's middle name might suggest he was a Democrat. More seriously, he thought it odd that this was the first time patient and physician were to meet, given the gravity of the circumstances. Robby seemed a quiet man, totally self-possessed, and not at all overwhelmed by his surroundings—or his patient.

"Mr. President," Dr. Robby had said, "let's get down to business, if we may."

Williams nodded and smiled, glad Robby was not intimidated by him.

"I've reviewed the entire record presented by Commander Bolling and concur completely with the information you've apparently been provided, including the assessment of the status of your cancer"—he looked directly at the president—"and the potential outcomes."

The president nodded again. "You're confirming that I've been in capable hands, and I'm grateful for that."

"I only wish that Commander Bolling had been more capable of persuading you to proceed with treatment eight months ago," Robby said.

"Not his fault—mine entirely." Williams smiled, as if in confession. "Call it the lust for power, and I don't regret any of it." *Well, maybe I do.* "Proceed, Doctor."

"I would not recommend the robotic surgery in your case, sir, because of what might be awaiting us—"

"Stop right there. If it makes any real difference in how soon I can fully resume my duties, I prefer the robotic protocol."

"Ill-advised, sir, because if the cancer has spread, my challenges will be all the greater, not to mention the longer-term risk to you."

"I'm more concerned about the next four years, Dr. Robby."

"I understand." Robby lowered his eyes. "May I plead with you to reconsider?"

"I am touched by your concern—maybe you're a Democrat after all," Williams said with a broad smile. "But I need to be back in the saddle as soon as possible."

"All right, sir. We'll comply with your wishes."

As Marine One continued its fourteen-minute flight, the president replayed the other choices he could have made. What it all came down to, he knew in his heart, was his insistence on keeping Joe Morrison on the ticket. Had he taken the advice of those closest to him at the time, perhaps he could have faced the media and the public in the spring of 2012—without Morrison on the ticket. Perhaps he could have had the robotic surgery then with a much more favorable outcome. People would have been more comfortable with the situation had they had more confidence in his VP. Though largely unsaid, most of the government, the media, and the voting public simply assumed that Joe Morrison would never sit in the Oval Office, and he hoped the fates would not prove them wrong.

Damn it, he chastised himself in the quiet reaches of his mind. *Quit the 'woulda, coulda, shoulda' bullshit. Anyway, he will never be in charge.* In the end, he knew that keeping that vow was out of his hands. He reached over and clasped his fingers in Andrea's as the helicopter slowed to home in on the Johns Hopkins landing beacon and the waiting staff.

Joe Morrison heard his alarm go off at four thirty and rose quickly. A cup of strong coffee in hand, he shaved, showered, and dressed. To his pleasant surprise, Sharon awaited him in the foyer and gave him a long kiss.

"Well, Mr. Acting President, let's just straighten out that tie." She gave him a tender smile. She had believed in him since their early days in Texas together, and she was all for him now. "Give 'em hell, Joe!"

"Don't you worry, hon." In his black, cashmere topcoat, Morrison went out the front door, past the Marine guard, and climbed into the waiting Escalade. This morning, his motorcade had one extra Tahoe with Secret Service agents and two extra police vehicles. He assumed his path to the White House had been eased by other policemen already at their posts.

On the way down Massachusetts Avenue, they zoomed around Dupont Circle to link with Connecticut before dropping into the heart of the District and the White House. Morrison couldn't enjoy the quiet as they sped their route. All he could think of was how he'd felt the night before in the Oval Office when the official documents were signed. It was as if he were the necessary evil in the room, but with his game face on, he stood there and behaved exactly as he thought they desired. All the more, he wanted to be the one giving direction, not receiving it.

At the West Wing, he was pleased to see that Remy Carlson had also come in early. Though neither were strangers to rising at oh-dark-hundred, neither had ever been at the White House for a reason so serious as this one.

Because he had little to do, he took off his jacket, and planted himself on the leather couch. Coffee in hand, he cruised the HDTV channels for any early coverage of the president's sojourn to Johns Hopkins. Except for outfits like News Global, he expected coverage to be routine and minimal.

To entertain himself, Morrison tuned into the News Global cable channel as the morning crew revisited the few occasions when Section Three had been employed. Each time the vice-president was empowered, they noted, it involved a procedure like a colonoscopy, during which the president would be unable to meet his constitutional obligations for four to six hours.

In the present instance, one of the News Global couch people pronounced that the White House had described the procedure in routine terms, but the reality appeared very different, according to unnamed White House sources. Because the president was likely to be unavailable for nearly a full day, this was a truly unprecedented transfer of power.

Surprised, Morrison liked what he heard. Had he not involved himself in bribery, corruption, and murder to achieve his and the president's reelection, his conscience would be clear as he contemplated what could be a bright future.

Once again, Marty Cox and the others who represented liabilities to his potential destiny came to mind. There were many people who might have knowledge of a small piece of the puzzle, but no one he could think of was in a position to put it all together. The only person who could put him in handcuffs was Marty Cox, the agent on duty a few yards from where he now sat. As for the others, they might steam and vent. They might make wild, even accurate guesses, but, "Fuck 'em," he muttered aloud. "They can't prove a thing." Cox was another matter, but his gut told him he had further need of the veteran agent.

Morrison had never been closer to the fulfillment of everyman's political fantasy, and no one was going to take that from him if the brass ring was there to grab. The real irony was that Williams's own lust for power had placed his presidency in jeopardy, and, by extension, placed Joe Morrison nearer to the seat behind the Resolute desk. He was glad to have risen so early on this particular morning, even without much to do. The longer day allowed him more time to savor all the things that might be.

6.

Mac Smith, *the farm's* supervising instructor for both the weapons and defensive driving courses, spent over a week being annoyed about his assignment, but orders were orders, and the pay was the same. When the two young recruits showed up on the tenth of the month, completely unexpected and out of sequence, again he railed against the Camp Peary director, but to no avail.

"This directive comes from the top, Mac. Just do the fuckin' job and get it over with. These two people may likely be dead in a month, but don't let it be because you were too pissed off to train them well. Now, get on it."

Smith's greeting to Paul and Mare Gladston had been anything but welcoming. He kept them standing outside the administration building, like the raw military recruits he trained in the first years of the Iraq war. "I'm told," he began, with a full measure of disdain in his hard voice, "that you two young marrieds are the latest and best this agency can find. Is that so?"

"And I'm told, Mr. Smith," Mare Burdette Gladston answered, "that we are not to discuss anything with you or anyone else. You have our names and the courses we are to take, and that's all you need."

Smith's could feel his face flush from the heat rising inside of him, despite the forty-degree temperature clinging to the cold, swampy ground not far from Williamsburg. Rather than respond, he looked at Paul Gladston, and said, in the most sarcastic manner he could manage, "Does the little missus speak for you, Mister Gladston?"

"No, she doesn't, Mr. Smith. She speaks for both of us. Is there anything else you need to know?"

Smith took a deep breath and said, "I see you've been provided your own weapons. That's all right with me."

"You have a problem with our choices?" demanded Mare.

"Actually, they're quite good choices, but I was only wondering how in the hell the likes of you knew to make them."

"Could we get on with it?" Paul asked, and get on with it they did.

First, Smith put them through several rounds of calisthenics, followed by a good run before dinner. He let them know that the next morning would begin the same way and that he had no intention of teaching them what he knew about weapons, ammunition, and related equipment, or even defensive and evasive driving, without ensuring they were physically and mentally fit to handle the stresses associated with those skills. Smith made it clear to his charges that it would be a crash course, indeed, and he didn't care a bit if they crashed.

The time flew by, and the trio gained respect for each other. Paul and Mare came to know of Mac Smith's military career as a training machine. They learned of his unstinting service in Iraq and Afghanistan and of his prowess with every kind of civilian and military weapon imaginable. Smith learned a bit of their background, and was pleasantly surprised by their marksmanship with a rifle. All of it made it easier for him to teach them handgun safety and skill.

When the weapons training gave way to the CTTC: the Countering Terrorist Tactics Course, which involved defensive driving, surveillance, interception, and evasion, the pair found themselves behind the wheels of several different vehicles, ranging from a light truck, to a midsize SUV and a small sedan. On top of the weapons and vehicle training, Smith threw in three days of VIP protection basics.

"What's this all about?" Paul asked, surprised.

"No idea." Smith developed a grudging respect for the young man and his wife. *These two*, he thought, *could actually make it through the ops course, with tradecraft likely posing no challenge for either of them.* "I just do what I'm told." He proceeded to further instruct them on many of the fundamentals taught at Camp Peary and the Secret Service's Rowley training facility. "In fact, you two should meet one of my best buds, a Secret Service guy who is on the protection detail for people at the top. This guy's done everything and knows everybody—he'd be of help to you."

"Thanks," Mare said, "we'll take a phone number if you have it." She wrote it down when Smith provided it.

"OK, you two, get outta my sight," Smith growled after dinner on the twenty-third. "I want you gone first thing tomorrow." Then he smiled. "And if I see you around anywhere, you'll have to buy me a drink."

As the sun rose on the twenty-fourth, Paul and Mare threw their gear in the old green Volvo and headed back to Washington, where they hoped some real excitement awaited them. On I-95, a little north of Richmond, Paul's cell phone chirped, and he carefully put the device to his ear, mindful that Virginia's new laws were not friendly to those who did not use hands-free calling. It was Pete Clancy.

"Paul? How did the course go? You two ready for action?"

"Yep. Great stuff—we'll thank you later today with dinner on us."

"Sounds good. Hey, the only reason I called is that I keep hitting a wall with that Virginia plate number you gave me."

"What's that all about?"

"I'm not sure, but we'll talk more when you get back." The line buzzed off.

As the men and women on the Johns Hopkins helipad scampered to meet Marine One, its rotors slowing to a chilled whir, President and Mrs. Williams stepped off the craft to a rush of activity, but, in fact, no one knew what to do. Under ordinary circumstances—ordinary meaning that a landing chopper was a life flight where the patient was severely injured or comatose or both—staff teamed to spirit the patient as quickly as possible to some of the best caregivers in the world. On this particular occasion, it was clear the president would not board a wheelchair or a gurney as neither was necessary, but the staff had their procedures to follow.

All laughed in embarrassment as the president waved off the wheeled transport and shook hands all around while moving with the First Lady toward the security and warmth of the double doors in front of him.

After all the prep work and a last chat between doctor and patient, Averell and Andrea Williams embraced warmly despite all the lookers-on. A few photos were allowed for the record. When the president was comfortable on the transport bed, the nurse anesthetist said the same words she'd used a thousand times. "I'm going to give you something to relax you."

"What's it called?" Williams asked.

She said, "Versed," knowing her patient was not conscious of the drugs's second syllable. Then the second stage of anesthesia was administered, which, in the usual course of things, blocked any sensation of pressure or pain from the patient's memory.

Dr. Tommy D. Robby made his appearance after the patient had made his, and orchestrated the setup. He knew some professionals disliked working with him because of his directorial way—not that he ordered people around, but he made sure each step was followed to the nth degree. When challenged over the years, he simply said, "When a patient survives and does well, everyone takes credit, but when the patient dies, my name is the only one associated with the tragedy, and I'll be damned if I'll allow even one of my patients to die in this process." He was glad they all understood.

The surgical suite became smaller with the da Vinci Robot present. Robby said, "We want the fewest number of people in here, ladies and gentlemen. With this monster, there's hardly room for the center of our attention: the patient." He then instructed the nurses where to place Williams on the operating table so that the da Vinci could be wheeled into position—no small feat for so heavy a piece of electronic wizardry.

"Let's place the patient in the Trendelenburg position." To the physician who had taken over for the nurse anesthetist, he said, "And Dr. Ruhati, please pay close attention to his respiratory rhythms as we begin the pneumoperitoneum technique." Since the patient would be feet up, head down in a thirty- to forty-five-degree angle in the Trendelenburg position, pneumoperitoneum—the introduction of gas to inflate his abdomen—would increase the gravitational pressure on his lungs and heart, but it also reduced blood loss and allowed for more precise surgical portals. The pneumoperitoneum presence was not ordinarily a problem, but could become dangerous if not carefully monitored by the anesthesiologist.

Once the patient—the most important one Dr. Robby had ever served—was properly positioned and catheterized, the da Vinci robot was rolled and braked into position between his legs. It was absolutely essential for the patient to be totally relaxed, unable even to cough, as any movement could cause him serious injury.

A scrubbed and gloved assistant made several small incisions in the president's abdomen. Into one, he placed the camera, which was actually two lenses that produced a high-definition, three-dimensional image of all the tissue that was surgically manipulated by the two robotic arms inserted in the other incised portals. Other incisions were made, each for a specific role.

Dr. Robby sat behind the robot and effectively strapped himself in for the duration. For every surgery, and this was number 937 by his count, he began with a silent prayer for the patient's success. More than once over the past few weeks, he had reminded himself that his patient was the president of the United States, yet he also told himself that neither president nor pensioner would receive better care than the other.

Dr. Ruhati had signaled several minutes earlier—before the robot's appendages were inserted in the president's abdomen—that the Fentanyl had done its work, rendering the patient completely immobile. Respiration, heart rate, and cerebrovascular functions were all normal.

At precisely 7:45 a.m., surgery began and lasted a little under three hours. Because of the advanced state of the cancer, Dr. Robby had to employ the gallery of skills at his command in removing the prostate and preserving the nerve endings that permitted both continence and erectile function. From Dr. Robby's preop review of all the data, particularly the MRI scans, he'd have bet there was little hope of preserving two qualities of manhood most men would demand. The patient had simply waited too long. Robby hoped it would all be worth it.

In surgery, he felt his instincts were correct, and he made a mental note to strongly recommend that the president receive appropriate counseling for the good of his mental health. In his consultation with Williams a few weeks earlier, the president had supposed him a Democrat, a comment Robby did not acknowledge. *I am an ardent Democrat*, Robby thought, but that fact could get him no better result.

"How's he doing, Dr. Ruhati? Can you see his face? Is the intubation firmly in place?" Dr. Robby asked.

"He's doing fine. Don't you worry about it," Ruhati said, annoyance streaming through his pale green mask.

Dr. Robby proceeded to examine his patient's seminal vesicles, and, though he was sure they were engulfed with cancer, he had them biopsied, but exercised his discretion in removing them. With the nerve endings for erectile function all but gone, along with the prostate, the patient would not need the glands that produced sperm. Last, he checked the lymph glands associated with the vesicles and was distressed to see that they, too, were already cancerous. That in itself increased the likelihood that cancer had spread elsewhere through the lymph system.

"OK," he said to his assistant, "we have a bit more to work through, and then we can disengage."

"Yes, doctor, whenever you say." It was the circulating nurse.

The quick biopsies confirmed his judgment, and Robby moved on to examine the bladder and all the tissue surrounding the locus of the prostate. Fortunately, he saw nothing to concern him in the ten minutes he spent manipulating the robot's highly agile hands. He had to admit that for the president's condition, the robotic procedure was probably the best choice. The machine's adjustment capabilities were much more precise than those of a surgeon's hand, and, what was more, the robot's inventors found a way to filter out the natural human tremor present with even the best of the practitioners he knew.

As he signaled his assistant to begin the disengagement process, he felt comfortable that he'd done the best anyone could have, but he felt less certain about either the immediate- or long-term outcome.

While the da Vinci apparatus was wheeled away and the several small incisions, six of them, were sutured or super-glued, he formed the words he would need for his next conversation, that with the First Lady of the United States. The president was taken to the recovery room where he would continue in a restful state for a while longer before he was given a drug to reverse his fully relaxed mind and body.

Dr. Robby had been briefed before the surgery and was told that Mrs. Williams would be waiting for him in a private, comfortable conference room. When he arrived, he found it occupied by several staffers—obviously a personal assistant and some media intercessors. He knew they all studied him to discern the news from his expression. They excused themselves one by one, and, in less than a minute, there remained he and Andrea Williams.

"Mrs. Williams," he began, filling his voice with hope and satisfaction, "I believe we have had a successful operation and the president is now in recovery—doing nicely, I expect."

"'Successful,' you said, Doctor?"

"Yes, ma'am. We safely removed the president's prostate and the seminal vesicles, all of which were cancerous. There was no sign, however, of any cancer migration to his bladder or any other digestive tract tissue." He stopped, and his listener remained silent.

"There is concern, however," Robby went on, "that the cancer cells have progressed into other areas of his lymph system," he said.

"Are you sure?"

"We cannot be certain until we take the next step, which will be to perform needle biopsies of several of the more likely nodes to see how far it has spread—if it has—and then, we'll go from there."

"Go where?"

"I meant to say," he responded, intimidated by her flat affect, "we'll decide the next course of treatment."

"Doctor, are you telling me that had the president had this surgery a year ago, the outcome today might not have been so..."

Dr. Robby let his eyes find the carpet. "Of course, we can't be fully certain, but my experience tells me that this surgery and its outcome would have been highly positive had it been performed earlier."

"Is there anything else, Dr. Robby?"

The physician hesitated before speaking, but chose his words carefully. "Yes, there is, I'm afraid. The president may not have full control of his bladder, which means he will have to remain catheterized and wear a collection device for now."

A look of horror crossed the First Lady's face.

"I can tell you, Mrs. Williams, that it is not uncommon when the cancer has progressed to this degree. Most men accommodate themselves to this set of circumstances. You should know that there is a small chance that will not be the case, but I want you both prepared for the worst."

"And?"

"And he will not likely be able to have sex without therapeutic assistance."

"I'm not sure I know what that means."

"Perhaps we can discuss that aspect of it when we have a more complete view of the overall picture here."

"Yes, I see," she said. "What about his recovery?"

"He must stay overnight. Later today, we'll get him up and see how mobile he is once the anesthetics have worn off. He'll need a lot of rest. Tomorrow we can decide our best course."

"This time, Doctor, no matter what he says," she insisted, "his health is to come first before that damned Oval Office." She broke down, weeping with a bitterness few would ever see. "This disease has taken nearly all of the wonderful man I married, but the rest of him belongs to me—not to the nation. Do you understand me, Dr. Robby?"

"Yes, ma'am, I do," he said quietly, "and I will do my utmost to comply." He paused and then added, "but he is the patient—and the president."

"I know who and what he is, but we are going to save him in spite of himself." She paused to daub her eyes. "Now, let me compose myself, and, may I suggest that now would be a good time to speak with the president's press secretary, Jack Sennett. He will make whatever statement should be made, and you should be aware that it will not include most of what you have told me." She continued, now in charge of herself and her circumstances. "Let Jack speak for you, Doctor. It will be easier all around."

"And you?"

"I'm going to do what any lifelong partner would do. I'm going to wait for him to wake up and tell me he loves me and that's what I'll tell him." Her dark eyes glistened like polished onyx. "I always will."

Dr. Robby nodded and turned to call the number he had been given the day before. He was glad to know he would soon fade out of the picture. He had already discerned that the public had been misled, and he wanted no part of it.

"This morning, at approximately six thirty, the president underwent an exploratory procedure to ascertain whether there was a presence of cancer," Jack Sennett began from his post behind the podium in the White House Briefing Room. "The president is making all aspects of his surgery public so that every man in this country realizes that when it comes to prostate cancer, there is no need for fear or embarrassment, only the right kind of treatment by the best practitioners to be found."

Sennett looked up, basking in the warmth of concern that bathed the journalists present in the packed room. "The procedure was performed by the foremost expert in this field, who happens to practice at Johns Hopkins University Medical Center in Baltimore. According to hospital staff—whose identities are being withheld for privacy reasons—the procedure went exceedingly well. Although cancer was discovered in the president's prostate, all of it was removed, and he is expected to recover quickly. The First Lady was at his side all morning, and she has now returned to the White House for a brief rest before making another visit to the hospital this evening." Sennett looked up once again. "I'll take a few questions."

There was silence in the room, as if a more complete rundown was forthcoming. Chad Kent of News Global clamored for Sennett's attention but was less visible than Tony Duke of CNS. "Jack," the latter began, "you didn't tell us the extent of the cancer, how serious it was, and whether it had spread. Can you enlighten us a bit more?"

Sennett was stunned by the directness of what he considered a State Media correspondent, but was glad the question had not reached the heart of the matter. "Well, Tony, as I said, we are informed that all the prostate cancer has been removed, and as to the seriousness of it, my statement that the president is expected to recover quickly provides enough information."

More noise engulfed the room, and Sennett called upon several others identified as friendlies. Each found a way to toss the press secretary a softball and sound intelligent doing so. One of the questions involved Vice-President Morrison's activities for the day, and Sennett responded, inappropriately, that none were noted. He corrected himself quickly when laughter swept the room. Kent kept his hand up and shouted with the best of his colleagues. Finally, as if he had no other choice, Sennett called on him with a sigh.

"Jack, are you prepared to say that the president will be sufficiently able, mentally and physically, to resume his duties tomorrow morning?"

Sennett cleared his throat. "The precise time as to when the president will return to the White House has not yet been determined, but when that information becomes known to me, I will make it known to all of you. Thank you very much." He strode from the room, followed by the querulous noise of unanswered questions.

"And there you just heard White House Press Secretary Jack Sennett provide us with a thorough update on the president's condition at Johns Hopkins University." Peter Marsden was speaking on the CNS set, while a banner ran below him proclaimed, *POTUS cancer-free and expected to make a full recovery.* "All indications are, ladies and gentlemen, that the president has come through the previously announced exploratory procedure with flying colors, and, while no precise time has been set for him to resume his full duties, it is expected that will occur in due course."

Marsden turned to the polished high-top plexiglass module on his right where two contributors were manipulating iPads. "This afternoon, we have with us two experts on prostate surgery who will provide their assessments of the president's medical situation. Dr. Shabezz and Dr. Albright, both from one of the top-ranking DC hospitals, welcome. Tell us, Dr. Shabezz, about the president's diagnosis and prognosis."

"Of course, Peter, we know little about the president's exact circumstances, but running true to form, prostate surgery is straightforward, and the results are generally quite favorable."

"Dr. Albright?"

"Dr. Shabezz is quite right. Without more complete data, I must presume that the John Hopkins physician is tops in his field, and that the president received only the finest care. While we do not know which protocol the surgeon followed, either hands-on or robotic, the results should be similarly uncomplicated."

"Thank you both. When we have more, ladies and gentlemen, we will bring it to you live from the *Control Room.*"

"Sir." Remy Carlson didn't know whether to call her boss *Mr. Vice-President* or *Mr. Acting President.* She waited for him to look up from his desk.

"Yes, Remy, what is it?"

"Sir, it's time. The motorcade is ready, and the police are already blocking traffic for you."

"Do you believe it? They don't want me using Marine One because it might appear that I'm being presumptuous."

"I understand, sir."

"OK, let's go. Make sure you're in the car behind me. I'll be surrounded by the president's people—no one I can trust."

"You have me and, of course, Marty Cox. Don't forget."

"Yeah," he responded, pensive. "That's right."

Morrison exited the West Wing for the waiting motorcade of two bulletproof limousines and four black Tahoes, along with flanking motorcycle officers. As he stepped into the cold sunshine, he reminded himself not to be too hard on people—none of them knew the proper protocol as to how he should be regarded because no such protocol existed. In the Reagan years, George H. W. Bush was never declared acting president, and when Section Three of the Amendment was invoked by George W. Bush, Dick Cheney served in that capacity for no more than a full morning.

Morrison was deeply cognizant of the fact he'd already held *the office* of president for more than twenty-four hours and, as such, would merit more than a passing mention in the history books. He noted that the pundits were already dissecting him like med school students would a cadaver. *Eat shit,* he said almost out loud, as he stepped into the black Cadillac.

On the drive over to Baltimore, high-speed and without so much as a pause, fantasy answers to all favorite what-ifs crowded his mind. Yet he couldn't banish the ghosts nagging his daydream. They weren't the ghosts of Enrique McCord and Jerry James—people who became expendable. Poor Jerry, he recalled, was a party and personal loyalist who'd been in the wrong place at the wrong time. At SoftSec's offices election night as the guru who decided on the manipulated vote counts in Virginia, Ohio, and the others, Jerry knew too much. Morrison never knew what Marty did with him and the nameless others dispatched in the cause of an all-consuming national election. At this point, he didn't much care.

No, they weren't the ghosts of people he'd had killed. They were specters of terror—the terror of being caught, of being exposed, of being seen for what he knew he was: a common murderer.

When the limo pulled up to the great hospital, the first face he saw was that of Marty Cox, as the agent opened the rear door for him. Morrison realized Cox must have captured a glimpse into his hidden self. That his protector now saw a weakness in him frightened him even more.

Morrison forced a game face when greeted by Freddie Frederick, Sondra Thompson, and Jack Sennett—those closest to the president.

"Sir, welcome to Johns Hopkins," Thompson said. "We'll take you to see the president, but first, we should convene in the large conference room reserved for us."

Morrison paid more attention to the apparently somber moods of the three presidential staffers than to the words. In the conference room itself, he was further welcomed by a body of beribboned military officers and high-ranking national security people. *This is completely unnerving*, Morrison thought, and wondered what was happening. In all the greetings, nearly all were more formal than customary.

"Sir," Thompson spoke again.

Was it his imagination, Morrison thought, *or was there a measure of respect in her tone?*

"Sir, we thought this was a good time for all of us to receive a medical update from Dr. Robby, the president's surgeon, before going further."

With that, Freddie Frederick opened a side door and beckoned.

A distinguished-looking man entered. He had brushed flat, silver-gray hair and wore rimless glasses. A white shirt and tie cloaked by a starched, white and unblemished physician's coat completed the icon of an all-knowing surgeon. Morrison realized at once Robby appreciated an audience where uniforms were important. *Will my empty title matter to this man?*

Thompson introduced them, and the two quietly exchanged a few words before Robby turned and gathered the attention of the entire room's congregants. "Ladies and gentlemen," he began in a low voice. Immediately his listeners strained to hear. "The president is resting comfortably, but the official announcements aside," he said with a scolding glance at Sennett, "the patient is not doing as well as we might have hoped."

A collective intake of air lowered the oxygen level in the room.

Robby continued. "We are now twenty-four hours postsurgery. In the recovery room, the president was slow to respond to wakeful stimuli, and, while that is not uncommon, I was struck by the lack of mobility he later displayed when staff got him up to take a walk. Nearly all patients struggle with the first step or two, because they're tied to a catheter and are attached to the IV pole by two or three lines, but all things considered, they do pretty well." The doctor signaled with his hand to hold off with questions. "Remember that most of our patients are the president's age or older, so we have a pretty good idea of reasonable expectations."

As Sondra Thompson was about to ask the first question, the conference room door flew open and in marched First Lady Andrea Williams. The electricity was palpable, and the gathered company looked like burglars caught in the bank vault.

"When you talk about my husband's medical status, don't you think I ought to be in the room?" she demanded.

"I am so sorry, Mrs. Williams," Thompson stated, "but I thought you had received a private briefing."

"I have, Sondra, but I want to know how this will all be handled with the public."

"We will respect the First Lady's wishes," Morrison said, speaking for the first time. He noticed the silent acknowledgement that it was he who should be giving directions and no one else. "Please sit down, Andrea," Morrison added, not unkindly, as he held a chair for her. "Let's continue, Dr. Robby."

"Thank you, sir," he said with respect, but not deference, as one with all the rank. "As I was saying, men of the president's age and shape usually progress rather well after this surgery, and although nothing was discovered or dealt with that we haven't seen before, each situation is different."

"What are you getting to, Doctor?" Thompson asked.

"What I'm getting to, Ms. Thompson, is that if asked officially, I'd have to say the president is not ready to resume his duties."

"Why, specifically?"

"Physically and mentally, he simply has not bounced back as he should, and, as his physician, I'd have to say that throwing him back into the pressure cooker for even a few hours could be a fatal mistake—literally."

"Even with all the support one might provide a president of the United States?" Thompson pressed.

"In a word, no. Put another way, this patient is not lucid."

Again, the small crowd sucked in their breaths and their collective shock filled the void.

"Then you think Mr. Morrison should remain acting president." It was a statement, not a question, from Andrea Williams. "I want there to be no shortcuts, Dr. Robby. We will not hurry my husband to his grave just so that we don't excite the public."

As empathetically as possible, Robby said, "As his doctor, Mrs. Williams, we are in agreement. As to these people...?" He waved around the room as if to say, *It is out of my hands.*

Andrea Williams turned to her husband's vice-president. "Take charge, Joe. This is what you want," she said, matter-of-factly and without rancor. "You take the job, and I'll take my husband."

Morrison nodded to the First Lady. "Dr. Robby," he said, turning away, "would it be advisable to transfer the president to Walter Reed? There, they have a presidential suite more equipped to deal with some-one of his stature. The question is, in your best opinion, are good people and facilities there to care for him?"

Robby held his response while he thought about it, and the room was completely silent. "Actually, sir, that is an excellent idea, and there are components of Walter Reed that are the equal of any medical facil-ity. In this particular area, it has an especially well-trained staff. In any case, I will remain available to serve President Williams in any way I am able."

Morrison glanced at the First Lady. She remained expressionless. He nodded to the doctor. "Then let's do that. This will make the presi-dent's resumption of office easier all the way round."

Without any real standing to alter that course of action, Thompson directed Jack Sennett to compose a simple press release indicating that Morrison visited briefly with the president and would remain as act-ing president until sound medical opinion confirmed that President Williams could resume his duties. A transition back to normalcy was expected within a day, but, in the meantime, the president would be moved back to Washington where excellent care for his condition was available at Walter Reed Military Medical Center in Bethesda. Everyone in the room nodded in the affirmative, as if they'd just agreed on the terms of a mortgage.

Morrison left the hospital without accomplishing his principal mission—to visit with the recovering president and symbolically, at least, hand back the reins of power. Yet he was inwardly elated that for another day he had another opportunity to let people get used to the idea of him.

In the limo back to Washington, he directed Remy Carlson to have Thompson, Sennett, and national security key advisers brief him on all domestic issues the president had on his desk to resolve, and all military and foreign policy initiatives currently underway. "Tell them, I insist on being brought up to speed because, in truth, we do not know how long this will last."

When he finished a run of instructions to her and others, his favored Secret Service man in the front seat turned and, sliding back the soundproof glass, said, "Sir, we received word that the president will be moved within the hour."

"Thank you, Marty. And if there's no change in circumstances, schedule a visit for us at Reed tomorrow evening or the morning after."

7.

At the completion of the drive back into Old Town Alexandria, the cold day added rain to the palette of steel-gray skies and deep-shadowed streets. Nonetheless, Mare and Paul were glad to face their new world together and told each other so.

Pete Clancy was waiting for them with food and news. A plate of grilled salmon, asparagus, and leaf salad with pinenuts and berries greeted them at the dinner table, and they sat down to a bottle of good Riesling.

Paul looked at Mare and the two of them laughed.

Clancy said, "Did you two have a better hotel in mind?"

"Not at all, Pete," Mare said, with an appeasing smile for her host. "You remember what a beer did to us a few weeks ago. You see, we spent two months at an Amish farm with the best comfort food anyone could want. Meat, starch—and plenty of it—and a few veggies. Then, we head down to spook boot camp for a few weeks where the food is, shall we say, something out of the canned goods aisle of Safeway, and here"— she sighed—"we come to some damn fine food—with wine!" Her mirth unabated, she picked up her glass. "We, who are about to die, salute you!"

Clancy's broad smile took over his earlier look of disdain, and he raised his glass as Paul picked up his and joined in.

"Ditto all that, Pete." Paul took a fork load of salmon with his wine. "We also owe you a vote of thanks for the spy school stuff. We learned a lot from Mac Smith, and he gave us a solid contact in the Secret Service if we need one. All in all, our time there was a huge plus. But what about that Virginia plate number? You said you hit a wall?"

"I don't know what to make of it," Pete responded, "but it's smelling real bad for the White House on this."

"Yeah, but," Mare jumped in, "with the Prez in the hospital, doesn't that make our job a lot harder?"

"Maybe the other way," Pete suggested. "What I've been curious about is what role Williams played in all this. We have a pretty good idea that Morrison has been calling the shots, but on his own? We're about to find out, I think."

"Good thing a guy like him—even if we didn't think he was a murderer—is only in the job for a day or two." Mare wrinkled her brow. "This could be real trouble."

"I'll have to give this more thought. When I ran the plate several different ways, the same info kept coming up. The plate belongs to a select group of protection vehicles—not a small number by the way—under the White House and State Department umbrellas."

"In a way that makes sense," Paul said. "If Morrison is our main bad guy, wouldn't it stand to reason that his henchman is somebody close to him? Somebody whose schedule he, in some way, controls?"

"All true," Clancy agreed. "And soon, we may find out just how small the circle is, but we have to be a bit more patient on that." His operatives wore faces of dismay.

"Look, Pete, Morrison and his people killed my mentor right out in public, and no one was all that interested," Mare said. "Sorry, I don't mean you. Then, there's McCord in Cincinnati. And then, there's Amber—who knows what happened to her?" Her voice cracked.

"That's right," Paul said quietly. "If there was a way to nail this son of a bitch, I'd be goin' for the hammer right now, no matter what."

"I get it, but be patient a bit longer, I'm asking you." Clancy changed tone and direction. "In the meantime, troops, we have another job to do to earn our keep in this world."

"What's that?" Mare asked, obviously interested.

"I need the two of you to head over to Walter Reed, if not tomorrow then in a day or two. We'll concoct a plan tonight. There's some suspicion that in one or more VA hospitals around the country, they're falsifying records about patient wait times."

"Why would they do that?" Paul asked. "You'd think that highlighting a service problem would solve some budget problems."

"You'd think. But it's more like they want to avoid Congressional hearings."

"So we go to Walter Reed. Say, wait a minute," Mare said. "Didn't they announce the Prez will be there? How will we get in?"

"Not a problem for a veteran." Clancy looked at Paul. "Depending upon what you find there, we may send you to the VA Hospital in Cincinnati."

"Why there, especially? Not that I would mind, of course—that was home for a long time."

"Because our client thinks a stink might be there as well."

"So who's your—our—client, Pete?" Paul asked.

"For the moment, I'll keep that card close, but you'll know soon enough. We'll visit some other friends of mine tomorrow and get the two of you full sets of alternate ID documents. You'll need them."

Sondra Thompson had been part of Averell Williams's circle of close advisers for at least two decades. She met him when he was a young assemblyman from Buffalo, New York, where they both grew up. She knew he'd driven a Checker Cab around the city to put himself through Canisius College and later, through law school, and that information endeared him to her as an unusual political animal, one she never stopped serving.

An admirer of his patient persistence, his ability to capture a phrase, and his raw work ethic, Thompson climbed on the Williams wagon early and stayed with him through his trek through Albany, then to Washington as a member of Congress, and back to Albany for a stint as lieutenant governor and two terms as governor. There was no doubt in her mind, back then, that someday Averell Harriman Williams would be president, and it didn't matter that he was African American. Neither did it matter to President Williams that she was gay, and, for that reason alone, she could have walked a hundred miles for him.

That she had to walk not far down the hall in the West Wing at the request of Acting President Morrison, however, was the hardest thing she'd ever done. Although she had long before accepted Morrison for the lightweight he was, she knew how her boss felt about him, and she found each step toward his office painful in the extreme. That she would have to kowtow to an empty-suited Texan was galling.

Yet, she reminded herself, she had signed on to serve, and her job, for the moment, was to make certain nothing happened to damage the president or his legacy. Her mission, she knew, was to render Morrison harmless.

In the office occupying a corner of the West Wing, she was surprised to find only Morrison and Remy Carlson. Thompson had half-expected a small army of national security and domestic and foreign policy types, and she was pleased that Morrison had not begun to gather around him the trappings of power.

"Good morning, sir," she said, unsure how to address him, just as she knew others were uncertain about that particuler nicety.

"And good morning to you as well, Sondra. Please sit down. I've kept this meeting to the three of us because, well, it's less formal that way. I do think it's best, however, that I be brought up to speed on the hot-button stuff should I be forced to act on the president's behalf."

"Of course, sir. Where would you like to begin?"

"Foreign policy. Let's start there. Since Emerson Grantham resigned from State, how is Susan Davidson doing in the job?"

"Well, sir, she has had much experience overseas, but, of course, she's had little time to impact the situations in North Korea, Iran, Afghanistan, Darfur, or Russia. She continues to follow closely the president's desired objective not to attempt management of everything going on in the world."

"How is that approach sitting with the Brits and the Germans in particular? And Israel?"

Surprised that he would zero in on these key areas so quickly, she responded as candidly as possible. "Naturally, sir, all of those countries would prefer that the United States take a greater leadership role vis-à-vis the world's problem children."

"Naturally. But they're happier with us than with Bush, are they not?"

She hesitated.

"Are they?" he persisted politely.

"In truth, sir, the president understands that many of the world's leaders would prefer a Bush approach but with more *savoir faire*—with a bit more sensitivity for their own circumstances. President Williams feels his is the better approach because he believes other leaders will then begin to solve some of their own problems."

"Sounds good. What about Benghazi?"

Thompson felt as if she'd been slapped. *Why would he ask about that?* she wondered. "We think Benghazi is nicely under control, sir. All of the participants with direct knowledge of what actually occurred have been appropriately prepared to remain silent—or will adhere to the administration's position."

"Interesting choice of words, Sondra."

"Yes, sir. In any event, our media friends are avoiding the story, and we don't think Speaker Whitaker will pursue it once it proves politically irrelevant to the GOP."

"OK. What about domestic stuff? Anything I should know there?"

"You already know we're stalemated in Congress. We don't think Whitaker has the votes to confront us on much of anything. Sure, he can whip the House to repeal anything he wants to, but he knows it won't go anywhere in the Senate with Harrison Riordan as majority leader."

Morrison grinned with satisfaction.

Thompson noticed the reaction to Riordan's name and was not surprised. It was well-known that the old Missouri fox had been Morrison's rabbi during his few years in the Senate. "Harry will remain a good friend to the administration, I'm sure, sir."

"What about the IRS mess? Is that under control as well?"

"That, too, is being managed, sir."

"There's more, isn't there, Sondra? I mean there must be thousands of dicey e-mails to be discovered, and then there's the visitor's log here at the West Wing."

"I'm not sure I understand, sir."

"Sure you do," Morrison responded, a gleeful lilt in his voice. "You must be concerned about the years of e-mails emanating from the same Gordon Hellman who made over a hundred and fifty visits to this building."

Again, Thompson felt her face flush. "I am truly sorry, sir. I did not know how deeply into these matters you wanted me to go. I'm sure Mr. Hellman's visits to the West Wing have their own explanation."

"And you're hoping that you're not called to testify, I'm sure."

Thompson felt cornered. "Sir, if you ask me any more questions on this issue, you will then know more than President Williams himself, and if I report this information to you, you will lose your deniability."

Morrison stopped to think about it. "Point taken, Sondra. Thank you. Don't tell me, then, about this administration's directives to the IRS to harass conservative organizations and keep them from fund-raising before the last election."

The fog lifted and the real reason for the meeting became clear: *To let me know what he knew and find out how much I was willing to confirm.*

"And the e-mails?" he pressed. "Deniability is one thing. E-mails sitting on servers somewhere are another. There are exchanges that are likely incriminating."

"And the subpoenas from the House committees?" asked Remy Carlson.

"We'll do what the Nixon Administration taught all of us. Stonewall till the mortar crumbles. Then, when some other crisis dominates the news, we'll simply announce that a server or archival crash had occurred at some date in the past—at least, it will buy us time until after the 2014 Midterms."

"Are we cynical enough to think that'll work?" Morrison asked.

"Being cynical has nothing to do with it, sir. It always works when the media is on our side. Without them headlining the tacky stuff in front of the public like they did Watergate, Iran–Contra, and Cheney-Halliburton to name three, it'll go away quickly and the Republicans will look like a bunch of Area fifty-one looney birds. That's the plan."

"I'm glad we're on the same side," Morrison said.

Thompson cringed, but kept her game face. "Yes, sir."

"This is Peter Marsden, and we are breaking into our usual morning programming to bring you, live, the White House press conference about to begin. I can tell you that the Briefing Room is abnormally quiet this Monday morning, the twenty-eighth of January, as all the usual, hard-core media men and women gather for what some might describe as a hastily called briefing.

"There has been no advance word, no leak, no hint as to what might be forthcoming," Marsden's voiceover continued. "As the camera pans the room, you can see that the principal network and cable giants have had their best correspondents standing by ever since the announcement that President Williams has not recuperated as expected." Marsden cleared his throat, and in a hushed voice, said, "And I understand they're ready. Let's go there now."

A confident Jack Sennett strode into the room. His buoyant demeanor was matched by his youthful face and topped by unruly dark hair smoothed into place and neatly parted in a way a mother of one would love. His smile before the hard-nosed media types, the camera crews, and the world that awaited all the communication he needed to convey, but words were required, and he appeared delighted to offer them.

"Ladies and gentlemen, as you will recall from earlier sessions, President Williams was transferred to the Walter Reed National Military Medical Center on the twenty-sixth, approximately twenty-four hours after his surgery. Because of some slower than expected recovery responses, it was felt that Vice-President Morrison should continue as acting president, thus permitting the president additional time for a full and complete recovery. This was the action prescribed by Section Three of the Twenty-Fifth Amendment to the US Constitution, and the nation is grateful to the vice-president for his patient, circumspect, and competent service while President Williams rests without the high stresses of office.

"This morning, the White House is pleased to announce that the president is up and walking around, is fully aware of his surroundings, and is completely in touch with up-to-the-minute world and domestic events. Early this morning, in fact, he asked for the PDB—the Presidential Daily Briefing paper. At eight o'clock, one hour ago, President Williams and Attorney General Sweeney revoked the action of Section Three, thus allowing him to fully resume all his duties as commander-in-chief."

The clicks of cameras from the press pool punctuated the otherwise soundless room as Sennett continued. "Because of the president's surgery, he has several incision portals that must heal, and, in accordance with the best medical advice, he will remain at Walter Reed for a few more days. There, he will conduct the affairs of state as every American would expect of him, and he will be carefully monitored to mitigate any postsurgical issue that might arise. Vice-President Morrison has resumed his own constitutional duties. I'll take a few questions."

A cheer erupted in the room, with all media members, irrespective of their politics, joining the heartfelt support for the president. The few questions that followed centered on medical minutiae, and, soon, the press conference was adjourned.

"There you have it, ladies and gentlemen. To sum up, the president of the United States has resumed his full duties as required by the US Constitution, and the nation's business will soon return to normal."

"I worked a four-week detail here in DC a few years ago," Paul said to Mare as they drove to Walter Reed on Wednesday morning, "and I have to tell you, the streets and roads here could make you crazy."

"We've been married less than a month. Don't go crazy on me yet."

"That smile of yours is pretty darn distracting."

"Back to the roads?"

"When I went to the website for the Walter Reed National Military Medical Center—now there's a mouthful isn't it?—the directions referred to leaving the Metro and crossing Wisconsin Avenue, which we're on now, but somewhere up here, the road changes to Rockville Pike, but I'll be damned if I know where."

"Are you going to obsess about this?"

"No, but Rockville Pike is the actual address of the place, not Wisconsin Avenue. Walter Reed is as large as a government facility can get. In fact, it's the largest of its kind in the world, and, having worked in this town, I can tell you that approaching one of these places can be intimidating on any level, especially after nine-eleven. I can imagine how a veteran must feel, coming here with a disability of some kind."

"So what are you trying to tell me?"

"Walter Reed used to be an army facility, but, as a result of the base closure effort nine or ten years ago, it was eventually combined with the navy operation to form one coordinated medical command. According to the website, this center treats over one million patients a year."

"Holy crap, Paulie boy. That's a big number, one that allows for plenty of mistakes. So who's watching the henhouse?"

"There's supposed to be a command evaluation and investigation unit responsible for accountability."

"Are they doin' the job?" Mare asked.

"There's sure a lot of stuff to count and monitor."

"So our plan today is that you're an Iraqi tour vet suffering from PTSD, and you're trying to get an appointment to see a shrink, is that it? Why wouldn't you call or try it online?"

"Because we're going to try something different—assuming we get past all the security." Eventually, Paul turned right onto Wood Road, following the curve, from which they could see the small skyscraper that centered the facility. When they reached the guard gate, they showed the photo IDs Clancy provided and were directed to parking, which seemed like a mile away.

Inside the main reception area, Paul asked for the Behavioral Health Unit and was given thorough directions for the long trek. Once there, he said, "Sit with me here, and watch what I do, and if the opportunity arises, you'll do the same with someone else."

"Won't someone notice us?"

"From time to time, one or both of us will get up, go down the hall, maybe to the cafeteria, and return. There are so many people here, if we're discreet, no one will pay any attention."

First the two sat together and picked from the large pile of well-thumbed magazines. Then, Paul spoke to the man in the seat next to him, a grizzled specimen in his late sixties.

"Fought in 'Nam," said the older man. "Samuel Freeport is my name. Seventh Cav."

Paul gave Freeport his fake name and unit designation in Iraq, old code for military brothers. He felt bad about deceiving someone who had actually served when he hadn't. "Been waiting long?"

"Hey, man, I been waitin' here so long, I don't leave the building for haircuts." Freeport laughed, but it was in derision.

"Seriously, Samuel, this is the Behavioral Health Unit, isn't it?" Paul asked. "So don't they take care of us pretty quickly? I mean, this is my first time here."

The older black veteran looked at him in disbelief. "Are you kiddin' me, man? I've had to wait six weeks for this appointment, and they called two days ago to cancel it. Only because I went ballistic on the phone did they agree to see me, and I've been here since they opened this morning at zero seven thirty hours."

"Is it like this all the time?" Paul asked.

"All the time, man. Well, maybe just the last few years. Before that, it wasn't so bad, but the last few years, it's the same thing all the time. That's why I lost it on the phone. I ain't gonna put up with it no more. No, sir."

"Do you see the same doctor?"

"And that's another thing. Just because I been outta the army for so many years and they think I'm harmless, they stick me with some junior intern. Jeeesus! I'm tired a bein' jerked around."

"Well, I hope I have better luck."

"I just want the same treatment as the old Prez down the hall somewhere. I'll bet he didn't have to wait no six weeks to see somebody." Despite his frustrations, Freeport said his piece with a broad grin.

Paul chuckled at the veteran's good nature, shook hands with him, and said, "I think I'll go get a cup of coffee since I have a pretty long wait today myself."

Out in the hall, he said to Mare, "See what I mean? Let's disappear for a few minutes while I make some notes on that contact. Then we'll go back in and sit down with somebody else. I'll pick a spot with only one seat so we can't sit together. You find another spot like that, and we'll pick up two more contacts."

"How many should we get?"

"Let's get at least a half dozen today, and dump it on Clancy to see what he says."

For the next three hours, off and on with breaks for coffee and lunch so as to be seen as joining the waiting room afresh several times, Paul and Mare worked in tandem and separately. They made nine contacts between them.

"God, I can't believe it. All but one had the same story as Freeport's," Mare said after they compared notes. "That means that a lot of these guys, none of them playing with a full deck right now, are getting frustrated just seeing someone, and they're in and out of here like lit dynamite."

"You have to wonder what the suicide rate is."

"Yeah," Mare said. "That's a pretty sad state of affairs for a place dedicated to 'healing our heroes.'"

"One last thing," Paul said as he rose and walked toward the appointment window, "I'm going to schedule one, and we'll see what happens to me."

Mare laughed. "You'd better not be too convincing with PTSD. They might want to see you today. Then what?" Mirth would not leave her.

"OK, smart ass," he said when he returned. "Let's make our way back to the main lobby where we started and get the heck out of here."

The pair trudged back through what seemed to be countless hallways with myriad signage, all leading them out of the labyrinth. A crowd had gathered in the huge, open reception area. Pressing closer, Paul stretched his legs full out to see over the people in front of him, but nothing was happening. "Let's get closer to the main doors."

They snaked their way through and around the burgeoning crowd until they were within thirty feet of the exit. They were held back by a phalanx of uniformed and plain-clothes security men, but they could see no activity that accounted for all the people.

At that end of the lobby, the gawkers were mostly quiet and full of anticipation. "You'd think General Patton himself was about to walk through those doors," Mare said.

No sooner had the last word escaped her lips than the lobby doors were pushed open, and two men in black suits with earbuds walked in, their gazes scanning every hand and face in the crowd. Then came Acting President Joseph P. Morrison, followed by two more agents close on his rear. One of them glanced in their direction and paused for a fraction of a second, long enough.

"Oh my God, Paulie. Look!"

"Look at what? Morrison?"

"No!" she said in a hoarse whisper. "Look behind him. Tall guy. Blond hair. One of the Secret Service guys. It's Crew Cut!"

As if he'd heard them through the buzz of noise from the crowd, Crew Cut made a right-angle turn without breaking stride and stepped toward them, his eyes scanning faces and profiles with a honed instinct.

The line of onlookers bent away from Crew Cut, like magnets repelling each other. Mare placed herself behind a grizzled man with a cane, his height and size making her invisible. Paul could seek no such refuge. He kept his head directly behind that of the man in front of him, ensuring that no eye contact could be made with the agent, who was not more than four feet away.

Crew Cut stopped within a pace of the line while he inspected the shoulder and body movements of each person in front of him. Gladston supposed everyone there saw him as a stone-sober agent dedicated to the protection of his assignment. Only he and Mare knew Crew Cut as a serial killer.

❖

"Well, we have our marching orders, and I don't mind telling you that I'm glad to be getting the hell out of here." Paul began talking as soon as they loaded into the Volvo. He turned the key in the ignition, a figurative and literal kick start to another flight from danger. "Good thing no one called the police while we were skulking around," he said, referring to alley behind Pete Clancy's townhouse.

"You're in an awful hurry to leave a place you were in an awful hurry to get to," Mare said playfully, though she didn't feel all that sprightly at three in the morning.

"Don't be cute. We're leaving because Pete wants us back in Ohio, and we can't be sure Crew Cut didn't make us yesterday afternoon at the hospital." Paul drove up US 1 through Alexandria and picked up the George Washington Parkway on the way to I-495. There was almost no traffic, but, this being the nation's capital, there were always night travelers—just like them.

"One thing's for certain now. We know who Crew Cut is—well, we don't know his name, but we can now connect him directly with Morrison, and we already knew Nelson Evers and Enrique McCord, and probably Nathan Conaway and Amber Bustamente lost their lives because of the election. None of that was Crew Cut's idea." Mare spoke with conviction, but she knew her brave speech was far from the service of justice.

"Thank God Williams has recovered. Jesus, think of the alternative!"

"We're only a month off the Schenk farm, and your language is already deteriorating, Paulie boy."

"You should talk," he said, trying to concentrate on the parkway curves and his train of thought. "As I was saying, there's no indication the president had anything to do with any of Morrison's schemes. I don't know what we'll do if Williams was involved. It's bad enough he let Benghazi and the IRS happen, and he'll pay the piper soon enough, but, at least, he's not a murderer."

"But he didn't win the election. Hardy did," Mare insisted.

"We only believe that because Nathan Conaway told Amber Bustamente that's what they were going to do. We need some actual proof, and, until then, we can't do anything about the election, but we can see how far this goes."

"Yeah, I suppose that's why we're on our way back to Ohio. Without McCord or Nathan Conaway, we need to find out why the dog didn't bark in the nighttime."

"What?"

"You didn't read your Sherlock Holmes, Paulie boy. We need to find some sort of evidence that will prove the election was stolen. That's the smoking gun, or the dog that failed to bark in the nighttime, because it would connect the murders to vote fraud and McCord, and McCord to Morrison via Crew Cut."

"You know, we really lucked out with Pete Clancy," Paul said. "He's obviously connected, he's got work, and he's giving it to us, just in time to get us out of town."

"God, he sure seemed in a panic when we told him what happened yesterday."

"Yeah, he hardly seemed interested in the VA stuff after we told him about Crew Cut."

"True, but he still wants us to work in some time at the Cincinnati VA on Vine Street, to see if we get the same kind or reaction there as we did at Walter Reed."

"Remember, though, that's actually second on the list," Paul said. "We are specifically being directed to one precinct in Cincinnati and two in Portsmouth. The gurus seem to think that if the vote count was inaccurate in those locations, then all of Ohio may be in question."

"But how the hell do we prove that, one way or the other?"

"Don't know yet, short stuff, but we'll have to see what's what."

"It's four o'clock. Can we stop for something to eat?"

"Sure."

After a quick stop in Hagerstown for gas and morning munchies washed down with copious amounts of coffee, the pair headed west, the rising sun chasing them westward.

"Did you tell me you never closed your apartment in Mount Lookout?" Paul asked.

"That's right—I know I told you that."

"I hear you only when you tell me you love me."

"Oh, no! Now I really know what's first on your priority list. Listen, Paulie boy, we'll camp at my place—I told you my parents kept it for me—and, when we leave, maybe I can take some of my stuff, and my folks will see that the rest goes to people who need it."

"But there is a bed there?"

"Yes, Paul, there certainly is."

"OK. Right after lunch, we'll head over to Hyde Park and nose around the polling place. Do you know where that is?"

"Holy Redeemer? Yeah, it's an Episcopal Church—that's where I vote."

"So what's the deal with voting there? How does it work?"

"We actually mark a paper ballot—I was there only for the 2010 midterms—then feed it into a scanner of some sort, and then it's supposed to be shredded."

"You really fill out a paper ballot?"

"Yeah, just like the old days."

Seven hours later, with rising apprehension, they approached Mare's Ellison Avenue apartment off Mount Lookout Square. Mare remembered the night they left, accompanied by more than a bit of fear. It was right before the election, and Crew Cut was after them. He followed them down the street in the black Tahoe, in the SUV they knew killed Nelson Evers. Their race out of the city and toward Columbus was one she'd never forget, and one she never wanted to repeat. Leaving Columbus was even more harrowing, as their would-be killer came within a hair's breadth of ramming them.

Even so, she loved the familiar smell of the four-family building, and she was glad familiar things were still in their places. Her parents had done a good job keeping it up and paying the bills. How could she thank them? Mare was happier still that Paul was now a part of her life, and she had no hesitation in enjoying what he called "a nooner."

At Holy Redeemer on Erie Avenue in Hyde Park, Mare walked Paul up to the front door and, glad to find it unlocked, she took him inside. "When I voted here, they asked me to show an ID, which I did, and then I went to one of the four tables they had set up. After they checked my name off, I went to a little booth and, as I described it to you—I hope you listened that time, Paulie boy—cast my ballot."

"What do you mean by that? What exactly did you do with the paper ballot?"

"Oh, I slid it into a machine, which I guess was supposed to read and count my vote."

"And then you shredded it?"

"Now that I think it through, I didn't see that part of the process, so I don't actually know what happened to it."

At that moment, an elderly man slipped out of the daytime gloom of the unlit church. "How can I help you?" he inquired, startling them with his unexpected presence. His white, wispy hair seemed adrift in the stir of air that followed him.

"Yes, sir," Paul answered with the same respect he was given. He produced the simple credentials provided by the office of the governor. "We're here doing a spot check of voting practices in the state, and I wonder if you can help us."

"Of course, young man. I'm Thomas Callahan, the sexton, and I make all the election arrangements. What do you need?"

"We understand," Paul began, "that when voters complete the ballot, they slide them into a scanner, is that right?"

"Yes. The equipment is provided by SoftSec, a big electronic voting company."

"What happens to the ballot once it goes into the machine?"

"It's supposed to be shredded," Callahan said, but his words were slow in coming.

"May I ask why you're hesitating, Mr. Callahan?" Paul asked.

"Well, you see, the shredders didn't work that day," Callahan said sheepishly. "Someone tried to stuff too many Sunday Bulletins into the machine at one time."

"You mean they weren't shredded?"

Even more hesitant, Callahan asked, "Will there be trouble over this?"

"None," Mare reassured him. "What happened?"

"Well, I guess we never got around to it, and there's a stack of them in the storeroom back here."

"Are they bundled or loose or what?" Paul asked.

"Oh, I was careful to bundle them up since the people who man the polls are volunteers—they couldn't take them." Callahan emphasized the last few words as if that would be the worst of horrors.

"And who has had access to them?" Paul asked.

"Absolutely no one—I have the only key to that room," Callahan said with absolute certainty. "Let me show you." He turned and glided back into the gloom. Off to the side, there was an unobtrusive door with a sturdy lock. "You see? They have been secured properly." He turned to look at them both. "My only mistake was that I should have made sure they were shredded as soon as possible after the election. I'm sorry."

"Don't be, Mr. Callahan," Paul hurried to say. "With the authority of Governor McNickle's office, I will relieve you of all responsibility for these ballots."

Callahan hesitated. "Please let me see those credentials one more time." He took each set and held them under the light, inspecting them carefully. "Phew," he exhaled. "I'm so glad you came. It's been a few months, and I've been worried about them. You'll be sure to take care of them?"

"You bet we will, Mr. Callahan, and we owe you a vote of thanks." Mare gave the old man her best smile. She and Paul each picked up two bundles. "Do you happen to know how many there are all together?

"Just a moment. I have it here in an inventory book. There are 947 in total. It was a heavy day, as I recall. There are a total of 1,008 registered for this polling place right now." Carefully locking the door behind him, Callahan walked the burdened pair to the great double doors that welcomed all worshippers. "Thank you so much for coming."

Paul and Mare thanked the old man again, secured the ballots in their locked trunk, and headed over to the mammoth VA hospital at 3200 Vine Street. Once in the parking garage, they entered the huge red-brick complex and sought out the nonresidential PTSD program center.

There for only a few hours, they spoke to a number of veterans, using the same approach as at Walter Reed, and documented almost exactly the same results: four of five complained of waiting weeks for an appointment only to have it cancelled at the last minute. Universally, the veterans stated that the nursing and medical staff was the greatest—"If you could only get to see them," several said—but something was definitely wrong with their scheduling system.

"Seems like a pattern, doesn't it?"

"Yeah," Paul responded, "and it has nothing to do with funding."

FEBRUARY

8.

"The White House regrets to report that President Williams suffered a minor stroke resulting from postsurgical complications," Jack Sennett said from his podium in the usual venue. The room's silence was marked by the utter absence of clicking cameras and the jostling of equipment. "This medical event occurred at seven twenty-five a.m. today, February first, at the Critical Care Unit within Walter Reed's complex in Bethesda, Maryland. Physicians there have not yet determined the cause of the event, and state categorically that the president is not in a life-threatening situation. At nine o'clock, thirty minutes ago, doctors stated that he is responding to treatment and is expected to make a full recovery."

Dr. Robby watched the large LED screen in the Walter Reed conference room. As Jack Sennett's face disappeared from the CNS broadcast, he turned to Sondra Thompson, the other senior staffers to the president who were there, and the Walter Reed medical staff. "Do you bastards ever tell the truth? Sennett packed more lies into one paragraph than anyone I've ever heard."

His voice rose to a low roar, an uncommon state for the placid Robby. "This patient has suffered a major stroke, and not because of some complication. It happened because this facility did not adhere to the recommended protocol regarding the use of heparin and warfarin following surgery." Robby glared at the Walter Reed personnel present. "What's more, his likelihood for full recovery is fairly slim."

"Doctor Robby," Thompson replied, her voice shaking with every syllable, "we called you in from Johns Hopkins this morning for full consultation, but evidently, not early enough. I'm sorry for what you just heard, but until we get this completely sorted out, we simply cannot fully inform the nation—or our enemies around the world—as to the president's status."

"Why the hell not, I'd like to know! Have you people ever tried honesty?"

Thompson closed her eyes for a moment and caught her breath. "I wish it were that simple, sir. President Williams did not have time to reinvoke Section Three of the Twenty-Fifth Amendment," she said, but stopped, as if choking on the words, "and so, it is presently unclear who is president of the United States."

Robby's eyes were wide with new knowledge he wished he did not have. "I see."

"It is not that we can't be honest with the American people. It's that we cannot tell the world—and give our enemies the opportunity of a lifetime—that the most powerful country in the world may be technically without a leader." Thompson made the statement without drama, but, for a moment, it threw the room into utter silence, suspending even the breathing of its inhabitants. "We are now awaiting Attorney General Sweeney's arrival. He telephoned a few minutes ago, and we think there's a solution to that problem."

In complete charge of the situation and herself, Thompson turned to Robby. "Now, Doctor, what does the future look like for the president?"

"It has now been almost two hours since the event. In many cases, contrary to popular belief, many effects of a stroke reverse themselves within an hour or so if the patient is properly treated, and here, staff did a remarkable job postevent. However, there remains evident numbness on his left side, some confusion, and difficulty speaking. These are not good indications." Robby paused. "Given his age and his already compromised state after surgery, I'd have to say the future is highly uncertain."

"Where is the First Lady?"

A Walter Reed staffer answered, "She is with the president, Ms. Thompson."

Thompson nodded, and turned to see Attorney General Sweeney enter the room.

"I'd like all of you to stay, because it is important that no one leave this room with any other story than the one I am about to impart." Sweeney looked around the room and they all waited. His eyelids winking rapidly as he spoke, Sweeney continued. "When President Williams invoked Section Three on the evening of January twenty-third, he was in full possession of his faculties. The instrument he executed contains language, albeit somewhat ambiguous, suggesting that if some event occurred that prevented him from signing another document, the one he signed on the twenty-third remains in effect. I've already informed Vice-President Morrison, and he understands his present role constitutionally."

"General Sweeney," Thompson said, addressing him formally for the benefit of the audience, "you used the word, 'suggesting.' Is there room for debate?"

"Not much, and I am fully prepared to swear that over and above the actual document, the president was explicit in conveying to me his requirements."

"What made him think in those terms? Thompson asked. "I mean, no one was expecting this series of events."

Sweeney shifted on his feet, and glanced carefully around the room. "I don't want this misunderstood, of course, but the president wanted to avoid, at all costs, the invocation of Section Four of the Amendment."

"Because?" Thompson asked, not having been briefed on the relevant clause.

"Because Section Four puts the president on the defensive, legally."

Sweeney could see in her eyes that Thompson instantly understood: once the president surrendered the office to Morrison, it would be hard to reclaim it.

"I understand," she said to the attorney general, then turned to Dr. Robby, who had been listening intently. "Doctor, in all candor, what are the president's chances for a full recovery at this point?"

Without a moment's hesitation, Robby said, "The president's situation is not impossible. I've seen worse cases walk away to a long life."

"The odds, Doctor?" Sweeney persisted.

"No better than two in five."

"Do we have everything?" Paul asked as they planted themselves in the Volvo's front seats first thing in the morning.

"I sure hope so," Mare said, chuckling as she continued. "I think I have all my shoes—what else is there?"

"Exactly. How can someone so young and so little have so many shoes? Are we driving around with a Macy's outlet in the backseat?"

"Don't start, Paulie boy. You knew what you were getting," she said, enjoying the near-constant banter. What she loved about him was that he was never serious, it seemed, and when he was, he left no doubt about it. Like the times when he told her he loved her. She smiled to herself. "So what's our plan, travel guide?"

"Well, thinking about what we found out at the VA tells me that when we get back to DC, we'll have to bang out a full report and turn it over to Pete. We've come up with only anecdotal evidence, to be sure, but what we've heard says a lot. They've got a big problem."

"Hey, did you ever tell me about your scheduled appointment at Walter Reed?"

"I guess we were too distracted when we left the place. Me, the PTSD vet, will need to wait until March twenty-sixth to see the shrink."

"Now I'm nervous. You might go ballistic on your short little wife."

"Funny. Now, back to our plan. I think the VA business is finished for now," Paul said. "The voting gig is another matter. Whether we find anything in Scioto County today or tomorrow, we'll need to shoot up US twenty-three from Portsmouth and drop off the ballots we have at the governor's office—at least that's what Pete told me the last time we checked in. Oh, Christ!"

"What?" Mare jumped.

"We need to change that plan."

"Why?"

"Here we are, in town, so focused on the present, we forgot about the past."

"Meaning what?" she asked, and then answered herself. "Conaway. Amber."

"Exactly. Let's go."

"Where?"

"SoftSec. Let's see what's going on there." They made their way from Mount Lookout through Hyde Park and onto Madison Road, heading into the city. A few miles down, Paul slowed the Volvo and parked across from the SoftSec offices. "Since we're dressed as reps from the governor's office, maybe somebody will make another assumption."

Mare smiled, enjoying the fact they were no longer bound by OPM and NIS niceties. The pair dodged traffic and made their way up to SoftSec's second-floor offices, where they saw that the company was still open for business. "It's odd, I suppose, but I guess this is one more example of life moving on. McCord was the key guy here, but he's gone, and the company still runs."

At the receptionist's desk, Mare was further surprised to see Heather Lake, the snooty woman she thought a bimbo. She approached first. "Why Heather, you remember us? Marlyn Burdette and Paul Gladston?"

Caught totally off guard, it took a moment for Heather to recall her. "Sure, I remember you! Mare—right? But I don't recall this handsome fellow. Weren't you here with some black guy the last time?"

Mare didn't skip a beat. "That was Nelson Evers—yes. We're doing some follow-up work, Heather. Is Nathan Conaway around?"

Lake looked back at her like she had two heads. "Nathan? I can't believe you want to see him. Why, he and that other guy left here election night—over two months ago now—and they haven't been seen since. Same night Mr. McCord was killed. Can you believe it?"

Heather was much more talkative now than she'd been the previous summer, and Mare pressed the advantage. "Really? Just never came back?"

"Yeah, really. Left everybody here holdin' the bag, and we have all these contracts!"

"Who's running the company now that Mr. McCord is gone?" Paul inquired gently.

"Why, Mrs. McCord, but she's not here now."

"Did you say Nathan disappeared with another guy?"

"Yeah—that Jerry James who came here from DC to help with the USEAC contract. He was here for only that one thing though, so I guess it's no mystery that we haven't seen him."

"Well, thanks, anyway, Heather," Mare said. "We'll be in touch."

On the sidewalk, Paul suggested they head back to Hyde Park and check out Conaway's apartment. Once on the square, they found a parking spot in front of Teller's Restaurant and entered Graeter's, above whose ice cream store Nathan Conaway and Amber Bustamente had lived together.

Mare remembered it was the same supervisor she'd interviewed the previous summer when she was attempting to verify Conaway's residence. She could see at once the look of disgust on the woman's face.

"That'll be the last time I rent to young unmarrieds," she said. "They split up and disappear. No notice. No rent. So why should I help you?"

Paul gave the older woman his best smile. "You already have, Ms. Davis, and we're grateful for your help. I guess you're telling us you never saw or heard from either of them again."

"Not a peep."

"Since...?" Mare took over, sensing the manager might say more to her.

"Since the night of the election. He was some kinda electronics wizard, his girlfriend told me—she was in the store all the time. I can't believe it, in fact, because they seemed like nice people."

"Their stuff?" Mare asked.

"When nobody claimed it after a month and no rent money showed up, heck, I sold some and gave the rest to Goodwill."

Mare cleared her throat. "Nobody picked up mail—either Nathan or Amber?"

"Nope. There was a big pile of junk mail and bills, of course, but nobody ever came by."

"So no relatives of either one ever showed up?"

"Like I said. Nothing. It was like they died all of a sudden. Know what I mean?"

"I'm beginning to. Thanks," Mare said.

Back in the Volvo, they both stared straight ahead. "Off the grid, like hell," Paul said. "Before, we were just guessing. Now, it looks like they're dead somewhere. We just don't know where."

"Probably never will," Mare added.

"Well, that's four. Do you think Crew Cut got them too?"

"Dunno. It looks like it. Wish we could get a line on that Jerry James guy. If he disappeared, too, that would pretty well tell the tale, wouldn't it?"

"Why not call Pete and give it all to him?" Mare suggested.

Paul fished out his cell and gave Clancy a full update. "Pete says he'll check out Jerry James, but he's not totally surprised about the other two."

"Got it." She did not want to dwell on the implications regarding Nathan and Amber, and she could see that Paul was still thinking about it. "What do we know about Scioto County?"

"Yeah. Well, unlike the one precinct we checked in Cincinnati, there are actually two precincts in Portsmouth that already look suspicious, even before we see if there's any paper lying around."

"What do you mean 'already'?"

"Wait a minute, this is your town. Get me on US52 East."

Mare gave Paul the driving directions. "That's the way people used to go to Portsmouth. You can go SR32 to US224, you know."

"I want to go along the river. We have time, and you can consider this part of your honeymoon cruise." They both laughed hard at the notion of Portsmouth—in the heart of Appalachia on the Ohio River, in the middle of winter—being a lovers' destination under any circumstances.

"Back to business, Paulie boy."

"Sure. I'm going by memory now since you're pressing me for details, and I can't consult my notes, but—"

"Hey, no excuses. Remember what Mac Smith said at the spook school?"

"Don't be bustin' my balls, little bit. Here's what I recall: we're to check two sample precincts that vote out of the Cornerstone United Methodist Church near downtown Portsmouth. What's interesting is that they each have between eight- and nine-hundred registered voters.

In each precinct, Democrats outnumber Republicans by less than ten voters, so it's almost even up, and there's one idiot who's a Green Party voter, and in each, there's around six hundred fifty nonaffiliateds."

"So what's the big deal about that?"

"In an area of the country that's highly religious and conservative—where people have often voted Republican—that's a high number of Independents."

"So?"

"According to the secretary of state's office in Columbus, both those precincts went over ninety percent Democratic in 2012."

"Maybe they did," she said.

"And pigs fly. It's possible, but not likely—so let's find out."

The two-hour drive to Portsmouth, about 120 miles, became longer when they crossed over the river into Maysville for lunch at the Busy Bee. Even so, they rolled into the Scioto County Seat at two o'clock and went right over to the Cornerstone UM Church on Offnere Street. Unlike Holy Redeemer Church in Cincinnati, a gruff woman met them at Cornerstone and made it clear she couldn't care less about voting or the governor's office.

She said, "Look people, there's no one here to help you, and they might not if they were. Get yourselves over to the courthouse and let them do their thing."

They drove over to Seventh Street, trudged up the stairs to the Board of Elections, and asked to speak to the person in charge. They were pointed to Ms. Marlene McKillip, a woman with a firm look from head to toe. Both displayed their IDs and asked to speak privately.

McKillip took them into her office and asked what it was all about, but before either could answer, she played her high card. "This is highly unusual, I would say. I might have to call Governor McNickle's office."

Mare spoke up. "Feel free to do that, Ms. McKillip. We don't want you to be in the least bit intimidated." She stepped forward, picked up the receiver on the landline telephone and handed it to McKillip. "Here, I'll dial the number for you."

McKillip took a step back. "No-o, there's no need for that. I don't want to annoy the governor." She invited them to sit. "Now," she said, manufacturing a wan smile, "let's start over, shall we? How can I help you?"

Mare did not let up. "We would like to be discreet, Ms. McKillip. We're sampling a few precincts around the state from the last election. Here in Portsmouth, we've decided to focus on two of the precincts that vote out of the Cornerstone Church."

"What do you need?" McKillip asked, her voice wary.

"We want to know," Mare continued while Paul sat back, half-smiling, "if the voting process that day was followed to the letter."

"Of course it was," McKillip said in defense of her territory. "We attested to that fact to Kathlyn Hopkins, the secretary of state in Columbus."

"And you folks still use the combination paper ballot and scanner procedure?" Mare asked.

"Yes we do, and there's no violation of state law in doing so. The SoftSec people provide good equipment, and we had no problems with their machines."

"What about the paper ballots, Ms. McKillip? What happened to them?"

"Why, procedure calls for them to be shredded, of course."

"That's not what I asked." Mare matched McKillip's hard jaw with her own.

"Well...just a minute." McKillip rose to close her office door. "Are you actually from the governor's office or from the secretary of state's?"

"Does it make a difference?"

"Yes, it does. Please tell me which."

"Governor McNickle's office," Mare said, wasting no words.

"And why are you sampling here, may I ask?"

Mare, who had no idea why the two precincts were chosen, said, "Because somebody thinks there might have been some irregularity."

"Irregularity? Here?" McKillip's voice was shrill.

"No, Ms. McKillip, not here, but between here and Columbus."

With a look of relief, she said, "Thank God! I've been hoping someone would come."

"Why?" Paul couldn't help himself.

"When the voting results were announced by Secretary Hopkins on election night, something didn't seem right at all. The county totals were correct, as were the totals for each precinct, but the vote allocation seemed off."

"Why didn't you do something about it?" Mare asked.

"Look, Secretary Hopkins is a Democrat and legally, we report to her office."

Mare nodded. "I see. Don't rock the boat, huh?"

Embarrassed, McKillip merely nodded.

"The ballots?" Mare continued. "I'm betting they were never shredded, were they?"

"No. I have the entire county's ballots under lock and key."

"Then you best hold on to every last one of them," Mare directed. "Except two—precincts eleven and twelve."

McKillip eyed Mare with respect. "Good choices. Wait here. I'll get them now."

When the woman left, Paul looked at Mare. "With a pair of balls like that, how can you be a woman." It wasn't a question, but a statement of awe.

"Remember, Paulie boy. We're all victims of little tyrannies—but we don't need to be."

Forbes Flannery settled his long frame into the specially designed seat on *The FactZone* set and let the makeup person wipe the last bit of shine from his nose. The producer signaled three, two, one with his fingers and Flannery began. "Good evening, ladies and gentlemen," he said, zipping through the stock intro. "This will be an exciting discussion as we put in perspective all that we've heard in the past twenty-four hours about the president's stroke while in an extended recovery from surgery. President Williams is a decent man, and I suspect his biggest disappointment tonight is that while he intended to be a role model for men in taking care of such a highly personal matter, things have not gone the way he or anyone else intended. The fact is that for nearly all men, treatment for prostate cancer, including surgery, is highly successful, and men can lead normal lives in every way. That's one.

"Two is that the stroke allows Vice-President Joseph Morrison to continue as acting president, which is constitutionally permissible, but, as each day goes by, untenable. For the country's sake, we wish the president a speedy recovery, and that's all I'll say on that score.

"Three. Today, Speaker of the House, John Whitaker, formed two committees opposed by the Democrats, but necessary, in this reporter's opinion. The first committee will be chaired by a South Carolina congressman who happens to be a prosecutor with an admirable background. His committee will investigate one of two scandals that simply will not go away, even now that the election is over. That has to do with the IRS and its targeting of conservative groups for simply exercising their free speech rights. Notice that I don't use the word 'alleged' here, because there is no doubt that it was done. What the committee must ascertain is why—though that answer also seems obvious—and under whose direction. That this could go all the way to the president's inner circle is a possibility, and while it is regrettable that the president is presently unable to address this matter, the American people are entitled to know what happened and is still happening.

"Four. Benghazi. Like the IRS, this is a stain on the very essence of being an American. The IRS scandal reminds us all there is a thin line between a banana republic and us. All of us were appalled decades ago with Nixon's 'Enemies List,' but that small-ball scandal doesn't come close to what Americans now know can happen here.

"What's the connection to Benghazi? To some, there is none, but, to me, it has something to do with who we are. We failed to protect our consulate there for fear of offending the Libyans, whose government we established. Then we failed to protect or save our personnel there—four of whom were murdered in a most brutal fashion—because we didn't want to have a military incident in Libya that might inflame other jihadists in the region. In Benghazi, this administration failed to do the right thing—and then lied about it over and over again. In my view, this is as un-American as it gets.

"What ties these two issues together is the 2012 presidential election. How this administration behaved in both has everything to do with controlling people and events. Targeting conservatives prevented them from making their voices heard. Lying about Benghazi continued the fantasy of a successful foreign policy. One can only wonder what other agencies and policies have been perverted in the quest for reelection.

"And whether the president is able to respond is irrelevant. His operatives know all about the IRS and Benghazi. Now is the time for them to stand up and speak. As a sidenote, there's a rumor that Former Secretary of State Emerson Grantham—you may remember he resigned in December—has reached out to Speaker Whitaker via telephone. We can only imagine what that call was about.

"For me, the bottom line is that Speaker Whitaker had no choice about investigating these scandals the Democrats wish would go away. Some have criticized him for waiting so long. I do not. It has now become clearer that there is much to investigate. The last question I'd put to *The FactZone* audience is this: why is News Global the only major news outlet interested in getting to the truth of it all?"

Governor McNickle moved to the small conference table in his office as Ohio's secretary of state, Kathlyn Hopkins, made her entrance. McNickle was not looking forward to the meeting. He was a white, middle-aged Republican male in his second term, and Hopkins was a much younger African American female Democrat in her first term. With all the potential for a flashpoint, he had considered his approach carefully. Because he and Hopkins and their spouses had socialized on several occasions, he knew she could put aside politics when needed, but would she do so now?

"Governor?" Hopkins said in a shorthand that addressed the man and inquired after his well-being all in one word.

"Madame Secretary?" McNickle responded in kind, doing so in a light-hearted fashion. "Now that we've done the formalities... ."

"Will it be about some of your gumshoes raking up stuff in my backyard?"

"Our backyard, actually." McNickle adjusted his rimless glasses and leaned back in his chair. "Kathlyn, I know you well enough not to waste your time. We have a problem."

"Such as?" she answered, her tone wary.

"With three random samples, there's now good evidence that the presidential election—in Ohio, at least—was fraudulent."

"Those are big words, Ted." She inhaled deeply. "I hope you can back them up, because you are attacking me directly. You know that, don't you?"

"I don't know anything of the kind. This is not about you or your office. No one is accusing you of anything. Let me explain—"

"You had better," she interrupted. "Do I need my legal staff here?"

"No, you don't. This is now between us, and I'm giving you the respect you deserve to see how you want to handle it." He paused to look her in the eye. "If I really wanted to do a job on you, this meeting wouldn't have happened. There would have been a major press conference."

"All right," she relented. "You have my attention."

"In precincts in both Hamilton and Scioto Counties—historically Republican—how people actually voted bore no resemblance to the vote totals coming out of Columbus."

"How could you possibly know that!" Her fists were clenched on her lap.

"I have the proof right here. In Cincinnati, the paper ballots used were never destroyed because the shredding system did not function, and we have sworn testimony from a disinterested party that the ballots have been sequestered since election day. In one precinct, there are 1,008 registered voters and on November 6, 947 people cast their ballots. That total number was reported to Columbus, and Columbus reported that total number out. However, according to an audit performed by a big-six firm here, the paper ballots showed 678 for Hardy and 169 for Williams. The official numbers from Columbus are 652 for Williams, and the balance for Hardy."

"I'm listening."

"In Scioto County, we did two precincts voting in the same location. In precinct eleven, there were 853 total voters registered, and, on election day, 827 cast ballots. There, the ballots were locked up because the local voting officials did not trust the system to report the data accurately. So we have those ballots, and again, the totals agree coming out of Scioto County and Columbus, but the paper count shows 502 for Williams and 325 for Hardy. The official numbers are 796 for Williams and 31 for Hardy."

"OK, now what?"

"I want your office to authorize a sweep of a much larger number of precincts."

"I think not," she said. "Who's to say there weren't irregularities in Democratic precincts?

"If you look at Democratic precincts, I'm willing to bet that the numbers voting for Williams were inflated and the numbers voting for Hardy, deflated. Your party needed Ohio."

"Even if this fantasy of yours were true, what of it?" It wasn't a question, but a demand. Her tone attempted to trump his facts. "The electors cast their votes, their ballots were counted, the House and Senate in Washington ratified the counts, and the president duly took his oath of office nearly three weeks ago. We can't put the toothpaste back in the tube."

"Don't you see, Kathlyn? Someone or something got between the voters at their home precincts and your office here in Columbus. And we owe it to Ohio citizens to let them know their votes were counted correctly and properly."

"Don't get pious with me, Ted! You wouldn't give a damn if the situation were reversed."

"I'll tell you why I'd give a damn. If you were governor with this information, and I refused to do the right thing, I'd expect you to have that press conference, convene a grand jury, and all the evidence available would be pointing at me, because the buck stops with the secretary of state. So pious has nothing to do with it—if you have some problem with me helping you to save your skin..." He let the thought trail off.

Hopkins sat still, and McNickle could see that she was remembering something.

After a long minute, she said, "You know, Ted, there was an interesting contract let by the US Election Assistance Commission in early 2012, and back then, I thought it was strange."

"Strange?"

"The USEAC gave the work to SoftSec and it involved monitoring the vote in several states. Look," she said, her eyes riveted on McNickles', "we never had this conversation."

"Keep going."

"I wouldn't have paid any attention to it but an NIS investigator came around asking about Enrique McCord and SoftSec—that's when it bothered me." She lowered her eyes. "Ted, do you realize how much of a problem this will cause me in my own party?"

"At this point, your party should be the least of your concerns—the party isn't going to go to jail for you or anyone on your staff. If, on the other hand, all of this was done without your knowledge, and in fact, came from somewhere on high...?"

"I don't like where this could go. Averell Williams would never do such a thing. There was a high probability he was going to win. It would have been stupid."

"Actually, the probability was this would be a tight race, and it doesn't look like he won Ohio's eighteen electoral votes. Maybe it wasn't Williams at all, but some overzealous staffer."

"That remains to be seen. That person would have had a helluva lot of strings to pull." After a moment's pause, she said, "Why not proceed in a way similar to what you described? Announce it. I'll be standing behind you with an unhappy face. Then, we can see where it all goes."

"Not quite. I'm not willing to embarrass either of us without more information. Let's each of us pick ten more precincts and see if we get lucky with proof, one way or the other."

"What about other battleground states? How far are you willing to let this go?"

"A crime occurred—maybe more than one. Maybe vote fraud. Maybe more."

"Oh, come on!" she retorted in complete disbelief.

"Do you want to find out?"

"You didn't answer me. How far will this go?"

"Wherever it goes. Our responsibility is to the people of Ohio," he said.

"As long as it isn't about unseating Averell Williams and making a Republican president of the United States."

Most Capitol visitors were unaware that John Whitaker maintained two offices—one for his district constituents in Longworth, and the ceremonial Speaker's Office looking out of the West Front. It was to the latter place he had come to reflect on the unprecedented goings-on at the pinnacle of the nation's power center. He needed time to center himself and to ensure that, in the days ahead, he remained grounded to the principles that had accompanied him throughout his public life.

Piercing his trance-like concentration was the insistent ring of his old-fashioned desk phone. Reluctantly, he glanced at the bank of lights signaling the call's likely importance and was relieved to see it was line two. He picked up the phone, expecting a pleasant interruption. As soon as he said, "Hello," he knew it would be an interesting, if disturbing conversation.

"Hey, Mister Speaker, this is your Columbus correspondent reporting in."

"Hi, Ted. I'll bet you're calling with some news I'd prefer never to hear."

"That depends, on your feelings about high crimes and misdemeanors," Governor McNickle said.

"I had a heads up on what might be coming, so go right ahead."

"Nothing's conclusive yet, my friend, but your instincts were dead on about the vote. The three precincts I had your gumshoes check—one in Cincinnati and two in Portsmouth—point strongly to a large-scale manipulation of Ohio's vote. Getting all of this to the surface won't be easy, John. You're aware, I'm sure, that my secretary of state, Kathlyn Hopkins, a fervent Democrat, will go along with me only as far as she has to, and then, it'll be out-and-out war."

"Where does it stand now?" Whitaker asked.

"At the least, we agreed to pick ten additional precincts each to see if the count was tampered with in any location where we can show, without a doubt, what the vote really was on November 6. We're in the midst of that audit as we speak, but I'm betting that traditionally Republican precincts will show smaller margins for Hardy, and Democratic precincts will have had Republican votes shaved for Williams. No real doubt about it."

"Damn. I had foolish hopes that our system of voting in this country remained sacrosanct. What about any other states, Ted?"

"I was told about some sort of last-minute federal contract with SoftSec to monitor state votes, presumably in other states as well. The stated purpose—you're gonna love this—was to ensure against fraud."

Whitaker laughed out loud. "Does Kafka live or what?" He laughed again, but there was no pleasure in it. "What was this special contract all about, do you know?"

"This came from the USEAC."

"Wait, the USEA who?"

"The US Election Assistance Commission, one of your federal monsters designed to help us poor dumb folks in the states," McNickle said. "Apparently, the USEAC deemed SoftSec the preferred provider to over a dozen states. They were to have monitored the vote in each of them. It should be no surprise to you that these were all battleground states. And this agency, by the way, reports to none other than Acting President Joseph P. Morrison, last I heard."

"Holy hell! The noose tightens."

"Noose?"

"Figure of speech, Ted," Whitaker said. "Needless to say, I hope your guys can nail down the numbers, and soon. And can you get me all you've got on the USEAC grant or whatever? I'll start something on this end."

"You bet. Hey, before I let you go, is it possible this whole thing could play out in a way nobody intended?"

"Meaning?"

"Who is going to be president of the United States when it's all over?" McNickle asked.

"For now, I hope its Averell Williams."

Their conversation ended, but its import turned Whitaker's stomach. Over his long career, he'd been a faithful adherent to the American system of government, which meant long rough-and-tumble battles over dearly held principles, and he'd always been glad to jump in and wage political warfare with the best of them, with the full understanding and expectation that negotiation, compromise, and more negotiation were all part of the legislative recipe. Sure, he knew, there were thumbs on the scale because of graft or dishonesty, but enough people with integrity always remained to ensure that, for the most part, the right thing happened in the end.

Raw politics may have jaded and sharpened the smooth edges of his ideals over his years in Congress, but he'd managed to comport himself through all of it in such a way that he could always kiss Janet goodnight, safe in the knowledge that no one could ever show him to be dishonest or disloyal, not to his wife and family, not to his country.

Most Democrats, he believed, were like him. They were decent, wonderful Americans, who happened to stand next to somewhat different principles regarding issues like immigration, abortion, voter ID, welfare, and America's role in the world. Battling fiercely over these and many other principles was the essence of American democracy, and as long as the combatants entered the arena in good faith, he was always content with the process and the outcome.

When someone, anyone—Republican or Democrat—sought to cheat the American people of their basic right of citizenship, the right to vote, the sense of betrayal felt overwhelming. Whitaker turned to look out one of his West Front windows, because he needed the reassuring sight he knew would be there. A mile away, straight down the mall, stood the cold, nearly white obelisk honoring the first president, and beyond, dim in the distance, stood the Lincoln Memorial. If his gaze could make a right turn at the Washington Monument, he would be looking straight at the South Portico of the White House, a home storied by over forty other great men and women.

When he thought of them and what they had given the nation, Republicans and Democrats alike, he could not let them bear the dishonor of Joe Morrison's high crimes. On a more personal level, what Morrison did might affect him in a way unlike any other American. At this point, however, could he change the course of events?

9.

J oe Morrison was already tiring of his role as acting president. Scanning his spacious, well-appointed, and richly paneled West Wing office, he vowed. *I can do better, and what I want is only a few steps away.*

Norton Sweeney entered, the door held open by Remy Carlson. Morrison smiled wryly as he continued tapping the empty blotter with the tip of a silver pen. It was as if he hadn't noticed his visitor's presence.

Morrison forced himself into the moment, stood up, and stretched out his hand. "You know, Norty, I can't tell you how much Sharon and I have enjoyed your company when you've been out to the house." He said the last words as if he lived in an ordinary suburb where a grill out was commonplace.

Sweeney shook the man's hand and smiled, but said nothing other than, "What can I do for you, sir?"

Morrison offered him a chair. "A lot. And I can do a lot for you as well; that is, if the opportunity were ever to arise."

Sweeney kept his tight-lipped smile and blinked briskly. With one hand, he touched the white-dotted navy blue bow tie at his neck. "What's on your mind, sir?" he said.

Morrison realized that the warmth he was fumbling to express for Sweeney was not reciprocated. Moreover, the man seemed uncomfortable, as if he'd prefer to be elsewhere. Of course, Sweeney and Williams went way back, and the attorney general had no reason to trust anyone but the president alone.

He plunged ahead because he needed Sweeney in his pocket, no matter how he was put there. "This morning I made the trip to Walter Reed before coming in." He let that fact sink in for a moment. "I think you know what I saw. The president is nearly comatose and unresponsive."

"The doctors say the president needs time and stressless rest." Sweeney blinked.

"It is now February eighth. His surgery was performed on the twenty-fourth, and he was due back in the saddle on the twenty-fifth."

"Your point, sir?"

"As sad as it is to say, Norty, I'm beginning to wonder if the old man is going to recover." Morrison looked across at his visitor's piercing blue eyes and wondered how much steel might be present in them.

Sweeney didn't answer right away. "I have known the president for more years than I can remember, and I am prepared to give him time," he said, touching his bowtie. "What's more, Averell Williams was duly elected and sworn in, and none of us should be in a hurry to make changes now." He put additional emphasis on his last three words.

"I can read the US Constitution as well as you," Morrison said flatly. "We are close to an invocation of Section Four."

"That clause in the Amendment is uncharted territory," Sweeney said respectfully. "It is too soon," he said further, as if he wanted to buy time for his friend. "If we reach that point, we must proceed with the greatest of care." He let his eyes rest on the empty desk.

"That's all I wanted to hear you say."

"In the meantime, sir, do you intend to make any response to Speaker Whitaker's formation of two special committees?"

"If I respond at all, I can tell you that I will create some distance between Benghazi and the IRS and this office."

"What do you mean, 'create some distance'?"

"Just that. I had no part in the IRS business but have reason to believe this administration is guilty as charged. As to Benghazi, Averell Williams made a mistake there, and, while I will leave him some elbow-room, I am equally aware that the story about a protest running amok over a video is plain bullshit. Emerson Grantham and I have had a good talk, and we both know that our political future is not rosy if it's tied to the Libyan mess Averell created." He could see Sweeney's color turning crimson.

"I can't believe you would do that! That would be disloyal."

"It has nothing to do with loyalty. If there's to be a Morrison Administration, I am not carrying that load of shit for anybody. Not Grantham, not Williams. Period."

Sweeney said nothing.

Morrison could see the man's facial muscles work to clamp his jaw. "And, by the way, you have reasons to be discrete, now don't you?" Morrison paused to let Sweeney ponder his meaning. "One of them is that you know Averell Williams may not have been duly elected at all." With that, Acting President Morrison rose and left his visitor sitting alone with secrets.

"Tony Duke," Peter Marsden said, speaking from the set of the *Control Room.* "Tony Duke, you're on the Hill. What do you make of the full-court press the GOP is putting on the administration while the president recovers from his stroke?"

"That's exactly it, Peter. The president is in a hospital bed at Walter Reed, and the Republicans are pressing ahead with special committees investigating the IRS allegations as well as the Benghazi question. Most here agree there's little to investigate, but that doesn't mean Speaker Whitaker won't take advantage of the opportunity to make political hay this season."

"You say many feel there's not much to these matters. I hesitate to use the word, 'scandal' with either of them, because the administration appears to have been rather forthright on both questions."

"That's right, Peter. Most major media outlets credit the Williams people with responding fully to all the requests the Republicans have made regarding the IRS and Benghazi both, but for some reason the GOP leadership won't let go of them."

Peter chuckled. "Yes, you'd think there was actually something to them. Before I let you go, Tony, do you know if there's any truth to rumors of voting irregularity in favor of President Williams in the State of Ohio?"

"There's some whispering going on about that, but Governor McNickle, who is Republican, has not yet made a public announcement."

"Do you think there will be some move afoot to discredit the president's clear-cut victory over Governor Hardy?"

"You never know, Peter, but in the political environment that seems all pervasive in the capital right now, almost anything goes."

Father Michael Pallison marched up the aisle with two candle and crucifix bearers, and, in a moment, the eight-thirty Sunday Mass at St. Mary's began.

Pete Clancy entered and took his usual place in the rear of the church. Under his arm was the church bulletin for February 10th, and he promised himself he'd read it later over coffee, but he knew it was a promise often broken.

As Father Pallison reminded congregants to silence their cell phones and seek pardon for their transgressions, two more men entered the rear of the church and took to the pew immediately in front of Clancy's roost. Observant congregants noticed the priest eyeing the latecomers just before a wry smile crossed his dark Irish face.

"Don't you guys worry someone will sic the political paparazzi on you?" Clancy asked the two men.

"Not as long as we have you to protect us," Andrew Warner said, and both he and John Whitaker shared a chuckle. "Can't you let a couple of sinners seek forgiveness in peace on a frigid morning as this?"

"God doesn't have all day, for cryin' out loud," Clancy said.

"He'll need a week for you," Whitaker said.

"Hey, you two, I need a minute afterward," Clancy said, and his companions nodded. There was no further need for conversation. All three men knew the routine.

Clancy marveled at the relationship shared by the three of them and the celebrant of the Mass. That, for over forty years, they had remained steadfast friends was, in itself, a small miracle.

When he thought of Warner, he wondered why so many men who ran the agency had been Catholic, from its OSS days to the present— *Was it the inbred intrigue of the Vatican they enjoyed?* The same was true for the Speakership, from people like John McCormack, Tip O'Neill, Angela Tesoro, and now, Whitaker himself. Even Newt Gingrich later converted. Whether or not they were of his faith made no difference to him, but it seemed somehow a comfort to know these men were practicing believers of some religion, not just lip movers.

With his three best friends in his line of sight, Clancy couldn't help but notice how each of them had aged. Pallison, of course, wore the invisible marks of torture with every facial expression, but he'd made food the surrogate for any other vice he'd ever contemplated. How the man could laugh his way through his days after spending a year as a North Vietnamese POW, Clancy never knew.

Pallison read from the gospel—something from John, perhaps.

Warner was the classic agency guy—tall, wiry, rimless glasses, steel-gray hair. While Jensen Roberts was the most senior African American in a cabinet post, Warner was a Williams appointee and had earned his super-agency slot every step of the way. When first the military and then, other institutions, had their eye out for nonwhite super achievers, Warner was always on the same short list with Roberts, and both men hated that. Either man could be at the top of anybody's list. From their Vietnam days, Clancy recalled that Warner was from a mixed marriage, and enough money lurked somewhere in the family to allow Warner the education befitting a brilliant mind.

Whitaker was not a pretty-face politician, but a man with features seemingly chiseled by a hard-knock early life. He kept himself fit and was clean-shaven, almost so that the startling blue eyes became all the more prominent.

The Lord's Prayer was recited, but Clancy heard only a few words.

He acknowledged himself as the youngest, shortest, and least in curb appeal compared with the two civilians in front of him, but he was glad he didn't have to carry the bags of worry Warner and Whitaker toted. He was also grateful he'd not lived Pallison's life.

Communion time came, and Clancy pulled himself into the present.

What they all had in common, almost as DNA, was their service as Army warrant officers in Vietnam. He, Whitaker, and Warner arrived in Vietnam in the spring of '71, Pallison in 1969. Pallison, who was not yet a priest, occasionally reminded his three buds that he arrived in Vietnam at the same time the number of US dead had just exceeded the total of all those killed in the Korean War—something over thirty-three thousand.

As warrant officers—that misty space between enlisted ranks and the officer corps—they served together as team leaders for the Army Security Agency linguists—men who knew Vietnamese and a smattering of Chinese, the latter to know if the Chicoms had entered the conflict. Inseparable for months on end, their fraternity came to an end when the North Vietnamese Army captured Pallison in the spring of '72 during the battle for Quang Tri City. No one heard a word from him. When the other three were evacuated, along with most US ground troops in March of '73, Pallison was left behind. In fact, they all thought he was dead when the 591 POWs were repatriated at the same time, and there was still no word.

Somehow, the North Vietnamese Army had learned Pallison was an intelligence officer, and they had conveniently not included him with the others in what the politicians called Operation Homecoming that March. Instead, the NVA tortured him for three more months, before using him as a bargaining chip in the Paris Peace Talks. Beaten and broken, he returned to the United States in the summer, and, after a few months in a VA hospital, he entered the seminary.

Clancy looked at his friend closely when the priest raised his arm in great pain to bless the crowd and bid them, "Go in peace to love and serve the Lord."

Mass ended at 9:45 a.m. The trio made its way over to St. Mary's Rectory and knocked on Father Pallison's rear door. His housekeeper welcomed them out of the cold—she knew they were regulars in the rectory kitchen.

"You know, the three of you could at least keep it down to a low roar in the back of church," Pallison said when he joined them.

"You have any hot coffee for chatty parishioners, Mike?" Clancy asked, ignoring the priest's remonstrance.

"Of course," Pallison replied with resignation. "You three know all my secrets from way back when." He laughed and welcomed his three closest friends, and everyone reciprocated the warmth that blessed their recurrent assemblies. "Sit," he commanded while rustling up coffee and danish.

"Turn off your hearing aid, Mike," Clancy said. "I need to have a conversation I never had."

"I never listen to you anyway," Pallison jabbed.

"I think we have a big problem, boys, and the goin' is goin' to get a lot tougher and nastier as the weeks go on."

"Don't bullshit me, Pete. I've got enough problems," Warner said.

"I wish it were, Drew," Clancy replied, "but this one won't go away, and you and Pallison can't tune me out. Look, I asked you guys for some time because I think John and I have come at the same puzzle from different angles, but neither of us has seen the whole thing."

"OK, let's see some cards," Whitaker said.

"When we last talked, John, you knew about the McCord and Evers killings." Clancy turned to Warner and Pallison, whom he knew always listened, and gave them some of the basic backstory.

"And?" Whitaker said.

"There are others. Two. Maybe three."

"How do you come up with that?" Whitaker shot back.

"The two kids I sent on your behalf—under Governor McNickle's umbrella. They're the ones who—with Evers—unraveled the whole thing in the first place."

"Say more," Whitaker said.

"I dropped you a hint last time we talked. Enrique McCord was the CEO of SoftSec, which has electronic voting machine contracts all over the United States. SoftSec also had a contract with the USEAC to 'monitor' the election process in certain places to ensure fairness. Right! Our guy interviewed Ohio's secretary of state, what's her name—Hopkins?—who wondered out loud about the ethics involved. Well, all throughout the investigation, McCord kept throwing around Joe Morrison's name like they were brothers."

"Jesus Christ!" Whitaker said.

"Hey, watch it," Pallison said.

"You're not supposed to be listening," said Warner.

"Sorry, Mike," Whitaker said. "I just heard some of this from Ted McNickle—they're canvassing a larger part of the state's precincts to see if the fraud pattern holds."

"What fraud pattern?" Warner asked.

"It appears Ohio may have been stolen from Hardy. If that's true, it would be unreasonable to assume it was only Ohio." Whitaker looked directly at Warner. "In Democratic precincts, they inflated their numbers by shaving votes from Hardy and, in Republican precincts, they gave Williams strong minorities or surprising victories. In other words, where black voters bolted for Hardy, their votes were made to look like the Williams vote in 2008. Sorry, Pete. Go ahead."

"That makes more sense." Warner nodded. "I couldn't believe African Americans would be taken in—again—by this crowd."

"And this from a Williams appointee," Whitaker teased.

"The Democrats don't own all black hearts and minds even though they think they do," Warner said. "Some of us have decided to leave the plantation—it'll only be a matter of time before the rest figure it out." He rarely spoke out on race issues, even with men closer to him than most of his own family.

The others nodded with quiet respect.

"So it was clear early on that McCord and Morrison were tight," Clancy continued. "But then, we run into that kind of stuff all the time when the high and mighty are involved." Clancy paused to give Whitaker and Warner a hard glance and waited for the chuckle in response. "Then one of my managers began getting telephone threats— all about how she better get her 'nigger' in line—meaning Evers. Sorry, Drew. And a few weeks later, he's run down by a Tahoe."

Whitaker sighed. "Keep going."

"Looking back, I wish I hadn't played by the rules, but I couldn't tell you guys anything when it was happening." Clancy looked down at his danish. "Anyway, here it is: McCord's techie, a guy named Nathan Conaway, had a gabby girlfriend who told my two Conaway bragged that he and McCord were doing something really big for the vice-president."

"Meaning what exactly?" Warner asked.

"Fixing the election, Conaway told his girlfriend, plain as day." Clancy looked at Whitaker. "That's why, John, when you asked for some people to go to Ohio to sample some precincts and I told you I had only the two? Same two kids. They're good."

"What else?" Warner asked.

"When the kids were back in Cincinnati on your behalf," Clancy said, nodding at Whitaker, "they got the bright idea to check up on Conaway, the techie, and his girlfriend, Amber Bustamente. It seemed odd that neither of them surfaced when the locals were investigating McCord's death. Your staffer, John, didn't know about them because there were no news stories out on them."

"So where are they?" Whitaker asked.

"That's the whole point—they're nowhere. When my two went to SoftSec to nose around, they were told that Conaway and his election partner—a guy named Jerry James—also disappeared that same night. The girl at the office assumed James took off because the election was over, but she said that Conaway had left them holding the bag with a number of contracts—especially bad because of McCord's death the same night as Conaway's disappearing act. Next, the Gladstons, my two operatives, checked out the girlfriend's apartment—actually, where she and Conaway lived—and, according to the landlord, they simply vanished that same night—election night. No notice. No nothing."

"What about James?" Whitaker asked.

"Nobody knows anything about him—just that he was from DC." Clancy looked at Warner. "Maybe your outfit could check it out, Drew?"

Warner pulled out his cell phone and made an electronic note to himself.

"Or mine," Whitaker chimed in. "That name is familiar. He's a politico of some type."

"So that's four suddenly out of the picture—five deaths if you count Evers," Clancy summed it up.

"Holy hell," Whitaker said. "This is worse, or better, than I thought."

"How can it be both?" Warner inquired.

"Right now, Joe Morrison is vice-president and acting president. When he resumes his duties as the number two, there appears to be enough evidence to begin impeachment proceedings."

"How do you do that with a VP?" Clancy asked.

"It's never actually been done before, because the incumbent resigned—remember Spiro Agnew?"

"Then what's the problem?" Warner asked.

"We need a president. While Morrison is acting president, technically, there is no VP, and we can't allow the top leadership to be removed," Whitaker said.

"That's a hell of a choice—keep a murderer in the chair because it's a crazy world out there and the country needs a leader," Warner said, then turned to stare out of the rectory window.

"So you wait until Williams comes back, then?" Clancy said. He noticed that Warner seemed preoccupied.

"No choice, really," Whitaker stated.

"Your two operatives," Warner said. "These the two I might have heard about?" he asked, looking at Clancy.

Clancy nodded, "Yep. Now the dots connect."

"Anything the rest of us chickens need to know?" Whitaker asked.

"You already know, John. Your tasks were delayed because... ."

"Got it," he said, nodding to Warner. "Thanks." Quiet interrupted their conversation for a moment. "And all this time, they were where?" he asked Clancy.

"Hiding out at an Amish farm in Pennsylvania."

Whitaker became serious. "Why didn't you take this all to the right place, Pete?" His question was not unfriendly, but his tone said it needed to be asked.

"What right place? You know, you can't just walk into a police department and swear out a warrant against the vice-president of the United States. Think about it. NIS reports to OPM and OPM reports to the VP, as does the USEAC. The guy holds all the strings. And though we had some reason to believe the killer somehow worked for Morrison, we didn't know the connection. Now we have part of the answer."

"Which is?" Warner grew more curious as the conversation went on.

"It's one of his Secret Service guys—I don't have his name yet, but John, when I sent these two to Walter Reed for you, they saw the killer walking into the hospital as part of Morrison's protection detail." Clancy let that all sink in. "And by the way, guys, I did inform my OPM boss about everything, names of all the players included. I suspect that information got to Morrison, and that's why all the witnesses are now missing and why somebody went after my two investigators. I also wrote private letters to the Inspector General's office of OPM, a friend in the FBI, and two media outlets—and nothing."

Warner turned to Whitaker. "You said you'd have to wait until Williams is back in the saddle."

"Yes. That would make things a lot easier. What of it?"

"Now this is really off the record," Warner said quietly, as he looked at each of his companions in turn. "Seal of the confessional, Mike?" They nodded. "What if Williams doesn't come back?"

In the Cadillac Escalade he preferred, Joe Morrison enjoyed the silent ride from the West Wing to his residence in Bethesda. For the past few weeks, his motorcade had attracted additional vehicles and outriders, and all traffic stopped for him wherever he went. Tonight, he looked forward to an evening with Sharon and the children because, he suspected, events in the near term would likely change their lives in ways he could not foresee.

His mobile phone chirped, and he knew it would be a call he should take. There were less than a dozen people who had his private number, and Remy Carlson had assigned a distinctive tone to each caller. The first four bars of *The Battle Hymn of the Republic* told him it was Harrison Riordan, the venerable majority leader of the Senate, Morrison's mentor when he joined the body as the junior senator from Texas in 2006.

"What do you say, Harry?"

"Why, Mr. Acting President, how are *you* feeling these days? It must be a heady experience, indeed."

"It sure is, Senator, and do you know you are the first person to address me by that title?"

"Hah. I do have to say, that's a title a bit hard to get all the way through," said Riordan's gritty voice through the ether. "Maybe that's why the author's of the Twenty-Fifth Amendment intended the tenure to be brief."

"That's a thoughtful remark, Harry. Are you going anywhere with that?"

"Indeed, I am, my boy—I mean, Mr. Acting President. Many of us are wondering if we are receiving accurate news about the president's recovery."

How smooth Riordan could be when he chose. "Now you know there are some secrets I must keep, even from you, but it's been seventeen days since Averell's stroke. Surely you can connect some of those dots yourself."

"I do not want to connect those dots, Joe. Williams's shoes will be hard to fill, and my advice to you is not to be in too big a hurry to slip them on."

"I don't know who you've been talking to," Morrison said. "But let's all remember that the most powerful country in the world is effectively without a leader. I may have the constitutional authority, but the president's staff and you guys would likely hamstring me if I tried to do anything they you didn't wholeheartedly support."

A buzz filled the silence. "You have a point there, but I should tell you that if a crisis arose, the right people would rally round."

"That's comforting to know, but for some reason, I can't quite believe that's the only reason you called—to tell me I'd have help." Morrison regretted the bit of sarcasm that laced his words.

"There is something else, now that you bring it up. There are pretty nasty rumors coming from a few places now that there was something wrong with the election, and that you are somehow connected with it."

Morrison's voice rose, and he regretted that too. "What the hell do you mean? Something to do with what, for Christ's sake?"

"I didn't mean to press your buttons, Joe," Riordan said, his words belying his exact intention, "but it's out there."

"What is 'out there'?"

"That you had some sort of relationship with this Enrique McCord, and that he was found murdered election night."

"You know damn well that I had a relationship..." Morrison let the damning words hang. "And what do you mean, 'murdered'? I heard it was a road-rage thing."

"I didn't know you kept up with motor vehicle mishaps in Cincinnati, Joe."

"Don't sound like a prosecutor, Harry. Ricky McCord was a political fan—an acquaintance. That's all."

"So you say, but that night in your study, you suggested something a bit closer."

"And what if I did? Not a one of you uttered a syllable of surprise or concern. You were willing to do anything to get us reelected."

"No one," Riordan said, working to clear the pebbles from his throat, "could have foreseen what has happened. Now, some might think your hands are less than clean, shall we say."

"You've never been an altar boy, Harry. Don't be one now."

US Senator Daryl Perelman was seventy-two years old—his youthful looks and physical fitness to the contrary notwithstanding—and as anomalous as anyone can become and remain in his seat. A Democrat for nearly thirty-six years, he became an Independent in 2008, when he borrowed an old line, "I didn't leave the party, the party left me." For favors owed and deserved respect, he retained his perks and power. Nonetheless, he was careful in his offhand conversations with leaders of either party, especially the standard bearer for senate Democrats. So when his desk phone jangled, and his assistant announced that Senator Riordan was on the line, Perelman sat up and prepared to spar.

"Why you old rascal, Daryl. I never thought I'd have to go through your assistant to get to you," Riordan said in mock dismay.

"You leave me no choice, Harry. When it's you, I always need a minute to get my guard up."

"Hah. You're always ready for a good conversation, and that's why you're held in such high regard."

"Good God, this must be important. The butter is already melted." Perelman laughed.

"It is, indeed, important, and you will no doubt have a keen role in the drama playing out before us."

"I'll play dumb here. Which drama is that?"

"Always the careful chairman of the Senate Judiciary Committee. The drama to which I'm referring, my friend, is the one now on stage at Walter Reed. As much as I have admired, and even loved, our Averell Williams, I'm thinking his term is about over."

"You don't feel uncomfortable planning the funeral too soon?" Perelman asked.

"Let's not be too seemly here. People like you and me have stayed in power because we looked ahead, saw what might be coming, and prepared for it."

"So you must be thrilled that your protégé may become president."

"Thrilled isn't the word for it. Let's be frank. Joe Morrison is a good ol' Texas boy, but he wasn't ready for prime time when Averell insisted on him back in '08. And if, by fate's twisted sense of humor, Joe becomes president, we have to think about how to protect him—and the country."

"Meaning what, exactly?"

"Meaning that we support Emerson Grantham for vice-president," Riordan said.

"Nice idea, but then we'd have two people with overheated hormones vying for the top spot in 2016. Not a pretty picture—and one that might guarantee the Republicans a win."

"You're right on that one, but at least, we'd have over three years to let nature take its course."

"If you're thinking that far ahead, then you've thought about the IRS and Benghazi messes, haven't you?" Perelman asked.

"You know, Daryl, you haven't lost a bit of your edge, have you?" Riordan said, his tone warming. "That's exactly, right, and that's the real reason why I called."

"I'm listening."

Riordan cleared some of the gravel from his throat. "If Averell, say, exits the stage, and we have a new president, that would be the best time to work a deal with Jordy Marshall and John Whitaker."

"Meaning?"

"Meaning that both scandals will go away in trade for something sizable on the budget, health reform, or immigration."

"I understand now. You think that if Williams is gone..." Perelman let his voice drift, but then hastened to add a question he'd been waiting for Riordan to broach. "And the aroma wafting up from the sewers about big-time vote fraud in November? What about that?"

"That, too. The nation must move forward, as we did after Roosevelt and Kennedy. If Williams passes, maybe we can work it out that the burning bags of dog shit left on our porch will go with him."

"I hate to mix a metaphor but, you know, even crocodiles can swallow only so much..."

10.

United States Constitution
Twenty-Fifth Amendment

4. Whenever the Vice-President and a majority of either the principal officers of the executive departments or of such other body as Congress may by law provide, transmit to the President pro tempore of the Senate and the Speaker of the House of Representatives their written declaration that the President is unable to discharge the powers and duties of his office, the Vice-President shall immediately assume the powers and duties of the office as Acting President.

The Roosevelt Room was chilly. Across the foyer, the Oval Office had been closed for over three weeks, and it was as if someone had turned off all the heat at that end of the West Wing. Vice-President Joseph P. Morrison, as acting president under the terms of Section Three of the Twenty-Fifth Amendment, had called the group together, and there, face-to-face, sized up the room.

Side-by-side were Attorney General Sweeney, his natty bow tie slightly askew, and Secretary of Defense Jensen Roberts, the only hold-over from the Bush Administration, and the only African American at the core-cabinet level. Both men were Williams loyalists, to be sure.

On the other side of the table stood Susan Davidson, the newly minted secretary of state. A former professor from the Kennedy School of Government at Harvard, Davidson had no strong personal loyalties, only to party and political philosophy. A few feet away stood Marvin

Gillespie, the ancient and largely ineffective secretary of the treasury, but a highly persuadable man.

Entering at the last minute were Senate Majority Leader Harrison Riordan of Missouri and Speaker of the House, John Whitaker of Ohio. Neither man was a keen supporter of the president, but Riordan, at least, was a Democrat. Whitaker was invited only because he had to be—he was politically astute and careful. Riordan—Morrison's rabbi for nearly a decade—was the only person present on whom he could count.

"My friends, in a few days, it will be two weeks since President Williams' last recorded lucid moment," Morrison began. "I don't mean that to sound harsh, just realistic. I visited him today at Walter Reed. In fact, I happened to be there when the First Lady was also in his suite. It is a difficult situation, indeed." He let his voice break and paused for effect.

"I spoke with both Dr. Robby and Andrea Williams, and neither believes the president can recover fully, if at all," Morrison said. "Of course, the First Lady hopes against hope, but, as the doctor spoke to us, she nodded her understanding of reality. In a separate conversation with me, Andrea said, 'End this charade. Either let him recover in peace, or let him go in peace.'" Morrison's voice and tone had their effect on his listeners.

"I fully realize that I serve as acting president under the terms of Section Three of the Amendment, but that status severely limits my ability to act and serve this nation as the people expect. Our economy, the Russians, the ongoing threats in the Middle East—none of them have taken a break out of consideration for us and President Williams. I am therefore asking for your assistance in invoking Section Four, which keeps my status as acting president, but accords me greater official *gravitas* for any actions I deem necessary as leader of this nation." He paused. "Your thoughts?"

Roberts spoke first. "I have now served two presidents in a cabinet position and, constitutionally, I'd prefer that the situation remain unchanged. Section Four places the president on the defensive. While I am open to reason, it appears to me a bit unseemly to proceed just yet."

"Mr. Vice-President," Davidson said. "I will vote with the majority of the principal officers of the executive departments. Like you, I think the likelihood of President Williams returning to duty, fully fit and able, is very small."

Marvin Gillespie cleared his throat and created a few verbal noises hardly anyone could hear. Morrison thought he heard words of acquiescence.

Sweeney stumbled over the first few sylables to leave his lips, but soon found his voice. "Sir, s-sir, you solicited my views some days ago, and I have to say, regrettably, that the time may have come to act," he said, blinking rapidly. "Let me be clear that I have been pleased to serve in President Williams's cabinet and would be pleased to continue to serve. Similar to Secretary Davidson's view, I will support a consensus. However, I should point out that the wording of the Amendment is vague as to the meaning of the word 'principal.' Does it mean each and every secretary at the cabinet level, or does it mean the core secretaries of Justice, Defense, Treasury, and State? Having said that, I do not see that there's time for Congress to legislate as the Amendment specifies— and there is no president to sign a bill into law. You doing so would be seen as a conflict of interest, not so?"

"So you'd prefer, for the sake of appearance and stability, that a majority of the cabinet be on board?" Morrison knew that Sweeney hadn't said that at all, but, having thought it all out, he knew that that was the only realistic option.

Sweeney cleared his throat. "Why, yes, sir. That would be most acceptable." Sweeney then cast his gaze at the legislators. "And you two?"

Riordan didn't wait for Whitaker. "As much as I admire, respect, and love Averell Williams, the country needs an unquestioned leader. An invocation of Section Four gives both the appearance and substance of leadership. Of course, should the president rally and be deemed fit by qualified medical personnel, every last one of us would be happy to see him return to the Oval Office, as would the entire nation."

"By God, Harry, we actually agree on a key point," Whitaker said to general laughter, which took the emotional chill off the room. "The

House will not oppose a change in status at this point, much as we'd all prefer, as Harry said so well, that Averell Williams return to office." He turned to look directly at Morrison and said nothing, his famous half smile frozen in place.

"None taken, John. It appears there is consensus in this room." Morrison was about to continue, when Jensen Roberts held up his hand.

"Excuse me, Joe. Let's make it unanimous."

"Thank you, sir," Morrison said. Then to Sweeney, "Norty, may I prevail upon you to draw up the proper documents? We'll convene a full cabinet meeting this Friday, the fifteenth. If there's no change in the president's status, I'll ask for an up or down show of hands. In the meantime, I will feel free to converse with each of them on the matter."

One by one, each person shook hands with Acting President Morrison as they left the room. For Whitaker and Morrison, however, the interchange was perfunctory and wordless. On the way out, Whitaker made a point to be next to Jensen Roberts and whispered, loud enough for Morrison to hear, "I suspect many prayers will be said between now and then."

When the Roosevelt Room contained only Morrison and the ghostly portraits banking the walls, he looked around, taking in the field of his victory, fully appreciating that he was about to achieve the objective he craved, one for which he had committed bribery, fraud, and murder. Calmly, he exited from the rear door, stayed to his right, and strode back to his office. Remy was behind him, and, as they passed Sondra Thompson's busy enclave, he wondered how Carlson would do as chief of staff.

Despite his success with key Cabinet members, there was no reason to celebrate. *Just savor it*, he told himself. *Celebrations will come later.* As he shut the door behind him after letting Remy go for the evening, he knew there were dragons yet to slay. He somehow had to allay his concerns, if not his conscience.

Sweeney may already have been neutralized. The difference between his attitude when the notion of Section Four was first broached and his behavior today was truly remarkable. It couldn't be a change in loyalty. No, the phone call about his sexual habits had finally done its job, and the man's knowledge about the election fix had actually worked to lock him in. Check one off, Morrison was certain.

Warner was another matter. Even though Cox said he'd scared the living shit out of the agency head and his wife, he doubted the man would be easy to manage. Warner would require a different solution.

His biggest problem was Marty Cox. Cox would be forever tied to him whether the agent realized it or not. There was no escape, because there was no place to go. Cox couldn't turn on him because he'd have to turn himself in, and Cox, like most other feds Morrison knew, would never jeopardize his family and pension. What to do? He needed Cox, and no one else, for the Warner problem, but then what? How did he rid himself of the man when the time came?

As for the young NIS couple, Morrison thought he shouldn't be too concerned. They knew next to nothing, and there was no one alive who could connect him to any crime. Would any law enforcement body seriously believe an allegation about election fixing from two unknowns against the president of the United States? And any other crime? Of course not!

Besides, Morrison concluded, even if an accusation were leveled, if no one in State Media gave it credence, it would quickly fade away.

The mid-February sun had just set in the front windows of the townhouse on South Fairfax Street where Pete Clancy was preparing a good Italian dinner while his two houseguests laid the table and decanted the wine. It had been about five weeks since Mare and Paul Gladston had arrived from the snowy Amish farm in western Pennsylvania, and, thus far, everything had worked out well.

First, putting his expertise out for hire had been a success. Clancy had nearly forgotten the stresses of NIS and the master–slave relationship with OPM. Being responsible for several thousand employees had lost its appeal. The two people and a few other stringers on his new payroll suited him well, and, no doubt, other NIS people might join him. It didn't hurt, of course, that he had served in the army with two people who had done well in the political world, but, since early January, there had been other jobs as well. Soon, however, he expected a nice flow of referrals, which meant a nice flow of revenue.

That afternoon, Mare had helped him mix the ground beef and pork, along with bread crumbs, Italian seasoning, and eggs to form meatballs slightly larger than golf balls. After baking them on a cookie sheet for fifteen minutes, Mare dumped them all into the sauce Clancy was simmering. Now, as the Barilla Spaghetti No. 5 finished its eight-minute swim in the boiling pot, it occurred to him it wasn't just the pasta that was ready to boil over.

He yanked the colander from its hiding place to drain the noodles and replayed his Sunday morning conversation with Warner, Whitaker, and Pallison. He couldn't believe all the wrong things that could happen.

What stayed with him from their talk was one of the last things Warner had said, and he thought about the implications. So deep in thought was he that when his cell phone buzzed and rattled on the ceramic tile counter top, he almost dropped the hot saucepot he was taking off the stove. Glancing at the caller ID, he knew he had to answer.

"Talk about karma, for God's sake," Clancy said. "I was thinking about what you said the other day."

"That's what I'm calling about, Pete. Can I drop over?" Warner asked.

"You? On a Friday evening? Won't Nancy be waiting?"

"Too many questions, and spooks don't have much of a social life."

"You can drop by if you want, but, you know, I have two houseguests."

"Are they the two I might know something about?"

"Yes. What do you want to do?"

"That's perfect—on several levels. See you in ten minutes."

"Only if you'll join us for some spaghetti."

"You're on—I'll call Nancy and fall on my sword."

At the Clancy house, the salad and steaming garlic bread completed the picture of a warm winter meal when the door buzzed. Clancy answered it. "Mare and Paul Gladston, this is Andrew Warner."

"Andrew Warner of the—" Mare began to say.

Clancy shushed her. "Not so loud," he said in a low, conspiratorial voice.

Everyone laughed and shook hands.

"Let's sit down," Clancy said. "Somebody say grace."

Paul pronounced a fluent Protestant blessing in the name of the Lord and was surprised to see both Clancy and Warner bless themselves along with Mare. "What is this? A Catholic convention?"

Laughter graced the table.

"Gotcha, Paulie boy. This time, it's you who's outnumbered," Mare said, apparently in reference to their time in Amish country.

"Drew, you called this meeting," Clancy said after pleasantries and pasta had been served

Warner told them what had transpired at the White House within the previous hour–that the cabinet voted to initiate Section Four, which gave Joe Morrison, the man all of them knew as a murderer, a tighter grip on the presidency. "Jack Sennett should be convening a presser right about now," he said, looking at his watch, after the trio had heard all the details.

Clancy rose and turned to the News Global channel. Barnes Ward was hosting the six o'clock spot and alerting the public of a special White House announcement expected soon. With the camera remaining on the Press Briefing Room, full and noisy, Ward speculated on what might be coming while the world awaited Jack Sennett, late almost always. Then, he turned to the wall-sized monitor on the wall behind him as Sennett began.

"Today marks the twenty-first day since the president's surgery for prostate cancer and, while the actual procedure was a success, President Williams has not rallied as doctors had originally anticipated. While he is conscious and communicative, all concerned feel that it is not in his or the country's best interest that he return to his duties as president of the United States at this time. Therefore, today, Friday, February fifteenth, at five thirty p.m. the full cabinet voted in a clear majority, as specifically required by the Constitution, to activate Section Four of the Twenty-Fifth Amendment. While the title and status of acting president remain the same, this change allows the vice-president to act more fully in carrying out presidential duties, thus sending the message to all here and abroad that the United States is not without its constitutionally mandated leadership. Acting President Morrison will serve in his present capacity until further notice. There will be no questions." The camera followed Sennett out of the room.

"So there it is," Warner said, a certain sadness in his voice. "The thing is that everyone in the Cabinet Room would agree—if you asked them—that Joe Morrison is the most unqualified man ever to be president, but no one has the will to oppose him. What no one in that room knows is what we know—that the man is a criminal, and the words, 'high crimes and misdemeanors' do not even begin to describe it."

His three listeners remained silent. Clancy spoke, his words solemn. "You didn't come here to have dinner, did you, Drew?"

"No."

"Let's have it."

Warner looked around the room and swore each person to secrecy. "I'm trusting you two on this," he said looking at Mare and Paul, "because I trust this man, and I understand you both know as much or more about Joe Morrison and Enrique McCord than I do."

The Gladstons nodded.

"Here's what you don't know. Late last summer, Vice-President Morrison called and asked me to set up a meeting place for him and persons unknown to me. All things considered, given who I serve and the business I'm in, it was not an unusual request. Morrison asked to make sure the meeting was neither observed by outside parties nor recorded by people on my staff."

"Go on," Clancy said, fascinated.

"We are who we are," Warner said, shrugging his shoulders. "So of course, the agency recorded and filmed the entire encounter, but I never looked at the tapes because I had no reason to do so at the time." He inhaled deeply, as if he were any other middle-aged, graying man short of breath. "During our conversation on Sunday," he said, looking again at Clancy, "I remembered that private meeting and became curious about it, only because it was Morrison and it happened about the time your man, Evers, was murdered in Cincinnati." Again, he paused to gather his thoughts. "This morning, I finally got hold of the material from our archives and viewed the entire tape."

"Can you play it for us?" Mare wanted to know.

"That might not be prudent at the moment, but let me tell you about it briefly." In a summary that took less than three minutes, Warner described for his audience a visit made by Morrison to a safe house in suburban Washington. There, he directed the conspiracy to steal the 2012 presidential election with the owner of SoftSec and his techie. The eyes of his listeners were wide with awe. When he finished his sketch, the room stayed silent until Warner himself broke it. "That son of a bitch!"

"Jesus H. Christ," Clancy said. "Drew, do you realize what you have? It's the smoking gun—the only one! There's no other direct evidence putting Morrison right in the picture. Everything else is indirect, purely circumstantial."

"That's right—and goddamn it, we had it all along!"

"Now what?" Paul asked.

"Now, I don't know who to trust. With Morrison in a position to pull any string he chooses, we have to be careful." Warner looked directly at the Gladstons. "I understand you two fared pretty well at Camp Peary. Mac Smith gave me the rundown."

"Yes," Mare piped in, "and we neglected to thank you."

"No thanks necessary. You can return the favor by signing on to do a little protection work for me and my wife."

"Aren't you already well protected?" Clancy inquired, gesturing to the street outside.

"Yes, and you'll meet my team. But Morrison's people don't know you."

"One of them does," Paul said, "and he hasn't forgotten us."

"Then you'll know who to watch for—and you'll be the last people he'd expect."

"Did your cameras catch the agent accompanying Morrison that night last year?" Clancy asked.

"No, he never went inside, but now that we have a good idea who he is, my team can consider a preemptive action."

"Nothing terminal, Drew. This agent these two call 'Crew Cut' is the only live witness we have. You may have a tape of Morrison with McCord, but Crew Cut is the guy who took him to the meeting. We need to talk this through with our other friend."

"Could we cut the spook stuff?" asked the irrepressible Mare. "Is your 'other friend' somebody all that special?"

Embarrassed, Clancy exchanged a glance with Warner, who nodded, almost imperceptibly.

"Our friend is John Whitaker, Speaker of the House."

AHW dead of a stroke at sixty-seven. Morrison to become president.

So screamed the banner across the bottom of millions of TV screens and through the ether to cell phones, tablets, and other devices around the world. Reminiscent of Walter Cronkite at the death of John F. Kennedy nearly fifty years earlier, Peter Marsden of CNS strained to hold his emotions.

"Ladies and gentlemen, it is difficult to carry on this morning when our hearts are so heavy with loss. We have just learned that President Averell Harriman Williams, sixty-seven years of age, was struck down—not by an assassin's bullet for America's first African American president as many had feared—but by an invisible, deadlier foe. It was a major stroke, but not, doctors said, a result of surgery so much as the president's inability to rally from the earlier stroke suffered several weeks ago. First

Lady Andrea Williams was at his side when the president passed away at six seventeen this morning, Friday, February twenty-second. It is one of history's ironies that today is Washington's Birthday.

"Doctors hastened to state," Marsden continued, clearly tuned into a voice in his earbuds as well, "that ordinarily, prostate surgery is nearly always successful with the survival rate among the highest of all cancer treatments. While there was a hint that the president may have known about his circumstances longer than he let on, all of that is now history as Joseph P. Morrison of Texas is about to become the nation's forty-fifth president of the United States.

"Our cameras are focused on the East Room at the White House where members of the Cabinet, the leadership of both houses of Congress, Republican and Democrat, and members of the Supreme Court have gathered. The East Room, you will recall, has been famous since before Lincoln's time. It's a ball room, state dining room, and sadly, a funereal space when circumstances have demanded it. Today, however, it is living testimony to the continuity and the resilience of our Constitution. A leader passes on, and a new leader takes the oath. And that is what will happen momentarily.

"Ah, now I see it." Marsden's voice turned almost to a whisper, as if he were standing in the room with the silent, gathered crowd. "Acting President Morrison has entered the room. It is nine o'clock, Eastern Time, and, in a moment, as required by Article II, Section One of the Constitution, he will repeat the thirty-five-word oath and become President Joseph P. Morrison.

"I see the chief justice there with the same Bible used by President Williams nearly six weeks ago. They join together near the podium. Let's go there now."

Taller and older than Morrison, the jurist held the Bible and said, "Please raise your right hand and repeat after me." Phrase by phrase, they spoke the sacred words, as the over one hundred senior government officials, justices, and members of the diplomatic corps looked on. First Lady Andrea Williams and Sharon Morrison, along with the two Morrison children stood quietly by to hear the fateful text.

"I do solemnly swear that I will faithfully execute the Office of President of the United States, and will to the best of my ability, preserve, protect and defend the Constitution of the United States."

With a second's hesitation, there was polite, but not thunderous applause. It was as if the crowd instinctively knew there should be joy that the Republic lives on, but that a tragedy occurred in order to prove the point.

Morrison stepped up to the podium as people seated themselves. "Thank you all, and especially First Lady Andrea Williams, for being here at this extraordinary moment in our nation's history. Averell Williams served his country ably for the past forty years, first in New York State, and then at the national level. His mark as president will not be that he was our nation's first African American elected to the highest office we can offer, but as a dedicated citizen persisting in his pursuit of the American dream—for his family, and for everyone's family. We will miss him.

"As for me, as vice-president, I never expected what happened to us early this morning. Because we anticipated the president's recovery, even if slowly, we proceeded with the business of government as if he was simply on an extended overseas trip or on a long vacation to his beloved Adirondacks retreat. While the fates have dealt us this terrible blow, it would be unlike Averell Williams, and unlike Americans, to mourn the past without marching to the future.

"My solemn intention is to proceed along the path blazed for us by President Williams, and you can mark those words. The hallmarks of integrity and transparency will not change with the sad event that has brought us here today. This does represent a new beginning, however, and I hope to work with the other party to put the issues and purported scandals behind us rather than allow them to divide us."

Morrison finished his left-to-right pan of the crowd. CIA Director Warner was not in attendance—an easy absence to notice. Morrison let his gaze rest on Former Secretary of State Emerson Grantham, who returned the favor with a tight smile.

"And that's all I need to say this morning," Morrison said. "Now, we must come together to grieve for our fallen leader and help Andrea

Williams find peace and comfort in the days ahead. May the good Lord give rest to the soul of Averell Williams, and may He bless Andrea and the United States of America."

Peter Marsden jumped in with a voiceover. "There we see President Morrison give the now former First Lady an embrace, as his wife and children surround her. He then takes her arm and walks her out of the East Room, no doubt to continue making detailed preparations for the presidential funeral three days from now."

With the camera on him back in the CNS studio, Marsden said, "As yet, we have few details about the funeral of our forty-fourth president, but as soon as they are released by the White House, we will bring them to you."

That morning, the solid, rusty red townhouse on South Fairfax Street hosted illustrious company once again. Andrew Warner sat in Pete Clancy's living room absorbing the news bulletins as they bannered across the screen. Feet from the street, ostensibly invisible behind the cream-trimmed windows flanked by operable Charleston green shutters, Warner relaxed with his feet on an ottoman. Outside, across the street, his bodyguard sat in an unmarked black Lincoln, from which he could maintain a clear view of the property and its front approaches.

Warner and his host flipped back and forth between CNS and Peter Marsden and News Global and Lew Michaels. Finally, they settled on Michaels, whom they considered the more reliable reporter.

On the screen, Michaels stood outside the White House, attempting to catch one or more dignitaries for a quick interview. "Senator Riordan," Michaels called out, "could we get your views on today's events and what they mean for the country?"

"Yes, you can, young man," Riordan said, his pebbly voice spilling onto the airwaves like so much hot asphalt on a roadway. "As you likely know, I've known this president since he was a freshman senator from Texas not too many years ago, and I believe he will do his job as president in a fit and able manner."

"Damned with faint praise," Warner said from his chair in Alexandria. "If that's the best his rabbi can do for him, then Joe Morrison has one helluva swim ahead of him."

"Senator, because you've known him perhaps the longest of all your colleagues, maybe you'd venture a guess on who his choice for vice-president will be," Michaels continued as they stood on the White House drive.

"Hah!" Riordan hugged his black cashmere overcoat closer to himself. "You get right to it, don't you, Lew? And that, of course, is the question of the hour. For President Morrison to best serve this nation, he will need an able number two, and, right now," he rasped, "I don't wish to speculate over his successor in the vice-presidency while poor Averell Williams should be the subject of our mourning."

"That is kind of you to say, Senator. There is talk, however, that you yourself have launched a small campaign on behalf of Emerson Grantham. Would you care to comment on that, sir?"

More gravel and stone bits swirled around Riordan's jaw. "No, I would not, but I should say that Emerson Grantham could occupy a fine, fine spot on nearly anyone's short list."

"A good many qualifiers there, Senator, but thank you. Now, here's your counterpart in the House, Speaker Whitaker." He shifted his and the camera's attention. "Sir, will the Republican Party be able to cast aside issues like the IRS scandal and the Benghazi cover-up as a sort of down payment to unify the country on the death of President Williams?"

"That's an interesting perspective, Lew." For the camera, Whitaker displayed a serious, unsmiling demeanor. "Naturally, the entire country wants to unite behind a new president, and we hope to find ways to work with the other party to put these issues behind us. But"—he looked in Riordan's direction as he spoke—"the previous administration doesn't get a free pass and neither will this one, until the public regains confidence in the integrity of our government. That's all I have for you today."

"Now there's a hint for anybody who was listening carefully," Clancy said in Alexandria.

"And if we cool our heels for not too much longer, John will practically jump off that screen and find his way here," Warner said. "Where are the kids?"

Clancy chuckled. "They're upstairs but will be down shortly, I expect. Last time you saw them, by the way, you talked about—"

"Yes, and I want them to start today. With Morrison having all the strings at his fingertips, I think we need to implement the plan we discussed."

As if on cue, Mare and Paul descended from the upper floor.

"You missed Morrison's swearing-in," Clancy said.

"Didn't miss a thing," Mare responded. "They can swear him in all day long, and he is still not our president. He was not elected to the job and, guilty as he is of high crimes, he has no right to the chair in the Oval Office."

"She sure is a shy one, isn't she?" Paul teased, and they all tried to laugh, but couldn't.

"But you're right, Mare, and we'll have to decide how to go about fixing this little problem," Warner said with conviction. "In the meantime, Pete and I were just talking about you two. I'll check with my wife to see what's on our social schedule, but I'll want you to complement my protection detail for all the reasons we discussed the last time."

"Sir, we're at your command," Paul said.

Warner rose and opened the front door a bit and silently signaled the man across the street next to the bare-limbed beech. After a few seconds, the sentinel entered and stood in the front hall while Warner introduced Agent Daniel Jorgensen all around. Warner stood aside and tapped a button on his cell, and then spoke for a few minutes.

Rejoining the trio, and with Clancy listening in, Warner sighed. "Unbelievably, Nancy—that's Mrs. Warner—says there won't be much going on socially for a few days until early March. She wants us to go to Kennedy Center for something called Nordic Cool. It's a play of some sort—she promised it's less than an hour and a half, thank God."

"I've heard of this show," Mare said. "It sounds, well, different, but interesting. Something each agency head needs to see, I'm sure," she added with a touch of irony to match his sigh. She looked at Paul. "I hope you noticed, Mr. Newlywed, that even guys all the way up like Director Warner here have to indulge a spouse."

"Gee, thanks for the heads up," Paul said with a gallows-humor grin.

"Seriously," Warner said, "if ever there's a time when I'm vulnerable, it's at occasions of this sort, and the Kennedy Center event will be no exception."

"You're being overly cautious, Drew, but probably a good thing." Clancy glanced through the sidelight. "John's here."

"We'll talk more when I have more details," Warner said to Clancy's young operatives.

After Warner's man returned to his post and Mare and Paul excused themselves for a lunch out, the three old friends worked their coffees at the dining room table. There was some desultory conversation about the ceremony of an hour earlier. Regarding Morrison's pious patter in the East Room, Whitaker let curses season his distaste for Washington hypocrisy at its zenith, and Clancy echoed his view.

Warner reached into his briefcase and pulled out two small, thin packages, identical in appearance. He handed one to each of his friends. "Let's watch one of them."

Clancy slid one of the DVD's into the slot on his MacBook Pro.

Warner continued. "Actually, I was wrong about something. Originally, I thought there was only one camera active inside the house, when there was another one on a tree in the driveway. Of course, that late at night, with no outside lights on the house and no moon, you'll see only the briefest glimpse of Morrison entering through the front door. It's not evidence of any kind, to be candid."

Warner paused as they watched the first three minutes of the DVD. They heard a car engine shut off in the darkness, then a few steps in pea gravel followed by the metal scratch of a screen door opening. Then, in a flash, they saw the back of a man's head and shoulders as he entered a house. In two seconds, he was gone.

"Now, here's the smoking gun, if ever there was one," Warner said. "Watch. Check the expression on Morrison's face."

The hidden camera captured Morrison stepping into the light of the dining room where Enrique McCord and Nathan Conaway had been waiting. Introductions were skimpy, a preliminary to the demonstration of a crime.

Morrison was dressed in slacks, a polo neck, and a plantation hat he wore pulled low. Even so, it was clear who was speaking. The video and audio were so good that the three men could have been watching something live in the next room.

"So let's skip all the other pleasantries," Morrison began. "When we're finished, you'll be escorted back to Dulles and dropped there in time for your flight to Cincinnati. And this meeting never happened. Are we clear on that?"

There was hurried acquiescence. Conaway began, as if he were a software salesman at a techie convention. "The best way to demo this, sir, is by example. These three laptops represent a mock-up of the 2000 presidential election setup in Florida. I don't need to tell you how that turned out. On this computer," he said, pointing to the leftmost one, "are the results for all the counties as they were originally reported to Tallahassee. So here you see Volusia County with 45 percent of the vote for Bush and 55 percent for Grayson. Here's Palm Beach County with 36 to 63 for Grayson, and Gadsden with 32 to 66 for Grayson. On the other side, here's Santa Rosa County with 73 percent for Bush and 26 percent for Grayson; Walton County with 67 to 31, Bush; and Okaloosa, 74 to 24 for Bush.

"So, on election night, sir, Bush apparently had a lead of 1784 votes, and, technically, he won. But that small margin triggered a recount, with Bush eventually winning by less than 600 votes."

"We know all this, Nathan. Where are you going with it?"

"Let's say this second computer, the one in the middle, was me sitting in my office in Cincinnati—but electronically, it was in between each county and the state capital. If we wanted Grayson to win the election—and avoid a recount—here's what we would have done, and we have two choices. We either inflate Grayson's win in the counties where he did win, or we shave votes from Bush where he won strongly but wouldn't miss a few thousand here or there, or we could do both."

"Do both," Morrison suggested.

"OK. Remembering that we need to avoid a recount, Grayson has to win the state by about sixty thousand votes. I recommend we do not change the state's totals, only who gets which votes."

"Agreed."

"There are sixty-seven counties total in the state," Conaway said. "So let's say that in Volusia County, already strong for Grayson, we give him two thousand more votes, and we do something similar in Jefferson, Leon, Dade, Saint Lucie, and Palm Beach Counties. With a few clicks here and there, we come up with twenty-four thousand votes. Now let's go to the strong Bush counties I mentioned, along with others, and we come up with another eighteen thousand. "

Conaway's voice rasped with excitement. "You might remember that Republicans won fifteen of the twenty-three congressional districts in the state. By turning over more votes, one way or the other, from the other forty-some counties, Grayson would win our mock election by about sixty-seven thousand votes, give or take a few. And the Democrats would win twelve of the twenty-three congressional races. And that all appears on laptop number three, here on the right, representing the Tallahassee official counts."

Morrison pulled up a chair behind Conaway and sat down, mouth hanging wide open. "It would have been that easy?"

"Well, in 2000 the right software wasn't in place in many of the states we would have needed."

"According to what you just showed me, Grayson needed help in only one."

They continued on like this for several minutes.

"This is incredible—better than I thought," Morrison said. "It's good you're ready to go in all those states, Nathan, but when we get right down to it, perhaps we'll target a smaller number someplace where we want it to count the most." The vice-president became ebullient. "After all, we don't want to be greedy, do we?" With that, he stood up and slapped the backs of both men, as if they'd enjoyed a good joke after a round of golf.

"All that'll be necessary, Joe," McCord said, "is for someone with the right political savvy to give us guidance on where to turn the votes over to the Williams–Morrison ticket and how many to turn to make it appear reasonable."

"And you're sure there can be no trail?"

"If you think about it, sir," Conaway said, "with electronic voting, and no paper, how could there be?"

Morrison nodded. "I'll see that you get the expert you need. You'll be doing all of this from your Cincinnati offices, Ricky?"

"Yes, sir."

"That'll make everything easy," Morrison said, upbeat and smiling.

Warner stopped the DVD and several seconds of astonished silence followed. Then he said, "There's only a minute or so more, but nothing so damning as what you have already seen."

Elated, Whitaker said, "Not only does Morrison lead the plot to steal the election, his last comments seem to suggest that he might already have been thinking ahead to when these two witnesses had to exit the stage."

"And he refers to the expert he'd send," Warner said.

"That would be Jerry James," Whitaker said, his voice like nails going into a coffin. "And do you know who James is—or should I say, was?" He savored the certainty of the moment. "James began his political career working on one of Morrison's first political campaigns in Texas. He was a loner. One of those math and analytical geniuses people loved and hated at the same time."

"You're saying James was the other victim on election night?" Clancy asked.

"You bet," Whitaker said. "Morrison put them all in the same place at the same time, and then he had his guy take them out." All emotion left his voice. "The man is the definition of ruthless—in the most brutal sense of the word."

"And all this is called civilization?" Clancy said.

"Who said so?" Whitaker asked. "I'd say we've been civilizing ourselves for at least three thousand years—but we are far from civilized."

"And our problem is that Morrison is now the president of the United States," Warner said. "If there's one small dot of bright light here—at least from my vantage point—it's that it seems clear Williams himself was not involved." He cleared his throat. "Look, guys, unless absolutely necessary, this DVD goes nowhere. I gave it to you as insurance, but I don't want my agency compromised. For all the CIA has been accused of, political murder of US citizens in the United States has never been on our to-do list."

His friends nodded. Clancy said, "You two are within his reach."

"He hasn't gotten away with it yet," Whitaker swore. "So, here's what I think we need to do..."

The somber voice of News Global anchor Barnes Ward filled the family rooms, kitchens, and bedrooms of millions across America, and millions more around the world as he described the scene at the US Capitol, "America's temple to democracy," as he called it. The News Global cameras caught the panorama from a point northwest of the West Front's plaza down and along the building's facade, catching the gleaming Roman structure in the cold Sunday morning shadows. Because the sun had not yet eclipsed the dome, patches of ice and snow were visible. Mourners, thousands strong, began to form a line.

"Nothing if not majestic," Ward said. "The Capitol Building rests with the patience of the republic as it waits to receive the body of its fallen leader, Averell Harriman Williams, forty-fourth president of the United States, sometime later this morning. I should note at the outset that this president's funeral will be different from other state ceremonies the nation has witnessed. In Lincoln's and Kennedy's, for example, there was a period of lying in repose in the East Room of the White House, but that was at a time when the residence was far more open to the public than is possible today.

"Some have thought, nonetheless, that having the lying in state begin today seemed a bit hasty, given that the president died only the day before yesterday. We are reliably informed, however, that these arrangements were made at the specific request of former First Lady Andrea Williams so that as many people as possible could come to the Capitol this weekend to pay their respects before the funeral service at the National Cathedral tomorrow afternoon.

"As is customary on these occasions, President Morrison has already signed an Executive Order declaring tomorrow, Monday, February twenty-fifth, a national day of mourning. That means that all federal offices, buildings, and museums will be closed out of respect for the late president. He has also committed the resources of the US Government to accommodate Mrs. Williams's requests, and that series of events is what has brought us to you this morning. Of course, all US flags in the nation and at all our embassies and installations abroad will be lowered to half-staff for the next thirty days.

"The fact that we are waiting here at the Capitol highlights another key difference in this state funeral. In many earlier observances, when the president's remains left the White House, the body was transported in a slow procession up Pennsylvania Avenue, then turned on Constitution Avenue to the Capitol. In this instance, that procession will occur tomorrow instead, but in reverse. More on that aspect later.

"To provide our viewers with a bit of the backdrop for this historic occasion," Ward continued while the screen showed a series of old tintypes and photographs, "the last lying in state of a president was for Gerald R. Ford in early January 2007. Before now, there have been twenty-nine such honors bestowed on American citizens, not all of them presidents.

"As some of our history buffs might already know, Abraham Lincoln was the first president to lie in state in the Capitol Rotunda, in April 1865, despite the fact that the dome above his catafalque remained unfinished. Since then, ten other presidents have chosen to receive this honor, and many of their funerals have been modeled after Lincoln's, most notably, that of John F. Kennedy. Averell Harriman Williams will be the eleventh president to lie in state at the Capitol Building."

Given a cue in his earbud, Ward continued his recitation of history while awaiting the hearse's arrival at the Capitol. "Many would be surprised to know that two of our most famous twentieth-century presidents did not avail themselves of a lying in state. Franklin Roosevelt's family decided that it would not be seemly for FDR to have all the pomp and ceremony surrounding his death while our boys died by the thousands overseas. Harry Truman's family also declined a state funeral, preferring, instead, a more private ceremony when he died in 1973.

"I've been told that we should expect the arrival of President Williams's remains any moment now." Ward paused while the camera held its focus on the Capitol Building's large underground reception area. "Earlier we spoke of President Kennedy's funeral. It's been said that sometime in the twenty-four hours after his death, First Lady Jacqueline Kennedy decided his funeral arrangements should be closely modeled after Lincoln's. Late that Saturday evening, two noted historians entered the National Archives, so the story goes, only to find they could not turn on the lights because they were on a timer. With flashlights, they searched until they found Frank Leslie's *Illustrated* and *Harper's Weekly,* both of which detailed all one ever needed to know about Abraham Lincoln's arrangements.

"And now, I'm told that the hearse has arrived at the Capitol. If possible, we will be able to view that process via the network pool camera. Yes, there it is," Ward said. "Representatives of the US Military—army, navy, air force, marines, and coast guard will serve as pall bearers—body bearers as they are called officially—as they carry the president's casket to the space of honor in the Rotunda."

The camera held the shot as the military escort of three men and two women moved through the imposing entry and deep into the Capitol's interior, accompanied by an armed honor guard. The clicking of their cadenced walk echoed off the marble and limestone surfaces.

"In a few moments," Ward said quietly into his mic, "the president's remains will be placed in the exact center of the Rotunda, which is ninety-six feet across, and exactly one hundred eighty feet and three inches beneath the top of the dome itself. Looking down upon it all will be Constantino Brumidi's *The Apotheosis of Washington,* an image of

Washington enthroned in the heavens. It will be an irony to some that one-time slaveholder George Washington will look upon one of his successors, the great-grandson of a slave.

"Another note of interest is that in Statuary Hall, not far from where the president will lie, the black Belgian marble statue of Martin Luther King Jr. will be present for what he must have imagined when he said he had a dream: an African American elected to the greatest leadership position on earth, and now, supremely honored in death."

Mare and Paul found a place in the line already snaking out from the Capitol's entrance to the Rotunda. "Do you have some feeling how many people are already here?" Mare asked when she checked her cell at 11:26 a.m.

"More feeling than in my feet? God, it's cold." Paul took a deep breath and walked his feet up and down. "When I asked one of the Capitol policemen as we came up, he thought there were about forty-five thousand already here, and they're expecting maybe a quarter million."

"When you asked him, where was I?" Mare said curiously. "I don't remember you talking to anyone.",

Her auburn hair was tucked under a knit, white winter cap with a pom-pom gracing its peak. He bent to see her eyes as she was shielding them from the sunlight that came over the Capitol Building. "It was while you were gawking like an Indiana tourist in town for the first time." He laughed.

"Shhh! Notice how quiet people are? And so? It's my first time here—I'm not embarrassed to be a tourist. Every American should see this, but not under these circumstances.",

"You know," Paul whispered, "if there had been any clue that he was involved with Crew Cut in any way, I wouldn't be here."

She nodded. "I feel the same way. The IRS business and the Benghazi thing aside for now, you couldn't help but admire him even if you weren't a Democrat. Averell Williams seemed to be a decent guy—a pure politician all the way, but people respected him because of what he accomplished to get here."

"Yeah, he was no slouch, that's for sure," Paul said. "I'm glad we came. I'll feel a whole lot better going after the other guy. Won't you?"

"You got that right, Paulie boy. Ugh!" She shivered. "Hope it doesn't get much colder." She looked away from the Capitol, around Paul's shoulder, and saw that in the brief time they'd been there, the line had doubled.

"This is Barnes Ward as we bring you the closing ceremonies at the Capitol's Rotunda this Monday morning. It has been estimated that something over a hundred and fifty thousand people will have made their way around the casket of President Williams atop the storied Lincoln Catafalque between noon yesterday, throughout the long, frigid Washington night, and throughout the morning today, until one o'clock, when public viewing will end.

"Some past state funerals have drawn more mourners, it might be noted, but in each of those other instances, the lying in state period was nearly a day longer, and in more clement weather. For today, there is an expectation of light snow within the next few hours as the temperature drops below the midthirties."

Ward contributed other bits of funerary trivia to the national knowledge base as millions in their homes, bars, and restaurants watched with rapt attention the unending line of mourners gazing at the face of President Williams for the last time. Otherwise, the network pool camera studied the armed honor guard surrounding the Lincoln Catafalque while, intermittently, individual network cameras portrayed the crisp, overcast day shrouding the nation's capital.

For a few minutes, Ward broke away from the scene to update the viewers, albeit with brevity and circumspection, on the ongoing Congressional inquiries into claims of IRS abuse, negligence in the handling of the Benghazi massacre, and hints of abuse of PTSD patients by the Veterans Administration.

"A few minutes from now the last mourners will make their way through the Rotunda, pass by their dead president and his guard of honor, and the large, bronze interior doors will close to public view," Ward continued as the News Global screen flashed solemn images of the Capitol scene to viewers around the globe.

"Over the past twenty-four hours, we've seen the world's great leaders pay their last respects, leaders from all major faith walks offer the nation their words of blessing and comfort, and American political leaders of both parties make their public peace with the man they loved or fought in life. Their words might best be summed up by what Senate Majority Leader Harrison Riordan said as he ended his brief remarks, 'Men like Averell Williams pass this way but once, and we are all the better for having made his acquaintance.'

"The last of the mourners have now left the Rotunda, and we now see the honor guard responding to an officer's soft commands to disengage. Another group of five body bearers will carry the coffin down the east steps of the Capitol to the waiting horse-drawn caissons, originally built in 1918 to carry a seventy-five millimeter cannon.

"Always of interest is the riderless horse that follows immediately behind the president's casket. A pair of boots is reversed in the stirrups as part of a tradition that goes back as far as the funeral of President Zachary Taylor, or perhaps, some historians think, to that of William Henry Harrison in 1841. Why all the military symbolism, you might ask?

"State funerals are under the auspices and direction of the Washington Military District because such ceremonies involve the Commander-in-Chief. Of course, the family's wishes are given much deference, but what you are seeing in the procession that follows is largely dictated by long military tradition. Let's watch."

On the high definition screen could be seen the minute details of the gold fringes of the red, white, and blue flag moving rhythmically as the black-lacquered caissons, glossy even in the dull light, moved slowly up Constitution Avenue. The only sounds were the rasp of the steel-rimmed wheels on the asphalt and the steady clip-clop of the eight horses. Those tempted to turn up the sound on their sets were drawn more closely to the eerie procession before them. Following the military marching units was the long line of black limousines, the first of which carried Andrea Williams and a military escort. Following them were government and military leaders, as well as the representatives from forty-odd countries.

At the White House, the president's casket was transferred to a waiting hearse. With a soft voice, so as not to startle the News Global viewers, Barnes Ward outlined the rest of the journey up Wisconsin Avenue to Washington National Cathedral. "And now we see, as expected, President Morrison's vehicle, along with an assemblage of protection presonnel, join in the somber line."

As the cortege proceeded up Wisconsin Avenue, Ward said, "It is further ironic that services for our nation's first African American president will occur not many yards from the sarcophagus of Woodrow Wilson—our twenty-eighth president. Wilson, as some historians point out, did much to slow the social integration of blacks that had begun to advance under President Theodore Roosevelt.

"We are told that the Reverend Mortimer Gurley will represent the African American Methodist-Episcopal congregation where President Williams often worshipped during his years in Washington. Traditional Protestant hymns and Gospel music will be performed by The People's Choir, a large group of men and women from all races and Christian faith walks. All living former presidents and their wives are expected to attend, and the cathedral will be a who's who of notables from around the world. President Morrison is expected to say a few words eulogizing his predecessor. As you might imagine, security will be tight, and the Secret Service will be ever-present. Afterward, the military escort will take the president's remains to Union Station, where Andrea Williams will accompany her husband back to Buffalo, New York, for interment there.

"Let's watch now as the services begin." Ward listened and watched along with his audience as *Eternal Father, Strong to Save* preceded the reverential prayers and blessings that rang through the cavernous, Indiana limestone edifice.

President Morrison rose and spoke of the qualities that made Averell Harriman Williams stand out among the leaders of his time.

"Above all," he said, "he was a man of the utmost decency and integrity, considerate of the First Lady, his staff, and his countrymen—to the point where he put the nation before his own health. For all of us who follow him, we must pledge ourselves to public lives of decency and integrity above all."

11.

Later in the afternoon, as the sun began its slow descent, Remy Carlson stood in her new office, the one that had been occupied until recently by Averell Williams's chief of staff, Sondra Thompson. As she gazed out her window, Carlson felt justifiably proud of her elevation to chief of staff to POTUS. Despite the early gray beginning to highlight her yellow hair, she knew she had accomplished much in her forty years.

That had been in part because she had made sure that over her five years as senior factotum to the then-vice-president, she knew where all the power buttons were in the West Wing. One she was never certain about, however, was the unusual closeness between her boss and Marty Cox.

Cox had a long and distinguished career as an agent with the Secret Service, the organization sworn to protect the president since McKinley's assassination in Buffalo, New York, in 1901. For nearly a fourth of those 111 years, Cox had been a rising star in the agency. Because of his age more than anything, he'd been assigned to Joe Morrison not long after the Williams–Morrison Administration began in 2008. She would have thought that once Morrison became president, he'd have opted for a younger, reflexively sharper cadre of men and women to protect him.

But no. Less than a week into the Morrison presidency, he made it clear to her that Cox was to remain on his detail. Not only that, Cox was her go-to guy for all security matters. Likable and competent though the Secret Service man might be, Carlson wasn't sure what their bond was all about. She snickered to herself that it sure wasn't sexual. She knew no men more masculine than Joe Morrison and Marty Cox. *But what was it all about?*

Carlson put it out of her mind when Cox appeared in view and passed her as he strode up to Freddie Frederick's desk and asked to see the president. After exchanging nods with Cox, she stopped to listen to his exchange with Freddie, the veteran keeper of the clock.

"Agent Cox, you know there's a protocol involved here. You don't just walk up and ask to see him."

"C'mon, Freddie. It's Marty, and I didn't come right off the boat, you know." He stuck his thumb in the air, pointing toward the Oval Office. "He called me. I think I'm expected."

Too professional to reveal her surprise, Freddie didn't skip a beat. She picked up the intercom phone and when Morrison answered, she said, "Agent Cox to see you sir." She put down the receiver, looked up at the tall, still blond specimen before her, and nodded toward the door without another word. At Carlson, she merely smiled, a quiet acquiescence to the new world order.

Cox walked up to the deeply inset door to the world's most powerful enclave, knocked lightly, and walked in.

"Come sit in the chair here, next to the desk," Morrison directed. His attention had been focused on the myriad of briefing books from the Departments of State, Defense, Treasury, and Justice, but his thoughts had been of his conversation with Andrea Williams, one that left him with warm acid in his throat, though he knew she could not have intended it.

"Joe," she had said, "I know Averell did not do well by you, and I hope you'll forgive him for treating you the way he did. In spite of what your feelings about him must be over these past years, I hope you'll do him—and me—one last favor. Help me plan a leave-taking from Washington that will be honorable and respectful, but not drawn out. I would hate that, and I think he would, too. Let us leave the city with dignity."

Morrison was only too happy to speed the Williams's exit from the public spotlight. He wanted no more reminders, from Andrea or anyone else, that by his predecessor's design, his vice-presidency had been the most leisurely of modern times. Morrison quietly vowed to secure his power, and that would begin by ensuring that Marty Cox eliminated any obstacles to that objective.

Cox sat down without taking airtime to speak. He waited for the new president to focus on him.

"You may not recall it, Marty, but this office has had microphones embedded in the walls and furniture since at least Lyndon Johnson's time." Morrison chuckled. "I'm having fun giving that warning to all my visitors—kinda like the warning on a pack of cigarettes."

"Yes, sir," Cox said, without laughing.

"All I wanted to say, since I'm not sure when we'll next have a chance for a word, is that when we last spoke, you may recall me mentioning there was one individual who required your special attention."

"You mean Dir—" Cox stopped when Morrison held up his hand, palm facing him. "Yes, sir, I believe my memory is the same as yours but I don't know if I can finish that assignment for you, Mr. President."

Joe Morrison caught the contempt and, yes, fear, nuanced in the man's words. "This is not optional, Marty. It is imperative that we both see things through to the end. After all, you have your family to consider, don't you?" The new president knew his words were loaded with meaning that would clamp Cox's insides in a vise.

"Family considerations are not part of this," he spoke firmly.

"Let's make sure that's not the case at all," Morrison responded, sure his listener heard all the messages in those words. "We're clear then?"

After a long pause, Cox said, "Clear."

"Soon, then?" Morrison asked, as if he were asking a clerk in a bookstore when a particular bestseller might arrive.

Cox did not respond, but rose from the chair and looked down at his boss from his six foot four inch height. When their eyes locked, he turned and walked out of the Oval Office.

❖

In Alexandria, Pete Clancy and the Gladstons labored over dinner preparation of a fresh salad, stuffed green peppers, and boiled potatoes. "A perfect dinner for the end of a blustery day," Paul said, while Mare chuckled and replied that it was difficult, food-wise, living with two guys.

"A nice piece of grilled salmon would do, once in a while," she needled. The trio then resumed what had become a daily exercise in friendly banter.

"You two have now been with me over six weeks, and, when my wife was here, I wouldn't have put up with guests for more even six days."

"Are you dropping us a hint, kind sir?" Mare asked.

"Not at all. Look, we have a fledgling business going here. We're getting more and more work, and you two are handling the lion's share of it. At the moment, I can't pay you what you're worth, quite frankly, but what we've agreed upon for now, and room and board works for me. Besides, it's convenient not to hunt for each other when a job calls."

"We're on the same page, Pete," Paul agreed. "We've been so busy with what you give us to do that, what with travel, it would be silly for us to live someplace else—that we can't afford right now—so as long as we're not in your way."

"But you're newly marrieds, and you need some privacy."

"You give us plenty," Mare said, "and living here hasn't stopped us from, ah, expressing ourselves."

"Could we get back to the salad, please?" Pete said, blushing, and they all laughed.

Something caught their attention on the flat screen TV attached to the wall across the island. It was tuned to News Global and the scene was at Union Station. Without anyone saying a word, they all began to watch.

To the near-ancient Harry Riordan, Washington, DC weather had always been a coin toss, and today was no different, he reminded himself, as his black Lincoln Town Car, a perk for the Senate majority leader, nosed its long hood close to the guard station at the foot of the

TurnAround

White House drive less than one hour after the funeral service for the late president. "One minute, you boil like a lobster in a steaming pot, and the next, you freeze your ass off!"

"Yes, sir," the driver said.

"Sorry, Jackson, I was talking to myself—a privilege of old age." Riordan coughed out a laugh. "Besides, I tell my colleagues it's the only way I can have an intelligent conversation anymore."

The driver chuckled and lowered his window to present credentials for Senator Riordan and himself. Waved in with a courtesy salute, the eight-year old Lincoln rolled with familiarity toward the entrance doors to the West Wing.

Riordan was dismayed that another vehicle was already there, one belonging to Angela Tesoro, former Speaker of the House and current nemesis to John Whitaker. Politics did, indeed, create strange bedfellows. Riordan steeled his game face. In a few minutes, he'd be talking to one of his altar boys—now the president of the United States—but, in so doing, he'd have to put up with Tesoro, Maryland's least attractive personality and a harridan of the first order. With the late President Williams not yet in the ground, Tesoro was in a hurry to shape the new power structure. Riordan shook his head, knowing how powerless she truly was.

Jackson opened his door into the subfreezing air, and Riordan stepped out, grasping his black wool Brooks Brothers overcoat as if it would ward off both the cold and Tesoro. He propelled his rickety frame across the five yards of asphalt and pavers and in the doors, where he walked through a metal detector and endured the wand, painful as it was to extend his arms, while the uniformed Secret Service Officer checked him out.

Off to the side stood the seemingly ever-present Marty Cox, the new president's favorite protective escort. He nodded to the tall blond machine, and ambled through the foyer. Glancing to his left, he noticed that the office of the vice-president was vacant. He nodded and smiled. Morrison had claimed his seat in the coveted, nonrectangular office up the hall.

In another few steps, Remy Carlson greeted him and took him to the anteroom where Congresswoman Tesoro waited. The two veteran

201

legislators and political combatants par excellence nodded and exchanged halfhearted greetings. The ensuing silence filled the space until Carlson, who had disappeared momentarily, returned to usher the pair into the world's most famous office.

In the Alexandria kitchen, the trio found themselves caught into the surreal scene unfolding.

"This is Barnes Ward, and here we are at one of the capital's landmarks, the venerable Union Station, a convenient distance from both the Capitol and the White House. It was built when travel to and from Washington was done by train, and even now, it is used daily by many thousands of travelers and workers in the city.

"Today, of course, it has the sad duty of hosting the final departure of President Averell Williams from the city and capital that loved him so well. Here we see what the police have estimated to be a crowd of over a hundred thousand people who have braved the end of another near-freezing Washington day to bid their leader a warm farewell.

"As you will see more clearly when the sun floats near the horizon and dusk is upon us, many thousands are carrying lit candles for this vigil. In moments, the hearse and honor guard will arrive for the transfer of the president's casket onto a special Amtrak train expected to leave the station shortly after six o'clock.

"Some have assumed that the president would be buried at Arlington National Cemetery. While many famous persons have been laid to rest in Arlington, including generals, justices of the Supreme Court, and senators and congressmen, only two presidents lie there: John F. Kennedy and William Howard Taft, the only man to serve as president and chief justice.

"We understand First Lady Andrea Williams took Arlington into consideration when these arrangements were being made, but she is reported to have said her husband's family had their start in Buffalo, New York, after the Civil War, and that is where he will go. Interestingly, he will be interred at Forest Lawn Cemetery on Delaware Avenue, where many of the city's mayors have gone to rest, and where another president, Millard Fillmore, is also buried."

The Oval Office seemed especially quiet as President Morrison walked forward to greet his former colleagues in the legislative branch and bid them to sit on either couch while he chose one of the leather side chairs favored by his predecessor. "How can I help my two old friends?" His tone was regal.

"It is we"—Tesoro glanced Riordan's way for a sign of support—"who are here to help you, Mr. President."

Morrison did not invite her to a first-name intimacy. He simply waited for her to continue.

"What I mean to say, Mr. President, is that Senator Riordan and I are prepared to assist you in the transition in any way possible. This is a terrible time for our country, one in which we should all unite to support your office."

"But not so terrible that we meet as President Williams is leaving town for the last time." Morrison paused. "Then I suppose," he continued, irony lacing his words, "that we should postpone this meeting until Speaker Whitaker can be present."

Riordan laughed out loud, his voice cranking up like an old engine. "Sir," he began and attempted to clear his throat of old cigar residue. "We, of course, would love to meet with John Whitaker to discuss your legislative agenda, but being of the same party, perhaps Angie had another purpose for our call."

Tesoro was slow to take the cue, known as she was to detest both Riordan and his young protégé. After a moment's hesitation, she said, "Well, Mr. President, you'll recall that when Gerald Ford assumed the office after Nixon's resignation, he was faced with the same historic choice now facing you."

"One of several, as I recall," Morrison said, baiting her.

"I meant, of course, his appointment of Nelson Rockefeller as vice-president."

"Sir," the pebble-strewn voice of Harry Riordan joined in, "you may also be aware this will only be the second time that Section Two of the Twenty-Fifth Amendment has been invoked. Already, you will go down in history as having been involved in three of the nine occasions the amendment has been called into action."

"And that means, I must nominate a candidate to be approved by both houses of Congress," Morrison said. "Rest assured, my friends, I have tutored myself in the nuances of the amendment's history over the past several weeks when it became clear it would be the subject of much discussion."

Riordan allowed himself a slight smile as he acknowledged his former acolyte's sudden constitutional acumen. "Then you will appreciate, Mr. President, that in times of potential crisis, such a candidate must be one who will immediately gather support from all quarters."

"And that is why you are here, I presume," Morrison answered, not looking directly at either of his visitors.

"Yes, it is, Mr. President." Tesoro said, her voice laced with anxiety.

The voice of Barnes Ward could barely be heard above the cadenced footfalls of the honor guard. "The silver-gray hearse has now arrived, as we can see, and First Lady Andrea Williams has left her limousine, escorted by a senior military officer, the Williams's not having any other immediate family. She is waiting patiently for the military body bearers—pall bearers as most people would call them—to begin their procession through Union Station's main entrance.

"As we began this portion of the coverage, someone mentioned to me that, with the dignitaries and royalty dismissed, the president has been turned over to the people for their own good-bye. Until now, this crowd, nearly half African American by all appearances, has been utterly quiet. The only sounds our microphones have picked up are the metal clicking and clacking one might expect as the rear door of the hearse opens and the removal of the casket takes place. The only other sound, as if in smart salute to a leader, has been the snap of the flags at half-mast around the station's plaza."

In the Alexandria kitchen, Paul and Mare were intent on the scene playing out, the only presidential funeral they'd ever seen.

"I am told that some in the crowd have begun to sing," Ward said onscreen. "But it is not a dirge or spiritual as some might expect. Let's listen." As the cameras zoomed in to capture the feeling of the throng, the mic picked up the words, "Nearer, my God, to thee, nearer to thee!"

There was no other sound. "E'en though it be a cross that raiseth me. Still all my song shall be nearer, my God, to Thee!"

"Most know this tune, as it was probably played and sung as the RMS Titanic went down in 1912," Ward whispered through the hymn.

"Though like the wanderer, the sun gone down. Darkness be over me, my rest a stone; Yet in my dreams I'd be nearer, my God, to thee..." The cameras caught the breaking voices, the glinting eyes, the streaming tears of a final farewell.

Angela Tesoro pressed on, politics as usual. "And that is why we have come to recommend that you seriously consider Former Secretary of State Emerson Grantham as your vice-president."

"Why am I not surprised," Morrison said—not asked—chortling through the words. "Tell me why he is the only candidate you both wish to put forward."

Riordan took command. "Mr. President, as Angie said, you need someone to help unite the country behind you, and Secretary Grantham, is respected by many. With the support of former President Harper, he will draw instant respect for your administration, both here and abroad."

Morrison's voice betrayed the absence of energy he felt for their proposal. "But Secretary Grantham deserted President Williams when he needed his stature to help insulate his policies from attacks arising out of the Benghazi mess, not to mention the rest of the Middle East. As I read the daily intelligence briefing, it seems we've been slow in acknowledging this ISIS group—the offshoot of al Qaeda. That will be next year's crisis, I'm guessing, and I will have Secretary Grantham to thank for it. I'm not sure those are factors that recommend the secretary."

Tesoro looked as if she'd been slapped. Her jaw visibly tightened. "But Mr. President," she stammered, "he is a foremost policy expert in so many areas, and—"

"May be of immense benefit to us should my administration need his advice."

"Mr. President," Riordan said, returning to the fray, "we hope you will not dismiss his candidacy out of hand."

"No, I will not, Harry. Grantham is not the only one deserving consideration." Morrison paused.

Riordan at last discerned what Morrison's main consideration: he wanted no competitor in 2016—least of all Emerson Grantham.

Tesoro smiled with pleasant sanctimony.

"I believe that the American people want this to be a thoughtful choice, not one of mere convenience, and certainly not one that would ignite a party fight in a race over three years away," Morrison said. "Toward that end, I believe that appointing you, Harry, and your counterpart in the House, Speaker Whitaker, to head a committee before which a number of candidates are brought forward and considered will be seen as the most democratic approach." He paused to look Tesoro's way. "But don't worry, Angela, you will always have your say." Morrison glanced at the grandfather clock striking the hour.

Riordan and Tesoro rose and, after a word or two of appropriate leave-taking, retraced their steps out to their waiting limos. Riordan could not restrain himself, however. "There is definitely a new game in town."

"Yes, there is, Harry, but *this* goddam Texan cannot be allowed to master it."

"This is Forbes Flannery, and you are now entering *The FactZone*, where journalists report the facts so that the decision in the voting booth is all yours. And it's the voting booth that I want to talk about tonight." Flannery's silver-gray hair gleamed in the studio lights as his intense blue eyes targeted the red dot under the camera lens.

"There is news out of Ohio these past few days that tells a most interesting story about last fall's presidential election. Although calls have not been returned from Republican Governor Ted McNickle or Ohio's secretary of state, Kathlyn Hopkins, a Democrat, sources in Columbus tell us that over two dozen precincts in Ohio—from Cincinnati, Portsmouth, and the Cleveland areas—all show huge voting disparities. Specific figures are not yet publicly available, but it appears that while the total number of votes coming out of each precinct and country are correct, there are vast differences between the party split reported by Columbus and how the votes were actually cast.

"Please take note, ladies and gentlemen, that this is not to disparage Ms. Hopkins or her office, but it is to suggest that after voters cast their ballots, an unknown person or persons tampered with voter choice in such a way as to shift large percentages of votes to the late President Williams and away from his challenger, Governor Hardy of Colorado.

"If Ohio did not actually vote for the Williams–Morrison ticket, then what about Virginia, Florida, and Colorado?" Flannery intoned his words with sadness. "It is a distinct possibility that the late president and the current incumbent did not actually win the White House this past November 6.

"It is truly unfortunate that this news has to break so soon after we lay to rest a president beloved by so many. His funeral in the Capitol and the interment ceremonies in Buffalo told the world the degree to which the man was revered. Quite frankly, it is difficult for this reporter to believe that Averell Harriman Williams, a man who worked his way into the Oval Office from truly humble beginnings, would have sullied his record with the vote fraud apparently perpetrated upon the American people.

"All of this leaves *The FactZone* with two questions, the answers to which the voters demand to know. First, if fraud was committed, who is responsible? Second, if President Williams did not win a second term, there is no President Morrison, and what do we do about it?"

John Whitaker sat in Pete Clancy's South Fairfax Street living room and took his gaze from the screen to speak to his host. "That was the first salvo."

"You've spoken to McNickle then?"

"Yes, and his office dropped it in News Global's lap. He and Hopkins are at odds—as you would expect—but the evidence is clear and convincing. Although she is fighting him on the matter, he will insist via emergency legislation, if necessary, that the entire state be immediately and thoroughly canvassed."

"But for the end result to be conclusive, would you have to have paper ballots to compile in each precinct?"

"Correct—and that's the problem. There won't be extant paper ballots in each precinct. Most will have been destroyed, but we are going to push the point as far as it will go."

"But, John, even if Ohio's eighteen votes truly went for Hardy, that doesn't change the result of the election," Clancy said.

"You're right. The electoral vote was 332 to 206. That's a difference of 126, which means that 64 votes have to switch."

"OK, so that's Ohio and...?"

"Virginia, Florida, and, from there, either New Mexico's five or Colorado's nine would give it to Hardy," Whitaker said.

Clancy eyed his companion in wonder.

"Nothing to be impressed about, old friend. It's my job to count noses—and electoral votes. So now we have to get some things going in those other states, and I'm working on that now."

"Why? Even if every state tumbles Hardy's way, the electoral votes have been cast and certified by, by *you*, for Christ's sake, and the Senate. You can't make a pickle back into a cucumber. We know Morrison did all this and committed murder to boot—why not go after him on that?"

Whitaker shifted his posture so that he and Pete were eye-to-eye, their faces not two feet apart. "Where are the kids?"

"Out. The Warners decided to sneak out to a movie. It's a test run."

"Good. Here's what I want to do. One way or the other, we will create enough pressure on Morrison to resign, which will put his vice-president—when he names one—in the seat. That will avoid a constitutional crisis the country does not need."

Clancy was furious. "Spoken like a true politician. Jesus Christ, John. Williams and Morrison had no right to take their oaths of office last month, much less occupy them! So, to hell with a vice-president of Morrison's choice. One tainted apple gets to choose another? Bullshit. We need to get Morrison out of office before he has a chance to anoint Emerson Grantham or anyone else as president. Maybe before he has a chance to commit another murder."

"Christ, keep your shirt on! You're right on all counts, but there's a problem with all that clear-cut logic."

"What's that?"

"I guess you don't remember the law, my friend."

MARCH

12.

" **F** ebruary is gone, Mr. President, and the country wants to know your plans for a vice-president." Shelly Ingber dived right in after the ritual pleasantries in an Oval Office where he now felt like he might not fit. Unseasonably warm weather had greeted him on the morning walk with his spaniel, and he supposed the sixty-degree temp was perfect for the last of the tulips, the azaleas all around, and possibly the cherry trees around the tidal basin. Nevertheless, his entry into Joe Morrison's new domain was like a face splash of ice water on a cold morning.

Ingber had served the previous occupant of this room for four years, and, before that, in high offices from Albany to Washington. No stranger to political egos, he was nonetheless shocked at how quickly the Oval Office had changed, from paintings to furniture and sculpture. The Remington was gone, and he suspected the fabled Resolute desk might soon be consigned to a General Services Administration warehouse. He was surprised most by the look in Morrison's eye when he addressed the political matter.

"I can read a fuckin' calendar, Mr. Ingber, and please don't join the Riordan and Tesoro parade to rush me into a marriage with Emerson Grantham. Those two couldn't even wait a day after Williams's funeral before they pounced with their uninvited advice."

Ingber winced at the reference to his former client and idol—not even a warm mention of the man's first name or the courtesy of his title. "I understand, sir, but it has been eight days since the president's death, and I did not come here to pressure you into Emerson Grantham or anyone else. I was thinking only of 2016."

Morrison exhaled. "You're right on that score, Shelly. Sorry I barked at you. Sit down." He waited until Williams's campaign manager was comfortable. "So that you know my thinking, here's why I don't want Grantham anywhere near me for the next three years."

"I'll think I understand your mindset, sir," Ingber said. "Emerson Grantham was a part of a previous administration, and you believe that a number of the world issues you've inherited—Iraq, Afghanistan, North Korea, Israel and Hamas, and Putin—to name a few—are on somebody else's scorecard. You do not want your administration identified with Grantham, the architect of the policies that got us where we are."

"Nicely put. The fact is—and I don't want to put you on the spot here—Averell Williams was the real architect of those lead-from-behind policies around the world, but it's in our best interests to let the public think Grantham—the presidential wannabe—was the man who made our bed for us," Morrison said with disdain.

Ingber smiled at the man's acumen for political intrigue. "Right again, Mr. President. Fostering that image will keep Grantham out of 2016, and that's the best of all worlds."

"Call me Joe when we're alone, Shelly. We'll work better together that way, and I like my friends to call me Joe."

Ingber cringed at the word, "friend," but he had one more presidential race in him, and, distasteful though it was, Joe Morrison was a Democrat and, for the most part, that was all that mattered. He told himself he'd have to swallow a lot of bile, but it could be worth it. "Why, thanks, Joe. I look forward to working for your reelection. And one thing that will help it, if I may, will be to pick the right VP."

"Anybody you have in mind?"

"Our party has always been in the forefront of inclusiveness—at least the public thinks so—so why not steal a march on the Republicans. They surprised us all in choosing Olivia Johnson Smith the last time, so we need either a female or, certainly, a Latino."

"No gays, Shelly."

"Excuse me?"

"You heard me. I may be a Democrat, but there's no reason to get that far out in front of the public."

"Perhaps. So let's see, then. With you being from the west, it's not such a big deal anymore to balance a ticket geographically, but to some in a close election, why push the envelope, eh?" Ingber continued. "Senator Marta Rodriguez from Florida—"

"Two southerners?"

"You may have a point there—we'll poll test that whole question. I take it Angela Tesoro is not on your short list?" Ingber asked with a chuckle.

"Oh, Christ, don't even mention that woman's name. I'm not Catholic, but her husband must be ready for sainthood."

"Then how about Senator Sharps Washington from New Jersey?"

"Ah, a black? Hey, that's not a bad idea. He will keep the entire northeast in our pocket. They'll be loyal to Williams, that's for sure. And once again, we'll lock up that vote."

Ingber enjoyed his newest client's convenient memory. As one of the few to tumble to Joe Morrison's complicity in stealing the last election, hearing him talk about the African American vote as if it couldn't be managed anyway was a presidential memory trick he planned to file away. "For sure. We don't want the Republicans to take even five percent of it."

"OK, Shelly, we're on the same page. Obviously, we need to talk again, but why not quietly check out Washington and Rodriguez? I'm in no hurry to appoint anybody, but we have two or three weeks, anyway. Let's have Jack Sennett float a few names to our buddies in State Media, and that'll keep interest up without us having to make a rash decision."

"Sure thing."

"Oh, and make sure they're clean. No dirt of any kind."

"You bet," Ingber said. "Speaking of dirt, what do you plan to do about the IRS, Benghazi, and the VA stuff stinking up the place?"

"All of it is bullshit. So we screwed up in Benghazi—they can all piss up a rope for all I care. That's done. As far as the IRS is concerned, they better figure out how to not get caught again. Those people aren't that sharp, so you may have to help them. As to the VA crap, that's all it is as far as I'm concerned. Get with Riordan and Angela Testosterone and cook up a deal with Whitaker and Jordan for more money for vets.

Maybe we can all look good on this one." Morrison paused. "Look, Shelly, you, Remy, Jack, and the rest of the crew need to make all this stuff go away."

"Got it, chief," Ingber responded, all the while thinking Richard Nixon would have been proud of Joe Morrison.

"The key thing is that what happened before November 6 is ancient history and doesn't matter. Right?"

Ingber nodded, hoping Morrison's convenient memory might somehow become reality.

The sun skulked behind the clouds, showing its face only occasionally as Friday crept toward noon. Mare and Paul had been out for a morning run, showered, and left again, but returned to the South Fairfax Street enclave with a promised lunch of Red Octobers, chips, and soda.

"I didn't know you could get these here in DC," Paul said, referring to the wrapped, warm sandwiches in the bag he carried.

"A Pennsylvania refugee, no doubt," Clancy said.

"What's on these, anyway, and do we need a defibrillator?" Mare teased.

"If you'd grown up near Clintonville, Pennsylvania, dear lady, you'd have a passion for thinly sliced ham, salami, provolone, chipped lettuce, tomatoes, light onion, Italian dressing, all lightly toasted," Paul said.

"Jesus, you sound like a commercial," Mare said.

"You need to clean that mouth before you eat with it," Paul retorted.

"OK, lovebirds, let's not let the honeymoon be over already," Clancy said. "Rather than talk about the sandwiches, let's eat the damn things while they're still warm, and tell me about your gig with Warner last night."

"You want a full written report?" Paul asked.

"Nah," Clancy responded. "Enough to know how much to charge him." He gave his employees a Cheshire grin.

"So much for friendship," Mare teased.

"Friendship, hell. We gotta eat," Clancy said. "How else can we afford these gourmet lunches?"

Everyone chewed.

"So tell me about it already."

"Well, it was straightforward enough," Mare began. "Mr. and Mrs. Warner wanted to see some indie movie in downtown Alexandria, and we went with them."

"Well, not with them, exactly. We were three rows behind them," Paul said. "This was at the Alexandria Old Town—"

"Yeah, I know it," Clancy said. "It was refurbed at the end of 2012, and it's a pretty nice venue. Four hundred seats, though, and hard to check out."

"You got that right," Paul agreed. "I went to the earlier show to look around and check the restrooms, exits, and every door that opened. The manager was a little spooked by the whole thing. It looked OK, but protecting people in theaters would not be my choice of an easy gig, let me tell you."

"Ditto," Mare said. "There were about seventy-five or eighty people there, a helluva lot for this Polish war film, *Remembrance*, the ending of which left me guessing, I might add."

"Never mind the movie. It's about the holocaust. Drew's wife is ethnically Polish and a Jew by religion—that's probably why she got him to go," Clancy said.

"Wow—now there's a combination," Mare said. "He's an African American Catholic and she's a Polish Jew. Talk about a clash of cultures!"

"It has worked for them for over thirty years," Clancy said. "About the movie, though. The fact that this was a spur of the moment thing is both good and bad."

"Meaning?" Mare wanted to know.

"Meaning that with no prior planning," Clancy said, "the event had no chance to be leaked, even accidentally, so the likelihood of an attack would be low. It's when more people are involved in a far more public venue that the risk goes up."

"You mean like this thing we're supposed to do at the Kennedy Center in a few days," Paul said.

"Like that," said Clancy. "Hey, let's catch the noon news to make sure the world didn't end."

"Funny," Mare said cautiously. "OK, let's see what Lew Michaels has to say."

On the screen of the kitchen TV, the newscaster offered his polished, prepared prose in the measured tones his viewers enjoyed. "This town is abuzz with the full-court press the GOP is putting on this administration, fledgling though it is. Not only are the hearings continuing on the IRS and Benghazi—if those two weren't enough to garner attention—now Speaker Whitaker has added concerns about VA treatment of veterans."

"Thank you, Lew," said Meredith Ramirez, working the noon slot. "Can you tell me more about the VA charges?"

"Here's all I know, Meredith," Michaels said into his lapel mic. "A number of congressmen and senators have received letters from veterans around the country complaining about long waits to see doctors, cancelled appointments, and, worst of all, allegations that some vets committed suicide while waiting to see their VA psychiatrists."

"Is this systemic or confined to one or a few locations?" Meredith asked.

"It's too early to say. What we've heard is that here in Washington, Walter Reed has had some of these issues—ironically, they began to surface when the late President Williams was a patient there—and then, in the Speaker's own district, the VA in Cincinnati is said to be plagued with these same problems."

"Thanks, Lew. Dare we move on to the loudest whispers of all?" Meredith asked. "About election fraud? First, we heard a few days ago that Ohio may well have voted for Governor Hardy, and those eighteen electoral votes should have gone in the other column. Then, we began to hear that other key states—Florida, Virginia, New Mexico, and Colorado might have had their electoral votes stolen as well. If true, ladies and gentlemen, then we—the American people—did not elect Averell Williams president of the United States on November 6.

"Worse"—Meredith's voice rose, filling the air—"word has begun to come to this desk from a number of sources that, not only was there widespread election fraud in November 2012, but that President Morrison was a key player in orchestrating that fraud. Those are big charges, but, if true, they will certainly heighten the intensity of conversation about impeachment. Wow! Talk about a series of developments over the past forty-five days that no Hollywood scriptwriter would have dared pitch. Well, keep it right here, ladies and gentlemen, because it will be here at News Global that we'll give you all the news."

The atmosphere in the kitchen became quiet despite the News Global commercials pounding the volume level.

"I guess that was the second shot," Clancy muttered, erasing the silence.

"What?" Mare asked.

"Forbes Flannery's piece about Ohio the other day was the first," Clancy said. "This is the second."

"Like in a game plan?" Paul wanted to know.

"Yeah. Something like that," Clancy said, still preoccupied.

Mare didn't wait. "C'mon, Pete. You're holding out on us. What the hell is going on?"

Clancy exhaled. "I guess if anybody has a right to know, you two do. Let's see. How do I put this in context?" He paused to frame his words. "The American people, you know, haven't changed much in two hundred years—with one big exception. We've always been led by the nose—even in Jefferson's time—and in the first hundred years or so, it was because good political speakers wound our clocks, and newspapers of every stripe whipped people into the frenzy of the day."

"Oh, God, is this another of your history lessons?" Mare teased.

"It is, but one you should know," Clancy responded, rubbing his jaw in thought. "Otherwise, you won't understand what's happening around you in your time." He took a breath and looked directly at his students. "With the advent of technology—newspapers, the telegraph, then the telephone, the Atlantic cable, radio, television, computers, cell phones, and all their spinoffs—did I miss anything?—we've become more and more attuned to the immediacy of information, and the faster we get it, the more we want." He cleared his throat.

"An unfortunate side effect is that with all the information coming at us, our grasp of it is becoming shallow," Clancy said. "Our sound-bite mentality has translated into how we view each other, as well as the icons of our time—they're prettier and prettier, more and more telegenic. We even attempt to design our children, weeding out imperfection and impurity—our definition of ugliness."

"Where are we going with this, Pete?" Mare's brow wrinkled.

"Now—whether we want to accept it or not—we have become so much the victims of peer pressure news that, well let me give you a few examples. I know this is unpopular, but I'm waiting for some grad student to do a study of all the photos of George W. Bush that were published by our one national newspaper during his eight years in office. I swear they found darn near every ugly frame of film and used it as his facial photo in their news stories about his administration."

"So? What of it?" asked Paul.

"So, over a number of years, if you were repeatedly shown unflattering photos of a prominent person, don't you think that would subliminally affect your opinion of that individual?"

"Maybe," Paul said.

"No 'maybe' about it, because we already accept the notion that if you repeatedly see favorable ads about cereals, cars, or people, you will develop favorable views of whatever the marketers have been trying to sell you."

"Yeah, and?"

"Wouldn't you suppose the opposite must be true—ala George Bush, for example?" Clancy asked.

"I liked President Bush," Mare said, "but that's a stretch."

"If every news outlet—except News Global—every newspaper, most opinion makers, Hollywood stars, late-night TV hosts—if they all derided him, mocked him, and denigrated him, don't you think even some hardened Republicans would begin to have their doubts?"

"I suppose so," Mare said.

"The same with his positions and policies, wouldn't you say?"

"What does all of this have to do with Morrison?" Paul insisted.

"That's easy," Clancy said. "For over four years now, the majority of opinion molders in this country, admittedly leaning to the left—have been shaping our views of Averell Williams and Joe Morrison pretty favorably, wouldn't you agree?"

"Definitely," both Mare and Paul said at the same time.

"So that means there's a strong reserve of good opinion about Morrison, even if it's transference from Williams, or a desire for the country to unite behind the president, even if he had been considered a gaff-prone lightweight in some quarters."

"OK, so then what?"

"What that means is that, right now, it would be hard to make a direct attack on this man, because public sentiment would not warmly receive criticism of Joe Morrison unless it was really bad stuff. Do you see what I mean?"

"Go on," Paul said, looking at Mare.

"In other words, right now, Joe Morrison can do no wrong, and, at the moment, the public might agree with the president—the IRS, Benghazi, and the VA garbage all happened under another president, and we should all let bygones be bygones. That's what State Media wants us to think."

"Yeah, I see that," Paul said.

"So, it will take a little time and some hard work for the media types to walk away from their love fest into the cold dawn, and see the evil that's really there."

"So it *is* a game plan," Mare said.

"Of sorts. Like a striptease. The American people need to see a little more every few days, and, pretty soon, they won't be able to take their eyes off it."

"Wow," Mare said, "that's really cynical, Pete."

"You think? Listen, little one, that's how the other side has been playing us all along, and we all fall for it. We go for the name, for the personality, for the glitz, even when it makes no sense whatsoever."

"Oh, c'mon, Pete, that really is over the top," Paul said.

"Oh, really? Let me give you two—a couple of so-called conservatives—but one example. Whenever you hear somebody went to Harvard, Yale, Columbia—to name three—you're really impressed, like whoever you're talking about is somebody we should pay attention to."

"People are impressed by those schools," Mare said. "What's wrong with that?"

"What's wrong with it is they are, reputedly, extremely liberal institutions that don't even keep up a pretense of teaching history, philosophy, or sociology in any kind of balanced manner—moderates and conservatives at these places are as rare as Christians in Mecca. If that's true, many of their grads likely carry, espouse, and spread the same distorted points of view. So why the hell are people still impressed with that bunch of biased, one-sided bastards?"

"I get your point," Mare said. "I never thought of it that way."

"Am I naïve to think that in spite of everything, the American people still elected Bush twice?" Paul asked. "Even if you want to debate 2000, there was no question about 2004?"

"But look what happened in the next two elections—look what State Media did for the liberals they loved, and then to the Republicans?" Clancy said. "Hell, they even jumped into one of the debates to side with Williams."

"So you're telling me we're playing a waiting game with Morrison?" Mare asked.

"Yes, I guess that's what I'm saying."

"And we have to wait," Mare couldn't help herself, "because Joe Morrison is the president and State Media is still on a honeymoon? Jesus H. Christ!"

"I don't think the good Lord has anything to do with this," Paul said.

"Right," Clancy agreed.

"At least, there's nobody else Morrison needs to kill," Mare concluded.

Jordy Marshall skipped his greeting. "Are we meeting here in the Speaker's office so I didn't have to go to the other building? If so, I thank you for considering this old man's legs."

"We are meeting here," Speaker Whitaker said, taking a serious tone, "because it's the biggest deal you and I will likely face in our political lives."

Marshall raised his eyebrows in question. "You know, John, I've been around this place so long, nothing is 'the biggest deal' anymore. Please pardon me for not getting too excited."

"Look, you old Kentucky scoundrel, we've got to handle this exactly right, or they'll put one over on us again."

"So give me the script, but don't call me 'old.'"

"In a few minutes that truly old scoundrel, Harry Riordan and his pal"—Whitaker traced the last two words with sarcasm—"Angela Tesoro will be here. I told them you and I had something we needed to talk about. They probably think it's about immigration or health care, so they're in for the shock of their political lives."

"How do you want to approach this?"

"I'm going to lay it out, piece by piece, and, whether they agree or not, one of our people will draw up a bill of impeachment while a lot of this is leaked to the media," Whitaker said.

"Why do you want to leak it?"

"We need people shocked and pissed off. Otherwise, Morrison will stay in office, and God knows what will come next from that crazy bastard."

"OK, I'm on board, but you know what this will look like."

"Yeah, I know." Whitaker looked up as one of the wood-paneled double doors opened to reveal Missouri's ancient majority leader and Maryland's former Speaker parade in. Riordan made no pretense of chivalry and entered first.

"It's into the spider's web we go," Tesoro said, her only deliberate attempt at humor.

Whitaker laughed, not to be baited. "The same web you spun a few years ago, Angie." They all laughed, even Tesoro.

"To what Republican thrust do we owe the honor to parry?" Riordan's cement mixer growl brought the meeting to its point. He sat, his white, wispy hair in free-range mode.

"I suppose I ought to start, inasmuch as it will be in the House that action is begun," Whitaker said.

At once alert and unwilling to wait for Whitaker to complete his thought, Angela Tesoro demanded, "What action?"

"You must never have played in Little League, Angie," Marshall said. "Sometimes you have to stand in the outfield and wait for it."

"When I was a girl, we weren't allowed to play in Little League with the boys. Now, I play with the boys all the time," she said, satisfaction gleaming in her eyes. She hadn't realized the double meaning of her words until she said them, but it was too late to beat Riordan to the punch.

"I do hope that there is no recording of Mrs. Tesoro's startling confession. Is there?" He raised is right eyebrow in mock concern, and tried to smooth his rumpled suit.

"Oh, for God's sakes, Harry," Tesoro said, "would you cut the bullshit for five minutes and remember who you came with."

"Oh, I remember, and my colleague has a point," Riordan said, looking at his Republican hosts. "What's all this about?"

"Impeachment of the president," Whitaker stated without preamble or varnish. "I think you two should both sit down," he said to both, but principally to Tesoro. "The question is, should we impeach him for complicity in the five murders he committed or, if that is too much for the American people, just the crime of fixing the 2012 national election?"

Tesoro was breathless. Her lips began to move, but no words came out for a few seconds. "You can't be serious, John. This is overreach. Why—"

Riordan lightly placed his gnarled hand on Tesoro's left sleeve, and she stopped in midsentence. "I've heard some bits about, shall we say," he said, and cleared the stony mud from his throat, "voting irregularities." He ended his thought abrptly to avoid words suggestive of murder.

"But it's no surprise to you, Harry, is it?" queried Whitaker, without giving away to Tesoro their earlier conversation indicating at least a tenuous connection between Morrison, fraud, and the killing of SoftSec's owner, Ricky McCord.

"No, I suppose not," Riordan acknowledged weakly. "But what I heard some time back was speculation, and now you're talking about five people?" Even with the mildest exertion, Riordan's face grew cherry red.

Whitaker saw that his words found their target with Riordan, an old-time politico and always a Democrat, but never one to put party above country. "Let's see if I can lay all of this out—it's complicated and elusive, but it's there. First, we have compelling evidence that Joe Morrison cultivated a relationship with Enrique McCord, owner of SoftSec. With a little digging, I'm sure we can demonstrate that Morrison's courting of McCord goes back to last spring—maybe March or April of 2012. Why and how it happened is anybody's guess." As he spoke, he looked directly at Riordan's chiseled face. The man's eyes were nearly buried in a sea of wrinkled skin. Riordan was in the room, to be sure, but his mind floated elsewhere.

"McCord somehow secured a contract with the US Election Assistance Commission," Whitaker said. "Soon, we'll know the answers to these two questions: how did Morrison meet McCord, and how did McCord get on the USEAC's radar? How this contract was ever allowed is beyond me, but it purported to let SoftSec 'monitor' vote counts in a number of states, ostensibly to ensure against vote fraud. Maybe the fact that, in 2012, the USEAC reported directly to Morrison had something to do with it."

"And you're telling me fraud occurred anyway. We can put a stop to that, John!" Tesoro said.

"It's all over now," Whitaker said. "The real purpose of the contract—not as it was let by the USEAC—was to get between the local precincts and the state capitals and their secretaries of state—and that allowed the votes cast to be redistributed electronically to achieve the end Morrison wanted."

"But why would he be so hot to get reelected as vice-president? My God, John, that idea alone argues against it." Tesoro was on a roll. "Williams didn't pay ten cents worth of attention to Morrison and with good reason—Jesus, did I just say that?—so why would Morrison be so willing to go out on a limb to get Williams reelected?"

"That is the question of the hour, isn't it?" Whitaker responded, while Harry Riordan and Jordy Marshall nodded in unison. "It's almost as if he knew Williams might not live."

"That's crazy, John! How the hell would he know that?"

Whitaker shrugged his shoulders. "I don't have to supply a reason, Angie. Those are the facts, however."

"Not so fast," she said, her partisan vigor returning. "What you've said is grist for the right-wing media, not for the courts. Do you have anything more? You said something equally preposterous about murder?"

"Take a breath, Angela. Let the man speak." It was Riordan, surprisingly.

"Oh, believe me, the proof of a relationship between Morrison and McCord is there," Whitaker said. "The contract existed. The method to pervert the vote is easy enough to demonstrate. Proof that it occurred already exists aplenty in Ohio, and samplings from other key states show the same thing."

"The alleged murders?" Tesoro persisted.

"Let's do this chronologically," Whitaker began. "As part of the vetting process for the USEAC contract I mentioned, SoftSec's McCord and his people underwent background investigations by OPM's contractor, NIS. The girlfriend of a key SoftSec employee, a guy named Conaway, reported to the NIS people—one of whom was an investigator named Nelson Evers—that Conaway bragged to her about McCord's relationship with Morrison and that plans were underway to fix the election."

His three listeners remained silent.

"At about the same time, according to a personal source I have with NIS, Evers spent some time at the IRS's Covington facility and got a clue, first hand, that the allegations Jordy Marshall received from one of his conservative constituents was likely true: the IRS was indeed targeting conservative organizations and denying their nonprofit status."

"So where is this going?" Tesoro demanded.

"According to my source, Evers was about to make some noise about the IRS mess in Covington—along with allegations that the election was going to be fixed," Whitaker continued. "Shortly thereafter, Evers was run down and killed at a Frisch's restaurant in my district. Witnesses said it was a black Tahoe with out-of-state plates. That was in the summer of 2012, but no one noticed a connection, except some people with NIS."

"Why didn't the NIS or OPM people take this forward?" It was Tesoro looking for a goat.

"We know that NIS took the allegation of potential fraud to OPM, and OPM presumably reported it upward," Whitaker said.

"To whom?" Tesoro demanded.

Riordan remained silent, but a slight smile creased his ancient lips.

"If you check the chain of command, Angie, that report would have gone to Vice-President Joseph P. Morrison."

"Oh my God!" Tesoro's eyes wandered into the distance as if contemplating doom itself.

"Stay with me now, because it gets thicker," Whitaker said. "Not long after Evers's murder, Conaway's girlfriend—her name was Bustamente—reported to the NIS people that a black Tahoe with Virginia plates was watching her apartment. Driving the car was a tall man with a blond crew cut."

"There are a lot of black Tahoes around," Tesoro said weakly.

"On the night of the election, Ricky McCord left his office when the race was called in favor of Williams," Whitaker raced on. "On his way home, somebody ran him off the road, killing him. The police put it down to some sort of road-rage thing. There were no witnesses."

"A crazy coincidence," Tesoro protested.

"Because it was a hit-and-run, the police did as much evidence processing as they could. Even though McCord's Mercedes became a fireball when the car exploded, the rear bumper and a quarter panel blew off intact. Forensics people recovered fresh black paint slivers that tied it to a black Tahoe."

Tesoro sat, stunned.

"The two principal NIS investigators who developed and reported the fraud in the first place felt it necessary to escape Cincinnati and Columbus in the middle of the night. They were chased by a black Tahoe, and, at one point, they saw the man driving it," Whitaker said. "He had a blond crew cut."

Riordan sank in the leather chair, his breath becoming labored.

"Though the NIS pair went off the grid for a few months, the driver of the Tahoe learned where they were. The NIS people recorded his Virginia plate number—a car logged to the US Secret Service."

"Jesus!" was all Tesoro could manage.

"It gets better, Angie. While doing some private investigative work on this VA scandal, they were at Walter Reed when the president was there recovering from surgery. When Morrison entered the lobby on one of his visits, the man closest to him in his protection detail was overly tall and had a blond crew cut."

"Is that all?"

"There's more. Not long ago, CIA Director Warner and his wife were at Tyson's Corner doing some shopping and they were almost run down in the parking lot by a large SUV. Black paint bits extracted from the director's overcoat matched it to a black Tahoe."

"He would kill someone here in Washington?" Tesoro seemed stunned that such was possible within the beltway. "Someone is responsible for all this! Those NIS people—they should have taken it all the way."

"Apparently, they did," Riordan said. "And OPM took it to the very man who could squelch anything or anybody pointing to him." His voice dropped to a whisper. "And to think...,"

Whitaker's voice was flat. "There are indications that both Evers and the head of NIS tried to leak this to higher-ups and the media, but nobody paid attention to something they must have thought so vile as to be impossible."

Tesoro awoke from her daymare. "We can't let the government change hands this way," she said. "The solution is simple. Morrison names a vice-president and resigns, ala Nixon. Whether Morrison is further prosecuted, I'll leave to others to manage. Then we can all go on and put this in the past."

Riordan looked at his party companion as if she'd had too long a drag on a roll of pot. He turned away from her and his opposites and stared at the wall.

"Not a chance, Angie," Marshall said, his jowls moving in rhythm. "In the first place, it appears that Williams and Morrison were never legitimately elected, so that's number one. In the second place, I'll be Kentucky-damned if I let that lowlife son of a bitch have a constitutional privilege he has no right to have—and to give that prerogative to a murderer will never happen."

"Then what's the alternative?" Tesoro began, spewing sarcasm with her words. "Are we to sit down and tell the American people that we need a quick do-over? Do we call Governor Hardy, and, like they say in Senator Marshall's home state, 'Y'all c'mon down'? So I ask again, oh, you men so smart, what are our choices?"

Riordan sat up and eyed Whitaker directly. "It's all up to you, John. If you initiate a Bill of Impeachment, then you'll have to lay all your cards out there." He cleared his throat. "As stunned as I am by what you've said, nearly all of it is hearsay and conjecture—what you say follows a logical thread, but it doesn't make it a fact."

"To me," Tesoro hurried to say, "It's the biggest power grab in history, and you'll never get me to vote for it."

"Not exactly, Angela," Marshall piped in.

"How do you mean?"

"The 2012 election and Joe Morrison—it doesn't get much bigger than that."

"Senator Marshall, Senator Marshall," a CNS reporter called out. "Is it true, sir, that the Republicans in the House are considering impeachment action against President Morrison?" The woman didn't wait for an answer. "Is it also true, Senator, that Republicans want Morrison out, so they can somehow claim the White House?"

A man used to the badgering and baiting of unfriendly media pundits, Marshall immediately perceived that the CNS reporter would be more effective at spreading information than he could ever be. With an evident sense of drama, he paused on the Capitol steps and faced his questioner. "What is true, Ms. Cole, is that if the leadership in the US House of Representatives takes up a bill of impeachment, it is likely there is sufficient evidence to do so, and it will be presented before the American people. As you know, however, it is one thing to be impeached by the House—which your audience should understand is like being indicted—and another thing entirely to be convicted by the Senate."

"It has been alleged, Senator," she continued, clearly oblivious to the answer, "that President Morrison, barely in office a few weeks, may have orchestrated the greatest theft of a national election in our history. Can you comment on that, sir?"

"No, I cannot. As I said, the Senate will take up the matter if the president is impeached by the House, and not before then."

"Do you have any comment, Senator, on former Speaker Tesoro's claim that charges of election fraud and other high crimes are a total falsehood? That whatever has been alleged is no more fraudulent than what the Bush campaign perpetrated in 2000?"

"If Speaker Tesoro mentioned other high crimes," he answered, with a slight emphasis on the word, *other*, "you'll have to seek elaboration on that point from the lady herself." He offered the camera a slight smile. "As to her comment about the 2000 election, I must say that the Speaker's wanderings into the land of hyperbole stun the imagination. You are well aware, Ms. Cole, that every investigation of the 2000 election, including one by a major cable network—was that yours?—and two national newspapers, all with liberal reputations, erased all doubt that George Bush was the duly elected president of the United States."

"Speaker Tesoro also says that, had he lived, the Republican Party would have tried to take down America's first black president."

"One has only to hear charges of that kind to understand why Americans are so polarized. A plain fact should be acknowledged. The late president is no longer in office, and to my knowledge, Republicans had no plan whatsoever to impeach him. On the other hand, what remains to be seen is whether the man now in the Oval Office was properly elected to anything at all on November 6, 2012."

"Those are strong words, Senator, and the American people will want you to back them up."

"I understand, Ms. Cole, that Senate Majority Leader Riordan has declined all comment on this matter, and I now join him in that wise approach."

13.

Joe Morrison wondered if Averell Williams ever found the Oval Office lonely on a Sunday night. Presumably, Freddie Frederick and Remy Carlson were enjoying the few hours they had to themselves before another high-stress week in the West Wing. *I know next to nothing about their personal lives.* He roamed the halls alone. *Thank God, if there is one, they know nothing about mine.*

The ceiling and lamp fixtures seemed to throw off light so much colder, harsher, and brighter when night surrounded the near-vacant building. Except for the security squad always present, the political hive was bereft of the throbbing rhythm of action present twenty hours a day Monday through Saturday. The uniformed Secret Service officer, Jake Goodson, a widower who preferred the evening shift, stood and nodded a surprised greeting when Morrison walked in and out of the empty office of the vice-president. *Maybe I should have been happy there.* "And good evening to you," Morrison mumbled to his smiling protector.

Back at the center of the arena, he sat down at the Resolute desk and had the White House operator find Harry Riordan for him. Ordinarily, he would have expected to hear him churning the gravel at the back of his throat in a greeting loaded with heavy humor within a few seconds of pinning the phone to his ear. He waited for a long minute, and hung up. Hitting the button for the operator a second time, he said, "You know, I just tried to speak to Senator Riordan. Did I lose the connection?"

"Oh, no, Mr. President," the operator said in a surprised voice. "There was no answer. I was coming back on the line to tell you, sir."

"No answer. You're certain, miss?"

"Yes, sir. I'm sorry, sir."

Morrison hung up, not wanting the operator to hear his fury. "That son of a bitch! How dare he not answer a call from the president of the United States?"

Fuming, he sent several blue-bound folders marked *Top Secret* skating across the blotter, coming to a stop only when they knocked over the six-inch high twin flag stand that held one of the United States and Texas side by side.

The desk phone chirped, and he reached to pick it up, thinking the operator had located the majority leader. "So you finally call?" he said into the receiver and realized, as the words poured from his mouth, that the caller might not be his old mentor.

"I'm glad you were waiting for my advice, Mr. President," said the voice of Angela Tesoro.

The electronic reproduction of her voice dripped a sweetness Morrison never noticed in person, and though her voice and manner caught him off guard, he exhaled slowly to recover his composure. "Why, you know I always hang on your every word, Angie," he said, attempting not to overdo his own version of Texas sugar.

"You don't fool me, Mr. President," Tesoro said, continuing in a light tone, "but I'm glad I caught you under the circumstances."

"Under what circumstances?"

"Under the circumstances, Joe," she said in an entirely different tone, "that you are about to be impeached."

"Oh, bullshit, Angie! That's Whitaker putting on the pressure so he can extract a deal on taxes or the budget or health care or whatever the hell is on his mind these days."

"You underestimate him," she said dispensing with title or *sir*. "He and Jordy Marshall went over the highlights of what they think they have on you regarding the 2012 election. And he has the votes, Joe."

"So what do they think they have?"

"Jesus, they think you masterminded the theft of the election, and, what's more, they think you had a bunch of people eliminated in the process."

"Oh, for Christ's sake! How can you believe that bullshit? This isn't *House of Cards!* It's like the IRS, Benghazi, and now the VA crap—all politics. The public won't even give it a yawn because our media friends won't give it air."

"Don't be so sure. State Media will only be loyal unless it thinks there's an even juicier bone out there to gnaw on."

"OK, I'll play along for a minute. What do they think they have?"

"They can connect you with Enrique McCord and, probably, with the contract McCord had with the USEAC. They know the Ohio vote went for Hardy, not us. They think they can connect you with whoever killed an NIS investigator, McCord, and some other people. That's the short of it, but it's enough to raise a stink from here to kingdom come."

"You spoke in generalities, but not with evidence, Angie. There's a big gap between that and impeachment, and, for Christ's sake, have you forgotten we control the Senate? There won't be the votes to convict, no matter how stirred up things get. Bottom line, Angie, is there is no proof."

"Joe, for God's sake! They're pretty sure they know the guy on your protection detail who did all the killings."

"That's crazy. Somebody in the Secret Service? People will laugh out loud. The Republicans must really be desperate to think that one up." He stopped, but he heard his own breathing through the silence. Then the tall grandfather clock softly chimed its reminder that ten hours had passed since noon. "Well, I'm truly grateful for the heads up, Angie, as ridiculous as this is. I'll remember it, by the way, when we retake the House in the 2014 midterms."

"Mr. President it's not the midterms we should think about," Tesoro said, a trace of sadness clouding her voice. "You need to name a vice-president now, and the public will be with us. They believe they elected Democrats in 2012, and if...if anything happens to you, we need someone to succeed you."

"Not that it will be necessary, Angie. Harry Riordan will spike their guns. Of that, I have no doubt. Having said all that, who is on your short list?"

Tesoro, the grizzled, grating veteran of three decades of political wars, plunged ahead. "Sir," she said, letting sweetness creep into her words, "you have an opportunity to let historians put your name alongside words like 'wisdom' and 'foresight' in the same sentence..."

"Cut it, Angie," Morrison retorted. "If you're about to pimp for Grantham again, forget it."

"Sir," she said, trying not to plead, "Emerson Grantham is a former senator from Connecticut and a former secretary of state, not to mention that he's first cousin to former president Jefferson Harper—"

"Grantham is an Ivy League entitlement snot, and I will not be party to having another one of those in office. Look what they gave us! And by the way, I'm pretty sure he's not even a second cousin to Harper, so check your material."

"Joe, he will lend credibility to the office and a Morrison Administration," she said, returning to barroom bargaining. "It will keep our party in the White House—now and later."

"You're way ahead of yourself, Madam Speaker," he said coldly. "I plan to be here for the rest of this term, and I expect to win when I run in 2016."

"What about the vice-presidency?"

"When all this impeachment bullshit is over, we'll do exactly what I said the other day—we'll have a committee review a list of the best and brightest, and only then will I make my decision."

"Joe, I hope it's your decision to make." Tesoro hung up without another word.

Five days later, in the president's private study off the Oval Office, Joe Morrison sank down in the red Moroccan leather couch and tuned his forty-two-inch HDTV to the Friday evening broadcast of his least favorite newsman. He knew, however, that Forbes Flannery commanded the largest evening audience segment, and what he said on the air drove public opinion.

The FactZone's polished acrylic set lit the News Global studio in New York as Flannery opined the opening of his usual evening slot. "This past Monday, House Speaker John Whitaker allowed the democracy's constitutional machinery to clank into gear as hearings began on the Bill of Impeachment against President Morrison. And what five days of hearings they have been with several more to come next week! Whether the House votes for, or against, the Bill, the evidence laid before the congressmen on live TV before the American people has been both stunning and damning.

"That as vice-president, Joseph Morrison controlled and manipulated the 2012 election process seems reasonably clear. All by itself, that crime may throw the country into a constitutional crisis never before seen in our history. Even if the president is ultimately found guiltless, the public will have no faith whatsoever in our system of elections.

"That Joseph Morrison may have directed the murders and/or disappearances of at least five people with knowledge of his alleged crime remains less clear. It is also an open question whether there is enough evidence to indict the man close to Morrison who is alleged to have been directly responsible the brutal crimes described.

"Never before in our history have impeachment proceedings been so squarely targeted to a series of criminal acts falling within the clear meaning of the constitutional phrase, 'high crimes and misdemeanors.' Not in 1868, when the first President Johnson was impeached for what most would consider purely political reasons, and not in 1999, when another president was impeached for behavior considered outside the constitution's purview. The Senate acquitted both those men. Will President Morrison be the recipient of a third acquittal?

"So far, the evidence is compelling, but circumstantial. No credible eyewitness has come forward with the pointed finger of damnation, and neither has any indisputable form of evidence developed that places the proverbial smoking gun in the hands of President Morrison. Therefore, *The FactZone* predicts the president will be impeached by the House before the middle of next week, but absent convincing first-person testimony or the equivalent thereof, the outcome of the trial in the Senate remains unclear."

Morrison muted the sound as Flannery ended his monologue, and began to process what he'd heard on the news and what he'd observed in the broadcast hearings. It had been obvious during the all-day, every-day hearings that the two NIS investigators could make only the most tangential connection between him and Enrique McCord, and despite a parade of other witnesses and experts, the closest anyone could get to him was a possible ID of Marty Cox as a rogue Secret Service agent. That meant he needed a way to isolate himself from Cox once he was sure all the dirty work was done.

The rest of the testimony would be viewed uselessly circumstantial and speculative, as Flannery suggested, and, as his own staff had predicted. What Flannery did not say was exactly what did not make itself known at the hearings: that no irrefutable evidence of the McLean, Virginia, meeting in the summer of 2012 existed. That meant Andrew Warner was the only man alive—aside from Marty Cox—who could possibly tie the entire string together: McCord, election fraud, the murders.

Could that lying bastard have relevant evidence after all? He pulled a cell phone out of his pocket and hit speed-dial number two for Marty Cox.

Nearly a week later, Paul and Mare found themselves alone in Pete Clancy's house when they returned from a brisk spring walk.

"Do you think yesterday's vote in the House will change the director's plans?"

"I don't know, Mare," Paul said. "It's not every day a president of the United States is impeached by so lopsided a vote."

"When all Republicans and over half of all the Democrats vote for impeachment, that makes the seventy or so Democrats who supported Morrison awfully lonely. With nearly three hundred and fifty votes for, you'd think there'd be a lot of pressure on the senators from the same states."

"You'd think so, but it doesn't always work that way," Paul said. "Senators have six-year terms, and if they're Democrats who are not up for reelection right away, there might be pressure on them to support their party. Since they control the Senate right now, I'd guess it could go either way."

"So tonight's the night, then?" Mare asked.

"Why do we have to wait until tonight?" Paul countered. "Pete is out of the house so we can..." His voice trailed off and his eyes rolled upward to their third-floor rooms.

"Look, Mr. Fixated, I was talking about our gig with Warner," she said, noticing his uncomprehending look. "You know, Paulie boy. It's Wednesday—lucky number thirteen—and tonight we go with the Warners to the Kennedy Center for that show Mrs. Warner wants to see."

"Oh, yeah. Of course. That means..."

"Right. You'll have to put on a black tie and I'll be dressed like you've never seen me."

"Oh, God. So that's what the shopping trip was for."

"You bet, studman! But I bought you that nice black suit, so you better look sharp for me."

Paul looked back at her in mock rebuke.

"Wouldn't want me checkin' out some other hot prospects, would you?"

"Well, if it's going to be that way," he said, pulling her close, "then we'd better take advantage of our opportunity right now."

"Not here! My God, we're in the kitchen. What if Pete comes back?"

"Kitchen? Dining room? Front hall? What does it matter? I'm gonna get you any way I can."

"Then you better put on your running shoes." With that, she broke away and made a dash for the stairs up to their nest. On the landing up to the third floor, Mare slowed her run just enough. Actually, she was on the first step to the third floor when he came up behind her, and she felt him burying his face in her auburn hair. She turned her head up to him.

Paul kissed her, his lips exploring hers, and then their tongues met. His hands slid under her arms and he cupped her breasts, and her whole body rose up in his clasp.

Mare felt her nipples respond to his touch through her top and sports bra, and he began to undress her then and there. "Just what do you think you're doing, Paulie boy?" she asked, her voice husky with desire.

"Exactly what we both want to do," he whispered. Somewhere on the floor below, he heard the kitchen door open and close. Mare looked into his deep green eyes, taunting him. He swept her up in his arms, and like newlyweds, he carried her up to another threshold.

Later in the afternoon, they passed her top and bra on the stairs when they went downstairs, and Mare's face turned much redder than her beautiful hair. She smacked him on the chest in mock reproach.

Back in kitchen, Pete looked up from his labors near the boiling pot on the stove. With a broad smile, he asked, "Have a nice afternoon?"

The atmosphere in the residence of the nation's First Family belied the bright sunshine that seemd to suddenly envelope the city. The unseasonably warm weather promised that the cherry blossoms would be more spectacular this year than last. Gardens around the White House were abloom, but nature's mood could not lift the pall on the Morrisons.

"Honey," the First Lady purred, "I know this must be hard on you, but must we let it dominate our every minute?"

Joe Morrison reached out to his wife from the large brocaded chair in which he had planted himself only the minute before. "I came up here, Shar honey," he said, holding her hand, "because this unfortunate nonsense is important, and I didn't want you to endure it alone."

"But it won't do any good for us to fret about it. Right, Joe?"

The president nodded absently, his focus being on the large HDTV not ten feet in front of him and tuned to Peter Marsden and CNS. The cable network and its anchor had been his favorite for at least a decade. Ever since he became aware that CNS, all three major networks, and media outlets like the fabled New York newspaper subscribed to talking points from a civilian blogger with strong White House ties, he was all the more comfortable with it.

To get the good, the bad, and the ugly, he tuned to News Global and their team of journalists who put it all right out there. It was clear News Global was beholden to no one. For the moment, he wanted to see that

CNS was following script, and, for the most part, he kept a small smile on his face while holding Sharon's soft, sweetly scented hand.

"This is Peter Marsden here in the *Control Room*," began the four o'clock news hour. "On this Wednesday, March 13th, the president may well be able to hold his own despite the bipartisan support for the Bill of Impeachment in yesterday's vote. The Senate, of course, is not bound by that vote. Since this is only the third time in our history that body will try a president for high crimes and misdemeanors, a prediction about the outcome for President Morrison is not at all clear. Going by past performance, however, it would take a mountain of overwhelmingly convincing evidence for the Senate, acting as judge and jury, to convict him.

"In other words, President Morrison can sleep well knowing that most legal experts believe no piece of evidence presented before the House will take the senators beyond reasonable doubt. Supporters of the president want to know more about the two NIS Investigators who unraveled the alleged plot and about the man they seem to identify as possibly responsible for crimes against perhaps five people. CNS will keep its viewers completely up-to-date as the Senate now takes up this most unusual case."

The First Lady interrupted her husband's thoughts. "That should make you sleep a little sounder, dear, but it's terrible that your enemies have to go to such lengths to pull you down. They couldn't possibly have any real proof, could they, Joe?"

"Real proof? Of course not, honey. I don't know how such proof could exist, and I'm glad you haven't wasted your time watching all this garbage on television."

"Gosh, no! I couldn't listen to those lies for one minute. I just hope your defenders in the Senate and in the media will stick with you until it's all done and gone."

"'Done and gone.' What good words, Shar honey. Hey, that reminds me. I think I need to call one of those defenders right now."

The sun was beginning its descent as Morrison glanced toward the Palladian window of the White House family room, and Sharon rose to leave. He took care to ensure she was out of earshot before pulling the nondescript cell phone from his sweater pocket and hitting number two on the "Favorites" list. Surprised not to receive an answer until the sixth ring, he demanded, "What took you so long, Marty?"

"I couldn't get to the phone."

You're lying, he thought. "Listen, Marty, we're tied together like a pair of Siamese twins, so don't go getting any crazy ideas. What are you doing right now?"

"What is it that you want? Natalie's out of town with the kids on spring break, and I've been home doing a lot of thinking. I don't want any part of this."

"Too late for cold feet, Marty."

"People starting to point fingers at me, Joe. Can't you do something about that?"

"It's not that easy, and I'm doing my best for us," Morrison lied in return. He waited, but hearing no response, said, "This is the last time I'll remind you of what has to be done."

"I haven't forgotten, but like I said, Joe, I want out."

"We have only one chance to avoid goin' down," Morrison said. "That's to make sure one particular individual is not in a position to offer evidence, if he has any."

"He's protected, and it won't be easy."

"Finish the job, Marty. It's now or never."

The evening's plan seemed straightforward, Paul thought, when the lead agent of Director Warner's security detail, Daniel Jorgensen, called late in the afternoon. He and the Warners would leave their Northern Virginia home around 7:10 p.m., and with a tail car and two agents, take a somewhat circuitous route to the Key Bridge before crossing into Georgetown to pick up the Whitehurst Freeway. According to Jorgensen, it would be Virginia Avenue to Twenty-Fifth Street, and then to the Kennedy Center on F. "Simple," he had said.

By design, the Gladstons were to take any other route they chose, and they would meet in the garage. If they could not sync there, they would go upstairs to the Chinese Lounge, where they were expected.

When Paul and Mare dressed for the evening after a quick pasta dinner and a salad—but no wine, they discussed their options. Mare's words trumped his idea. "You know, Paulie boy, as long as we live in DC, and as long as I'm an American, which means for as long as I live, I want to enter the District over Memorial Bridge."

"Why is that?" he said absently, as he tied and tugged his black bow tie.

"Because when you cross that bridge—especially at night—and see the Lincoln Memorial, it gives me the chills. You know, Nelson Evers told me once that most people back in Fairfax, Ohio, didn't realize that if you get on US fifty there, you can drive all the way to the Lincoln Memorial; and he said, one day he was going to do just that."

Paul stopped when he noticed the change in her voice. He saw the tears streaming down her cheeks, and remembered how close she had been to her black rabbi before his murder. He recalled her telling him how Evers had always meant to see the face of the man who'd freed his ancestors from two hundred years of bondage. Paul walked over to her and held her close. He didn't need to say a word. He let her carry on for a few minutes, and then said, "C'mon, we'll be late," in a voice he hadn't expected to be so thick with emotion.

Stepping back from him, Mare kept her eyes downward, lifting them to give him a teary, broken smile. Then, with lightning speed, she donned a black satin dress that was not overly long. For a few minutes, she fussed with her holster so that the folds of the dress covering her bodice would conceal it nicely. Once or twice, she practiced reaching in to pull out the Kimber in one smooth motion.

Paul finished dressing in plenty of time to admire his wife and partner, absolutely stunning in a vision of shimmering black, capped in an auburn halo. He resisted the hormonal impulses coursing through him to take her clothes off and spend the evening at home.

His Walthers PPK safely tucked in the small of his back, Paul led Mare down the stairs where Pete Clancy waited like a beaming, over-protective father.

"Now you know why they went to the movie. In a somewhat similar venue, it was a warm-up for tonight with you, the Warners, and his security detail working closely together in a much larger arena. Follow the protocols they showed you, and you'll be fine. Good luck."

Mare and Paul thanked him for getting them ready for the assign-ment and headed out the door. In the District, they paused briefly to gaze at Lincoln and the people who'd come to see him as they made their way to the assignent.

"Ah, the gods are with us," Paul said. "I'm sure that's them up ahead." They positioned themselves behind the tail car and, in a min-ute, were at the entrance to the Lincoln Center garage. At that point, the tail car peeled off. Paul knew the driver of that vehicle would place itself near the exit from C level while the agents left the vehicle and provided security with Daniel Jorgensen inside the Center.

The Gladstons propelled their Volvo down the ramp to C Level and found the exclusive spaces nearest the garage elevators that were set aside for VIPs. They parked a few spots away from the Warners and covered their backs while Jorgensen led them to the elevator bank.

Paul and Mare knew the drill: Once up in the Chinese Lounge, Jorgensen would survey the two dozen other VIP donors expected, more women than men according to the list, and once he felt comfort-able with them and the safety of the room itself, the Warners would enter, accompanied at a distance by the Gladstons. No one in the room would know there was any connection between them and Andrew Warner and his wife.

The Warners moved easily among the group in the lounge, evi-dently recognizing one or two of the other concertgoers. As Paul observed them chatting, he began a more careful scan of those pres-ent. Ever since the whole waterboarding scandal under the Bush Administration, the director's staff knew there would be those who might consider themselves proxy angels of revenge on the man or his family.

The threat to the CIA director in this room with this group should be nil, Paul concluded, because the Warners' decision to attend this concert was neither publicly announced, nor was it mentioned to their inner circle. Also, this group appeared older, refined, and, typically, less given to revolutionary or impulsive behaviors. No one present betrayed any sign of malevolent intent, and neither did anyone match a profile of an assassin from a hostile entity.

Paul slowly absorbed every detail. There were nine men in the room, not including Warner, Jorgensen, and himself. Of the others, all of them older men, no one stood out, except one who moved stooped over and looked like a bird of prey with heavy black glasses perched on his beak. Aside from Nancy Warner, the women present were in their seventies and richly dressed, but not for escape. When he'd processed the room, he breathed a sigh of relief, and then took a few steps to the entrance leading to the box tier of the one-thousand seat Eisenhower Theater. He wanted a look at that setting before Director Warner went through to the concert hall.

As he made his move, Paul noticed Mare stop, fascinated by the room's chinoiserie. The deep reds, shadowed by blacks and contrasted by lacquered finishes that imitated ancient porcelains decorated a world to which neither of them had ever been introduced. The room was darkly beautiful, and, like Chinese art, politics, and life, much existed in shadow. Then he saw her move closer to the Warners while he turned to check out the vast space beyond where he stood.

The room went completely black. There were soft, startled cries of surprise. Paul heard metal against metal and supposed the sound came from one of the older men who'd been pulling a small oxygen kit. There were mixed, low noises as the crowd instinctively clustered and moved toward the exit. The standard emergency beacon washed the room in a strange twilight.

Paul knew Jorgensen would lead the Warners back through the door by which they had entered, but the door opened inward. It might be difficult if the small crowd suddenly rushed in that direction. Paul turned and moved toward those bunching to exit, He could hear the older, frightened voices.

Every blip on the screen of normal had to be regarded as a potential threat, and the lights going out suddenly qualified. He could not see the Warners, and, given Mare's height, Paul lost her in the darkened space. He assumed she'd have closed in on her targets to help propel them from behind.

Then, a metallic voice, possibly pre-recorded and trained to soothe rather than panic, mingled with the sounds of the room's occupants. "Ladies and gentlemen," it purred from the hidden speakers, "we are experiencing a malfunction in one component of our electrical system. There is no emergency. You may remain where you are until it is remedied, or you may depart at your discretion. You may guide yourself to the red exit lighting if you wish. Please exercise care."

No calming effect resulted. Paul heard and felt the crowd shuffle, almost in unison, urgent whispers accompanying their shift. The two-wheeled oxygen trolley rolled. Then, Paul heard a sound like an airlock opening, but couldn't tell whether it was close by or emanating from the speaker. In a moment, there were murmurs of concern. *Had one of the older people stumbled?*

"Oh my God," sirened a voice creased with age. "I feel blood! Oh, my God! Where's it coming from? What's happening?"

Mrs. Warner's voice cut through the din. "Drew! Drew! Oh, God, Drew!"

Paul pushed forward until he came to the dark, still form, lying on the deep-hued carpet, black scarlets mingling in a new pattern barely visible in the light.

Jorgensen knelt beside his man. He said to Paul, "Take her. Get Mrs. Warner to the car. Security and an ambulance are on the way."

"No!" shouted Nancy Warner, "I'm not going anywhere. I need to be here with him."

"Please, Mrs. Warner." Jorgensen tone seemed to say she could no longer be of comfort to her husband.

"Mare," Paul called out, and as if on signal, the lights came on, and people in uniforms of several sorts burst into the room. Because the official people didn't know who he was, Paul was shoved with the rest of the patrons toward one corner of the room.

"No one moves. No one leaves!" shouted one man in a DC Police uniform.

"Wait! My wife, my wife has disappeared!" Paul called out.

"Stay put, fella, or you won't like what happens next."

"Jorgensen!" Paul called out, but Warner's chief protector was busy with all of the official music, directing the medicos and, at the same time, cluing in the uniforms that the man on the floor was the Director of the CIA. He knew Jorgensen had his priorities. Paul had his. "Mare! Mare!" She was nowhere to be seen.

"Quiet!" the small crowd's protector warned.

"We were part of his protection detail," Paul barked into his face.

"Yeah, right. Well, I guess you didn't do it very well then. That guy looks dead to me."

"But my wife and I work for him, and she's gone."

"Not my problem, pal. Get back, or else."

"But it's my problem!" Paul shouted, lunging forward with an elbow to the man's jaw. With all the confusion around Warner, no one noticed an extra suit moving in a frenzy. In a half second, Paul loped past Jorgensen, kneeling over Warner's inert body. The agent looked up at him and nodded ever so slightly.

Warner was dead. But how? Who? Where was Mare? She was gone. It was a reality Paul refused to accept. He bounded out the door into the Hall of States and moved in the direction his instinct told him to go. The lights were now full bright and cast a cold, white swath across the broad expanse. He moved with the thick, loud crowd into the Grand Foyer.

Repeatedly, he called out for Mare, but no one turned in his direction. In the uproar, his voice did not carry. She couldn't hear him, and he couldn't hear her. Where did she go? Why did she leave the room? His heart pounded as he pushed ahead.

For some reason, the crowd seemed to gather around the three-thousand-pound bust of JFK, and, as they did so like activated electrons surrounding a nucleus, Paul scanned every face, every head, every dress. No alluring smile, no auburn hair, no black satin anything!

A tightly packed group of Asian tourists were in his path. Every urging of his being pushed him toward the building's south side, but the chattering gaggle was in his way. Then he saw something odd near the emergency exit at the far end of the foyer.

The stooped over man in the Chinese Lounge, the one with the large black-framed glasses, now ran, tall, fully erect and, in front of him, was Mare! She was running, but didn't look back. She didn't scream for help. What was happening?

He pushed hard to slice his way through the gaggle, but the crowd would not give. He shouted for her, but the two of them flew out the door into the dark of March. They were gone! She was gone!

The next thing Paul felt was a bolt of lightning. Instead of breaking through the Asian thicket to save his wife, he felt the marble floor yank him downward. Screaming Mare's name, he heard only the echo of his own voice as the floor pulled him further down and under, into another world where his senses seemed disconnected from him. Light and dark alternated in gauzy waves as he felt himself being dragged backward. Time did not exist. Mare did not exist. Only disabling pain.

Slowly, he swam up to the floor and burst through it, opening his eyes when somebody shook him awake. It was Pete Clancy. "Who? What? Mare! Pete! What the hell is going on?" Paul thought he yelled, but his throat allowed only a whisper.

"You're in custody, at least for another minute or so."

"Custody? Where am I? Why are you here? What about Mare?"

"Whoa! First, you're still at the Kennedy Center. They're processing the scene and want to talk to you. I'm here because Jorgensen knew to call me, and I hope you're damned glad. After you knocked that guy over in the Chinese Lounge and bolted, they thought you were the assassin. You're lucky you weren't shot." Clancy didn't scold his operative; he was matter-of-fact.

"What was I supposed to do?" Paul said, his voice a hoarse whisper. "I saw the guy that did it and went after him. He had Mare! Hey, why am I handcuffed?"

Clancy motioned to a uniform who stepped forward and freed him.

Paul rubbed his eyes and head. "What the hell happened to me?"

"Never been tased, eh? Well, now you know. They tried to subdue you, but you were crazy to plow through the crowd and try to escape, they thought." Clancy chuckled. "The only way to stop you—without hurting you—was to give you a jolt."

"Without hurting me? Are you kidding?" Paul said nothing for a few seconds but rubbed his arms. "Oh, hell, Pete, never mind me; we've got to find Mare."

"It'll be a bit before they can look at the security tapes—it seems they went out with the lights, but so far, there are no witnesses, except maybe you."

"Then, let's get on with the damn debrief," Paul said, trying to get up. "We need every fed in town looking for my wife."

"That won't happen, kid. You and Mare don't exist. You aren't feds, and you aren't law enforcement officers. As far as the agency is concerned, you weren't even official. To all of them, you're nobody."

"Then look, goddamn it, Pete!" Paul clenched his teeth. "I want you to call in any goddamn favor you're owed in this town, because this is Mare we're talkin' about, not some nameless cypher!"

"Settle down. I want them, too," Clancy said gently. "I already made my calls while you were snoring away. People want to help, but they don't know where to go, what to look for. So let's clear your head and sift out the details we need."

Paul pulled his six-foot-plus frame into a sitting position and wiped his eyes some more, then took a long swig of ice cold water. Clarity came back and, at once, questions were flung at him. For the next forty-five minutes, badge carriers from DC Police, the FBI, and the CIA all peppered him with demands for his observations from the time they entered the building until he saw his wife running out the door.

It was frustrating to listen to the three agencies argue about pre-eminence and jurisdiction. Finally, the FBI wrenched control of the investigation, and Paul focused his attention on the agent in charge. At once, the Q&A proceeded in a logical, chronological order without tangents. Paul flipped on his memory switch and spit out every detail he had absorbed, principally the few minutes in the Chinese Lounge before and after the murder.

Paul turned to Clancy. "My God, Pete, I'm so sorry about Director Warner. You guys were close. What happened exactly? How did we fail?"

Clancy responded, "First, he was shot through the heart from the back with a silenced weapon and a dumdum—he bled out in seconds. He had no chance." Clancy paused momentarily, eyes shut, as if in prayer. "Don't worry," he added, his voice a vow, "we'll get the bastard!"

Paul listened.

"Second, you didn't fail. There was no reason to think anybody knew Drew Warner was even here—had to be somebody who knew his schedule."

"It had to be somebody who could find out at the last minute," Paul said.

"Yeah," Clancy said, his eyes going distant. "Yeah, somebody federal with a need to know. Somebody on high!"

"Oh, fuck! Crew Cut!" Paul cursed, over and over. "It was him. He was the stooped old man with the wig and the black glasses. It was him all the time. Oh, Jesus, Pete, I missed it, and he's got Mare. She's a hostage somewhere."

Clancy nodded to the agent, who had identified himself as Peter Spinelli. "Now we know where to look. Get to the Secret Service and oh, for Christ's sake, we don't even know his real name yet. Jesus! We need the name of the agents on the president's protection detail, and we need them now!"

"Fat chance of that, Clancy," the agent whined. "Nobody demands that kind of info about the president's security people. They don't give that out for any reason."

"This isn't any reason!" Clancy shouted. "The director of the CIA was just murdered in the Kennedy Center, in all likelihood by a Secret Service agent assigned to the president. Figure it out, pal, and fast."

"What the hell do you want me to do?" There was fright in Spinelli's brown eyes.

"Get that fucking director of your agency to talk directly to the fucking director or whatever he is of the US Secret Service and get that fucking information before anybody else gets murdered on our turf by our people," Clancy yelled. "Got that?"

"Yessir," Spinelli said in one swoosh of sound. "I don't know exactly who you are, but it sounds like you know what you're talking about."

The air was blue and cold, and Paul had never heard Pete Clancy raise his voice, much less, apply an old English adjective to help the agent understand.

"You bet, my friend," Clancy said. "The dead man here was one of my best friends, and you don't want to know who else might be his friend."

Spinelli thought a minute. "OK, bud, you made your point. Now back off, and let me get to it."

CIA Director Assassinated at Kennedy Center

The early morning hours generated reams of copy for the network and cable news crowd, the columnists, the scare hawkers. State Media wasn't sure what to do with it, but soon found a hook: "Top Administration Blacks Dead. A Plot?"

Amid the confusion, alarm, and mayhem, all in the context of an impeachment process halfway through, there was no mention of a kidnapped woman. For Paul, the hours were the hardest to bear. No word, no Mare. Despite Clancy's pressure on the feds, there was no immediate response from anyone with the power for justice. Too many silos, too many icons, too many turfs to pass through, over, and on.

Paul wanted to prowl the city, and, Pete's warnings aside, he climbed in the Volvo and drove back over to the Kennedy Center where at midnight, the place was locked up tight. As he drove around the building's maze of roadways and access drives, he spotted an FBI van with several men around it, talking.

Paul pulled up.

At first, he was met with suspicion, one agent's right hand at the ready for trouble. "How can I help you?" The question was not inviting.

"My wife. She was kidnapped here tonight when Director Warner was murdered."

"Oh. You're Gladston? Over here." The unidentified agent led him to the group of men, who stopped speaking immediately and waited to find out what the newcomer was all about. Then punctuated only by blinking lights, the same senior agent on whom Pete Clancy disgorged his spleen stepped out of the darkness.

"You! I thought we released you a few hours ago. What do you need?"

Paul let the harshness of the man's question fall flat on the tarmac. "I need my wife, Agent Spinelli."

"Why shouldn't we think she was involved with the assassin? She ran out of here, didn't she?" Spinelli asked.

"You stupid son of a bitch!" Paul spat. "My wife and I uncovered a little problem with murder and election fraud you seem to have overlooked, and we were engaged to spend time with Director Warner. And you want to think my wife went along with this guy willingly because she was part of it? Have you watched too many fucking TV shows with twisted plots about good guys and bad guys, Mr. Spinelli?"

Spinelli said, "Hey, just a minute."

Paul looked around the group. "No, you 'just a minute.' I assume some of you guys are married and love your wives. Well I love the woman I married two months ago, and I know she would have shot the bastard who killed Warner if she'd had the chance. You sure you're not stickin' up for this guy because he's Secret Service? Because he's another hotshot fed like you guys?"

Spinelli took a step forward.

"Sure. Go ahead," Paul taunted. "Take your punch. Beat the hell out of me if that's what you want, but how about usin' that energy on the guy who murdered Warner and took my wife? Huh?"

"OK, calm down, Mr. Gladston. Look, we have every agent in the city on this one and don't think the CIA isn't bringing more pressure to bear than you can. We're sorry about your wife, but we live in a crazy world, and Christ, you never know!"

The tension in the circle evaporated.

"All right," Paul said in a much lower voice. "Can you guys tell me if you found anything here? Anything to help?"

"You already know how Warner was killed. Your wife must have been too close, and he must have known who she was."

Paul nodded. "This guy's six four or so, with a blond crew cut, but obviously in a makeover tonight. We never did get his name."

"Nothing else. No name yet. We're looking at the camera tapes now. So far, we have the same bent-over older man, gray, straggly hair, with black glasses. That's all. We're hoping to tag him coming from the garage or going back there with your wife. Either way, if we're lucky, we'll see what vehicle goes with him."

"This guy knows all your systems. He knew how to get hold of the director's schedule, and that's practically top secret," Paul said. "Somehow, the son of a bitch knew how to kill the lights for the entire Center. So, I'm guessing he also knew where to park his vehicle to be out of camera view. So far, whenver he's shown up, it's in a black Tahoe with Virginia plates. If any of that's any help."

One agent stepped away and spoke into his phone.

"I wish we could give you more, Paul, but until we get something from up top—and we all have to admit, the director of the CIA is a high-profile target for a lot of people—we've got nothin'."

"I know I'm not FBI," Paul said. "Only OPM and NIS, but we all have the same rule."

"What's that?" Spinelli asked.

"None of us believes in coincidences."

"Good thing you're up early," Clancy said when he found Paul pacing the yellow and gray kitchen at six in the morning. "I got a call from John Whitaker late last night while you were gone. He's going to be out and about today and wants you to be with him."

"No way. I'm have to use every bit of energy I have to find Mare. Any minute now, we'll be getting a call from Spinelli telling us they've got Crew Cut's name and address, so I've got to be ready to go."

Clancy looked at Paul's face, full of determination and resignation at the same time. The chances were that Mare was already dead. If the kidnapper was Crew Cut, Clancy reasoned, Mare would be an object of his revenge, nothing else. He had no reason to keep her alive. If Warner's murderer was an agent from a foreign power, Mare would have been killed moments after they left the Kennedy Center garage.

Clancy leaned forward to grab the edge of the gray granite counter with both hands. His heart still hurting over his wife's early passing, and, over the past few years, he built a shield of defense for his emotions. Now in one night, losing a friend of forty years and, probably, the sweet wife of Paul Gladston, his heart hurt all the more. He wanted to hug him, not so much for comfort, but to steady him and keep him from doing something foolish. In a short space of time, he'd come to think of his guests more like the children he never had.

"You know, Paul, they aren't going to call you," Clancy said choosing his words carefully. "It would be against protocol. Even if it was the wife of one of their agents, they would not likely let him accompany a team on the raid."

"But," Paul began, the blood rising in his face and voice.

"Sorry. When you're in a spot like this, it's easy to think you're the exception to the rule, but the fact is, no one is the exception." Clancy paused to let his words take hold. "I'm sure that once they've gone to Crew Cut's house, we'll get a call, but only after they're sure of what they've got."

"I'm sure now."

"But they can't be. Look at it from their side. Without the string of circumstantial pieces only you and Mare provide, there's nothing to concretely identify Crew Cut from the man on the moon. Only you two believe the man you saw in Cincinnati and New Wilmington is the same man you saw briefly in the VA lobby here in DC. Paul, that's it."

"I see what you mean, but, I'm sure," Paul said slowly. "Period."

"OK, let's leave it there," Clancy said with a finality to draw Paul's close attention. "In the meantime, you need to be at the Speaker's main office in the Capitol at ten o'clock sharp. With all the BS you'll have to go through to get to him, you'd better leave here at eight thirty at the latest."

In the Leesburg four-over-four colonial owned by the bank and the Cox family, the Secret Service agent spoon-fed Cheerios and milk to a bound Mare Gladston in the cheery, spring-green kitchen.

"What the hell do you think is going to come of this?" Mare spat at her captor.

"One of two things, Miss Pain-in-the-Ass. Either you're going to be my ticket to an immunity deal or you're going be under spring mud somewhere in the countryside."

"You mean like Amber Bustamente and those others in Cincinnati?"

"That fat chick?" he said, a snarl on his face and in his voice. "Yeah. Her. Her boyfriend and the other geek. Yeah," he repeated. "Just like them."

"Killing nice people a hobby of yours, shithead?" Mare spat a soggy Cheerio in Crew Cut's face.

Cox slapped her. "Don't think you're gonna get a cushy deal if you get out of this alive, bitch. I won't like killing you just like I didn't like doing the others. Some orders I don't like to follow."

"Welcome to the world, pal," said Mare, unwilling to ease up. "Life's a bitch, ain't it?"

"Nice mouth. Look, Marlyn Gladston—isn't that what your license says?—you don't have any idea about the world I inhabit. Or the shit I have to take to feed my family, pay for this"—he said, gesturing to the house around them—"and planning for a future—"

"Some future Nelson Evers has. Or Amber. Or the others, big man. Don't tell me about your sad life. You work for Morrison, don't you? How bad can that be?" she asked and saw the hate in her captor's eyes.

"You think workin' for that guy is a good deal?" he screamed. "Let me tell you, missy, when the vice-president asks you to make a call, then do a little more, and a little more after that, it's so easy to make the man happy who controls your life and career."

"Yeah, tough," Mare said, taking no pity. "You guys are supposed to have a pair. You're supposed to do the right thing, even when these fuckin' politicians want you to cross the line."

"What you don't understand is for some of these guys, there is no line! C'mon. Get up."

"Where are we going?"

"Where they won't find me—or you."

A few minutes before ten thirty, Speaker of the House John Whitaker and a key staffer left his ceremonial offices on the Capitol's West Front and made their way across the vast edifice to liberty where a duplicate set of offices was reserved for his counterpart in the Senate. Along with them, as additional minders, went Paul Gladston and two members of the US Capitol Police. Whitaker was one of three to be so accompanied—the other two were the president pro tempore of the Senate and the Senate majority leader. As Whitaker no doubt expected, he was interrupted innumerable times by constituents giving him a thumbs up, a good-natured rib, or a discrete "Rockefeller salute." Used to getting the finger from so many, the Speaker smiled politely and went on.

The small parade arrived at the high-gloss varnished door of Senator Harrison Riordan of Missouri at eleven o'clock, and Whitaker—alone— was ushered into the senator's inner sanctum. Paul and the two Capitol policemen flanked the outer door and waited.

Whitaker was not especially surprised to see three powerhouses in the room. Arrayed before him like the Trinity were Connecticut Senator Daryl Perelman; the near-ancient Wilson Revere, senator from West Virginia and president pro tempore; and the raspy Riordan himself.

"The people's humble representative is vastly outnumbered, Harry. I was expecting his eminence," Whitaker said offering a mock bow in the direction of Wilson Revere, "but I'm pleased to see my good friend Daryl Perelman."

"I thought," said Riordan, as the lime, sand, and gravel began to churn, "it would be helpful to have Daryl here inasmuch as he will take up your infamous b-bill," he said with distaste, "right after lunch."

"My friend," said Perelman, "and I say that in quotes, wants to persist in his dreamy belief that I remain a Democratic stalwart, subject to the pressures of the party, but in coming here today, I do so as a true Independent," Perelman said. "And furthermore, as chairman of the Judiciary Committee, I plan to be as fully objective as the members of the House of Representatives and the people of the United States have a right to demand."

"No presumption intended, my good sir," scraped Riordan's voice like a file across hardened steel. "That's exactly why you are here, Daryl. Now, John," he said as he turned to Whitaker, the grind in his throat having no small amount of condescension in it, "what is it that you have to tell us that your members haven't already voted upon?" His question expected no good answer.

Whitaker smiled. "Gentlemen, I come here, I know, out of normal order, and ordinarily, I wouldn't presume to speak *ex parte* to my good friend, Senator Perelman. However, you should know that there is a smoking gun—God I hate that phrase—but we were not permitted to enter it into evidence in the House proceedings."

"Then," Riordan jumped in with an amazingly clear voice, "you should not be tainting our proceedings without a compelling reason."

"The compelling reason, Senator Riordan," Whitaker said, using the formal address deliberately, "is the murder of CIA Director Andrew Warner last evening. I have reason to believe that he died to ensure that a key piece of evidence never surfaced."

"What could you talking about John?" Revere asked.

"You gentlemen may not be aware of this, but Drew Warner and I go way back—all the way back to Vietnam days, and, once in a great while, Drew might share something with us that might not otherwise become public."

"Us?" prompted Perelman.

"There are two other guys who served with us back then, and we've stayed close. The killer didn't know that."

"So what possible evidence do you expect the Senate to consider?" Riordan spoke forcefully. "What the House heard and what you told me and Angela remains a lot of conjecture, to tell you the God's truth." He looked at both Revere and Perelman.

"When I spoke with you earlier, Harry, I did not know this evidence existed because Drew Warner didn't realize he had it." Whitaker threw the next words out like a terrible trump. "He made me promise not to use it, but his murder changes all that."

Only the ticking of an ancient mantle clock broke the silence. "When all the noise and stink arose about the vote in Ohio and four other states in particular, along with the coincidental murders of some people key to that election, Warner remembered receiving a call from an occupant of the West Wing to arrange a secret meeting for him—that was in the summer of 2012."

"Averell Williams would never be a party to something like that," Perelman said, "and I knew him from the time he was a State Assemblyman out of Buffalo way back when. You may not like his political philosophy, John, but you could never fault his integrity."

"Did I say the request was from Williams?" Whitaker asked innocently. "Harry, get your staffer to set up a DVD player for us—just us."

Riordan reached for a phone and crackled an order. The foursome sat quietly for the two or three minutes the aide needed to sync the office's DVD player with the HDTV imbedded in a bookcase across from Riordan's conference table.

When the aide departed, Whitaker took a DVD from his pocket, inserted it in the player, and hit the requisite button. In a moment, it began, and the rapt party zeroed in on the screen as the figure of Joe Morrison entered a well-lit dining room from some darkened space. As the minutes rolled by, the veil of circumstantial evidence lifted from the eyes of Riordan, Revere, and Perelman when they saw Morrison put Enrique McCord and Nathan Conaway through their paces. At the end of it, they saw Morrison confirm their presence in the Cincinnati office on election night.

Whitaker spoke. "When Warner remembered Morrison's not-all-that-unusual request, he began the retrieval process for the tape of that meeting and, of course, was stunned at what he saw. What he saw," Whitaker repeated with some emphasis, "and what you have now seen, was Morrison in a room plotting with two men who had key USEAC contracts with battleground states, which allowed them to manipulate the votes in any precinct in any state, all without a trace. One of those two men was murdered on a public street on election night, and the other has since disappeared, like the election results, without a trace."

Whitaker's listeners turned ghostly gray as their voices left them. Riordan looked chastened. Revere, who'd seen far too much in his career, seemed disbelieving, but accepting, and Perelman appeared flattened, then scared. Whitaker saw Perelman's mind calculating as if it were an old-fashioned, pull-lever adding machine. As the machine achieved each sum, Perelman nodded, ever so slightly.

"And Warner showed you this DVD?" Perelman asked.

"He gave a copy to me and one to another friend—he knew it was insurance. He must have known Morrison was tying off loose ends, and he had more than a hint of it the night someone tried to run him down in Tyson's Corner. That's why he had some extra protection last night."

"I most heartily wish it had done him some good," Riordan said. His demeanor was one of a master bitten, betrayed by a stray dog he had taken in and fed.

"Then at the end of the day..." Revere began to say.

"Yes..." Perelman's voice trailed off, but he looked at Whitaker with new respect.

Mare watched as Cox maneuvered the black Tahoe off the I-95 exit ramp and headed west on the two-lane toward and past the Spotsylvania Military Reservation. At US 208, he made a sharp left and drifted south for several miles toward the little burg of Snell at the junction where Morris meets Courthouse and Partlow Roads. Not all that far east of there, an unpaved lane took off to the north where, a mile or so inland, a small A-Frame cabin nestled. Cox said he and Natalie built it when they were first married and thought their honeymoon would last forever.

The A-Frame logs, Mare noticed, showed their age, and she suspected the place was a bug- and bat-bothered getaway that Cox's wife no longer found appealing. All the way east on the Dulles Toll Road to 495 and then I-95, she wondered about the man who now held her prisoner. Except for her hands being tied in front of her, she had not been blindfolded or thrown on the floor in the back. That was both good news and bad news. Good news, perhaps, because when all was said and done, he had no intention to harm her. Bad news, just as likely, because he didn't care what she saw—she would never live to tell about it. They talked off and on the whole way, and, except for the slap—and she vowed to kick him in the balls for it—he took care to treat her with some modicum of respect and privacy.

At first, when he grabbed her in the dark after shooting Andrew Warner, she thought it was Paul running to shield her. The assailant—at that point, she had no idea who he was—whispered that she'd better not make a sound or she'd get what Warner got. Not one for heroics, Mare went along, but thought she was only buying time, that she'd be beaten and raped before a bullet in her head erased her being. It was surprising to her that none of that happened.

Mare was almost getting used to thinking of him as Marty Cox rather than, 'Crew-Cut.' *Funny how differently we think of people when we know their names.* She would never feel sorry for this man or take his side, but she was beginning to understand that Marty Cox was the real prisoner in the drama. He had been trapped by his own job security and career aspirations, all of which he was willing to put before his love of family and country.

In her short years in the workforce, Mare saw and heard about many instances where an individual's undying loyalty was to a person, not to an institution or an idea. Oh, people talked about their devotion to freedom, she knew, but when a choice had to be made, loyalty to self or someone else reigned, and not always in that order. Her first-hand experience with Enrique McCord and Marty Cox, their slavish devotion to Morrison who was, at best, a two-bit politician people saw as a shallow stream, taught her that the possibility for criminal or immoral conduct rose in direct relation to the iconic status or fame of the principal. "Mare's Law," she was convinced, was not built on empty observations.

McCord was one example, but he must have had a conscience at the end—why else dispose of him? As for Cox, Mare saw that over time, Morrison's first demands—requests, Cox called them—were small, just a little over the line. Then, when Morrison had sucked him in, there was no retreat, no exit, no option. Cox had to do what Morrison wanted or else give up everything he'd ever worked for. Entitlement trumped common sense. Like any addict, once Cox took the step from one kind of crime to murder, he had nothing to lose.

Poor bastard, she thought, as he released her seat belt and untied her, *he doesn't know this can have no good end for him.* "Well, what do you think you'll be able to get for me, Marty? I'm nobody. They won't bargain with you," she said not believing she would say it.

"Sure they will, and I can give them Morrison. That's the big story! And you'll be my shield when the time comes."

"Don't count on it. If you want points, your best bet is to let me find my way to civilization while you disappear. You know all the routines the feds have—you can go off the grid for months, years even. Paul and I did—hell, you came within a few feet of me at that Amish auction."

Cox looked at her. "Are you shittin' me? You two were there all the time?"

"Yeah—and we could have stayed right there and had a good life."

"Maybe you should have, missy," he said, as he tied her to a wooden kitchen chair. "I don't know what I'm gonna do. It's looking like none of my plans are workin' for me. That fuckin' Morrison has had it all his way, and he'll probably get away with it."

"You got a point there. He might," Mare said. The satellite radio news station on in the Tahoe blah-blahed about nothing else the whole time they were on the road. "You think Senator What's-his-Name from Connecticut will vote for Morrison?"

"You mean Perelman? Hell, I don't know who owns who on the hill these days, but Perelman is one of the honest guys."

"You can never be sure, though, can you?" Mare said, shifting tactics. At the end of the day, Cox was a serial murderer, no matter what his miserable excuses might be, but she was fascinated with the killing creature a few feet from her.

He stared through the window for what seemed like minutes. After a while, a serious, almost sad look washed his face. He reached for his cell and punched a single digit. He walked away from her toward the big window looking into the forest.

"You on a break? Good. Hey, I got a problem. Remember the cabin? Yeah, well, I've got somebody here. Yeah, special situation—you know the drill. Can you buzz on up here and watch somebody for a day? OK. Not until tomorrow morning sometime? Great. I'll be gone by then, but that works. Key is in same spot. Hey, man, no need for any special treatment here. Yeah. See ya."

Although she could hear only half the conversation, it was like Cox was reading a script for a play, but his voice was devoid of feeling, like the verbal display of a flat brain wave. She felt as if death itself lurked in the shadows, waiting for its moment.

THE IDES

I n the constituent office, where he much preferred to work and serve,
Speaker Whitaker was at his desk thinking about the morning schedule and, in particular, how to avoid the media types, all of whom would
be vying for hot observations he might care to offer. Whitaker knew
there were two key questions hanging in the balance. If there was doubt
about President Morrison's guilt, would he be permitted his right under
the Constitution to name a vice-president? And second, if Warner's DVD
was played for the Judiciary Committee senators, why was it not in evidence before the House vote?

Dodging the media was not the end in itself. Though he would
never admit it, he enjoyed the give-and-take, the banter, and sometimes, the camaraderie some—very few—politicians enjoyed with the
media. Some of his predecessors had the knack: Tip O'Neill and Carl
Albert did, to name two. Both Presidents Roosevelt knew how valuable
such a skill could be, and they used it to the hilt.

In this case, however, he knew the president was guilty beyond
doubt—bribery, election fraud, and serial murder were short phrases
that summed it up nicely. All of that meant the first question was irrelevant. As to the second, how would he explain that a friendship of forty
years permitted him access to the most critical piece of evidence of all?
And had it not been for that friendship, might the president be acquitted? Worse, the media might follow the course of events to their most
logical conclusion and ask the next question, the answer to which was a
nightmare for him and all others who had ever been in his position. He
had no intention of dealing with that, the most awkward question of all.

His desk phone purred. Seeing the originating number and caller, he picked it up instantly. "Why, Senator Riordan, you're the last person I expected to call me today."

"And a good morning to you, John. I should warn you, you're on the box, and Daryl is here with me."

"Are you fellas on recess?" Whitaker asked, his question pointed at Senator Perelman.

"Yes, we are, John. I realize this is short notice, but I think the three of us need to head over to the White House."

"For what reason? I'd rather talk to every member of the liberal press than to spend even a minute with that bastard."

"John," Riordan broke in, "one way or the other, Joe Morrison will not be president for long, so, for now, we all need to put on a game face and go."

"I'm not sure what that encounter would produce," Whitaker said.

"A resignation," Perelman said with certainty.

"Why would Morrison even deal with us?" Whitaker asked. "There's been no news report that your committee has seen the DVD. And in any event, my company is not necessary to your mission."

"John, I know you're angry, personally angry, about Drew Warner's death," Perelman said, "but I hope your grief will not cloud your wide-angle judgment on this. If we can secure his resignation—get him out of the office—the country will be better off if it is spared what's on that DVD right now."

"You want to give him a chance to go quietly in the night?" demanded Whitaker, his voice rising. "A year ago he was an empty suit we all had to put up with for the sake of politics. Hell, I understood that. My party has occasionally had the same problem. But Joe Morrison has now become the most despicable character in our nation's history—he makes Aaron Burr look like a Boy Scout by comparison. What are you guys thinking of!" The latter wasn't a question.

"We're thinking of our country, as you usually do," Riordan said, his voice clear and firm. "We've just had a president die and, less than a month later, we'll have a president leave office under a cloud. I can't imagine Joe will be eligible for a pardon—this is no itty-bitty felony like the Nixon mess—so Joe will pay for what he's done. Yet, putting the nation through all of this nastiness while he still occupies the office somehow besmirches each president before him—and it will taint those who follow."

Whitaker remained silent while the buzz on the line occupied the time. Finally, he said, "I understand, Harry, but I am not sure I should be there."

"It's me again," Perelman said. "You should be there because it's your evidence. You have dug up all that would otherwise have been buried. There's more than an irony to your presence, John. It may be the only piece of justice you'll ever extract—to see him agree to leave."

"And if he doesn't?" Whitaker asked.

"That would be unthinkable," Riordan affirmed, his voice clear and strong. After a moment, he added, "Let's meet in one hour—at the East Underground Entrance."

"As I think about it, boys, it might appear to me you want me along so that it's a Republican who lowers the boom on a Democrat. You may despise him, but he's a Democrat, nevertheless. Harry, you don't want to be seen as betraying your party, and Daryl, you old rascal, you want to avoid being the first to convict a president of high crimes. Do I have that right, my friends?"

Dead silence reigned for ten long seconds before Riordan spoke. "You got me there, John—and Daryl too, I suppose—and we'll owe you."

"Damn right you'll owe me. There are two issues in particular I want to put in the rearview mirror."

"You mean the pipeline? The medical devices tax?" Riordan tried to make his words sound sweet, even inviting.

"Oh, no, Harry—you won't get away that cheap. I'm talking about true border security tied to immigration reform."

"Well," Perelman was quick to say, "we can handle that."

"And then, there's abortion-on-demand up until term—that's got to stop, and I want your commitment right now that when I come to you with a bill restricting third-term abortions in this country, you will give it your unqualified support."

"My God, John, you're asking way too much."

"It's our God, Daryl, and I'm only asking what the vast majority of people want. Joe Morrison has never respected life before birth and, now we know, not after. Aren't you ready to do the right thing?"

"This will take more, ah, conversation, John." Riordan rasped and coughed as if he would choke. "There are two dozen left-wing Democrats who will vote against such a measure."

"The rest will vote 'Aye' when the time comes, and so will most Republicans. That means there are at least sixty-five votes in favor, but Harry, you have to let the bill come to the floor."

"I'll agree to let it come to the floor, but I can't vote for it," Riordan said.

"Your voters will pay you back for that, but that's your problem. I'll work with you on other issues. What about you, Daryl?"

"I can support a well-worded prohibition, with the standard exceptions."

"With provisions against abuse, yes. Harry? Are you on board?"

"Agreed," Riordan said, barely churning the lime and gravel. "Will you be this difficult next week?"

"I don't plan to be, Harry. I know it's not something you're used to, but Republicans and Democrats will start to work together again."

"You drive a hard bargain, John."

"For once, I may hold some good cards. OK, fellas, I'll go to the White House with you—still against my better judgment, but perhaps, because of what you have not yet said, Daryl."

"What's that?"

"I'm guessing you already know the Judiciary Committee's vote—yours, Harry's, and the rest—will be for conviction. Do I have that right?"

"Let me just say," Perelman answered, "I would rather avoid voting to convict—for the first time in American history—than nearly anything else on earth."

"An hour, then?" Riordan persisted.

"I will meet you at the West Wing."

Paul spent the first hours of daylight contacting everybody in he knew in law anywhere in Washington, and every person with any clout appearing on Pete Clancy's exhaustive list. It was to no avail. Paul slammed his palm so hard on the gray granite island that it stung for minutes afterward. When his cell chirped, he lost no time in answering what could be the only call he wanted to receive: good news about Mare.

"Paul, I need you again this morning," John Whitaker said. When there was no immediate response, he said, "Paul, are you there?"

"Here, Mr. Speaker. I'd hoped it was about Mare. Sorry, sir."

"I'm the one to be sorry, Paul. I wish for all the world I could be giving you good news, but I'm not the one to do that in any event. Right now, despite Mare's predicament—and I have to believe she's safe, by the way—I need you with me on a short trip to the White House."

"With respect, sir, do you really need me there this morning?" Paul's voice was plaintive, with an emphasis on the "me."

"Well, I can't take the old guy you work for," Whitaker said, attempting to lighten things up. "I don't have Secret Service protection and I'm going into the lion's den, as it were. Someone young and quick is what I need today, and that's you, my friend. What's more, I want you to come armed. Even though you'll have to surrender it at the entrance, you'll have me covered going and coming."

"Understood. Sorry for trying to beg off, sir."

"For a lot of reasons, I thought you'd want to be along on this ride, Paul, so saddle up." Whitaker gave him instructions where to meet so that he could enter the White House grounds in the Speaker's limo.

Whitaker smiled as he realized his mind had played a little trick on him. A place, a person, a thing can evoke entirely different feelings depending upon its association to good or evil, he knew. While Averell Williams occupied the White House, he felt on a fool's errand whenever he entered the West Wing. Not because there was anything evil about that occupant of the Oval Office. It was because for the most part, he and Williams were so far apart politically as to make most meetings futile. Nearly all turned out to be photo ops, and he had been merely a prop for Williams to play politics, a skill at which the president had been the acknowledged master.

Now, as his limo pulled through the gates for the first security check, he looked ahead through the windshield and didn't see the gleaming white icon of the world's superpower. He saw a cold, guileful bastion of lies and crime. It gave him no comfort that Paul Gladston sat next to him, armed and ready to protect him. "Who would protect the nation if we fail here today?" Whitaker demanded of his conscience, under his breath.

"You said something, sir?"

"Sorry, just thinking out loud. You know, Paul, I wanted you here this morning not only because you might want the pleasure." His voice was low and compassionate. "I thought—and Pete did, too—you needed something to do until Mare shows up." He acknowledged Paul's nod. "By the way," he said, offering a jaded smile, "this ought to be the easiest gig you'll have for a while, so enjoy the magnetic tug to power, if only for a moment."

"I will, sir, and you were right—I needed something to do this morning. And it's too bad evil has such a powerful pull."

Whitaker looked back at his young companion, and understood the full meaning of Paul's insight.

"Here's something you might appreciate," Whitaker said, handing his companion a polished, red pamphlet. In response to the question in Paul's eyes, he said, "I was at The Heritage Foundation the other day and picked this up. See the title? *Does Your Vote Count?* It's important to know that some smart people have figured out that this most basic right of ours is in jeopardy. In my opinion," he continued, glancing at the Washington Monument as they passed it, "the right to vote is the sum of all our rights in the US Constitution and all its Amendments. If we lose that right, we lose everything."

The Speaker paused. "You know, Paul, the first part of solving a problem is identifying it, and the Heritage people have done their part. What we're doing here today is dealing with one of those problems."

He turned his gaze toward his earnest protector, and nodded, as much to reassure himself as anything else when the car crunched to a halt.

Sprung with adrenalin and conviction, Whitaker and Gladston exited the limo and approached the bulletproof double doors to the West Wing. Inside, they bore the scrutiny of the uniformed Secret Service personnel, and Paul gave up his weapon, as all nonauthorized individuals, law enforcement or otherwise, were required to do. The Speaker did not bother to introduce his bodyguard to Senators Riordan and Perelman, who waited patiently. He took note of their expressions when they saw the young man produce a Walthers, and let them draw their own conclusions.

All four marched down the hall behind Remy Carlson, who had come out to greet them. The mood was somber, given the fateful proceedings currently on temporary adjournment across town. At the foyer in front of the Oval Office, Carlson nodded to Freddie Frederick, who in turn gestured Paul to a comfortable seat.

Paul looked around, taking in every detail. He had to admit that power's orbit was hard to resist, and the effect was unreal. It was totally quiet, as if the outside world—the real world—existed only in another universe. Paul sat down on one of the blue-and-gold chairs and fixed his eyes on the door fifteen feet in front of him. He saw it close and heard it latch, then nothing. The minutes became like weights thrown on his shoulders. Then, he closed his eyes and thought of the only thing that really mattered to him. *Where is she?*

In rural Virginia, Mare kept her eyes on the single-glazed kitchen window not ten feet away. Dawn had arrived at the old A-frame several hours earlier, and the bright, cold morning sun began to fill the room. She could easily imagine the thin crust of frost on the ground outside, the bits of gravel on the long-untended driveway frozen in place, the few animals out foraging for what little was there.

There was no sound save the occasional click of the thermostat running the propane furnace. Even so, it did not take the chill off the morning. Her hands and feet were numbing from the polyrope binding them tight. Despite the blanket Cox had thrown over her when he left a few hours before sunrise, Mare felt the lonely cold of a death from starvation, if not a bullet to the head.

She thought about the phone call Cox made. Who was coming? How would he—more probable than a she—feel about her? About being alone with a bound female deep in the woods? Cox had not bothered her in any way, but how about his friend?

As she sat in the unpadded kitchen chair, repeatedly scrunching her fingers and toes to keep the blood flowing, she thought that with a little effort she might be able to hobble, stumble, wiggle her way to the window and maybe even break it. But to what end? She would expose herself to winter's last blast. And who would hear her if she called out? She had never felt so alone, and, despite her natural abhorrence of tight crowds, she desperately wanted to be at a Cincinnati Reds game on Opening Day.

One way or the other, Mare knew she couldn't stay there long. When Cox left, he said good-bye as if he were speaking to his wife as he left for work. It was the most natural thing in the world, but it seemed so final. He had the fabled thousand-yard stare in his eyes. He was a man obsessed. Would Cox ever return? If he did, then what?

In the absolute silence, her ear became attuned to any sound. A creak in the wood timbers of the house? Expansion and contraction of the metal ductwork for the heating system? As the sun began to fill the woods with light, robins called to one another. She could almost hear their wings, wishing she could be one of them.

Then, there was the crunch of gravel as a vehicle rolled slowly to a stop not far outside the A-frame's back door. The muscles in her stomach tightened. She closed her eyes, concentrating on the sounds. First, there was the double click of a car door opening. A truck, maybe? Then, as if the driver looked carefully all around before leaving the vehicle, she heard the door close. Then, stillness. Unhurriedly, his steps—a half dozen at the most—reached the small square wooden porch.

She fixed her gaze on the old-fashioned wooden door, paneled on the bottom, four lights on top. It wore a coppery coat of old varnish. Cox's wife must have hung the curtain across the door years ago, and there it stayed ever since, now askew and unwashed. Of all things, she thought about how clean, even sterile, her surroundings were on the Amish farm from which she had come two months before. She wished she were there.

A large shadow blocked the curtain's filtered light. The man was large, and he fumbled with the old Kwikset lock, once shiny brass, but now wearing a dingy sheen.

She could see the little thumb knob turn as the key found its tumblers, and fear gripped her heart. The door opened, slowly at first, and then wide.

Inside the Oval Office, Joe Morrison stood behind his desk, as if Resolute would somehow protect him from the forces of democracy. At first, he made no attempt to come from around the wooden bastion, then decided he had no choice since there weren't three chairs close to the fort. He gestured to the twin couches and he walked to one of the two leather chairs between them.

Behind him, the fireplace roared, but did nothing to warm the frigid atmosphere. The president tried to catch the eye of his ancient mentor, Senator Riordan, but the old man studied the fruit bowl on the coffee table between the facing couches. "How can I help my old friends?" he began, hoping the words did not seem as hollow to his listeners as they did to him.

"Mr. President," Riordan said, his throat attempting to sift more gravel, "we are here on a most unpleasant mission."

"How so, Harry?" Morrison looked at Daryl Perelman, too, staring ahead into an unknown distance. "The Senate hasn't begun its trial," he said, guffawing at the word, *trial*, "and there isn't anything but wild conjecture on which to vote." He shifted his stare to Whitaker.

"We are now in possession of incontrovertible evidence of your guilt, Mr. President," Riordan continued, "and we are here to save you and the country much anguish and embarrassment."

"What evidence could there possibly be?" Morrison demanded.

"Just this," Whitaker said and produced a retina display iPad from his case. It was already prepped. "Most of what you'll see here, Joe," he said, refusing to address Morrison by his title, "isn't grainy video at all, so the incriminating detail will be all the more crisp for you—and the world—to see." He handed Morrison the iPad, who took it to his lap, a little clumsy with the engine of disaster now in his hands.

Riordan, Perelman, and Whitaker studied Morrison as he viewed the CIA video of his visit to the McLean house in the summer of 2012. Together, they heard Morrison's voice in the dining room of the agency safe house, but within a few seconds, Morrison's eyes widened, then narrowed into a look of disgust and perhaps, hatred. In less than a minute, he flipped the iPad closed and all but tossed it on the coffee table.

"That slimy son of a bitch," Morrison said in a loud voice, unable to restrain himself in the face of betrayal. "That cocksucker! He said there'd be no record!"

"You're the son of a bitch," Whitaker spoke, trying to control his anger. "You killed them all, didn't you, Joe? And this tape proves it."

"It proves nothing," Morrison said, nearly shouting. "I'll embargo this tape. It was made on government property using government services, and the agency head gave me his word!"

"Gave you his word?!" Whitaker all but shouted. "So you killed Drew Warner." It was not a question.

"Harry, you don't believe any of this, do you? Daryl, you're an old Democrat—you can see this is more right-wing bullshit! Now they've gone too far!" Morrison's eyes were wide and glaring.

"That *is* you on the video, isn't it, Joe." Perelman spoke gently, quietly, but his words weren't a question. "We didn't come here to debate your guilt or innocence," he continued in the same tone a doctor might use in describing a likely fatal outcome, "but we did come to offer you a face-saving exit from"—he gestured with his hands and eyes—"this office."

"What do you mean, 'an exit'? According to Article Two, Section One of the Constitution of the United States," Morrison announced, standing fully upright, shoulders back, "I am the president of the United States!"

"You weren't elected to anything on November 6," Whitaker said. "But for your theft of the election in Ohio, Virginia, Florida, New Mexico, and Colorado, you would never have achieved the two hundred and seventy necessary votes. Governor Hardy was elected, not you."

"Tell that to the Electoral College! Tell it to the Congress—all of you," Morrison said, pointing to Riordan and Perelman specifically, "voted to certify the results. So, tough shit, boys!"

"This video will be out on YouTube this afternoon if you do not resign your office immediately," Whitaker said.

"That's your best option, Joe," Riordan offered. "I have to say, it pains me to give you that option. You were a young senator I took under my wing, and what monster did I raise?"

"Oh, fuck you, Riordan. You knew what you were doing. You wanted influence with a rising star who might become president. Well, you blew it, pal. I *am* president. That tape isn't going anywhere. If I have to have all three of you arrested for treason, that will be no problem for me."

Whitaker looked into the eyes of his companions and couldn't discern whether it was disgust or fear he saw there. "Don't even think about it." He turned to the president. "I'm giving you ten seconds to give the right answer to our offer. And by the way, think of the video as Drew Warner's revenge."

"It appears to me, Joe," Perelman joined in, "that you don't give a good damn about the country or the Constitution, but I recommend you not insist on a trial. I suspect that in both the Judiciary Committee and the full Senate, the vote will be unanimous. Though I am saddened to preside over the first conviction of a sitting president in US history, it would be a just outcome." The anguish in his voice was palpable.

Morrison stood in front of his chair, his eyes on the Resolute desk, the literal seat of power in all the world. He said nothing.

"Time," Whitaker said, and turned to walk toward the door.

In the foyer, Paul sat still, his lap empty of reading materials because there weren't any. Except for a biography of Averell Williams, which Paul suspected would be replaced by another's, there was nothing to command his attention. The minutes ticked by. Not a sound came from behind the door recessed into the artificially thick wall three long strides in front of him. *What was going on in there, anyway?*

To the right of the door sat a woman who had been introduced as Ms. Frederick. She, too, sat stony-faced and busy with her laptop squarely in front of her so that she could see down the hall from which most guests might approach. She could easily look left and right, and occupied an ideal protective position. Paul appreciated the fact that someone had thought it all through.

Once or twice, he tried to kindle an exchange, but to no avail. She was either too busy or she'd concluded he'd never be back. Why waste time, he decided she thought. He smiled to himself and decided to relax, inasmuch as it might prove to be more than the usual ten minutes allowed for what a president considered a bothersome interruption. At least, that's what Speaker Whitaker had told him.

It all happened at once. Paul saw Frederick look up from her desk and peer down the hallway over his right shoulder. Her eyes and slight smile told him she saw someone coming whom she knew. In a moment, the look on her face changed from a welcome to one of surprise. Paul could see that she tried to take her gaze from the hall while she looked around her desktop. *Did her movement seem a bit frantic?* Sensing something amiss, Paul began to rise and was halfway to full height when the new visitor appeared, walking straight toward the door leading to the Oval Office.

The giant of a man, well-muscled, with short, fading yellow hair marched along as if he owned the place. Paul felt his leg muscles turn to momentary mush when he realized he was within a few feet of Crew Cut. Up close, without a crowd of Amish around, the blond goliath let his over-sized frame dominate the space to the left of Frederick's desk.

"Marty," she said, her voice under control, but on the edge of a quaver, "I didn't think you'd be in today, and another agent has the duty. Is there something I can do for you?" When she finished the question, she pushed a quick glance in Paul's direction, causing her visitor to turn around.

For a moment, Paul's eyes locked on Crew Cut's face and its sharp-edged features. He saw that despite the man's cold, blue eyes, devoid of care, he was connecting images. While his jaw muscles jerked, a small snarl curled his lips. The man's brain must have played a quick slide-show of stills. There was one in a racing car north of Columbus, one in an Amish auction barn in New Wilmington, and one in the Walter Reed lobby.

"You prick!" Crew Cut said, taking a step toward Paul.

Instinctively, Paul reached behind him only to find his holster empty. Crew Cut did the same. The way his arm contracted slightly told him that the Secret Service agent had been allowed to keep his firearm. Crew Cut now intended to use it.

In the nanosecond before Crew Cut fully extracted his hand free of his suit jacket, Paul stretched for the only thing within reach. It was the heavy, hardbound autobiography of Averell Williams. With all the strength he could manage, he rammed the spine of the book into the bridge of Crew Cut's aquiline nose, while he found his adversary's right hand with his left. He heard bone snap and hoped the man would soon choke on blood.

With momentum in his favor, Paul crashed full force into Crew Cut's chest, hoping to leverage the two-decade difference in age to his advantage. Off balance, Cox fell rearward, the lower part of his back catching the corner of Frederick's desk. When his body fell across the glass-covered surface, the laptop and every other item went flying.

The two men rolled toward the middle of the desk as Paul found a grip on the agent's forearm. Crew Cut tried to torque his man all the way over.

Paul's strength drained away. Other voices filled the airspace, but Paul could not make them out. As a flash of Mare crossed his mind, Paul grabbed hold of what force he had left, and swung Crew Cut's gun-laden hand away from Frederick and himself. In the small room, the explosion out of the barrel jangled all his senses.

Seeing Whitaker turn to leave the room, Morrison yelled, "Wait!" and dashed the four steps to stop him.

Whitaker was too quick for Morrison, however, and he reached the portal first. At the moment he pulled the door open toward his right, Morrison managed to rush through around Whitaker's left, blocking the Speaker's exit.

A loud crack shattered the moment as Morrison turned to face his accuser. Morrison held his hands up, palms forward, as if in surrender, and began to form his lips into a word when his chest exploded in tissue, bone, and blood.

Whitaker felt the blast of gore a fraction of a moment before Morrison grabbed his shoulders, his fingers clasping the Speaker's jacket in vain hope of support. Whitaker stood stock-still, speechless. He looked into Morrison's eyes. Devoid of strength to make even a sound, his lips seemed to ask, "Why not me?" As he fell to the floor, Whitaker saw his eyes, once a brilliant blue, drain of all life.

A frightened voice called out, "Mr. President!"

The two older men ran up behind Whitaker and pulled him backward into the room. Breathing hard, Riordan held Whitaker fast while Perelman made a point of stepping in front to shield the Speaker from whatever else might happen.

Only seconds had passed. Crew Cut was not finished. He used the desk as s springboard to throw so powerful a left-handed punch into Paul's right eye that it clenched shut in rhythmic pain as he fell on his back.

The colossus was standing over him. Then, as he tried to focus, all he could see was the barrel of the gun.

Marty Cox pointed his pistol at Paul's head. "It was you who fucked up this whole thing."

Paul closed his eyes, not wanting to think about a bullet tearing through his face and erasing every memory of Mare.

"Marty!" a voice roared, breaking through the haze. "Marty!" the voice commanded. As if responding to an order, Cox turned to face a smart-suited woman with a gun. A single shot split the moment.

EPILOGUE

I n the White House Medical Office two floors below, Paul tried to lay still on the gurney while Dr. Jeremy Bolling cleansed the deep gash next to his right eye and injected the area with a numbing agent.

"This will take about eight stitches, Mr. Gladston."

"Do what you've got to do, doc, but what the hell happened upstairs?"

"The president was shot."

"Was that who—?"

"Yes, I'm afraid so."

"Sorry, Doctor Bolling," Paul said, reading the man's name on the badge clipped to his shirt, "but I can't share your grief."

Bolling nodded. "I understand, but two losses in a month can't be good for us." He glanced at his watch. "Let me crank you up into a sitting position, Mr. Gladston. You should then be able to watch the screen."

"Watch...?" He felt woozy, but shifted his concentration to the HDTV mounted to the wall. It was tuned to CNS and, across the bottom, scrolled the banner, "President Shot By Rogue Agent." He could see Peter Marsden was talking away, his lips moving faster, it seemed, than the electronic media could carry the sound.

"If this isn't the most important story for our nation over the last one hundred years, I don't know what is, ladies and gentlemen. Averell Harriman Williams died unexpectedly from surgical complications less than a month ago. In the intervening weeks since President Morrison's swearing in, there have been persistent rumors about voting and other crimes committed during the last election. Impeachment proceedings were underway. Now, this morning, at eleven oh two a.m., President Joseph P. Morrison was assassinated by a lone gunman—possibly a rogue

Secret Service agent—who somehow gained entrance to the West Wing. We will report details as they develop."

"Can't you get News Global, Doc?"

"Not in this White House."

"Seriously? Somebody will have to rethink that." Despite the anesthetic, his skin stung as Bolling skillfully worked the sutures.

"Be patient." When he completed the work, Bolling leaned up to the TV and flipped the channel button as he walked out of the room. Over his shoulder he said, "I'll be back in a minute."

"This is Barnes Ward with a News Global Special Broadcast concerning the assassination of the impeached president, Joseph P. Morrison, by Secret Service agent Marty Cox. Agent Cox, we have been reliably informed, served on the president's protection detail and may have been involved in crimes alleged to occur on Morrison's behalf. One source has suggested that President Morrison may not have been the intended victim at all, but the then Speaker of the House, John Whitaker. It is uncertain whether we will ever know the truth of the matter, since Cox was shot and killed while preparing to fire his weapon again, immediately outside the Oval Office. Whatever Cox's intent, it is interesting to note that he shot President Morrison on the fifteenth day of this month—the Ides of March, when a few thousand years ago, assassins murdered a tyrant at the seat of world power. Stay where you are, ladies and gentlemen. I have just received warning that the ceremony is about to begin. Let's watch."

A little dizzy still, Paul sat straight up as Dr. Bolling returned to watch with him.

"Funny, isn't it?" Bolling asked.

"Funny?"

"I never get used to it. Funny that the ceremony is taking place not far above our heads."

"According to the Presidential Succession Act of 1947," Barnes Ward said in a low voice as the camera traced the small crowd of White House and other personnel entering the Roosevelt Room, "a law that has been changed several times since the founding of our nation, when there is no sitting vice-president, the presidency does not devolve to a senior cabinet member or the president pro tempore of the Senate as many still believe. It was thought at the time," he began, pausing in mid-thought, and then, continuing. "I'm sorry about that, but I am informed the stage has been set and the players are in position." He shifted his gaze to the HD wall on his right.

"Now comes Justice Antonin Scalia, probably the first person on the court the Secret Service was able to round up on a moment's notice. You see him there clad in judicial black, and entering from the right is John Whitaker, about to become our forty-sixth president. Let's listen in."

"I, John Houston Whitaker, do solemnly swear that I will faithfully execute the Office of President of the United States, and will to the best of my ability, preserve, protect, and defend the Constitution of the United States, so help me God."

"And the world breathes a collective sigh of relief," Ward whispered, "as this constitutional crisis has been averted. We will never know, of course, if when all was said and done, whether Joseph P. Morrison would have been convicted of high crimes and misdemeanors by the US Senate—the first time in our history. Many may come to feel that was a good thing. Now, President Whitaker, with only his wife, Janet, at his side, will offer his thoughts on this most historic day."

"Americans have borne many burdens and, at times, have suffered much in the nearly two hundred and forty years of our existence as a nation," the new president said. "That we have weathered the many storms is testimony to our persistence in the face of crisis and adversity. Despite what we have endured these past weeks, we will persevere now as well. As a great American writer is thought to have once said, when we are broken and heal, we are all the stronger in our broken parts. That will be true for us today and in all of our tomorrows, of which I expect there will be many.

"No longer do I represent a congressional district in Cincinnati, though I will love her always. No longer do I serve in another branch of government, though I will respect it always. No longer do I identify myself first as a Republican, though that party's principles will always serve as a guiding star. Now, I am one American who serves all

Americans, and I am not beholden to one party's views or one set of private interests.

"How well we have learned the lessons of the last two hundred years will determine how well we take our country forward to better times. Yes, times will be better when we encourage companies to hire, and to hire at good wages. Times will be better when we assimilate all peoples who seek to join us in one country with one national language. Times will be better for all when those who have so much share just a little bit more with those who have so little. Those who want more, however, those who seek the blessings of a capitalist society, will have to take their education responsibly and work hard at jobs for which they are skilled. And as those times get better, we should respect all who live among us, even the unborn. As Governor Hardy said in the last campaign, what we are all about at the end of the day is human rights for all—nothing less.

"With your help, my friends, and with the grace of Almighty God, we shall do no less."

"You can hear the small group's burst of applause," Ward continued. "No doubt, there will be much applause across the nation and the world as people see before them a man with experience and conviction who says he will work with and lead all Americans, not just those of his race or party. Now, for further analysis and reporting on what happened this morning, I will turn to..."

"Mr. Gladston, are you all right?" Bolling asked as he saw tears streaming down Paul's cheeks.

"Yes, sir. I never thought this day would come. Now, if only—" Cut off in midsentence, he saw a familiar face at the door, but for the moment, could not place the man to whom it belonged.

"Paul Gladston, you lousy newbie!" the voice boomed. "I have somebody here who insists on seeing you." Then, the man laughed out loud as he stepped aside to let Mare step into the room.

"Mare!" Paul shouted with glee, then reached up to his sore head as she ran forward and threw her arms around him.

"Cooling your heels at the White House, huh, while I'm in captivity and in fear of my life," Mare said in tones designed to pull a leg.

"What! Who the hell...? My God, Mac Smith," Paul said. "Camp Peary! What the hell is going on?"

"A story for another time, laddie." Smith grabbed Bolling by the arm and steered him from the room.

Paul pulled Mare close to him again.

"What about your head?"

"Forget it."

"So what do you want to do this afternoon, Paulie boy?" she whispered heavily into his ear.

"Just wait. Just you wait!"

ACKNOWLEDGMENTS

TurnAround could not have been written without the steadfast support of family and friends. For advice about writing in general and working with publicists and publishers, Paul Kengor, acclaimed author and professor of history at Grove City College, has been of immense help. Dale Perelman and his wife, Michele, are always there as friends, readers, critics, and all around advisers, and added to them are many other friends who have informed, kidded, goaded, and encouraged me along the way.

A key, perhaps, unwitting contributor to this effort has been The Heritage Foundation. Its booklet, *Does Your Vote Count?* should be required reading in every county Board of Elections office across the land. I'd also like to thank each library and service club that allowed me to come and speak about *Turnover*, the precursor to *TurnAround*. Listening to American voters firsthand and understanding how precious their rights are to them motivated me to write, as Paul Harvey used to say, "the rest of the story."

Finally, I could not have written this book without the quiet and enduring support of my wife and children, who still cheer me on as I make my way through life's third act. For them, "Thanks" will never be enough.

Made in the USA
Coppell, TX
21 June 2021